take me in bangkok

KD ELIZABETH

TAKE ME ABROAD BOOK TWO

VLM

This book is a work of fiction. Names, characters, places, and incidents are the product of the author's imagination or are used fictitiously. Any resemblance to actual events, locales, or persons, living or dead, is coincidental.

Take Me in Bangkok Copyright © 2022 by K.D. Elizabeth

All rights reserved. The scanning, uploading, and distribution of this book without permission in any form is a theft of the author's intellectual property and not permitted. If you would like permission to use material from the book (except in the case of brief quotations embodied in critical articles and reviews), please contact the author at kdewrites@gmail.com. Thank you for supporting indie authors.

The use of this book is permitted for noncommercial purposes only.
First Edition: September 2022

Vivre Libre Media and the author are not responsible for websites (or their content) that are not owned by the either the publisher or the author.

The author is available for speaking events. You may reach out for more information at kdewrites@gmail.com.

ISBN:
ISBN-13: 978-1-956045-06-2 (paperback)

Editing: Cassie Pearse
Proofreading: Red Leaf Proofing
Cover Design: K.D. Elizabeth
Print and E-book Formatting: K.D. Elizabeth

*For they
who face their fears.*

I
THE FLOWER

CHAPTER ONE

ALESSANDRA

I'm already regretting the flight before boarding has finished. The plane is tiny, two rows of double seats crammed so close together the aisle is really more a general concept than a reality. My point is, if someone made a bet with me to throw a ball from one end of the plane to the other, I could totally make it.

I stare at the twelve inches of space between my aisle seat and the one across the tiny gap and realize with sickening dread that if anything happens on this flight, they'll know the reason none of us made it out alive is because we all got trapped trying to shove our way down the narrow aisle.

At least on the flight from Rome, I could pretend I had *some* space. But not here. They must have made a mistake. Wrong plane. Something. This one has to be heading to some super small, remote town, not the party capital of Thailand. Ha ha. Funny. I laughed. Now please get me off.

No one comes to rescue me. No one announces over the

loudspeaker that they've accidentally put us on the wrong plane. Everyone just keeps trucking their crap down the aisle like everything is fine.

Yup, okay. It's official; this flight was an incredibly stupid idea, on top of the already idiotic decision to cart myself off alone to Thailand. Maybe I should just—no. I'm not leaving. I'm not. That would be proving my brother right. That would be listening to the demands of the Chief Marketing Officer of my family's company, who insisted multiple times that this was the worst possible time for me to take off for an indefinite leave. Too bad for him; I need this break. I've needed it for months, and if I'd pushed it off much longer, I would have had a breakdown.

And my butt is already in this seat. I'm suffering through this Bangkok-Phuket flight if I have to white-knuckle it and chug three vodka sodas to make it through landing.

My gaze snags on the tiny window one seat over and then quickly veers away. I think of how soon we'll be hurtling through the air and shudder.

I'm not afraid of flying. Really. Don't have a problem with it at all, actually. When we fly over land, that is. I could live on a plane, really, if I had to. I swear. But flying over water? Not so much.

I don't do water. And when I say I don't do water, I mean I'm deathly afraid of it. Ponds, lakes, streams. Rushing water, still, shallow, deep, freshwater, saltwater—it doesn't matter. The only kind of water I can tolerate is a glass of it in my hand. And showers.

Even the showers took two years to tolerate. I'm now

the world's fastest speed-showerer. You're welcome, environment.

But above all, I *really* don't do the ocean. You can sink and sink, down, down, down, with no hope of ever swimming back up to the surface. No one would ever find you.

And the color! People think the ocean is blue. And it is. Near shore. But in the real ocean, the middle-of-nowhere-no-one-can-save-you-now ocean, the water is black. Impenetrable. Cold.

We are not made for deep water. We are land animals, through and through. Every moment we spend in the ocean is a second nature bestows upon us like the most regal of kings. *That privilege can be revoked.*

So that's why I bought myself a one-way ticket to Thailand.

I don't *like* being terrified of water, despite the fact that I do have a very good reason for my phobia. In fact, I'm beyond sick of it. Sick of my brother's pity, my estranged father's derision, the snickers behind my back at parties, all of it.

And the press! God, the press is the worst. My family owns one of the largest media companies in Italy, and let's just say that our competitors love mocking my absurd fear for clicks and views.

Yes, I know. Poor me. Alessandra Vitale is so blessed the only thing she worries about is stupid water. I get it. I acknowledge all that. Which is why being afraid of it is even *worse*.

All the wealth, privilege, and opportunity mean nothing when you feel like you're not even a whole person, although they do make it easier. And that's how I feel when I stare at a fucking pool. Pathetic. Worthless. Less than. Making a big deal out of nothing. Because my family is affluent, it's like I have no right to complain about the fear that has debilitated my life since I was eight.

So here I am, in a country as synonymous with water as I can imagine. Being on the other side of the planet doesn't hurt, either. No one knows me here. I can get over this fear I utterly despise in private, without interference from anyone back home.

If I can, you know, just make it to my destination.

"Excuse me. I'm in the window seat."

"Oh, sor..." my voice trails off as I look up to discover an absolute giant of a man standing in the aisle. His shoulders are so broad he blocks out the row opposite us. He's actually stooped over to avoid banging his head on the ceiling. That's how absurdly tall he is. Curiously, though, his face is turned away from me. Even stranger still, he carries nothing with him. No carry-on or bag, not even a computer case. It's like he just walked right on to the plane as is. Weird.

"I'll just get out of your way," I say, unbuckling.

"You can have the window seat if you want," he says, his voice barely more than a rasp, his tone so low I have a hard time understanding him, especially since English isn't my first language. Although I pretty much speak it fluently.

"No, no! That's your seat," I say hastily, not wanting him to realize that I specifically chose this seat, and if I have to sit that close to the window, I'm going to expire. He frowns, still looking away, and it occurs to me that with his size, he was probably hoping I'd take him up on his offer. Well, too bad.

He moves back a few steps so I can step out into the aisle. I'm decently tall for a woman, but I feel tiny in comparison. Without a word, he slides into the window seat, his knees touching the seat before him. I wince; he definitely would have preferred the aisle seat.

I slide in next to him, trying to ignore the intensity of the man sitting next to me. He seems coiled. Anticipating something, somehow, and vaguely irritated by everything around him. I open my mouth to introduce myself, thinking to apologize, to explain why I really need the aisle seat, but one look at the determined set of his jaw as he stares straight ahead, not even acknowledging me, and my mouth slams shut.

Fifteen minutes later, we take off and are speeding south. Most of the short flight will be over land, so it's possible to trick myself into believing everything is fine. I flick idly through the in-flight magazine and consider pulling out the book I'm in the middle of reading, but I'm too wired, too dreading the landing to pay attention to anything right now. When the flight attendant comes past with drinks, I consider it but then ultimately shake my head in refusal; even if it would relax me, alcohol is the last thing I need right now with the way my stomach churns.

Then we start the descent. My stomach burbles. Oh, God, here we go. I obsessively plotted out the flight path yesterday, so I know that we've just moved past the mainland of Thailand and are now flying across the water in the direction of the tiny peninsula where Phuket is located, which is pronounced like "poo" and "keht."

All that's keeping me from that infinitely deep ocean is this cramped metal tube.

Yeah, you know, I really should have had that drink after all. If I was tipsy, this would all seem funny. Or at least surreal. Then I could pretend it wasn't happening. Now I can only sit here, stone cold sober, and freak out.

The plane lurches downward. I barely hold back a scream. I *really* should have taken her up on that vodka soda. Hell, I should have bribed her to leave the whole cart.

Don't do it. Don't do it. Don't—I look out the window. My breath catches: nothing but water as far as I can see, shining up at me. Did you know if you fall into water from even a few feet, you can die? I do. You splat. It's like jumping out of a building and landing on concrete. If I fell out of this plane right now, it would be the end of me.

Okay, so looking was a bad idea. That's fine. I'll ignore it. That blue blob in my peripheral vision doesn't exist. Nope. And I'll just ignore the popping in my ears that means we're descending. Flights land normally all the time. This one will, too. This is no big deal.

What I need is a distraction.

Glancing at the man next to me—and definitely not out the window—I ponder a way to start a conversation. He hasn't moved the entire flight, hasn't looked up from the battered paperback he must have pulled out of a pocket somewhere. That must be nice. Women's clothing never has pockets that large.

Still, I now have an icebreaker. Who doesn't want to

talk about books? And thank God for it, too, because the plane gives another drop. My hands fly to my armrests; my gaze veers toward the window. Oh no. Even closer.

"Enjoying the book?" I say, my voice high and frightened even to my own ears.

He says nothing, his thumb flicking to turn the page. Apart from that, he doesn't move, not even an inch. How does he do that? This guy could be a statue. I stare at the strong jaw, which clenches ever so slightly under my gaze.

A very *attractive* statue, I'd wager.

I wonder what he looks like. His face was averted when he sat down, and he hasn't turned to me the entire flight. An increasingly large part of me wants to know, and not for the simple sake of having a distraction.

"Is this your first time in Thailand?"

He shifts uncomfortably in his seat, still refusing to look at me. Really? He intends to just *ignore* me? Who does that? It's as if I don't exist.

"It's my first time in Thailand," I say, as if we're actually having a conversation and not playing an impromptu game of who-can-annoy-a-stranger-more. "I was supposed to be on this flight yesterday, but they lost my luggage when I arrived, and I had to spend a night in Bangkok. Can you believe that? They found it, though, so at least there's that. And I got to see Bangkok, which was way larger than I—"

"Look, ma'am," my seatmate sighs in the distinctly masculine drawl that Hollywood movies have convinced me all cowboys must surely sound like, "I'm not here for idle chit chat, okay?"

He flicks another page, having delivered this brutal remark without even looking up from his paperback.

What the hell is in that book, the recipe for eternal life?! Excuse me for trying to make a little polite conversation. Message received. No distractions coming from this guy. Mind your own business, Lessa. Don't go accosting some stranger for help if you're actually serious about getting over your fear yourself.

I turn my attention to the seat in front of me, my teeth grinding together with the force necessary to keep them from chattering. I can do this. Only a couple minutes more and we'll be on the ground. The plane is not going to be swallowed up by the ocean. That is ridiculous. The pilot probably makes this exact flight multiple times a week. Maybe even multiple times a day.

I'm pitched sideways as the aircraft encounters a pocket of turbulence. Despite my best efforts, a small whimper escapes me even though my lips are slammed together.

The plane lurches back the other way, obviously leveling itself out, but it doesn't matter. Sweat breaks out on my forehead, under my arms, even behind my knees, but I'm cold, so very cold. My hands have become claws, digging into the soft skin of my wrists so harshly I don't need to look to know I'm drawing blood. My vision tunnels to the tiny writing on the seat in front of me: "In case of emergency..." Oh, God, don't look at that, don't think of it, anything but that. This is normal. It's fine. We are *fine*. I'm not fine. Oh, God, I'm going to faint—

"Hey."

My seatmate has to repeat himself another three times

before I even realize he's addressing me. "Hmm?" I grunt, not looking at him, my entire attention locked on the cupholder of the tray before me. I'm holding it together, but barely. The slightest distraction and I'm going to unravel.

"Look at me."

"Hmm, no, that's fine."

"*Look* at me."

The forcefulness of it—the kind of tone that leaves no question whether it will be obeyed—is so unexpected my gaze snaps to his in an instant. Before I've registered his face, my eyes land on the water out the tiny window behind him. We're so *close*. The water is merely feet below us, and I can't see a landing strip. We are definitely crashing.

My vision tunnels to tiny pinpricks; fainting has become a certainty.

"Christ."

With the last of my dwindling vision, I look not at him but at the window as he slams down the shade. A large hand falls on mine that is currently burrowing its way into my left wrist. His hand is hot, or maybe mine is simply freezing, but the contrast is so stark I'm able, just for a moment, to forget our imminent demise.

"Look at me."

And finally, unexpectedly comforted by the warmth, the strength, of the hand on mine, I do.

I gasp in shock. His eyes are incredibly beautiful. Brilliant green, with specks of aquamarine near the iris. Warm, shallow water. I know that color of water. It's peaceful. Safe. Still. Why on earth do I find that association *soothing*?

But I do; a wave of peace rolls through me, pulling me back from abject terror.

Something in those gorgeous eyes flashes for the briefest instant. In my best state, I doubt I could identify it. In my current one, it's a lost cause.

"Breathe," he growls.

I gasp, dragging air into my lungs for the first time in who knows how long.

"Again."

I breathe again, staring at this guy, whoever he is. He orders me to breathe a third time and I do. There is no question of not obeying; he could order me to do anything in this moment and I would.

He falls silent when it becomes apparent I've regained the ability to breathe. But to my surprise, he doesn't look away, nor does he remove his grasp on my hand. We fall into silence, unaware of the roar of the plane, the chatter of the people around us, the announcements over the loudspeaker. Calm descends over me, silently, softly. And only then do I become aware of it.

An energy, an electricity, a bond passes between us, one that feels strangely irrevocable. I will likely never see this man again, but he saved me just now, and we are linked for life. Does he feel it, too? I stare deeper into his eyes, searching desperately, and something, some instinct tells me he does. He recognizes it. I'm certain of it.

But then his eyes flash again. They harden. And I feel it like a physical blow to the gut as he breaks that tenuous bond, tears right through it, shatters it to pieces and then stomps on it until there is no hope of ever repairing it. This man wants no link with me. I gasp, stunned by the rejection. He looks away and removes his hand in the same instant the plane's wheels hit land.

Gradually, my environment reasserts itself into my consciousness. I stare, dazed, at the head of the person in front of me as we taxi to the gate. Did any of that really happen? I sneak a glance at him; his jaw is tight, fists clenched atop his thighs, his gaze resolutely staring forward.

Oh yeah. None of that was my imagination.

Still half-stunned—or maybe that's just the adrenaline crash—I grope for words, a sentence remotely capable of describing the gratitude I feel toward him, but before I manage a single word, he unsnaps his seatbelt, shoots to his feet and then, without a single glance at me, steps over my entire body, shoving forward the seat in front of me, much to the annoyance of the man sitting in the seat.

He's halfway down the aisle before I unbuckle. By the time I make it off the plane, he's disappeared.

CHAPTER TWO

ALESSANDRA

"Welcome to the Golden Lotus Resort, miss. If you follow me right this way, we can have you settled shortly."

I can't believe he just disappeared like that.

"Miss?"

I mean, he practically ran out of the plane! It's like he regretted helping me.

"Miss? Is something wrong?"

I just wanted to thank him. He didn't even give me the chance.

"Miss? Miss?"

A hesitant hand on my shoulder snaps me out of my brooding. Blinking, I turn to the resort employee who's staring at me like I've completely lost it. Frankly, after that flight, I may have. Why didn't he give me an opportunity to thank him for helping me out of my panic attack? I could have bought him a cup of coffee. Offered to share my driver. Something. Not that it would have been necessary, but still.

I would have liked to do something nice for him like he did for me. The guy essentially just rode off into the sunset like in one of those Western films I was secretly obsessed with as a kid.

Maybe someone here can tell me who he is. He didn't have any luggage with him, right? That must mean he lives here. Phuket can't be that big.

Cheered, I smile at the employee and say, "Sorry, it's been a long two days. I'm afraid I'm a little out of it."

He smiles. "No worries at all, Miss. The time difference is enough to bother anyone."

"I think I should still be sleeping right now."

He gestures to the man standing off to the side of the entrance, who steps forward to begin taking my luggage. Turning back to me, he motions for me to follow him and says, "My advice to you is to spend as little time as possible in your room today. That way, you won't fall asleep until this evening. Tomorrow, you'll be on our schedule, no problem. How long will you be here?"

"Two months, I think," I say, although it depends on how long it will take me to get over my fear of water.

The man grinds to a halt, his eyes widening. "Oh, but you are Miss Vitale, then?"

I nod.

His face flushes. "Forgive me for not realizing. We were told to expect your arrival. Had I known, I certainly would not have touched your arm just now. But you looked out of sorts, and I thought you might need help and—"

"Please," I say resignedly, holding up a hand. "It's no trouble. And I would appreciate it if you could treat me as any other guest while I'm here. I'd like to ... blend in, if you don't mind."

The man frowns as if that's the last thing he wants to do. Poor guy is probably worried I'll report him. But just as quickly he wipes the frown from his face and nods. "Of course, Miss."

"And if you could share my sentiments with the rest of the staff here," I say firmly, watching as he pales slightly. I sigh. So much for relative anonymity on this side of the planet. "Never mind. I'll discuss this with the concierge."

He nods again, this time in obvious relief. "As you wish, Miss."

He leads me to the check-in desk and whispers something to the woman behind it, whose eyes widen. She jerks upright, plastering a smile on her face. I sigh again. I'll have to tell each person here to pretend I'm a nobody. It's kind that they're so dedicated to making my stay enjoyable, but I really just want to be treated no differently than the other guests.

"We are pleased to welcome you to the Golden Lotus Resort, Miss Vitale," she says. "A shame your luggage was lost. I imagine they were able to find it, yes? Did you have a nice flight in?"

A laugh escapes me. The concierge's smile freezes in well-concealed horror, as if wondering how she's managed to offend me already.

"It was very pleasant, thank you," I assure her. "And they did find my luggage. But I'm ready to relax."

"Well, we have plenty of space for that. Three pools, one of which has its own waterfall, and a spa, and of course the ocean is right outside. You can charter a boat whenever you wish, and if you'd like to plan an overnight excursion, we can schedule a meeting with our trip specialist to plan that. If you like to dive, we have dive masters who can lead you on as many dives as you wish, and if you aren't certified but would like to be, we have instructors who will have you diving in as few as five days. Of course, if that is not to your liking, we have snorkeling as well."

"Right," I say weakly, the sheer number of water-related activities making my stomach lurch in protest. "That all sounds wonderful."

The concierge perks up. "Shall I schedule something for you now, then?"

"No, no," I say quickly. "I mean ... I would prefer a few days of solitude first."

Make that at least a week of solitude, maybe even two.

"I see," the concierge says like she doesn't at all. "Well, we are pleased to welcome you to the royal suite during your stay here. It is a separate villa, away from the main resort. It has a private beach, accessible by key card, as well as its own multi-level pool and waterfall. You may also avail yourself of the golf cart, and if you require a vehicle, please let us know. We can also arrange a driver for you."

"Oh ... wonderful," I say, feeling faint. All that extra water in my villa? No way was that in the room description. "I don't recall so many amenities when I booked my stay."

The concierge says, her voice tinged with pride, "It is our pleasure to offer you this residence. Our most special guests stay here. I believe even the Thai head of your company stayed here a few years ago."

"I was not aware of that," I say, working to hide my alarm. Our VP of Southeast Asia stayed here? So much for thinking I could get away from the office.

There is absolutely no way I can refuse this room. It would be the height of rudeness, and while the Italian press may have dubbed me Land Lubber Alessa, I've yet to give them an excuse to call me rude. I wanted to get over my fear, didn't I? Well, this is how I do that.

"That is so very kind of the resort," I say. The concierge, whose nametag I finally notice says "Malai" beams and begins typing away at her computer.

"Your things are already being arranged in your villa," Malai says without looking up.

"Thank you."

"And here are your keys. One for the main gate, marked one, one for the entrance into the building, marked two, and one for the entrance to your private beach, marked three. Be sure to lock the beach gate, for your own safety."

I blink at her. My safety? It's not actually dangerous here, is it? I want to ask, but am hesitant to unintentionally insult the staff, especially since they've already given me the mother of all upgrades. She probably just means to lock it so other hotel guests don't wander into my place.

But then she looks up from her screen and says, "And is there anything you'd like to put in our vault for safekeeping?"

"W-what? Is there—should I be concerned about theft?"

"Oh, no, Miss. Most assuredly not. It's standard policy

to ask all guests if they'd like us to hold something. Many people keep jewelry and currency, things like that."

Unnerved, I stare at her in silence. She merely smiles back, seemingly unaware of my discomfort. Maybe I really am reading too much into it. Still ...

"I would appreciate it if you kept my passport with you," I say, sliding it across the counter to her.

"Of course, Miss." Malai takes my passport and turns to the door behind her. I watch as she types in a code and enters; a giant vault is visible before the door swings shut.

Well then. This place really does take security seriously, doesn't it?

Malai returns a few seconds later. "Don't hesitate to call down if you need your passport for any reason. Is there any last thing I can help you with before Arun shows you to your room?"

"No, that's ..." I trail off suddenly as a pair of green eyes flash through my mind. "Actually, perhaps you could help me. I met a man on the flight here who happened to help me with something very important, but before I could thank him, he left. He had no luggage with him, so I believe he may be local to Phuket. He was extremely tall and had ... um ... really green eyes. I don't suppose ..." God. I have no idea what the man who sat next to me looks like. The eyes had been so arresting I didn't even notice the rest of his face!

Malai's professional smile remains frozen in place for a long time, likely wondering how to deal with such a vague question.

"I'm afraid that description brings no one to mind."

My shoulders slump in disappointment, but really, with that terrible description, what should I have expected?

Arun says something to Malai in Thai; she shakes her head sharply and says, "Arun does not know him either. He will drive you to your residence now, Miss. Enjoy your stay." She folds her hands before her in the traditional *wai* gesture that is similar to the *namaste* of India and bows.

"Thank you," I say, and turn to the man who greeted me upon arrival.

"This way, Miss."

I follow Arun through the lobby, which I finally have time to notice has an indoor pond with fish lazily swimming among beautiful pink flowers, their fuchsia petals turned up toward me. A small fountain bubbles from the center, the soft sounds of trickling water the only noise in the otherwise silent lobby.

I swallow hard. This entire place is going to be riddled with water, isn't it?

"I see you've noticed our namesake."

I blink at Arun.

He nods to the pond. "The lotus flowers. Beautiful, yes? Did you know you can make fabric from the stalks of the lotus flower? It is a process that was created in our neighboring country, Myanmar, but it is making its way here. Lotus fabric is more expensive than even silk and is the only fabric the monks of Myanmar wear. You know, the yellow fabric, yes? Those are our monks. In Myanmar, the color is ... what do you call it ... a dark red."

"Burgundy?"

"Yes, that's it."

"Wow," I say, the water for once forgotten as I stare at the flowers. "I had no idea. They're beautiful."

"If you like, we would be happy to arrange a demonstration of the fabric creation process."

"I would love that, thank you."

"My pleasure, Miss. If you step this way, I shall drive you to your residence."

Arun allows me to settle into the golf cart parked in the same spot where I arrived, and then we set off.

My eyes widen in growing astonishment as we wind through a formal botanical garden, laid out with exquisite orchids, and of course, more lotus flowers. There are many other plants that I cannot identify, too; whoever designed the garden was extremely talented. I may not be ready to dive right into the nearest pool, but I'll certainly be spending many hours in this gorgeous oasis.

As Arun steers the golf cart along a gently curving path, he tells me that this garden has existed for over a hundred years, and that some of the trees were planted in the original garden. The few succulents I keep back home seem pitiful in comparison.

"And here we are, Miss," Arun says when we've arrived on the far side of the garden. A door is set into the wall that Arun tells me is made of bamboo. It's so unobtrusive I might have missed it had I not known to look. "This golf cart I will leave here for your personal use. You can park it inside your residence. If you will follow me, please."

Arun takes my set of keys and demonstrates how to unlock the gate door and main door to my villa, which is three stories tall and could rival the largest in Tuscany. It is an obscene amount of space for one person. I follow Arun as he shows me every floor, each room more unbelievable than the last.

And there's the staff. A chauffeur, a chef to accompany the outdoor kitchen, complete with a wood fire oven, a masseuse on demand, a whole host of people I'll probably never meet who clean the rooms, and finally a stylist, who Arun introduces as Pranee.

"I'm honored to assist you, Miss Vitale. I can help you dress for dinner, if you like."

"I would appreciate that, Pranee," I say with a genuine smile. Dinner is always a formal affair in Rome; Pranee's offer feels like the first familiar thing since arriving in Thailand. "And if you're assisting me, I insist you call me Alessandra."

Pranee's face flushes, but she doesn't take me up on the offer. Arun takes his leave of us and Pranee informs me that I have some time before readying for dinner. I take a quick nap even though it won't help with the jet lag and wake refreshed.

Pranee helps me select an olive green sheath dress with matching heels and sweeps my hair into an elegant chignon before working on my face. She quietly replies to my attempts at conversation but isn't particularly loquacious; by the time she's finished my makeup, I'm plotting how I can hire her .

Pranee offers to drive me back to the main building, but for the first time since arriving in Thailand–no doubt thanks to Pranee–I'm feeling like I can handle this trip, so I tell her I'll drive myself. When I arrive, I'm directed to the restaurant, whose maitre d' informs me my table is not yet ready and that I can enjoy an aperitif at the bar.

Making my way to the bar, I glance up and freeze in shock. There he is. The man from the plane stands right in front of me.

CHAPTER THREE

ALESSANDRA

Why didn't the concierge tell me she knew him? I just asked her about him, and here he is, not even a few hours later in the actual resort itself! Maybe it's one of those client privacy things. They must be instructed not to give out information about who's staying at the resort. But no matter. Here I thought I'd never see the man again, and now I'm lucky enough to run into him again on the same day. What are the odds of that? It must be part of that travel magic; the way things line up when abroad that just couldn't happen back home.

His back is to me. I only recognize him because of the mirror behind the bar; one second was all it took for him to glance up and for me to recognize those eyes. His attention drops back to the drink before him, giving me a chance to observe him. He's easily taller than everyone else in the bar—and it's not just because he's a foreigner in Thailand, a country whose people are closer to my height. He literally stands head and shoulders taller than everyone else. Even in my heels, I'm level with his shoulders.

There's that strong jaw. That I certainly remember, along with how it clenched when I tried to talk to him. But apparently, now that I'm getting a good look at him, the rest of his face is perfect. Cheekbones that look like they could cut granite and a straight, proud nose give way to a surprisingly sensual mouth for a man who doesn't seem particularly passionate. Then again ... those full lips, currently twisted in an annoyed grimace, might mean there's more to him than meets the eye.

Then there's his clothing. While everyone else in the bar—myself included—is dressed to impress, he is dressed deliberately, almost mockingly, without care. His linen jacket is a wrinkled mess, worn negligently, as if solely because the resort requires a suit coat for dinner. His slacks are just as wrinkled, although I can tell that at one time the entire outfit must have looked fairly sharp, for both articles are tailored to his considerable size. Maybe that's why I first noticed him in this crowd; he's just not trying to fit in. And he doesn't.

My stomach twists with sudden shyness. Italy is chock full of some truly beautiful men, but there's something about this one ... is it the fact that he brought me out of my panic attack? Has to be. And yet ... if some other person had helped me, I wouldn't be feeling so strange. I both want him to see me now—looking my best and feeling just as good—and yet am still too embarrassed to talk to him, since I would have to acknowledge how freaked out I was on the plane.

Still, even if he is intimidating, I have to thank him. It's just basic decency. Maybe I can buy him that drink after all. Taking a deep breath for courage, I make straight for him. My mouth opens to get his attention, but before a word escapes, he suddenly pivots toward me. I nearly barrel right into him.

"Sorry for nearly running into you," I say, "I had no idea you were going to turn so quickly like that."

He says nothing, just frowns as he sweeps a long look down every last inch of me with those eyes. A shiver of feminine appreciation sweeps through me. God, his eyes are even more incredible than I remember. The color isn't even the only remarkable thing about them; a blatant, raw intelligence radiates out of them. This man suffers no fools.

Too bad I swore off men for the duration of my Thailand trip. If I'm here to overcome my phobia, then I need to focus on myself. No physical distractions. But wow, if anyone could tempt me to break that vow ...

"I didn't think I'd see you again," I say inanely after a few moments pass and he's still staring.

No response.

Feeling ridiculous, I say, "Are you a guest here? I figured you must live in Phuket since I didn't see you had any luggage on the plane. Have you been here a while?"

"No."

I blink. "So you haven't been here a while?"

He takes a slow, deliberate sip of his drink. "No. I'm not a guest here."

Why do I get the feeling that he wouldn't be caught

dead staying at the Golden Lotus Resort? But if that's the case, why is he here?

"Were ... were you looking for me, then?" I blurt out, then mentally kick myself for my stupidity. He couldn't possibly; the man made it clear he didn't want to talk to me when he practically ran out of the plane. It's just those damn eyes scrambling my brain. "If you're not staying here, I mean?" I finish lamely.

His expression somehow flattens even further. Seriously, this man could give Michelangelo's marble statues a lesson or two in stoicism. His gaze sweeps down my body again; this time what I feel isn't a frisson of excitement. It's dismay. He's still expressionless, but I could swear there's a hint of contempt in his eyes.

"Oh, yes," he says, his voice sounding like he's chewing gravel. There's definitely contempt in *that* tone. "I couldn't possibly be here for any other reason. I simply had to track you down after I disappeared from our flight without even asking for your name, let alone getting your contact information."

I reel back, shocked and strangely disappointed by this unwarranted rudeness. Even though he helped me, this guy's no hero, not with that arrogance. What a waste of an incredible body and an even more attractive face.

"Excuse me," I say coolly to mask my disappointment. "I came up to you to express my gratitude for helping me during the flight. I'm sure it would have been much worse had you not been there. So thank you for that. Have a nice evening."

Without giving him a chance to respond, I turn to leave and nearly collide with a waiter.

"My apologies, Miss Vitale," the waiter says, straightening his already immaculate white dinner jacket. "Your table is ready. If you would—oh. Sir, I didn't see you there. I'm sorry to say we haven't a table for you this evening after all. We've been busier than anticipated. My sincerest apologies, Sir, but perhaps you could return tomorrow and I'm sure we could accommodate you then."

And I don't know why I do it. Something in me must secretly be a masochist because before he can even open his mouth, I say, my smile so fake his jaw pops, "Oh, but then you must join me for dinner. It would be a pleasure."

He stares at me flatly. "You're too kind. I couldn't."

My smile widens. "Oh, but I simply insist. I couldn't possibly bear to think of you losing out on what will surely be such an exceptional meal. I'd lose sleep over it."

He suddenly straightens; I resist the urge to take a step back so I can see his face better. He towers over me, our chests inches apart. This man could use his very stature as a weapon.

"Well," he drawls in that cowboy accent, his mouth twisting with what might just be the hint of a smile, "if you insist."

Wait, really? My brows raise in surprise; I never, not for one second, actually believed he'd take me up on my offer. I quickly school my expression into a mask of casual disinterest, when in reality curiosity is about to eat me alive.

"Okay, then," I say slowly, half expecting him to change

his mind. "It being my first evening in Phuket, I would be happy to have a companion for dinner."

Without another word, he extends his hand toward me. I cock my head. What, does he want to shake hands and introduce himself? We sailed past that social nicety long ago. I place my hand in his and am surprised when he tucks it into his arm, pulling us together as if we're about to go into dinner like two characters in a regency era novel.

A bolt of electricity snaps between us. I stiffen, wondering if he feels it. A moment later, his bicep flexes under my fingers. Yep, he does, too. The bond from the plane, that instantaneous link that wove between us, returns with a vengeance. And here I thought he'd severed that link. Unnerved, my gaze flashes to his face in time to see him look away from me, his jaw tight.

This might have been a bad idea.

We remain in tense silence as the waiter leads us to the dining room. A second chair has magically appeared in the little alcove where they've placed my table. Candles flicker from the table, contrasting starkly with the deep red of the tablecloth and lending a distinctly romantic vibe to the setting. Yikes. They expect us to eat *here?* God. This guy keeps acting like I'm coming on to him. Eating here isn't exactly going to convince him otherwise, is it?

Mercifully, however, my companion doesn't comment on the table setting as we sit down. The waiter asks for my drink order and asks him if he'd like a refill, to which he nods without looking at him because he's staring full-on at me.

I stare right back, refusing to break the silence first. I'm supposed to be at this table, after all. He's the one who's here after he said multiple times he wants nothing to do with me.

The waiter returns with our drinks and then tells us our first course will arrive shortly. They've already decided our meals for us? Now I don't even have the excuse of holding up the menu between us to avoid his forceful stare.

I pluck my glass of red wine off the table and raise it toward him. "To the joy of meeting new people."

I taste the wine—excellent—waiting for him to respond to my slight sarcasm. He makes no remark, however, simply sliding his old glass aside and picking up his new one before tipping it just slightly toward me in a salute as he raises it to his lips.

"Really?" I say, exasperated, taking another sip of wine. "Nothing? You're just going to sit there the entire meal in silence?"

His lips twitch ever the slightest bit. "Yes."

"You must be joking."

He shrugs lazily, takes a sip of his whisky or bourbon or whatever suitable cowboy drink he's got. "I'm not a man of many words."

"Really? I had no idea. And here I thought that when you said—what was it? Oh, yes—you're not here for idle chit chat, that was just for show."

He gives me a considering look, placing his drink on the table. "So you do remember."

"Remember what?"

He leans across the table, those electric eyes rooting me

to the spot like a rabbit caught in a snare. "I. Don't. Like. To. Talk."

"And yet you agreed to dinner."

He straightens. "So I did."

We lapse into silence again. I search for another topic of conversation. I'll get this guy to crack during this meal if it's the last thing I do.

Speaking of which.

"What's your name?" I ask.

He just looks at me.

I sigh. "Seriously? We're not even going to do names?"

"You're the one who invited a stranger to dinner. Who am I to ruin your plans by introducing myself?"

"A convenient excuse."

He smiles faintly, lifting his glass again in another faint salute. "Isn't that what you're here for? A little adventure? A trip to get away? Some lighthearted fun with a stranger a world away from all your problems?"

If he only knew.

"Right, the dumb tourist looking for some cheap thrills," I say, trying not to feel insulted, although at least now he's finally talking. "And I suppose this is the part where you tell me my next job is to fall into bed with you."

He grows absolutely still, a coiled intensity stealing into his features. That wasn't what he was suggesting—this man has made it painfully clear from the start that he's not interested in me—but is he suddenly reconsidering?

Now I lean forward, smirking when his gaze dips to my chest. "I. Don't. Screw. Strangers."

His eyes flash with begrudging admiration as a startled

chuckle escapes him. He salutes me again with his glass. "Brutally put. If I'd been angling to get you out of that dress, you would have put me right in my place."

I scoff and make a gesture toward his large frame. "As if someone could put you anywhere you don't want to be."

He grins again; this time the admiration is genuine.

To ward off a smile of my own, I say, "I suppose I'll just give you a name myself, then. I can't just call you guy, right? Although, on the other hand, why not? We're never going to see each other again. So, Guy, tell me. Have you always been this taciturn, or is this a recent development?"

Guy taps his index finger on the rim of his glass, studying me. "Well, *Gal*, I'll answer your question if you answer mine."

"By all means."

"Have you always gotten what you wanted, or is this a recent development?"

I laugh, my first carefree laugh in what feels like ages. "Well, I suppose we have our answers."

Guy stares at me for a long time, so long I fall silent. The bond jerks tight between us. I swallow hard; every inch of my body feels like it's been lit on fire. His eyes grow hooded.

"Yes," he says quietly, "I suppose we do."

CHAPTER FOUR

ALESSANDRA

A week later I'm staring at the deceptive calm of my private pool and thinking yet again of Guy and our dinner. I've gone over it again and again so many times it's taken on a surreal quality, like it never happened.

For the next three hours, Guy and I worked our way through the tasting menu, teasing each other over seven courses. He, of course, wouldn't let me live down the fact that we were being served the tasting menu—not that I had actually selected the most expensive item on the menu. Another perk for the Vitale daughter, apparently, which I definitely didn't explain to Guy. I would have never heard the end of it.

I, in turn, made sure to comment on his inability to smile like a real person and his absurd proclivity for silence.

And the craziest thing is ... I had so much fun. In no way was I the only one enjoying myself. I caught that near-smile on more than one occasion. I never did find out why he agreed to have dinner with me, though. And I probably never will; after dinner ended, he left without another word, and I haven't seen him since.

What a strange way to start my vacation.

Pushing the thought aside, I stare at the water, my chin dropped down on my knees. On this side of the pool, opposite from the waterfall, the water is calm and peaceful. I can almost trick myself into believing it's beautiful when I'm not worried about plummeting into it. And that's a good thing, too, because today's the day I force myself to enter it.

After a week of rotating between the garden, the spa, and a chauffeured drive into town to see the lotus fabric-making process, I'm, well, bored. I wasn't wrong when I decided to head to Thailand to get over my fear of water. It's everywhere. But that's also the problem because *there's water everywhere.*

Most activities involve it in some capacity. It's alienating being unable to enjoy the entire point of being here. I haven't tried making any acquaintances because they'd inevitably invite me to do something with water and I'd have to turn them down. It's about time I did something about it.

I can do it. I can stick my feet in the shallow end of the pool and keep them there for five minutes. I can.

Rocking back and forth, as if I'll somehow magically end up in the pool without having to actually stick my feet in the water myself, I take a deep breath for courage and grab the side, my nails scraping the concrete as I force myself to extend a shaking foot out in front of me. It hovers over the water for one, two, three excruciatingly long seconds before, swallowing hard, I dip my toes in the water.

Oh God, it's so cold. Despite the blazing afternoon heat I shiver, hating the cool sensation of the water swallowing up my foot, eating it right up like I'm nothing, absolutely nothing. Just like before. Just like when the water closed over my head and—

No. That was then. This isn't happening now. I'm sitting on the ground, for God's sake. Nothing can possibly happen. Wanting to get it over, I shove the rest of my foot into the pool, my teeth grinding together, my chest heaving. Tears of frustration trickle down my cheeks. I hate this. It's pathetic. Look at me, crying over my foot in a fucking swimming pool. I swipe viciously at my face and shove my other foot into the water. The sudden movement disrupts the water, sending a little wave over my other foot. Water surges up my calf and I gag, my leg spasming. Every inch of my body yearns to get as far away as possible from this torment.

My heart pounds, so fast and hard it's difficult to breathe. But my feet are in now. I'm doing it. I have to lock my entire body so as not to jerk free. I grab my phone and jab the screen until I've set a timer for five minutes. Placing the phone on the ground next to me, I stare down at the water, my vision tunneling until I realize I'm not breathing.

Dragging air into my lungs, I rock back and forth again, trying to keep my legs still but unable to remain motionless. My entire body cycles from cold to hot to a fiery itchy sensation and then back to chills. I glance at the timer. Surely my time must soon be up?

It's been just a minute and a half.

This is actual torture. I am torturing myself. A soft sob

escapes me. I swipe at my cheeks again, thankful for my private villa after all. Not even the staff are here right now; I'm truly alone. No one can witness this humiliation.

Unable to stare at my feet another second, I instead turn my attention to the waterfall, watching the water cascading down and imagining myself able to enjoy it one day. I imagine myself being one of those people from those corny commercials for island travel, standing under the falls, their faces upturned and smiling. Those commercials are dumb, but they still work. I want to be one of those people, and damn it, I'll become one no matter how much it hurts to do it. If that means I have to sit here for a fucking hour with my feet in the pool, then I'm going to do it until I—

Beepbeepbeep. Startled, I snatch my phone. The five minutes are up! My feet are out of the pool so fast I nearly overcorrect and end up face-first right in it.

Not trusting my balance in this shaky state, I roll away from the pool and crab walk backwards. Once I'm a good ways away, I roll to my knees and then slowly, carefully, climb to my feet.

That's when it hits me. I actually did it! Every second of it was pure torture and I nearly threw up multiple times, but I told myself I was going to do it and then I did.

Maybe there's hope for me after all.

Exhaustion slams through me. I sway on my feet. Hell, I'm tired. I ran a 10K once and didn't feel this bone-meltingly exhausted. That's definitely enough for the day. I've earned a nap in the hammock I've spent my evenings reading in, if I do say so myself. But only after I wash the disgusting pool water off my feet. There is no worse smell in the world than chlorine.

When I come out of the bathroom, I hear a sound. Thinking it must be one of the staff, I continue making my way downstairs to the hammock. But as I reach the ground floor and hear it again, I stop; someone is crying.

Frowning, I follow the noise until I come upon Pranee sobbing in one of the ground level bathrooms. She's crying so hard she doesn't even notice my arrival, just continues weeping into her tissue, her face red and swollen. How long has she been sitting here like this?

Aghast, I consider her in mute silence as I weigh how to handle this. The Thais I've interacted with so far are extremely private individuals, especially compared to my home country of Italy, where everyone is practically one big extended family. I'm afraid that any interference would be unwelcome, but it hurts my soul to see someone in such pain, especially Pranee, whom I've come to love this past week.

"Um, Pranee? What's wrong?"

She shrieks, coming off the toilet so quickly my hands fly out to prevent her from toppling to the floor. Pranee blots her face and squints at me, hiccuping.

"Oh, M-Miss Vitale. I'm s-sorry to interrupt your—"

"None of that, now," I say firmly. "Tell me what is the matter."

"N-nothing—"

"Pranee."

She sighs, hands twisting her tissue. I reach across the sink and grab another one, then, thinking better of it, grab the entire box and extend it to her. She takes a few tissues and mutters a thank-you in her soft voice, which has grown hoarse from all the crying.

"Now, what is this all about?"

Her shoulders slump. "I'm fine, Miss Vitale. I should never have lost my composure at work. It's unprofessional of me."

"I consider you my friend, Pranee. I would hope you'd tell me if something were truly wrong," I say, worrying I'm overstepping some aspect of workplace norms in Thai culture. But to my relief, she doesn't take offense, merely sniffles, and then delicately blows her nose. I wait, letting her decide whether to tell me.

"It's my cousin," she says finally. "He's in the hospital."

"That's awful, Pranee," I say. "I'm so sorry to hear that. How did it happen?"

"It was a car accident."

I wince. My chauffeur has driven me around Phuket enough for me to understand that the driving here is even more hazardous than it is in Rome, and that's saying something. The last thing I'd want is to get into an accident here.

"Will he be all right? How did it happen?"

Pranee shakes her head. "I don't—it was an accident. They don't know how long he should be in the hospital, but it doesn't matter because ..."

She trails off, dropping her gaze to her feet. I wait for an answer, and then when she doesn't supply one, I prod, "Because what? Why doesn't it matter?"

Her face turns red. She glances around, as if taking in the entire property, and I know exactly what she means.

"It doesn't matter how long he should remain in hospital," I say slowly, "because your family doesn't have the money to keep him there."

Pranee's face reddens even further. I sigh, inexplicably exhausted. As a person of means, people often come to me to ask for help, sometimes even with malicious intentions, but it's the people I truly care about who refuse to ask for the help I could easily provide that is even more demoralizing.

"Pranee, how much does your family need to keep him in hospital?" I say bluntly. Sometimes it's easier to cut right to the chase in matters of money. She demurs; it takes me another thirty minutes of gentle but firm asking to finally get the sum out of her. It's an amount that would set back most people in Italy. In Thailand, it's even more disastrous.

But I am not most people.

"Okay, then," I say. Pranee sighs, her body wilting, tired from the emotional drain of her outburst. She refuses to look at me. "Pranee, I would like to help you and your cousin. Would you let me do that?"

She says nothing, which for me is as good as a yes. Taking her arm, I say, "Let's go into the kitchen. I'll make us some tea and we can put our heads together about how to solve this issue, yes?"

Pranee lets me lead her into the kitchen, where I go about making tea that pales in comparison to the way the chef here makes it, but is still warm and comforting. Thankful that we're between meals and the chef is therefore not here yet, I situate her at the counter and place the tea in her hands. She sips it quietly, barely registering it.

Placing my own cup in front of the chair next to her, I say, "I've forgotten that there's a call I must return. Can you wait here for ten minutes? Then I'll be back, and we can see about doing something for your cousin."

She nods vaguely, still lost in thought.

"You promise you'll be here when I return?" I say, just to be sure she won't run off in embarrassment for having shared her problem with me.

"Yes, Miss," she says, her tone tinged with fatalism, "I will be here."

"Good."

Without another word, I turn on my heel and head upstairs to my room, where I grab my purse. Doing a quick calculation on my phone, I head for the front door and then climb behind the golf cart. For once not ambling slowly through the garden to enjoy it, I push the cart as fast as it will go to the main building, where I march inside and head straight for the ATM.

This ATM, by virtue of being at a high-end resort, has a much larger daily withdrawal limit than most ATMs, but it still isn't enough. I carefully fold the bills into my purse, glancing around to make sure no one is watching me, and then head over to the concierge on a hunch, remembering the solid door of the vault the day I checked in.

The concierge, this time a man I've never met greets me with a *wai*, which I return.

"I'd like to go shopping at the outdoor markets today," I say. "I've just withdrawn the limit from the ATM, but I'd like more." I tell him the remaining amount I need for Pranee. I'm not thrilled about lying about my purpose for needing the money, but there might be a rule about employees accepting help from guests, and the last thing I want is to get Pranee fired. A female tourist wanting to shop, however, will go unquestioned.

The concierge's eyes widen. "Uh, Miss, the markets sell items that are much less, um, in price. I don't think such a large sum will be necessary for you to shop there."

"Well," I say conspiratorially, "I *did* happen to see a shopping street as well. And the items here are so beautiful. I prefer to shop with cash, you understand. It helps me keep a budget. With a credit card, all you do is swipe, and before you know it, you've spent your entire life savings."

The concierge laughs politely. "Very good, Miss. Yes, we have cash here we can provide you with."

"Perfect," I say, "please charge it to my room."

"Yes, Miss. If you will wait here."

"Certainly."

I wait as he types the code to the door behind him, then disappears inside for a few minutes. When he returns, he has a thick envelope in his hand. "If you like, I can arrange a driver and keep this here until you're ready to leave? It is a large sum."

"Oh, no. I can keep it with me. I'm alone in my place after all, and I like to budget out my shopping ahead of time," I say breezily. Then, with a flash of inspiration, I remember what a friend of a friend told me about the daughter of an oil baron who had threatened to disinherit her because she was spending so much shopping. "I like to put the money in little bundles for each store I plan to visit. Keeps me from overspending."

"Very well, Miss," he says, handing me the envelope with only the slightest hint of hesitation. "When would you like the car brought around?"

"Perhaps in two hours? That should be enough time," I say, resisting the urge to sigh. Now I really will have to shop, in order to sell my story. But it isn't as if the driver will follow me inside; he won't know that I'll pay with my card. And I need to buy gifts for my family back home, anyway, so I suppose it's not a complete lie, after all.

The concierge assures me the car will be ready, and I head back to my villa, feeling lighthearted for the first time today. My experience in the pool was exhausting and upsetting, but this issue with Pranee I can actually solve. My stupid phobia often makes me feel like an emotional cripple, unable to fully participate in life; at least in this instance my wealth can be used for good.

Returning my golf cart to its parking spot and locking both the gate and the main entrance with care—it *is* a lot of money—I quickly return to the kitchen, relieved to find that Pranee is still there, staring dismally into the dregs of her teacup.

"Okay, Pranee, here you go." I take the envelope and the bills from my purse and place them on the counter before her.

She stares at the money, her face going extraordinarily pale. Her mouth opens and then closes. Then opens again, but still no sound emerges. Finally, she manages to say, her voice strangled, "I couldn't possibly—"

"You can and you will," I say firmly. "I would like to do this for you. You were the first person to make me feel truly welcome here. It's because of you that I believe that I can accomplish what I set out to do here. So I want you to have this, as my thanks for that. And I want you to take the rest of the day off, go straight to the hospital, and pay your cousin's bill so there's no question of him getting the treatment he needs. I can do my hair and makeup for dinner tonight."

Pranee bursts into tears.

CHAPTER FIVE

ALESSANDRA

"Did you get everything sorted at the hospital?" I ask Pranee's reflection in the mirror.

She nods quietly, the brush taking another pass through my hair. "I gave them the money yesterday and paid my cousin's bill in advance. They say he can stay as long as he needs now. I can't—Miss Vitale, you saved his life."

"I'm sure he would have pulled through regardless," I say hastily.

Pranee begins pulling my hair up in an elegant twist at the nape of my neck. "No. You cannot know that, Miss Vitale. He was—the accident was very bad. He needed multiple surgeries that he will now receive thanks to you. I am so grateful."

"You're very welcome, Pranee," I say, watching her eyes cloud with tears as she continues working my hair. "I'm glad to be able to help."

Pranee remains silent, then, a moment later, says fiercely, "I will repay you every penny!"

"No, I don't want you to do that," I say firmly. "But if you really wish to do something, I would prefer it if you helped someone else one day, like I did with you. That would be better, don't you think?"

She stares at me in the mirror. We gaze at each other, and then her customary faint smile breaks out on her face. "I will do that."

"Perfect."

Pranee begins on my makeup. I close my eyes, letting her work in silence. A few minutes later, she hums in approval, her hands dropping away from my face.

"There, Miss. You look beautiful as always."

"Thank you, Pranee. You do an excellent job."

She flushes, her smile widening. Her dedication to her work is admirable, and even better yet, she's talented. She should have her own shop, a whole staff of girls working her particular kind of magic. If there's anything I've learned as a Vitale, it's to recognize an investment opportunity when I see one. Something tells me an offer like that would be rebuffed, however. Perhaps by the time I'm ready to leave, we will be familiar enough that I can pose the idea.

Rising from the chair, I survey myself in the mirror. This is the first time I've worn the midnight blue gown, although it won't be the last. In another week or so, I'll need to start recycling the outfits I brought. Although with all the clothing I bought yesterday to sell my story, I have longer than I originally anticipated.

"Have a nice dinner, Miss."

"Thank you, Pranee."

I drive myself over to the main building, stopping at the

fountain in the middle of the garden to run a hand through the water. After the first day I put my feet in the pool, I've made it my personal mission to sit by the edge of the pool and stick my feet in for as long as I can tolerate it. I can make it a whole five minutes now without it bothering me too much, but usually around eight minutes the itching starts, and I want to tear my feet from the water. The longest I ever lasted was about twelve minutes two days ago. I'm not sure what will happen when I start to put more than just my feet in the water, but that's a problem I'll deal with later.

But the other thing I do is dip my hand in the water of the main fountain whenever I drive through the garden. I don't hold it there for long, just a quick dip, and I always have to immediately wash my hands—sinks don't bother me, but actual bodies of water do—but I figure it's a good idea to get used to interacting with water sporadically. And it's actually just a tiny bit easier each time, although I still hate that awful sensation of feeling a limb being swallowed up by cool, impenetrable water. The force of it hitting my hand is awful.

Plunging my hand into the pond, I swish it around, scattering the few fish that were curious enough to get close. I'm not a huge fan of fish, but I try to channel them whenever I submerge a part of myself. *Be like a fish*, I tell myself, *You like this.*

That task complete for now, I flick the excess water off my hand and am proud when I shove down the urge to gag. If this continues, the very sight of water won't make me want to hurl up my most recent meal. I dry my hand on the towel I've taken to leaving in the golf cart and then continue my drive to the main building.

The waiter arrives with my first drink and an unexpected request.

"There is someone who would like to meet you."

"Really?" I ask, glancing around the restaurant, but no one appears to pay me any mind.

"Yes," the waiter says, "Mr. Chakrii is our most valued local guest. He dines here quite frequently and would like to extend an invitation for you to dine with him this evening."

"That's kind of him," I say, considering the offer. Surely it must be fine to dine with someone I don't know? They wouldn't let just anyone in here. And I've been rather lonely this last week; apart from Pranee and the rest of the staff, I talk to no one. The dinner with Guy was the last time I've had a conversation of any significant length with someone who's not here to do something for me. "I would gladly have dinner with him."

The waiter nods and leads me to a corner of the restaurant, up onto a small dais where a single table is surrounded by a semi-circle of waist-high plants that create a kind of pseudo-wall between the table and the rest of the restaurant.

A Thai man, probably around my father's age, sits alone at the table, his back to the wall. He stands as I join him, dressed in a brilliantly white three-piece suit that is open at the collar, his right hand gripped tightly around what I assume is a walking stick made of solid gold. Holy Mother. I try not to stare at it; that many ounces of gold must be worth tens, if not hundreds of thousands of euros. It's a rather blunt display of wealth, and the ostentatiousness of it makes me uneasy. If that walking stick is even three kilos, then it is worth over one hundred thousand euros. The lunacy of carrying around such an expensive object is so obvious as to make me wonder what real purpose he could have for using it.

Perhaps he knows no one would ever dare try to steal it from him.

"You are even more lovely up close, my dear," he says as the waiter pushes my seat in behind me. Once I'm seated, he follows suit.

"Thank you," I say, then really consider what he's just told me. "You've ... seen me before, Mr. Chakrii?"

He waves his hand carelessly. "I dine here most evenings, and a man takes notice of a woman like you. And please, call me Pravat."

I smile politely, not wanting to encourage his thinly-veiled advances. I'm not here for a fling, but to work on my phobia. Hopefully, I won't have to rebuff him explicitly.

"You may call me Alessandra," I say, extending the same courtesy.

"I did notice you dined here with a man about a week ago," he says, then pauses as if waiting for me to deny it. I taste my wine in lieu of answering. "Do you know him well?"

"No," I say, slowly, wondering why he'd ask such a question. "I don't know him at all. I heard that he could not get a reservation for dinner that evening, so I offered to let him dine with me." Then, for a reason I'm not sure of, I add, "I haven't seen him since."

"Really?"

"No."

"Curious," he says, lifting his glass to his mouth as he studies me. "It seemed a rather *intimate* dinner to me."

I shift uncomfortably in my seat, beginning to regret my decision to dine with this man. Why does he care about our dinner so much?

"We had an intense debate about politics," I say, searching for a suitable explanation for why it probably looked like we were disagreeing.

"Is that so? With a perfect stranger?"

"It was an academic discussion."

Pravat smiles, his teeth showing in a way that reminds me of a predator snarling right before it goes in for the kill.

"And you're having a nice time here?" he says.

"Yes, it's a gorgeous resort. The food is incredible as well, although I'm sure I don't have to tell you that."

He laughs softly, but it doesn't reach his eyes. "That it is. Will you be staying long?"

"I have no definite plans," I say vaguely.

"Are you intending to see other parts of my country?"

"I saw Bangkok when I arrived."

He nods. "Yes, a very dynamic city. I was born there, you know. I still keep a place in the city, and much of my work takes me there, but these days I find I prefer the slower pace of Phuket."

I'm tempted, sorely tempted, to ask him just what kind of work leads him to purchase walking sticks of that nature, but I don't dare. It doesn't take a rocket scientist to know he wields that thing like a club of power.

Sensing the direction of my gaze, his hand drops idly to it, and he strokes it slowly, his hand circling again and again, almost like he's considering using it for something other than walking.

"And are you unattached?"

"Unattached to what?" I say, deliberately misunderstanding him. These questions are weirdly personal for someone who is literally a stranger to me. Does he have some sort of agenda in asking me to dine with him?

His smile widens, as does the incongruously hard look in his eyes. "Are you married? Engaged? Seeing someone?"

I place my glass down on the table. "I beg your pardon, but I fail to see how that is any business of yours."

We fall into silence. I search for a graceful way to end the meal. This guy won't take any supposed insult to his character lightly, but spending another two hours eating with him sounds like a nightmare.

"You really are beautiful," he says idly, taking another sweep down my body. "In a refined way. Classy. Good breeding, I expect."

I bristle, disgusted by his comparison of me to a well-bred animal and infuriated by the insinuation that others might suffer from a lack of such *breeding*. My desire for politeness sails right out the window.

"Anyone can be taught manners," I say coldly, then pause, looking at him significantly. "Or perhaps not."

Pravat is not a stupid man. His eyes narrow as he registers my insult. He leans back in his chair, pulls a cigar from the inner pocket of his jacket, then holds it out to the side. A waiter materializes from nowhere and takes it from him with a hand clothed in a spotless white glove. He removes a clipper from his pocket and snips the end of the cigar before returning the clipper to his pocket. Taking a box of long matches from another pocket, he strikes one and holds it under the cigar, rolling it efficiently back and forth above the flame. This continues for a good two minutes; he pauses only to light a second match.

Then, with great ceremony, he extends the cigar to Pravat, who takes it without looking at him and puffs twice distractedly. He's still glaring at me, his dark gaze inscrutable. The waiter disappears. My feeling of unease grows, signaling it's time to go. The way he looks at me ... it's best if I leave. I don't know this person; accepting his invitation to dine with him was a bad decision. The playful animosity Guy exhibited a week ago is nothing like the anger wafting off Pravat now.

I rise. "You'll have to forgive me, Mr. Chakrii. I'm suddenly feeling poorly and would prefer to take my dinner alone at my residence. It was a pleasure to meet you."

"Sit down."

I gape at him, nearly collapsing back into the chair in shock before I jerk upright. "You misunderstand me, sir."

"I misunderstand nothing," he snarls. Pravat takes another puff on his cigar, as if deciding what to do with me. "It is a great honor to dine with me."

Glancing around the restaurant, I discover multiple tables are watching us covertly. Even one of the waitstaff positioned along the far wall stares. My unease transforms into outright alarm; does everyone know this Pravat?

Wishing to avoid a scene, I say quietly, and with as much respect as I can muster, "It is still an honor I must decline. I wish you a good evening, and a pleasant dinner."

Pravat takes another puff, then says, "If you so desire."

"It is." I step away from the table, drawing a few gasps from the tables around us as I make for the exit, my back rigidly straight in an attempt to mask my discomfort. I'd better lay low for a few days until the scandal dies down.

Pausing briefly to speak to the wide-eyed maitre d', I request my meal to be delivered to my residence in half an hour, then return to my villa. Pranee has already left when I enter my room. Quickly, I remove my outfit and change into something more comfortable. When the food arrives, I pick at it listlessly, still unnerved by what happened at dinner. I'm unable to eat the tiniest bite. Exhausted, I give up entirely and ready for bed. I'll sleep it off; tomorrow I'll have more clarity about the situation. I can decide what needs to be done about it then.

And I almost believe it, until a few hours later, when I'm jostled awake by someone in my room.

CHAPTER SIX

ALESSANDRA

I scream, or try to, but a hand slaps over my mouth. My hands form fists and I thrash out, seeking to hit my attacker, but in the dark and my sleepy confusion, my fists hit nothing but air. I kick my legs, shoving the blankets down so that I can launch off the bed. I swing out with a foot, this time colliding with the stomach of the person restraining me. The person gasps and the hold on my mouth loosens as I hear the person hit the ground. I jerk my face free and draw in air to scream.

"Miss Vitale! You must be quiet!"

I freeze. "P-Pranee?"

"Yes, Miss," she groans from the floor.

"W-what are you doing? Why did you wake me like that?"

Pranee peels herself off the floor. "I'm so happy you woke up. Miss Vitale, you must leave immediately."

My still-shaking hands fumble around for the bedside lamp. I've nearly found it when Pranee notices what I'm about to do and grabs my hands with hers. "No, Miss. You must not light it. They'll know you're awake and come sooner."

"Who? What? What are you saying?" I ask, slowly growing more alert. "Pranee, what are you doing here?"

"Miss Vitale, you must *listen*," Pranee says with such a sharp tone, I fall silent, blinking with sudden alertness. Pranee has never used a tone like that with me, not even close.

"Mr. Chakrii invited you to dine with him last night, yes?"

"How do you know—"

"Everyone knows that," she says hurriedly, "it's all over the resort. The guests, the staff, everyone."

"But why would anyone even care?"

"Because Mr. Chakrii is an important man! A very important man. In fact, the *most* important man on Phuket."

My mind flashes to the gold walking stick, the casual yet proprietary way he stroked it. Like the walking stick wasn't the only thing he owned.

"Well, I didn't have dinner with him," I say slowly. "Barely talked to the man for five, ten minutes."

"Yes, exactly!" she cries. "What you did was much worse. You actually left when he invited you as his special guest. Miss Vitale, you simply don't understand how stupid ..." she trails off, as if horrified she's called a guest "stupid," then rallies and says, her tone just as forceful, "How incredibly dangerous it was to anger him like that."

"I don't see how leaving a meal is such a big deal."

"But leaving the dinner is an insult! No one disagrees with the Dragon. No one. They especially don't get up and leave. And you did it at dinner; many of the people dining were his friends and closest business associates! This is a grave disrespect. He has lost much face because of you, intentionally or not. His position cannot allow him to tolerate such an insult. If he lets you go, others might think they, too, can insult him and get away with it. You must be made an example of."

"This is ... this is ridiculous," I stammer, my heart pounding. "What are you saying? What? This isn't some B-grade spy movie; this is my life! You can't possibly think he means to harm me?"

"But he will, Miss. He will. He has to. The Golden Dragon cannot ignore an attack, or else another serpent might attempt to sink its fangs into him."

I blink at her, barely able to make out her form in the darkness. "Golden Dragon ... Golden Lotus ... you mean ..."

"Yes, yes! The Dragon owns this hotel. You have insulted the man whose very villa you reside in right now! This is not like other hotels; you live here at the pleasure of Mr. Chakrii. It does not matter if you have paid to stay here. If he wants you gone, you are gone. You must leave before he comes for you."

"Pranee," I say, refusing to give in to such histrionics, "I am ... listen. I am not a normal person. What I mean to say is, I am the daughter of a very important family in Italy, yes? We own a very large company. My face is, um, frequently in the papers. This ... this Dragon or whatever can't just kidnap me or kill me. I'm too well-known. It would create an international incident. Surely Mr. Chakrii's pride is not so great that he would risk that, would he?"

Pranee is silent a long time, her faint breathing the only sound in the dark. "Miss Vitale. Many beautiful women go missing in this country all the time. Even, from time to time, the rich ones. It will be as if you simply disappeared, a tragic accident. Your country will mourn you. The people here, though, will know the difference. That is all that matters."

I swallow hard, unwilling to actually entertain any of this insanity but yet beginning to believe Pranee might have a point.

"Okay," I say, climbing out of bed, feeling an intense compulsion to move. "Okay. So, what, I need to leave? What proof do you have of any of this?"

She barks a startled laugh. "Proof? Your dinner was delivered here last night, yes?"

"Yeah ... so?"

"You didn't eat it, right?"

"How could you possibly know that?" I ask, a sick feeling unfurling in my gut.

"Because, Miss," Pranee says, her tone sad, "The Dragon instructed the chef to drug it so you'd fall asleep. The chef did, but you woke up right away when I touched you. You wouldn't ... it's a strong drug, Miss. You should still be sleeping."

"I can't believe this," I say, "you're saying he *drugged* me? Am I still sleeping? I must be. Who in their right mind would drug someone for canceling their dinner plans? I don't believe it."

"Miss Vitale," Pranee says, her voice serious, "Mr. Chakrii is *chao pho*."

"He's what?"

"He's *chao pho*. It means 'godfather' in Thai. You know what that means, yes?"

I shiver. "Yes. I know what that means."

"The Golden Dragon controls one of the largest *chao pho* gangs in the entire country, Miss Vitale. If he wants something, it's done. And that is why a mere person like you cannot simply insult him. He owns most of the important resorts in Phuket. His members extract all the money from the tourist scams. Anyone who isn't directly owned by him is likely paying him protection money. He's untouchable."

"I'm beginning to see why he had a walking stick of solid gold."

"Yes," Pranee whispers, "he uses it to remind people of how much higher he is than us. He is like a god. It is a symbol of just how much more he has than the rest of us."

I remain silent for a long moment, pacing back and forth, refusing to believe the situation really is that bad. I mean, a Thai mafia don? Really? My family is used to the mafia. You don't amass a huge company in Italy like my family has without coming into contact with the mafia.

But that's exactly the reason why I struggle to believe any of this. I'm an expensive target! I can't really be worth the trouble for Chakrii, can I?

"Maybe this is still blown way out of proportion. You could be mistaken about the drugs in my food, about all of it. I think in the light of tomorrow, everything will seem—"

"Come here."

"What?"

"Come here!" Pranee hisses. I shuffle closer. "Come to the window. Yes. Now stand in front of me. Don't move the curtain! Let me ... see that man?"

I peer through the crack between the curtain and the window, struggling to see whatever is—"There's a man down there!"

"Yes."

I stare at him, horror cutting through the skepticism I've felt since Pranee startled me awake. A man stands in the botanical garden across from my gate. He's around my height, but what he lacks in stature, he makes up for in bulk. His hands are clasped together in front of him, his feet spread shoulder-width apart. I don't need him to unbutton his suit jacket to know he has a gun holstered somewhere. This guy's a textbook security employee.

He doesn't move, his gaze boring into the door, as if he expects someone to come out of it at any moment. I swallow hard.

Or as if he expects someone to go through.

"H-he could be ..." I trail off, not bothering to finish whatever lame excuse that was about to roll off my tongue. Normal, innocent people don't stand motionless in parks two hours before dawn. This guy's got an agenda, one I have no desire to learn of firsthand.

"There's another one on the opposite end of the garden. Near the main entrance."

"What are they doing?"

"They're waiting."

"Waiting for what?" I ask, my voice turning up an octave.

"They're waiting for the Dragon to tell them to come in here and get you. Do you believe me now?"

"Y-yeah, I think I do."

"Good. We must go. Pack only your most important things; we must leave within five minutes. They could receive the order at any time."

"Why are you even helping me?" I ask, mystified. "If this is what he'll do to me, I don't even want to think about what he'd do to you for helping me. Wait, I definitely don't want that. In fact, you can't help me. I'll just hail a cab."

"You can't hire a driver," Pranee says, aghast. "Half of them are employed by the Golden Dragon, and the other half are terrified of him. You sneaking out in the middle of the night is as good as telling the Dragon your plans."

"Naturally," I say, throwing up my hands. "Of course they are. Well, whatever. I'll figure something out. I don't want to risk you getting into trouble. Only one of us should risk our lives, and apparently I already did that."

"Miss Vitale," Pranee says, "I *must* help you. I want to help you. You've saved the life of my cousin! You wanted me to help someone instead of repaying you, remember? Well, I choose to help you. I could not possibly leave you now, when you need help the most."

"That wasn't what I meant," I mumble.

"I don't care. Now, pack this." She shoves my carry-on luggage at me.

"What about the rest of my stuff?"

"You'll leave it."

"Right," I mutter, trying not to think about how much all of that cost. It seems a stupid thing to worry about right now, but those clothes are all I have linking me to home. The only things that feel familiar.

Pranee stuffs the suitcase full of clothing while I dress in a dark pair of athletic leggings and shirt, followed by my running sneakers. The suitcase is nearly full when at the last second she adds a red bikini I've worn maybe once. A swim suit probably is practical clothing for someone who's lived her entire life in Phuket, but I feel like a loser saying she might as well leave it. It's already in there, anyway.

We fumble around in the dark, using the illumination from our phone screens—but not the phones' flashlights—to see what we're doing. I stuff my wallet, computer, tablet, and the few books I brought into my small backpack, the only possessions I really cannot do without. We move so fast it feels surreal, like I'm still dreaming, like this is a nightmare I should be waking up from any second now, laughing over how real it felt.

It's only as I'm slinging my backpack over my shoulder that I finally remember.

CHAPTER SEVEN

ALESSANDRA

"Pranee!"
 "What?"
"My passport!"
She freezes.
"Oh no," I moan. "I left it with the concierge. It's in the vault."

Pranee says something in Thai that I can only assume is a string of curses. "You left it with them?"

"They told me it would be safest. I didn't think—I had no idea—you don't actually think they'd do something with it, do you?"

Pranee doesn't reply, which is reply enough. I clutch the straps of my backpack, trying to remain calm. The last thing I need is to freak out unnecessarily. There's no reason to believe it wouldn't be there. No way would Pravat steal my passport.

"Should I go—"

"No," says Pranee quickly. "You can't be seen in the

lobby. I'll go. You know how to get to the private beach, yes?"

My stomach flips. "I do," I say slowly, although I've never visited it. I may be doing better sticking my feet in the pool, but going anywhere near the ocean is absolutely out of the question. I just ... I can't do it. Surely there must be some other way to get out of here?

"Wait here ten minutes—ten minutes exactly—while I get your passport, and then meet me on the beach. I've brought my family's boat. It's pulled up on the beach. After ten minutes, go out to the boat with your suitcase and lay down in the back. Cover yourself with the tarp and wait for me."

Oh dear God no. "Pranee, I can't—"

"You must," she says with such a hint of understanding that I wonder how much she knows about my water phobia. Has she witnessed me torturing myself in the pool? "Ten minutes, remember?"

"O-okay," I stutter, my terror of stumbling out onto that beach much greater than a literal mobster supposedly wanting to hurt me.

Pranee disappears downstairs. I follow much more slowly, my clammy hands clutched tight around the handle of my suitcase and my backpack strap. Am I really doing this? Am I really fleeing in the middle of the night? How has my vacation gone so horribly wrong?

When the ten minutes elapse, I creep out the back door, which I haven't used before now, and cross as quickly and quietly as I can manage in my jittery state. My heart hammers in my chest. I quietly open the back gate just slightly enough for me to squeeze through. Pranee's already unlocked it and will re-lock it with the set of keys she must have stolen from the concierge.

I grind to a halt when my feet hit sand. Oh God. I can't do this. She wants me to walk out to that water? Actually put myself in it? No way. This is impossible. It's so dark. I can't even see the boat and using my phone to illuminate the beach is too dangerous. This is out of the question.

My mind flashes back to the sight of the hired muscle standing in the garden. There is simply no reasonable explanation for him standing out there, staring at my villa. I want to deny it, but I can't. Something is wrong. What am I going to do, just let him waltz in and carry out whatever he's planning to do to me? Try to sneak past him in the garden? Not possible.

If I can relocate to another resort, at least I can regroup. Find some reasonable way out of this. If it really does turn out that this Chakrii guy is after me, well, then I'll have to leave for Italy. If it's all just an overreaction, it shouldn't be difficult to return for the rest of my stuff or checkout over the phone.

I just have to make it onto the boat. Squeezing my eyes just, I drag in a deep breath for courage, my feet shuffling around in the sand. I can't even see the boat. How am I supposed to force myself into the water *and* find the boat?

My right foot suddenly slides into a depression, and my eyes fly open. Of course! I can't use a light, but I can use Pranee's footprints. I haven't used this beach once since I came here so none of them are mine. I doubt anyone else is allowed out here while I'm staying at the Golden Lotus, which means there can't be that many footprints. They must be Pranee's.

Stepping carefully, I blindly follow the footprints down the beach, inching along until the sand becomes firm. My heart lurches; the ocean roars in nearness. My feet slow down, dragging through the sand with dread, my suitcase banging along behind me.

Water suddenly surges over my feet as I shuffle along, soaking me up to my ankles. I gag and slap a hand over my mouth to keep from crying out, kicking uselessly with my now drenched sneaker in a futile effort to remove some of the water. It's cold, so very cold. I can't do this. There's no way I can find the boat. I can't wade through the water. It's just too—

A light clicks on in the house at my back. I freeze, terrified. Pranee knows not to flick on a light. Which could only mean ... they're looking for me. As much as I wanted to believe Pranee's fears are exaggerated, she was right; men are after me. If I have any luck at all, they'll search the house long enough for me to get away before they think to search the beach.

I must get into that boat no matter how much I'd rather run screaming from the water. My eyes finally land on the boat, illuminated by the light from the house. It's a decrepit dingy with an outboard motor I seriously doubt can get us anywhere fast. It's only feet away; I was right to follow the tracks.

But that same light also illuminates *me*.

I'm running out of time. This is just like the pool. Unpleasant, yes, but not impossible. I've been able to sit there with my feet dangling in the water for nearly fifteen minutes now; surely I can handle climbing into a boat.

Before I can let my fear get the better of me, I slosh the rest of the way to the boat. Water swirls steadily around my feet. My heart clenches and the tiniest whimper escapes me, but I force it down so far I know there will be an eruption later. As long as I'm nowhere near here when it happens, I don't care. But that doesn't prevent my heart from pounding and my breath from wheezing in and out of my lungs as I move one foot after the other.

My shaking fingers desperately clutch the boat as I hoist my soaked carry-on into the back. Luckily it's one of those hard plastic suitcases, but who knows if water's still seeped inside. I don't even care. Gingerly, I remove my backpack with all my electronics and gently put it in a dry patch next to the tarp Pranee mentioned.

Then, for lack of a better option, I roll myself inside the boat, trying to hit as close to dead center as possible. The craft still dips sharply; I whimper again as the gunwale dips closer and closer to the water. If this boat takes on water, I'm finished. Forget my backpack and suitcase, they're going to find *me* at the bottom of the sea.

But a moment later, the boat pops back up, stabilizing. My breath whooshes out in relief. With the last of my strength, I pull the tarp over me like Pranee instructed.

Then commences the wait. I hug myself, my fingers digging into my arms as I pray for Pranee to return. The water slaps the boat all around me, taunting me with how very close, how very defenseless I am right now. Any significant wave could slosh right over onto me and then they'll know I'm out here, because if that happens, I'm screaming my head off.

Eventually soft footsteps approach. I shudder, praying it's Pranee. What will I do if it isn't? During the wait, the light coming through the tarp has grown brighter as more lights are turned on in my former villa. They must know I'm gone by now. Any second now they could come out here.

But I don't dare lift my head to see if the person is Pranee.

"Miss, are you here?"

"Yes," I whisper in extraordinary relief, making to pull the tarp off me.

"Leave it for now."

"Did you get my passport?"

Silence. Stretching so long I have my answer.

"They took my passport, didn't they?" I say dejectedly.

"I'm sorry, Miss. You will have to contact your embassy. Please stay under the tarp until I tell you it's safe to take it off."

I don't bother with a reply. What is there to say? My life has taken a decidedly awful turn. There's a gentle shove as she pushes the boat off the sand, and then the boat dips again as she climbs inside. She draws two oars out of the boat beside me and begins rowing. My stomach lurches with every movement. Nausea claws up my throat; I slap my hand over my mouth again, determined to force it back. Long minutes pass with silent rowing before Pranee finally stops and slides the oars back into the boat.

"It's okay now," she says as she moves to the back of the

boat and starts the motor. It sputters, forcing her to pull back a few times before the motor finally turns over.

Throwing the tarp off, I sit up and immediately regret it. Nothing but water surrounds us as far as the eye can see. I look over Pranee's shoulder and can just barely make out the Golden Lotus Resort in the distance. Turning back to face the front, some lights from across the Bay of Phuket just barely twinkle, but they seem like miles away. They probably *are* miles away, and we somehow have to get there in a boat whose motor sounds like it might quit at any moment.

"What now?" I say in a small voice, unable to take my eyes off the water sloshing up near the lip of the boat. "Where do I go? Are you taking me to the police?"

Pranee aims the boat across the bay directly opposite the Golden Lotus Resort. "I would not advise that, Miss."

"Why on earth not? Of course I must go to the police. They need to be notified of what happened. Those men were sent to kidnap me, and—"

"The Golden Dragon has many employees working in the police force, Miss. I can take you, but ..."

"But Chakrii will be expecting that," I say.

Pranee nods. "It would be easy for him to find your location. He has spies everywhere. It is how he maintains his power. I worry that if I left you with the police, one of his spies would quickly deliver you to him."

My stomach churns with growing panic. I resist the urge to tear at my hair. "Then what do I do? Where do I go?" I ask, then answer my own question. "The consulate. They have an Italian consulate in Phuket, don't they?"

"Yes. I can take you there," she says, but there's a slight catch in her voice.

"Pranee, why wouldn't ..." I puzzle it through, then realize she's essentially already told me. "There's someone in the Italian consulate? Or are you afraid of someone seeing you helping me and then Chakrii coming after you?"

"I can take you," Pranee says quickly.

"No, no," I say. "That's it, right? Chakrii might find out. Of course. Don't take me to the consulate. I'll get there by myself. I'd hate it if you lost your job or worse because you helped me."

"But I can—"

"No, Pranee. You've already done so much as it is. I won't risk endangering you."

Pranee steers in silence for a few minutes. I'm lost in thought, trying to come up with a solution to the fact that I'm currently homeless.

"I can take you to the Green-Eyed Tiger."

My gaze jerks to her. "The what?"

Pranee glances at me, frowns. "The Green-Eyed Tiger is Mr. Chakrii's only enemy in Phuket. The one person he cannot control or intimidate."

"Who is he?"

Pranee shifts uncomfortably. "He is someone who will keep you safe until you can arrange a passport and a way out of Thailand. The Dragon won't bother you so long as you stay with him. He wouldn't dare."

"Why? I thought Chakrii terrified everyone. What does this guy have on him?"

"He has a ... collection of skills that have hurt Chakrii

before. Now they circle each other, each searching for a weakness to hurt the other, but they're both too powerful to defeat the other, so the war stalls indefinitely."

"What is he? One of those ... what did you call Chakrii? *Chao pho*? A godfather?"

"No. He's what you call ... a lone wolf? Is that the expression?"

"I believe so," I say. "You mean a person who works by himself? Keeps apart from other people?"

"Yes, that's it. He has a business, a resort, where he lives alone when guests are not there."

"Then why does Chakrii fear him?"

Pranee hesitates. "After he hurt the Dragon, people started coming to the Tiger, thinking he might help them. Protect them. And he did, in a way. Every once in a while the Dragon receives a retaliation after one of the locals gets hurt. A local who isn't affiliated with the Dragon. Sometimes one of the Dragon's shipments is misplaced, or one of his thugs ends up in the hospital. Things like that. The Dragon has lost much money because of the Tiger. He despises him. However, none of it has ever been tied back to the Tiger, so the Dragon does not dare provoke him. It would be a fearsome fight. The rumor is once he's finally provoked, the Tiger goes berserk. You know what that means, yes?"

"I think so," I say slowly. "A person who goes mad with fighting, making him unstoppable. A person who only later returns to himself when the battle is over."

"Yes, like that. The Tiger is like that. That is why we call him that name."

"And you want me to *stay* with this person?"

"Once he hears what the Dragon has done to you, the Tiger will protect you. He's protected others before. If we didn't have him, we would all be stuck under the Dragon's terror. With the Tiger, we can hope to be left alone."

"Hmm," I say noncommittally. We'll have to wait until we reach the shore before I can think about this. I'm too freaked out by being this close to the ocean to make rational decisions. I return to the bottom of the boat and pull the tarp back over me. This old thing barely cuts through the water, which is choppy enough to send it slamming up and down with every wave we encounter. I'll faint if I have to keep staring at the ocean around me.

It's a long haul across the Bay of Phuket. By the time Pranee finally pulls the boat up to a dock, I'm about two seconds from hurling right over the side.

"This way, Miss," she says, pulling the tarp back and grabbing my suitcase.

I follow much more slowly, unable to stand in my weakened state. Without caring how I must look, I crawl on hands and knees over the side of the boat and up onto the dock. I roll onto my back and stare up at the starless sky, surprised by my sudden sense of accomplishment.

I took a boat—no, a tiny little wooden thing barely *passing* for a boat—kilometers across open water with nothing but some rickety boards protecting me from falling into the ocean. I actually stuck my feet in the ocean, too! And I didn't faint! Or puke! I nearly did, but I didn't, so it counts!

I *can* get better.

A startled laugh escapes me.

"Are you okay, Miss?"

I climb to my feet and impulsively hug Pranee. "I *am* okay, Pranee. I really am."

"Okay ..." she says slowly, too polite to comment on why I'm suddenly laughing in the middle of this dangerous situation, "well, if you'll follow me, we are almost there."

Pranee leads me to a car, even older and more decrepit than the boat. If I get out of this situation alive, I'm going to buy her a new boat *and* a car because she more than deserves it. She loads my suitcase into the trunk and then opens the passenger door for me.

"How far is it?" I ask, staring out at the Bay. It's near dawn; the sky is already lightening. My would-be captors back at the resort know by now that I've escaped. "Will we get there in time?"

"Yes, Miss. It's just down the road."

Pranee pulls out, weaving around the other cars and motos zipping around in the pre-dawn light. I stare out the window, attempting to push back a wave of despair. What am I going to tell this guy? The truth? Fall at his knees and beg for aid? What if he takes one look at me and decides to use me as a way to get one over on his enemy? What will I do then?

I worry about it all the way down the road until Pranee pulls into the drive for what could charitably be called a resort. It's grown light enough to make out a faded sign proclaiming "Three Divers Resort." The sign dangles from a rusted chain on one side, the other half of the chain presumably already gone the way the rest of the resort is going. The pavement leading up to the entrance is cracked and uneven, grass shooting up from the cracks. It's barely wide enough for Pranee's car to pull through—and that's saying something, because her car is not exactly hogging up the road.

There is no formal garden at this place, that's for sure. What grass that still manages to grow despite the owner's clear efforts to the contrary is brown and sickly, with dirt patches scattered throughout the tiny yard where the vegetation has already given up.

The building itself, of course, is technically standing, but it could do with a coat or two or fifty of literally any color paint so that the stains I don't even want to contemplate the origin of would be hidden. There's not a single light illuminated anywhere. Zero signs of life. The whole structure is listing to the side, like the foundation is off.

If Pranee herself hadn't taken me here, I would have turned right around and disappeared as quickly as humanly possible.

This is the resort owned by a man who frightens the godfather that walks around with a stick made of solid gold? Really? How could he possibly cause a financial hit of any significance to Chakrii?

I stare at the sorry site in astonishment. It's not that this place is easily the least luxurious accommodation I've ever stayed at—although it so definitely is—or that I'm suddenly wondering if I'm kidding myself thinking anyone who can't even mow a lawn properly is somehow going to protect me from the Golden Dragon—which I for sure am—there's another reason entirely that has me so shocked.

And that reason is this: It's like this place doesn't *want* guests here. Like whoever owns this place has done his very best to make it as unappealing as possible. Or maybe it's more like the owner is trying to make a point; that amid all this beauty, there's still a lot of ugliness that everyone here would prefer to ignore. And since I've unfortunately and unwillingly come face-to-face with the ugly underbelly of Phuket, I kind of wonder if the owner has a point.

Pranee and I glance at each other. "You're, um, sure this is the right spot?"

She nods. "Oh yes. Everyone knows this is where he lives. My uncle even came here to ask for help with my cousin's medical bills, but the Tiger wasn't around."

"Wonderful," I say weakly. I stare at the building; no way this place improves in the bright of day.

"I will wait here for you," Pranee says without looking at me. Great, even *she* doesn't want to interact with this guy.

Well, what else can I do? I've already sailed across the ocean in a rickety boat and survived. How bad could this really be? I'm out of options. Pushing open my door, I pick my way around the uneven pavement and step up three cracked and uneven steps to reach the entrance. The doors have been pulled closed. How long have they been shut? Overnight? A week? Forever? Who knows.

I look for a doorbell and shockingly find one. Pressing it, no sound emerges. Right. Why on earth would I assume it works? Forming a fist, I knock on the door instead, then wait. Nothing. I knock again, then begin pounding, because fuck it at this point. A minute later I finally hear footsteps.

The door slowly creaks open. A man stands on the other side. He stares at me. I stare right back. We gape at each other in complete silence.

Then I just laugh. Because of course they call him the Green-Eyed Tiger. I would have, too. It fits everything about him.

Guy slams the door shut in my face.

II
THE TIGER

CHAPTER EIGHT

ALESSANDRA

"Hey!" I yell, both fists pounding on the door.

It's ripped open. Guy glares at me and folds his arms over his chest, his stance wide. Everything in him screams "fuck off."

"What are you doing here?" he snaps.

"No, what are *you* doing here?" I snap back, knowing it's an absurd response and not caring.

His nostrils flare as he huffs. "I *live* here."

I am going to kill Pranee. What the hell do I tell him?

He steps toward me. "Let me repeat myself. What are you doing here?"

I just look at him, trying to push back a wave of fatalism. I cannot tell this man why I'm really here. We did not get off on the right foot. He's been clear about how little he likes me. If he's this Green-Eyed Tiger, why would he endanger himself to help someone he doesn't like? What if I tell him Chakrii wants to kidnap me and he tosses me out on my ass? Sure, he helps other people in Phuket, apparently, but I'm not a local. I don't have to live with Chakrii the rest of my life. That's probably why Guy helps them; to keep some sort of peace in Phuket. To give people an honest chance to earn a living. I'm none of that. Why would this guy be moved to help me when he doesn't like me?

Or, my God, what if he's keeping his identity as the Green-Eyed Tiger a secret, and my asking him to protect me using his alter ego infuriates him? Pranee said nothing was ever tied back to him. He might see me as a threat if I told him I knew!

I can't risk that, and I certainly can't take the risk he might make me leave, even if Pranee's convinced he'll help me. At least not right away; maybe I'll get a better feel for him and then I'll be comfortable telling him later. For now, though, I have nowhere else to go. No one to help me until I can make an appointment at the consulate. Better to just act like I want a place to stay.

"I need a room."

His head snaps back, then his gaze hardens. "And you just happened to settle on my resort? How did you even find it? This is not your kind of place. Are you following me?"

I wince, hating how this must look to him. "No. I had no idea this was your resort. My friend's the one who brought me here."

His eyes flick to the car behind me. "And why did she do that? There are plenty of places more suitable to your taste."

His tone sharpens sarcastically on that last word, like my so-called taste is poor. I resist the urge to snap back that my taste can't be that terrible if he frequently dines at the Golden Lotus.

"I came to Thailand to get away from it all," I say, which is the honest truth. "At that last resort ... well, everyone knows me. I just want some anonymity."

He makes a derisive noise like he patently disbelieves me. Then his face stills in consideration. He flicks a gaze down my body thoughtfully. Zero chance I'll like what he says next, but I stare him down, refusing to give him the satisfaction of seeing my unease.

"I don't have room for you," he says, leaning against the door jamb.

I make a show of glancing around the deserted property. "Really?"

"The place is booked up starting tomorrow," he growls.

Yeah, right. "Well, then, I'll just stay here for one night."

That's all I really need, anyway. By tomorrow, I'll have an emergency passport and be on the first plane out of here.

He blinks at me. "You don't want to stay here. Just go somewhere else. Have your friend drop you off at the resort two miles down the road. That's three kilometers to you. It's beautiful. Right up your alley."

My mind races trying to come up with a reasonable excuse to decline. "Oh, no," I say, "I don't know whoever owns that resort—"

"You don't know me."

"—but I do know you, and I would much rather spend my money with someone I know. It's more personal, don't you think?"

"No. I don't think," he snaps, straightening away from the door jamb. That speculative look is back. "However ... I don't have room for you ... but I do need an employee."

I fold my arms over my chest protectively. Just what kind of employee does he mean? His gaze drops to my chest, and he scowls. "An employee?" I say, trying to ignore the sensation of those green eyes on me.

"Yes," he says, still irritated. "Someone to clean the rooms, the pool, and the yard. My guy just quit yesterday, and I need someone before everyone arrives tomorrow. You work for me, and you can stay where he was staying."

"Would I get a wage, too?" I ask, curious.

"Of course I'd pay you," he says, voice tight with fury. Great, I've offended the man who's reluctantly giving me a job and a safe place to stay. He rolls his eyes and adds, "Not that the wage would be a drop in the bucket for you."

I don't reply to that because he's not exactly wrong. I don't need whatever money he gives me, but I'll give it to Pranee and her family, along with the boat and the car. Someone might as well benefit from this shitshow.

But fine, whatever. At least he'll let me stay here. "Done," I say, and extend a hand.

His jaw drops. He thought I'd never take him up on his offer! He figured my spoiled self would never stoop to cleaning for a place to stay. Well, screw him. I may not have any experience cleaning rooms and taking care of grounds, but I'm a hard worker, and if this is the offer on the table, I'm taking it. I will figure out how to do what he wants from me.

And it's only for one, maybe two days, max. Then I'm

out of here. I'll leave so soon he'll even think he succeeded in scaring me off. Win-win for everyone.

I just have to sacrifice a little of that Italian pride that screams I can't let him win like this.

He stares at my hand like it's about to bite him, his head shaking back and forth. "No, you don't get it. You'd have to work. It's backbreaking stuff. Lots of lifting and scrubbing. You wouldn't like it."

Oh, I already know I'm going to hate it, but he's deluding himself if he thinks I have any intention of turning it down. I wiggle my fingers at him. "I'm sure I can handle it."

He swears under his breath, plowing a hand through his hair. I wait as he shifts on his feet, his gaze locked on the ground, as if berating himself for making the offer and trying to find a way to back out. But if there's one thing I do know about this guy, it's that he's got just as much pride as I do; he'll gnaw his arm off before being the first to back down.

"Fine," he grumbles, giving my hand a desultory shake. Electricity snaps up my arm, and he drops my hand like I've just electrocuted him. Whoa.

"So are we finally going to do names now?" I say, surreptitiously wiping my hand on my leg in an effort to rub feeling back into it.

He throws his head back and stares up at the sky, as if in disbelief he's gotten himself into this situation. Then his gaze drops back to mine; I'm instantly snared by the brilliant green. Damn, that's annoying. How on earth am I going to be able to work for this man when every time he looks at me my brain misfires?

"Ford," he grumbles. "My name is Ford. Walker."

"Ford?" I say, confused. Is this an American name or something? "You mean like the car?"

He says flatly, "Wow, yeah, I've never heard that one before. Is your name Ferrari?"

I snort. "No, it's Vitale. Alessandra Vitale."

Ford grunts and steps out onto the entryway. I resist the urge to step back, craning my head up as he towers over me. He cocks a brow in annoyance. "Are you going to stand there all day, or do you need help with your shit? Unless you've decided not to stay after all?"

Wouldn't he like that?

Before he has a chance to change his mind, I turn and march toward the vehicle where Pranee waits. She notices my expression and pales, leaping out from behind the wheel to jerk open the trunk.

"Why didn't you *tell* me he's your Green-Eyed Tiger!" I hiss as I drag my lonely suitcase out of the trunk, keeping my back to Ford because it doesn't take an idiot to know he's watching our every move.

Pranee looks guilty. "I feared you wouldn't let me take you to him if I told you. Everyone knows you two don't like each other."

"And how does everyone know that?"

"You two had words during your dinner."

I tamp down the desire to make an Italian gesture of utter exasperation. "Of course, of course. How could I forget the resort gossip? Was I watched the *entire* time I was at that damn place?"

Pranee's guilty expression somehow becomes even more guilt-ridden.

"*Riiight.*" I resist the urge to kick the suitcase, grumbling, "There are entirely too many people here with animal nicknames. No, make that too many people with stupid fierce predator nicknames. Next you'll be telling me some woman named Raptor is going to try to chop my arms off. People should be running around with their actual names so I know who the hell everyone's talking about. Not that he ever actually gave me his name until today, but still."

"I'm sorry this has happened, Miss," Pranee says sadly.

I sigh, my shoulders slumping. "No, Pranee. I'm not angry with you; I'm just frustrated. You saved my life. I'll never be able to repay you. Can you *please* call me Alessandra now? We're beyond friendship at this point."

Pranee smiles. "Okay, Alessandra."

"Finally," I say, feeling lighthearted for the first time since she shook me awake.

"Should I help you bring this up?" she asks, motioning toward my suitcase.

"No, I can handle him myself." Mostly.

Pranee glances over my shoulder. Her face turns bright red. It takes everything in me not to look at him. His facial expression must absolutely broadcast unpleasantness.

And I'm going to be living with him. No, *working* for him. This is ... not ideal.

"Well," I say, pushing that disconcerting thought out of my head. There will be time to panic over my new living situation later. You know, once this entire situation finally seems real to me. "I suppose this is goodbye."

Pranee bobs her head. "Yes, M-Alessandra. I will try to get the rest of your belongings to you."

"But not if it endangers you," I say firmly.

She nods. "Of course. I must keep a low profile at the resort."

"Pranee, I don't think you should go back there," I say, concerned for her safety. "What if they find out you're the one who helped me? They might hurt you. I couldn't stand that."

Pranee shakes her head. "I am unimportant. They won't think I could be involved."

"You're sure? You swear it?"

"Yes, Alessandra."

Impulsively, I pull her into a hug. She stiffens in surprise, then wraps her arms around me. "Be careful," I whisper.

"You be careful as well. Have the Tiger take you to the consulate; you'll be safe until you leave. Chakrii would not dare come here."

I watch as she pulls away, a sudden feeling of panic overwhelming me. What am I going to do without Pranee? Will I ever see her again? What if Chakrii discovers she helped me? I shudder, wishing I had a way to guarantee her safety.

"I didn't hire you to stand there all day."

I whirl on him, eager for the distraction, for the outlet to vent my frustration over my current situation. "And you didn't really hire me at all. I had to …"

He cocks one brow mockingly. "Beg me?"

I glare at him, furious with myself that I very nearly did just that. Grabbing the handle of my suitcase, I drag it up the walkway, my backpack slung over my shoulder. When I reach him, he's studying me.

"You don't seem like the kind of person to travel lightly."

"Hmm."

"Can't fit many green dresses in a tiny little suitcase like that."

I smile at him, delighted even though I know better. "Aw. Remembering our dinner? That's so cute."

He turns abruptly, heading toward the entrance. "Try to keep up."

I soldier along behind him, smirking at his back. When his shoulders stiffen, I have to tell myself he couldn't possibly have seen me. He's probably just annoyed in general. It's practically his default setting. I bet if Ford Walker ever laughed, his internal circuitry would malfunction and he'd explode.

And I definitely do *not* want to see that happen. At all.

By the time I follow him inside, Ford has slipped behind the front desk. I don't bother to hide my curiosity—curiosity that quickly turns to dismay. This resort needs major repairs. And actually, resort is a very charitable word to describe this place. I'm grateful to have a place to lay low, but still ... wow.

The building must have been constructed decades ago, and I would be shocked if it's been updated at any time since. The carpet and wallpaper are sorely outdated; the greens and blues that were probably cheerful at one point now seem sad and even a little grimy. Definitely faded. The atrocious decor really isn't something I should be fixating on when a criminal is trying to abduct and possibly kill me, but I just can't *not* notice it.

Two hallways stretch out to my left and right; the elevator stands right before me, which I will not be taking. If the elevator is anything like this carpet, which has three threadbare sections in the concierge area alone, I doubt it's been serviced any time recently. No way am I risking my life with that.

I can only imagine what the rooms are like.

"Heads up."

A set of keys come hurling at me. I barely manage to get my hand up in time to prevent them from whacking me in the face.

Ford jabs a thumb behind him, indicating the hall to my right. "Follow that down to the end. When you reach it, go through the door and follow the path around the pool to the pool house. On the opposite side there's a door marked 'Administration.' That's where you're staying. Once you've settled in your many things, you can come back here, and I'll give you your work for the day."

"What, no showing me to my room?"

Ford stares at me balefully. "You're not a guest, remember? Employees are expected to be self-sufficient."

"How could I forget?" I mutter.

"If you're not up to it, I could certainly point you in the direction of another place to stay. In fact, literally any direction would suffice. Walk thirty feet and you'll hit a resort.

Better yet, go back to the Golden Lotus. That's really more your style."

"What would you know about my style?"

"Plenty. I had the great pleasure of staring at it for over three hours, remember?"

"Why, Mr. Walker. That's two remarks about my dress in as many minutes. One might think you've got a little crush."

His jaw tightens. "Go unpack and be back here in fifteen minutes or you're fired."

I smile. "You can't fire me. You need me, remember?"

His expression darkens. "No. I don't need you; I need a cleaner. You, I think we can both agree, are not that."

Well, that kind of hurts. Even if he is right. I spin on my heel, refusing to give him the satisfaction of realizing his jab hit its mark. Heading down the hall, a dark chuckle echoes behind my back.

Following his directions, I push outside and walk out into the pool area, astounded to discover it's absolutely immaculate. Spotless. There's no cracked pavement here. No sickly grass shooting up everywhere. The pool itself must be Olympic sized and is so clean the whole area reeks of chlorine. It's so massive, in fact, I get the feeling the yard itself used to be larger but was dug out at some point to expand the size of the pool. Even I can tell this pool is state-of-the-art; absolutely no expense has been spared. The contrast between the pool and the rest of the resort is so jarring my earlier intuition that the Three Divers Resort is deliberately rundown just has to be true. No other explanation makes any sense. What is going on here?

I take a few nervous steps toward the side and peer down, down, down. How far down *is* that thing?! The deep end looks like it could easily be twice as deep as my height. Maybe even three times.

Oh God. He expects me to clean *this*?

CHAPTER NINE

FORD

I am the dumbest fuck.

Alessandra sashays down the hall, her suitcase banging along behind the graceful sway of the gently-rounded hips that would bring a lesser man than me to his knees. I've dreamed of those hips, that ass, and that long, wrap-your-fist-around-it dark brown hair. I've stayed up late, staring bleary-eyed at the ceiling, paralyzed by the memory of her little smirk right before she says one of her little remarks that infuriatingly puts me in my place. All that fire begs to be tamed, or perhaps inflamed even further.

I despise her for it. I resent this attraction to her. I don't want it. Italians are supposed to be passionate, so maybe that's why it's felt as though a comet has lit up my entire world from the moment she fell into it. And that would certainly be the easiest explanation. Who wouldn't be attracted to a sexy brunette with perfect curves and an accent any man would lose his head over?

It could be that. More likely, though, the real reason I

can't get her out of my head is that, for a while now, my life has been colorless. I've been going through the motions, keeping my head down. Forgetting. But it was fine. *I* was fine. Or I thought I was. But this woman, so beautiful, so graceful, so fucking classy, with that ability to cut me down to size with one little look of cool disdain, has only underscored how much I've lost. Namely, how much better a man's life is when he has a gorgeous woman to share it with.

I'd forgotten that. Purposely. Now I remember, damn her.

I should have never agreed to let her work for me.

No, back up. I never should have had dinner with her, no matter how incredible she looked in that damn dress. I shouldn't have wanted to needle her until I broke that cool reserve, just like some stupid adolescent boy.

And I never, *never* should have helped her on that fucking flight.

Everything leads back to that short hour on the plane. I told her I didn't want to talk to her, and that was true. I know when a woman expresses interest in me, and I've sworn off women. Better to offend them so they go away before their attraction deepens. This time was no different.

At least, that's what I thought. Later, when I realized she was talking to me to distract herself from her fear of flying, I felt like the biggest asshole. Couldn't even look at her, I was so ashamed. When she started panicking during landing ... shit. Couldn't take it. I took her hand, intending to distract her, but the only person I distracted was myself.

I've been distracted ever since. Fuck.

It doesn't matter a damn bit that she frequently pisses

me off; whenever she talks to me, the memory of those terror-stricken eyes and naked vulnerability—her genuine need for someone to save her—flashes through my mind and I find myself caving to whatever she wants just to ensure that look never streaks across her face again.

This fucking savior complex. How many times has it compelled me to involve myself in a situation that will only cause me grief?

I stare moodily down the hall long after she's disappeared. Why the hell did she have to show up here? As if I have any desire to be around her day in and day out. With any luck, if the shitty apartment in the pool house doesn't send her screaming, the backbreaking work my previous employee bailed on will.

That's the other thing that doesn't make sense about any of this. What the hell am I thinking? I have no explanation for why I agreed to let her stay here other than the uncomfortable truth that for the first time in months—no, years—I'm thinking with my dick instead of my head.

But that doesn't explain why *she* wants to be here. And it certainly doesn't explain why she showed up here at the literal crack of dawn.

The woman is stinkin' rich. No doubt about it. No one stays at that fucking resort without being beyond well off. But even if I'd met her on the street, I'd still know she was affluent. The wealthy always carry themselves that way. It's something in the way they move. The confidence, the assurance. It's different than the confidence I have, though, as someone who's earned it by surviving some truly awful shit.

There's an effortlessness to her, like she expects the entire world to move out of her way.

Probably because it does.

Thankfully, she doesn't have the entitlement that typically accompanies wealth. Not much, anyway. But, boy, can she turn on the disdain when she wants. Although I suppose I'm not much better, in a different way.

Still, none of that explains why she's here, either. It only explains why she shouldn't be. Women like her do not belong at the Three Divers Resort. In fact, I've made it my business to not attract people like her here.

Serious divers only come to TDR. That's the only kind of customer I want. Someone who doesn't care how shitty their room is because they know they're going to be on the boat most of the day, in town partying at night, and only in the room for a couple hours to sleep at most—assuming they don't end up in someone else's bed.

That's how I like it. No fussiness. Alessandra Vitale, on the other hand, is anything but a no-fuss miss. Something else is going on here, and I intend to get to the bottom of it. She genuinely had no idea I owned this resort. No one can fake shock that well. So what the hell is she doing here? Does she really want to get away from the so-called attention like she said? That seems like a stretch.

Muttering to myself, I pull out my phone and do a search. I only need to scroll down a few hits before I get the picture. This girl puts our spoiled American reality stars to shame. All the articles are in Italian, but the pictures of her looking drunk at various parties are enough for me to get the picture, so I don't bother translating any of them. She must have pissed someone off at the resort, and now wants to slum it with me. Fine.

I shove my phone back in my pocket, also shoving away the strange sense of disappointment I feel in learning she's another brainless party girl looking for fun in Phuket. She doesn't seem brainless to me; quite the opposite, in fact. Whatever. It's not my business. She'll hopefully be out of my life soon, anyway. Scrubbing toilets and cleaning pools will get old real fast for someone like her.

My fingers tap the counter. I stare at the spot down the hall where she disappeared. This complication could not have arrived at a worse time. For hell's sake, they're all arriving tomorrow. I specifically cleared this place out so there *wouldn't* be anyone else here, and now this shit happens. As if this week wasn't shitty enough; she'll only make it worse.

The guys are going to be all over her. No doubt about that. It's hard for *me* not to flirt with her, and I've sworn off women. Getting them to leave her alone will be a fuckin' nightmare. But at least I can control them. Alessandra, on the other hand? Yeah, right.

The image of Alessandra hooking up with one of my boys flashes through my mind. My hands turn into fists. Some uncivilized part of me screams to claim her in front of them the very moment they arrive. But the woman is nothing to me, even if I did help her on that plane. Even if we did share the one meal I've enjoyed more than any other in months.

Even if she is now working for me.

I came to Thailand to avoid these complications, found

them anyway, then lost them nevertheless. And it's not happening again, damn it.

Never again.

I glance at the clock. Twenty minutes she's been gone. What the hell is taking her so long? The room's a piece of shit; twenty minutes is nineteen minutes longer than any normal person needs to take one look at it and decide to bail.

What the hell is she doing?

Muttering under my breath, I take off down the hall. This show needs to get on the road. If I give her enough shit to do this morning, by noon she'll be gone. I'll still have most of the day to prepare for the boys arriving tomorrow.

I half expect to find her prowling through another part of the resort, sticking her nose where I haven't authorized her to go, but I don't. When I bang open the door to the pool house apartment, she's right there, slowly unpacking her clothes into the tiny piece of shit dresser shoved up against the wall. My eyes search for the green dress before I'm even aware I'm doing it.

Get it the fuck together.

I drag my gaze away from her suitcase, quickly scanning the room. It's been a while since I've been in here, before my previous employee moved in. Christ, it's a hellhole. This place badly needs repairs. But what money doesn't get sunk into maintaining the pool goes directly to keeping the rooms bearable. This little room is so far down the list of priorities, it'll probably never get fixed.

A guilty part of me considers putting her in the main building, but that would only put her closer to the guys, and that's a no-fucking-go. She'll just have to slum it. If she stays, that is.

I process all of this in a mere instant, like I've been trained. Alessandra drops the shirt she was lifting toward the dresser and whirls to face me.

"What are you doing in here?" she snaps.

"No. What are *you* doing in here?" I growl. "It's been twenty minutes."

"You told me to get situated with my things!"

I meant scaring yourself off from how shitty this place is. "I didn't mean spend all day putting the clothes of one little suitcase in that dresser. Throw 'em in there and come with me."

"Well, ex*cuse* me," I hear over my shoulder as I head out the door. Her footsteps patter along behind me as I make for the main building. My teeth grind together; I'm being the biggest dick right now, but a large part of me seriously believed she'd already be fucking off to literally anywhere else right now. Instead, I find her moving right in, getting all cozy, as if the shittiness of the apartment doesn't horrify even me.

"Okay," I say without looking at her once we've reached the linen closet on the ground floor. "The rooms on the ground floor need to be cleaned. Ten guests left yesterday, and my guy quit before he cleaned a thing, so there's ten of 'em that need to be turned over. I haven't had a chance to get to them with all the other shit I have to do. So clean them all, then change the linens, which are in this closet. Chemical closet has all the cleaning shit, and the pool shit. That's behind the door next to your apartment. Get that shit first and clean the rooms, then come in here for the linens. Then—"

"If I need to go to the closet in the pool house first, why didn't we start there? Now I'll have to go back."

I turn on her. She's folded her arms over her chest and is glaring at me. For the first time, I register that she's changed out of the dark clothing and into nothing but a pair of white shorts and a top, one of those ones that has the tiny straps on them instead of sleeves. It's definitely not a real damn T-shirt, and it's thin as hell, which I'm sure is cooler in this heat but only serves to practically serve her tits up to me on a platter, especially with the way her arms are folded under them right now.

My eyes narrow even as my traitorous mouth waters. She did that same thing back on the porch just a few minutes ago. Is she *deliberately* trying to distract me? Because it fucking won't work. Much.

She huffs and my gaze snaps back to hers. Something on my face must set her off, because she throws up her hands in a gesture that's the most Italian-like out of her yet.

"So, what, I'm not even allowed to ask questions? Isn't that what good employees do? Get clarification when they aren't certain?"

I lean toward her. "Good employees of mine are seen and not heard and follow my orders to the letter without asking questions."

Alessandra mutters something that I could swear is "damn cowboy," then says only slightly louder, "This isn't the military."

I stiffen, jaws clenching. "We started in here," I grind

out, "because my office is in this building, and after I'm done issuing your orders, that is where I'll return. You're capable of finding a chemical room, aren't you? I'll even give you a hint: there's chemicals inside it."

She makes a huge show of clapping her palms to her cheeks. "Wow, really? I had *no* idea. What helpful orders."

My mouth starts to twitch in a smile I'd rather die than show her, so I turn my back to her again and jerk a thumb over my shoulder back in the direction of the pool house. "Good. After that, clean the pool. The shit's in the pool house. But you already knew that, didn't you?"

When there's no response, I turn back. Alessandra is staring down at the floor, arms on her hips, her head shaking just the slightest bit.

"Well?" I ask hopefully; maybe she's finally cracked. "You gonna do all that or not?"

Her head whips up. She steps up to me, her arms folding over her chest. She has to crane her head back just to maintain eye contact. From this angle, I'm painfully aware of what her chest must look like. It takes my entire force of will not to let my gaze drop.

"Consider it done."

CHAPTER TEN

ALESSANDRA

I literally don't know how to do what Ford is asking me.

Clean a hotel room? What? I'm hopelessly underqualified to do this. I could manage to clean my own room, I suppose, but this is professional cleaning. There have to be laws about it, right? Like standards of cleanliness?

Not that the state of this place gives any indication that Ford cares about any of that.

But still. I'm way out of my comfort zone here. I drag myself back to the pool house—I'm not even going to *think* about the horror also known as the "apartment" I'm staying in—and find the chemical room. I push open the door and just stare. Yeah. I am so screwed.

He wasn't kidding when he called it a chemical room. There are stacks and stacks of boxes neatly labeled with the scientific names of chemicals crammed in every available inch of the place. A bunch of scary-looking tools are hung up along one wall. There's easily got to be fifty tanks that I'm pretty sure are used for scuba diving in a corner, along with a giant tank that must fill them. The whole room absolutely reeks with a strong chemical odor, so pungent I wonder if I should be wearing a mask. This can't be healthy to inhale, right?

Interestingly, though, the place is spotless. No spills, nothing out of place, everything maintained with an exact level of precision, almost militarily so. Hmm. By contrast to the rest of the resort, this is plain weird. Does Ford only care about the diving part of his resort? Actually, that would make perfect sense. Combined with that stellar personality of his, it's no wonder this place is deserted.

My English is excellent—my family shipped me to a boarding school when I was twelve and all they spoke was English—but I doubt I know scientific names even in my native language, let alone a foreign one. It doesn't take a rocket scientist to know that some of these chemicals are put in the pool's filter, but it probably *would* take one to know which chemicals in which amount are used.

Well, I'm not going to worry about it, anyway, because I can't do it. There is absolutely no way I can get near enough to that pool to clean it. I could maybe dangle my feet in the water while I skim leaves off the top, but that's about it. Just the idea of leaning over the edge of the pool with that long vacuum thing makes me want to hurl.

No matter. I'll just fake it for the couple days I'm here until I leave. Act like I've cleaned the pool when I haven't. It's so clean, I bet a few days without cleaning it won't even be noticeable. By the time it actually becomes a problem, I'll be long gone, and he can hire someone else, or, even better, clean it himself.

Assuming I can clean the other stuff well enough he doesn't immediately throw me out on my ass, that is. I scan the room hopelessly, looking for anything that feasibly is used for cleaning hotel rooms. My eyes land on a cart with a giant trash can, towels, and various cleaning supplies. Thank God. Even I've noticed those in the hotels I've stayed at. That must be what I need.

Grabbing the cart, I push it out of the chemical room, dismayed by its heaviness. I can move it slowly, but after a while it will be a misery pushing it.

I maneuver the cart along the path beside the pool, resolutely refusing to look at it as I go. I'll stick my feet in it later, maybe even go up to my knees, although the idea of doing so makes me nervous. My Thailand vacation may have been cut short, but that doesn't mean I can't go somewhere else after I get out of this country to continue making progress with my phobia. Maybe the Philippines. Or Singapore, since that's closer. It's not like Chakrii will follow me around the world for the rest of my life.

The one thing I don't want to do is return to Italy. Not yet, anyway. I'm not going back until I'm no longer afraid of water. My family's competitors will be forced to stop calling me Land Lubber Alessa if it's the last thing I do.

I make for the first room on the ground floor, which are all accessible from outside. The doors open almost directly onto the pool deck. That must be why Ford keeps the cleaning cart in the pool house. Maybe there is a method to his madness after all.

After I shove the cart into the first room, I fold my arms over my chest and glance around, keenly feeling my own inadequacy with regard to completing this task. I search my memory for any clue as to how our staff or a hotel employee cleans rooms, but it's just not something I've noticed. Obviously I'll need to clean the bed. And the bathroom. And probably this other stuff, but what's the order?

I pull out my phone and search how to clean a hotel room. To my relief, a bunch of sites come up assuring me a hotel room can be cleaned in thirty minutes. Well, that's good. That means all ten rooms will be done in around five hours. It's still so early, I'll probably be finished by noon.

Leaving the entire afternoon for the pool. Well, I'm not thinking of that right now. Nope. Hopefully, Ford will take a lunch break at some point, and if he asks later whether I've cleaned it, I can say I did it while he was on break.

Maybe this won't be too bad after all.

THE PLAN almost immediately goes awry.

I don't know what planet those websites are living on, but in no universe does it only take half an hour to clean a hotel room. Maybe if you've been cleaning rooms forever you can approach that level of speed, but me? Yeah no.

First of all, the sites tell me the first thing to do is strip the bed. But Ford told me to replace the linens after cleaning the room, so without even trying, I'm right away faced with the conundrum of whether to disobey his oh-so-important orders. Something tells me he's not a professional cleaner, either, so I decide to get the linens first.

I don't know how to change a bed, but another quick

search finds a ten minute video on how to do it. And it takes about two seconds to drag all the linens off the bed and toss them out into the entryway, so it doesn't seem so bad.

But the stupid fitted sheet on the bed refuses to behave. Every time I get one corner down, the opposite side pops off. What the hell! This is torture. It takes a good ten minutes just to wrangle the stupid thing on, and even then, it's clearly uneven. I'd be fired on the spot if I ever put in such sloppy work at one of the hotels near my family's compound. By the time I get the sheets, the bed cover, and all the pillowcases (another nightmare) fixed too, there goes the half an hour I thought it would take for the whole room.

Embarrassed it took me so long to complete the simple task—thank God Ford wasn't there to watch or I would have single-handedly confirmed his poor opinion of me—I resolutely look for trash and then dust everything, which the already-hated sites assure me is the next thing to do.

These tasks are much easier. Any old idiot can drag a rag around lamps and over tables, and an idiot is pretty much what I feel like at the moment. After the dusting is complete, I wipe down the same surfaces and then sanitize them with the bottle that thank every god in the universe is simply labeled "sanitizer." Only five minutes pass before it's all completed. If I can continue completing tasks that quickly, maybe I can get the whole process down to a science.

But the bathroom. It all goes to shit in the bathroom. And it's not because I have to search how to clean everything, which I do, or because I have to figure out which cleaning instrument cleans what, which requires additional searches also. And it's not because I have to waste another twenty minutes watching videos on how to clean stuff most people have been cleaning their entire lives. Any of that would slow down and frustrate me—which it does—but that all pales in comparison to the real struggle.

It's the shower. Cleaning it means scrubbing and then letting water run the cleaning stuff away. And *then* I have to polish the surfaces so there's no water marks. All of which requires being in close contact with running water way longer than any shower I ever take.

It's torture. I have to get in there and scrub while the water runs right there next to me. Right by my ear. Just inches from me.

I try shutting off the water while I scrub, which is fine, but I still have to wipe away the suds so no soap scum is left after the tub dries, which really requires running water. There's no getting around it. I try pushing the shower head all around in the hope of the water magically washing all the suds away, but it doesn't hit far enough back in the tub, and the shower head isn't detachable. I have no choice but to let the tub fill up enough to use my sponge to clean off the walls and the back of the tub. Then I have to let it drain, and then scrub the tub again while the water is still running so I can remove the last bit of soap scum.

It takes thirty minutes just to psych myself up to shove my arms into the tub. The water goes all the way up to my elbows, my face hovering inches above the water since I have to kneel over to clean it all. The water sloshes around with my every movement, sometimes even splashing my face. It's so horrible I start crying, then hyperventilating, then crying harder because I'm so angry scrubbing a tub makes me unable to breathe.

By the time I drag myself away from the tub—I'm soaked and shivering and so deeply unhappy I want to roll into a ball and cry—and finish cleaning the rest of the bathroom, nearly two hours have passed. Once I've finished replacing stupid crap like towels and shampoo, I'm so utterly, soul-deep exhausted, I want to just give up.

Fuck it. Chakrii can have me. I don't even care anymore. I can't do that another nine times. And I sure as fuck can't then go anywhere near a pool.

I should be proud I even put my hands in the water and got my face that close to it, but I'm not. I'm too exhausted and disheartened. I thought I'd started to make some progress with my phobia, but that ordeal proves otherwise.

Deciding to take a break—I can't go through that again, not right away—I drag myself out into the entryway and collapse onto the chair sitting outside the room.

"Taking a break already?"

I don't even bother looking up at him.

"You've only done one room, haven't you?"

I don't say anything, my gaze focused on the ground. As surreptitiously as possible, I shove my fingers under my thighs so he can't see they're still shaking with fear.

A long moment passes.

"Look," he finally says above me. "I get you're not used to cleaning rooms, but this isn't a task that can last all day, okay? The resort is empty now, but when people arrive tomorrow, you'll only have a couple hours to clean the rooms while we're out on a dive. I won't be able to clean any of them myself, since I'll be leading the dive. Try to figure out a system to make it go faster."

And then he leaves. I stare at his back, shocked. That was almost ... nice. Or at least considerate. Two personality traits I frankly thought him incapable of holding. When I felt him standing in front of me, I figured I was about two seconds away from an impromptu employee review.

Huh. Maybe he really *does* need my help.

But he's right; this process needs to go faster. It can't take over two hours to clean one room. It will go faster now that I've managed one room. But the showers ...

Those aren't going to get any easier.

Sighing, I climb to my feet, searching for the will to tackle the next room and wracking my mind for any excuse to delay the inevitable. Then I remember I have one. A quick glance at my watch tells me it's mid-morning. The Italian consulate in Phuket should be open by now. The embassy itself is in Bangkok, but I currently have no way to get there. The consulate can surely handle my situation just as well.

I search for the number, then dial, foot tapping against the cracked pavement while I wait for someone to respond. A few seconds later, a woman answers and with much relief, I explain my situation.

"So you lost your passport, Madam?" the woman says in Italian, my native language on her tongue making me so instantly homesick I can hardly breathe.

"Yes, exactly," I say, although that's not it at all. "I'd like to arrange a flight home as soon as possible, but without my passport ..."

"I understand perfectly. I can schedule an appointment with us so you can come in to get an emergency passport. Can you tell me your name, please?"

I tell her.

There's a long pause. I sigh. Here we go.

"You're Alessandra Vitale? Really?"

"Yes, that is correct."

"Oh," she says slowly. "I would have thought—"

"Someone else would be taking care of this for me?" I ask dryly.

There's another pause like it's finally hit her what she just said. "I just meant that I ... have your company's news app on my phone, Miss Vitale."

"That's kind of you. Is there anything else you need from me?"

"No, Miss. I will call you back as soon as I have an available spot for you."

"Oh ..." I say, surprised. "You mean I can't come in now?"

There's another pause. "Do you have an imminent flight?"

"Well, no." That's a whole other problem I need to solve. I have a bad feeling getting off Phuket won't be as simple as booking a commercial flight.

"Oh, well in that case ... it's just that we have a line of other people with emergencies, some of which are serious. Are you experiencing an emergency? Do you need immediate aid, or ..."

I hesitate. Should I tell her about Chakrii now? This must be an unsecured line. Pranee made it seem like

Chakrii could somehow hear even this phone call. But this is an Italian government agency! And I'm pretty much famous. Wouldn't *not* telling them put me in even more danger? They'd have to help me. It's their job.

I decide to risk it.

"Um, a man named Pravat Chakrii has tried to ... take me."

"Take you? Do you mean kidnap you?"

I wince. Hearing it put so badly makes it seem insane. "Yes. He had ... there were men outside my villa. They came inside after I had already fled. He's still looking for me."

"Where are you now?"

"Somewhere safe," I say hastily. "You don't need to worry about that."

"If you give us your location, we could send someone to assist you," the woman says in concern.

It's on the tip of my tongue to tell her, but at the last moment, something stops me.

"I can just come in on my own," I say.

The woman makes a skeptical noise. "We would be happy to host you, Ms. Vitale, until you have a way out of the country. In fact, if you are in danger, I must insist that we come to you immediately. We would be absolutely devastated if something happened to you. If you could just let us know where to pick you up—"

"That's okay," I say, feeling weirdly skeeved out. Man, am I becoming paranoid or does she really want to know where I am right now? "You said there are people with real emergencies. I wouldn't want to use my ... um ... fame to take resources away from them. I just need a passport from you so that I can leave. When's the earliest you can see me? Can I come in this afternoon?"

"We are fully booked today unfortunately," the woman says. "If you like, I'll speak with my superior to see if we can fit you in sooner, but it still may take a day or two, especially since you don't want to request emergency services. That is what you're saying, correct? You don't want us to come to you right away?"

I'm torn. Half of me wants to flee this murderous criminal as quickly as possible, but the other half knows it would create an international incident. Is it really so much to ask for a quiet getaway? What if they sent Thai police to pick me up, and it just so happened that one of the officers was one of Chakrii's spies? I don't know what to do!

"Ms. Vitale? Are you still there? Are you okay?"

"I'm fine," I say, still deciding. I glance distractedly around the resort, then shake my head. Who on earth will find me here? This is a place that doesn't want to be found. And Chakrii supposedly hates Ford, so he's kind of like my bodyguard, in a way. I know I'm safe here, but if they come and take me somewhere, I can't know for certain that I won't be in danger. I'd rather take a known level of safety here than risk a potentially more dangerous environment if Chakrii has people planted in the police, or even worse, at the Italian consulate.

My God, how the hell am I even considering this crap? This is a nightmare! What are the odds that my own country's government will harm me? Zero!

Still ...

"Just let me know when I can come in, and I'll come to you," I say.

"If you're sure, Madam," the woman says, sounding disatisfied. "I'll call you with an appointment time as soon as possible. Hopefully it will be no later than the day after tomorrow. Unless you change your mind about coming into our custody. This number is okay?"

"Yes, this is the number. Please try to fit me in as soon as possible. Have a nice day," I say and then hang up, not thrilled about my private number now floating around the consulate. With the way my luck is going, someone will leak it to the press back home.

I stare glumly at the next guest room awaiting me. And here I thought I'd have a quick escape.

CHAPTER ELEVEN

FORD

I find her in the kitchen the next morning.

"You're still here?" I ask.

Her back is to me; she stiffens, then jerks her head yes, her attention never wavering from the bowl of fruit she's assembling out of the fridge.

I lean against the door jamb, folding my arms over my chest. "I see you found the kitchen."

Slowly, she turns to face me. I flinch. Her face is haggard, deep circles ring under her eyes, which are red-rimmed and swollen. She's either been sobbing for hours or ... I have no damn idea. Something terrible.

"Are you okay?"

She shrugs, then turns back to the fruit. "Sure, yeah. I'm fine. Didn't sleep well."

Guilt flashes through me. She doesn't look like she didn't sleep well; she looks like she didn't sleep at *all*. I curse. Never in a million years did I actually expect her to stay in there. It's cramped, not exactly clean, and probably infernally hot; the air conditioner in there only worked so-so the last time I checked. And once the guys get here, which should be any minute now, it's going to be loud as hell at night.

"Look," I say, feeling terrible, "you don't have to stay in there—"

"It's fine," she snaps. "That's where you put me. The terms of our agreement, right?"

Irritation flashes through me. I'm not a fucking complete bastard! "Yes, and I can change them at any time."

"I'm fine," she says again. That phrase is starting to tick me off. But I know what's really going on here; she's as damn stubborn as I am, and neither of us wants to be the first to break.

Although, I suppose technically I just did.

But if she wants to suffer in there just to make a point, whatever. That's her choice. Everything else this woman has done has confused the hell out of me, so why bother trying to figure her out? Even if a small part of me really wants to.

Staring at her rigid back, I run a hand through my hair in frustration and ask a question the answer to which I already know. "Did you finish cleaning all the rooms yesterday?"

Her hands still. Very slowly, she grips the edges of the counter so tightly her knuckles turn white. "Yes, they're clean. I said I'd do it, didn't I?"

I frown. "Yes, you did," I say quietly.

For the life of me, I can't figure out why she did. I was in and out of the office all day yesterday, getting the boat and dive gear ready for when the guys arrive. Every time I went outside, there she was, excruciatingly slogging her way through the rooms. She's easily the slowest cleaner I've ever met, but she *did* clean them.

Is it a pride thing? Some sort of weird impulse to prove me wrong? It must have been. And I have to say that it worked.

She looked absolutely miserable every time I saw her. Exhausted and disheartened. But she never said a word to me, never complained, never even looked at me. And now, today, she's still here.

I'm impressed, despite myself. She's made no effort to hide the fact that she comes from wealth. Her life has not been one of cleaning. She couldn't have been more unsuited to the task. But she put her head down and ground it out. I can admire that quality in anyone.

And I hate to admit it, but she really saved my ass. When my employee up and quit two days before my guys were due to arrive, he left me in a huge bind. Sure, none of my men would have cared if their rooms got cleaned during their stay—we've all shacked up in shittier places, far shittier—but it's the principle of the matter, and with regular guests arriving right after they leave, I wouldn't have had time to place someone before they checked in.

How is *this* woman the same one from all those party pictures I saw just yesterday? She doesn't seem spoiled at all. None of this makes sense.

And it pisses me off. I'm already attracted to her, which is annoying as hell. I don't want to like her, spend time with her, or understand her. That's a complication I don't need, and more importantly, don't seek.

Even if it's a mystery, standing here now, I feel compelled to solve.

"Well, great," I grumble. "You clean the pool?"

"I did," she says softly, so quietly I can barely hear her.

I shrug. "Okay, then. My cook will be in later today to prepare dinner. You can help her with that. Other than that, you can have the day off. But tomorrow you'll have to start cleaning the rooms while we're out. Three of 'em. Oh, and clean the pool again, of course. I'll see you later."

I turn to go, but freeze when she says, "I have to clean the pool again?"

Turning back to her, I say, confused, "The pool has to be cleaned every day. It's a pool."

She blinks at me. I could swear her face pales. My eyes narrow. "Is that a problem?"

The fuck? Why would cleaning a pool be a problem after toiling in all those rooms? You'd think she'd welcome the opportunity to cool off after sweltering inside all day.

Alessandra folds her arms over her chest and jerks her chin up. My eyes zero right in on her tits; I'm physically incapable of not looking. Anger mixes with lust inside me, my gut clenching. Fuck it all to hell. I'm about to say something I'll later regret when I manage to lift my eyes to hers and realize she's not even looking at me. She's staring over my shoulder. And she looks ... nauseous.

What the hell?

"Is that a problem?" I ask again, my tone much softer.

Her gaze snaps to mine, then hardens. "No," she says, and turns back to her food.

"Okay," I say slowly, debating whether to push her on it and then deciding fuck it. Her shit is not my business. I need to remember that, damn it. "I'll leave you to it, then."

"Sure," she mumbles.

I give her one last look, then shrug again. I have other problems to deal with; Alessandra, my incomprehensible employee, is far down my list of concerns.

I ARRIVE at the airport in time to watch them land. I stand on the tarmac of the private airport, arms folded across my chest, as Jesse taxis into the hangar; he's still shutting everything down in the cockpit when Asher and Tucker bound down the staircase, bags slung over their shoulders.

I release the breath I hadn't realized I was holding. Damn, I missed them. Once a year is nowhere near enough.

Although as they like to remind me, my exile is self-imposed.

"Hey, man," Tucker says, extending his hand to me. I shake it, then pull him in for a one-armed man hug. "You doin' okay?"

"Yeah, sure," I grumble, which about covers it. We both know nothing about this week is ever okay.

A bag slams into my chest. I barely catch it before it falls to the ground. I glare at Asher. "Watch it, dipshit."

He gives me a bear hug, bag and all. "Good to see you, Car."

I roll my eyes. "You know I hate that shit."

He grins. "You're never supposed to like your nickname. And I didn't serve three tours with you just to start calling you by your real vehicle name now. You'll be Car until the day you die, my brother."

I toss his bag back at him, resisting the urge to smile. "It's absolutely terrible to see you, man."

Asher gives me a sloppy salute. "I'll eat any shit so long as it's served to me by some bikini-wearing Thai lady."

Jesse climbs down from the cockpit in time to yell, "And he wonders why he's still single!"

"Well," I drawl. "That sounds like a you problem, Ash."

Asher points at me. "No. My problem is that I'm two minutes into this country and not already holding a drink. Bro, you had *one* job."

Tucker laughs. "That's the first sense you've made all day, Ash."

Asher flips him off. "I say plenty of sense. I'm a sensical guy."

"You are not," I say. "Now if y'all could grab your shit, I can get to work on that drink of yours."

They follow me out to my battered Range Rover, toss their bags in back and then have a very important fight over who gets shotgun that Jesse wins only after I threaten to leave their asses at the airport if they don't hurry the fuck up. I tell them about the dives I have planned for tomorrow and by the time we pull around the back of the resort, I've forgotten all about her.

Until the car suddenly falls silent.

"What's wrong with y'all?" I ask, glancing around.

They're all staring at the pool over the row of hedges that separates the back of the resort from the parking lot. I look over and slam on the brakes.

Alessandra is stretched out in a chair wearing the tiniest red bikini I've ever seen, revealing every inch of the body I've been trying to forget since that damn dinner.

Fuck.

Her face is hidden behind a pair of large black sunglasses and her hair is pulled back in a tight ponytail that reveals the sheer perfection of her bone structure. She absentmindedly crosses one of her mile-long legs over the other, her toes sliding along her calf as she turns a page of the book she's reading. Even from this distance, I can see her skin glinting with sweat. My mouth goes dry, desire barreling through me so hard my fists clench on the wheel.

I want to swipe away every inch of that sweat with my tongue.

Tucker lets out a low whistle. "Damn."

Jesse's looks from Alessandra to me, his brows raised. "I'm sensing a helluva story here."

Asher's nose is literally smashed against the window, he's staring so intently. "I have died and gone to heaven."

He rolls down the window, leans his entire torso out the side, cups his hands over his mouth, and yells, "Hey, beautiful! You're the love of my life!"

Alessandra startles so badly her elbow jerks and knocks over the drink next to her, which spills everywhere. She shrieks and jumps to her feet, those magnificent tits swaying as she tosses her book behind her and swipes at her legs.

An instant later, Asher has launched himself through

the window and executed a neat somersault, rolling to his feet before I've even fully parked. Tucker and Jesse groan as he hurtles the hedgerow and in seconds is offering his grimy hankie he's pulled out of his pocket. He shamelessly dabs at her legs, going on and on about how sorry he is.

He's laying it on so thick even Alessandra stops to watch the performance, her expression slack-jawed. Even with the glasses hiding the rest of her face, I can tell she's flabbergasted.

Asher suddenly tosses his hankie over his shoulder and snatches her off the ground, yelling dramatically, "There's no hope for it. You need a good dunking."

He starts backing toward the pool, fully clothed and all. Idiot's probably got his phone in there as well. Alessandra shrieks and starts pushing at his shoulders. Jesse and Tucker chuckle. Even I manage a smile; this is not the first time Asher's dragged a woman into a pool. And while they always shriek and protest, they still inevitably end up in his bed. The rest of us couldn't pull it off, but Asher sure can.

My smile fades. I shove open my door; watching my friend's hands slide all over her has me seething with jealousy. This is *exactly* what I didn't want happening, fuck it all.

Asher laughs and pretends to lose his balance, then staggers backward another step toward the pool. His right foot has hit the edge when it all goes to shit.

"No! *No!* PUT ME THE FUCK DOWN RIGHT NOW!"

We all freeze, even Asher, who's now frozen just inches from the water, one leg extended back behind him, so surprised a woman is screaming at him he's forgotten how to move.

"RELEASE ME, YOU ANIMAL!" she screams again, then hauls off and slaps him across the face. Asher staggers forward a step, more from shock that a woman has hit him than from the force of the blow. She continues struggling.

"*Asher*," I snarl, hurtling the hedge myself. I've nearly made it to him when he finally snaps out of it, slowly lowering her to the ground.

The instant she's released, she takes three giant steps back, never looking away from him, like she expects him to suddenly grab her again. Jesus Christ.

"I'm so sorry," Asher says softly, his tone both horrified and bewildered. "I was just playing."

Without a word, Alessandra turns and grabs the towel slung over the back of her chair. We watch in unbearable silence as she wraps it around herself like armor and then grabs her phone and book from the table.

Then, with more dignity I've ever seen before in my life, she turns back to Asher and says coolly, "Your games leave something to be desired."

Jesse and Tucker join us as we silently watch her weave around the pool, her back regally straight. She disappears into the pool house.

"Well," Tucker says after a long moment as we all stare uncomfortably at each other. "That was fucked."

"I'd never hurt a woman," Asher says softly, pitifully, his entire body slumped over in dejection.

Jesse sighs. "Well, my dude, that was bound to happen

eventually. How many times have we told you to cut that shit out?"

Asher's still staring after her, looking genuinely heartbroken. He says nothing, just kicks at the water and swears, then glances at the pool house again. Suddenly, his expression transforms into one of resolve. "I'm going to go apologize again."

I slap him upside the head. "You will do no such thing," I growl. "Leave her alone, Asher. I mean it. You got that? *All* of you leave her the fuck alone. She's off-limits."

CHAPTER TWELVE

ALESSANDRA

I hide in the pool house. I'm not proud of it, but after the humiliation of freaking out in front of all those men, I can't bear to move from my infernally hot room masquerading as an apartment with air conditioning.

What an embarrassment. Of course I knew the guy was joking—I wasn't that far gone—but it's like my brain shut off.

I panicked, simple as that.

I sigh, undoing my hair tie and running my hands through my hair. If I had thought I was getting over my phobia, the last five minutes just proved otherwise. I could have just calmly told the guy to let me down. But no, I screamed my head off. Way to face your fear, Alessandra.

I went out there in my bikini thinking I could try going into the shallow end, just up to my knees, but before I did I wanted to read a little, calm myself down and also psych myself up to try. Then that idiot showed up and pretended to throw me in, which undid all my motivation. It'll be a long while before I'll want to try again.

And to think, tomorrow I have to clean his room. What a joke.

Flopping back on my bed, I grab my book off the bedside table and return to my thriller. I haven't done nearly enough reading on this trip so far. With all the work Ford expects me to do, I won't have much time to read, at least until I can leave this country. If today is my day off, I plan to take advantage of it.

I make it about ten pages, then slam the book closed, swearing. The truth is, I *don't* have the day off. Not yet. Not technically.

Because I haven't cleaned the pool.

I didn't clean it yesterday, either, even though I told Ford I did this morning. I straight-up lied to him.

What was I supposed to say, "Sorry, Ford, I didn't clean your pool because I vomited twice and had three panic attacks cleaning your showers and the very idea of getting anywhere near the pool literally made me cry?" Yeah, no. Like I'd want him to lord that over me.

Although yesterday he didn't bite my head off for taking forever to clean the rooms. And this morning he even gave me the day off, so he might understand if I told him the truth ...

But still. We're not friends, and while we're not exactly enemies, either, it's dumb to go around disclosing your weaknesses to someone like an employer.

I shut my book and stare at my door, fingers tapping the cover absently. Who are these guys? In the few seconds before I literally ran away, they seemed pretty close with Ford. When he kept mentioning guests, I thought he meant strangers, but these guys are clearly his friends. And there isn't anyone else here. What's up with that? Could he have deliberately kept the rest of it empty?

Since there's another two floors above the ground floor, I really, *really* hope that's the case. I might actually expire if I had to clean more showers. It's curious, though.

Not that I'll get any answers. Ford's made it clear that I'm not a guest here, and after what nearly happened in the pool, I'm too embarrassed to interact with them. I'll be gone soon, anyway.

I return to my book and read for a few hours, glad for the distraction and the quiet. I just get to the part where the first victim is murdered when my phone rings.

I startle, then shake my head. I've had quite enough startling for one day, thanks.

I answer.

"Ah, yes, Ms. Vitale. I'm calling back about your appointment at the consulate?" says the same woman from yesterday.

Finally! She wasn't joking when she said it would take some time. "Yes, hello. When should I come in?"

"I'm afraid we can't process you until the day after tomorrow."

What the hell? "You don't have anything sooner?"

"I'm afraid not," she says apologetically. "It's just that you said you don't already have a flight booked, and the families we've been processing have all already missed their flights. And we've had a few medical emergencies, typical vacation situations, you understand. It is the high season."

"Right," I say softly, wondering if I would have gotten faster service if I'd booked a flight in the first place, or at least told them I had. But then Chakrii might have found out, and something tells me the only way I'm getting out of here unnoticed is if I arrange private transportation.

"I really appreciate your understanding, Ms. Vitale," the woman says. "But again, I must insist that you consider us picking you up from wherever you are staying. We would be able to process you more quickly in that case. I've even spoken with my superior and we are prepared to let you stay in one of our residences here until you leave."

"What time is the appointment?" I ask to see whether I should take them up on their offer.

"The day after tomorrow at 5 pm."

That's a whole other day. "Five? Isn't that a bit late? Will the consulate still be open then?"

"We decided that it would be best, because of how well-known you are, for you to come in after the consulate has already closed. That way there won't be other citizens still waiting on services who might overwhelm you. I'm sure this has been a trying situation for you and we'd like to save you any additional stress. But again, we could push that up to this evening, if you like. We would have to rearrange some things, but I'm sure we could make it work. Just let me know where to send the car."

I don't like this. Not at all. They want to wait until it's already closed to see me? That's weird. And why do I feel like she's using the prospect of waiting so long to get me to jump at her offer to come pick me up now?

Jesus Christ. Maybe Chakrii *does* have someone on the inside.

"I can come in during regular hours," I say slowly. "It's no trouble. I'm sure people won't bother me."

"Well, we can certainly do that," she says. "It's just that we scheduled this time because all of the other appointments are full. Some staff volunteered to stay after so we could process you. We're busy tomorrow evening with an event, so we thought this would be the best solution. But if you like, I can go back to my superior and see if we can find another time."

Fucking Italian bureaucracy! I could be an old woman before they finally find a spot. "No," I say hurriedly. "I'll be there at five. The day after tomorrow. Thank you."

"Please be sure to bring a form of photo ID."

"You mean my face won't be enough?" I ask dryly.

The woman laughs nervously. "It's standard procedure, I'm afraid."

"Of course," I say. "I'll bring my driver's license."

Not that I ever drive anywhere.

"Perfect," she says. "We'll see you then."

I toss my phone on the bed then begin to pace. Now how am I going to get there? My only real option is to ask Ford to take me. But that would mean telling him everything, wouldn't it? He'll surely wonder why I need to go to the consulate. Maybe I could tell him I need to buy more cleaning supplies, and have him drop me somewhere, then take a taxi to the consulate.

But Pranee told me not to trust the taxi drivers.

I'll have to stick as close to the truth as possible. Tell him I need to be dropped off at the consulate. I'll say I need to get another passport because I lost mine shopping. He won't think twice about that explanation, I'm sure.

Glad that I at least have some semblance of a plan, I return to my book, wanting to finish it before I have to help the chef with dinner tonight. I skip lunch, still too embarrassed by what happened this morning to have the courage to head to the kitchen in the main building.

By mid-afternoon, though, I'm too hungry to put it off any longer. I'll just go around the long way if I have to. But when I peek my head outside my door, the pool is deserted. They're all either in their rooms or not here. Judging by how loud they were when they arrived, they must not be here.

In the kitchen I make myself a salad and cut up more fruit. I hope the chef is a Thai cook, because eating the same food I eat in Italy isn't exactly adventurous.

Taking my food outside, I fold myself behind the table in the back corner of the pool area. What few plants are still alive at this resort grow mostly around this table, likely because of the way the building blocks the sun for most of the day. More importantly, in addition to the ample shade, it's quiet. What really matters, though, is that it's the farthest table away from the pool itself.

A giant roar explodes from the hedge concealing the parking lot. A second later, the same guy from this morning comes flying over the hedge, and in three bounds dives right into the pool. He swims its length underwater, does some sort of flip thing and swims back, still below the surface. I imagine swimming all that way without coming up for air and feel queasy. I place my hand over my stomach, hoping I won't regret eating lunch. I hurled so many times yesterday I barely kept any food down.

The guy surfaces as the rest arrive, Ford bringing up the rear. They're all hauling tanks and have gear slung over their shoulders. They must have been on a dive; that's why this place was so quiet.

"Yo, Asher, if you think we're going to carry your shit in for you, you're about to get your ass kicked," one of the other guys says. He has brown hair that's shaved close to his head and dark eyes, but from this distance I can't guess their true color.

Asher, my lovely pool buddy, slicks his blond hair out of his eyes and gives him the finger. "After I carried your ass out of Raqqa? Really, Jesse?"

Jesse lowers his tank and slings the pack off his shoulder while Ford heads back to the parking lot. "Not this again."

"Yes! This again!" Asher scoffs. "I am never going to let you live it down. I saved your life, bro."

Jesse rolls his eyes and collapses into a pool chair. "And I am telling you, if that guy hadn't turned at that *exact* moment, I would have dropped his ass before he'd seen me."

"You were supposed to have already dropped him," says Asher. He pauses, then says more quietly, "Of course, had I not been late getting back, you probably wouldn't have had to drop him."

The third guy walks over to the outdoor bar, leans over it, and pulls out a bottle of whiskey. "Typical Asher.

Fucking shit up and then killing himself trying to fix it. You got the intel, though."

He cracks open the bottle and takes a long swig. Then he walks over to where Jesse sits, who says, "Give me that, Tuck."

Jesse drinks as Asher swims over to reach up out of the pool for it. He takes a swig, then rests the bottle on the ground.

"Chase had to drag us both once I got shot carrying you," Asher says quietly.

They all fall silent.

I glance from one to the other, unnerved by their sudden seriousness. The three of them remain quiet until Ford returns a final time from the parking lot. He lowers his gear, jaw tight as he studies them. I finally get a good look at his shirtless body and my eyes nearly fall out of my head.

The man is a work of art. Michelangelo's *David* has nothing on Ford. Every inch of his body is ripped with corded muscle. Did I ever really notice how massive his shoulders are? How did he even fit them in that tiny plane seat? And his chest ... I don't know how heavy a weight a person has to lift to get pecs that large, but I'm guessing it's a bunch more than my entire body weight. His biceps bulge as he begins arranging the dive gear.

Okay, maybe Pranee was right about Ford. Maybe he really is the Green-Eyed Tiger. *This* man could kill someone like Chakrii. Or at the very least be his enemy.

Ford suddenly turns and I bite back a gasp. Over the top of his left shoulder is a tattoo of a massive frog, its front legs reaching out around his neck almost as if it's strangling him. But the strangest part is that the tattoo is no mere frog but rather the skeleton of one, stylized in long spindly bones instead of the usual fat frogs I imagine when I think of one. It creates an eerie effect, foreboding.

There's a story to that tattoo. I shiver.

"Hey, Car, remember when Chase had to drag our sorry asses home?" Asher says.

Ford stills, his back still toward us. The three of them turn to look at him. Something snaps in the air, something heavy, emotional. I shouldn't be listening to this. I'm witnessing a conversation, or a memory, rather, of something truly private.

What do I do? Get up and leave? But then they'd know I've been here the whole time and heard everything. If I stay, maybe they'll leave and never realize I overheard them. But what are the odds they don't notice me? It's not like I'm hiding. All they have to do is look over and they'll see me. Would it be worse if I don't at least make the effort to disappear?

Indecision wars within me. I'm still trying to decide what to do when Ford turns back to them. And in the instant that he turns, I see devastation on his face.

"I remember everything," he says quietly.

Then his gaze snaps to mine.

CHAPTER THIRTEEN

FORD

Did she have to hear everything?

Apart from the worst of it, of course. But not even we discuss that part. It's too painful.

And she knew it. The instant our eyes collided, her face paled. The sympathy streaked clear across her face—as well as discomfort in having witnessed our conversation.

Screw her sympathy. And her understanding. She's not here to endear herself to me. If she does, I will be forced to admit to myself that I'm attracted to her. And if *that* happens, I'll be tempted to act on it.

That can't happen.

It only got worse when the boys noticed her. Asher practically fell over himself apologizing again, which she accepted more out of rote politeness than from true acceptance. I can't really blame her on that score; Asher should never have touched her like that, the stupid fuck. Tucker tried to get her to stay. Even Jesse seemed interested in talking with her, but Alessandra just mumbled something about helping the chef get ready for dinner, then promptly disappeared.

None of us saw her for the rest of the evening.

Shit, what a clusterfuck. If only she'd never showed up at this resort. Whipping back the covers, I roll out of bed, then pad naked into the shower. The freezing temperature does little to wash away any lingering dissatisfaction about Alessandra discovering my guys aren't here for fun. There's nothing to be done about it now. But that's the last she'll hear about it.

After the shower, I head for the rooms on the ground floor and rap on their doors. Jesse and Tucker are already up, but Asher, of course, is still in bed.

"Dude!" Asher groans. "Too early, dick."

I am pitiless. "You're the asshole who drank too much on a dive trip."

Asher rolls his eyes. "Some things never change."

"True," I say, "I suppose that's correct. Now get your ass moving."

He climbs out of bed, naked as the day. "Do I need to remind your commanding ass we're no longer in the teams?"

I smirk. "Some things never change."

He laughs, giving me the finger as he disappears into the bathroom. Grinning, I slam his door shut and continue down the hall to the kitchen.

Christ, I've missed them. I always forget how much until they return for the anniversary. How many more years will I have with them? Each year our reunion number dwindles as more men get married or no longer want to make the trip, but Asher, Tucker, and Jesse are the remaining holdouts.

I already know I'll be the last one.

My smile fading at the thought, I shove into the kitchen. Someone has to scrounge up some breakfast to haul out to the boat, and since they're my guests, it's my job. The leftovers from last night will be fine; none of us like to eat much before a first dive, anyway. We can just—

Alessandra stands there, staring at me. Something flashes in her eyes before she quickly hides it. Was that ... nervousness? What's that about? Shit, is she afraid of me, too, for that dumbfuck pretending to throw her in the pool? Christ.

"Hey," I say, compelled to apologize, "I just want to make it clear that Asher should never have touched you, you know, yesterday in the pool. He's never done well with thinking before he acts. But I knew that and should have known he'd do something when he saw you. He's always making a fool of himself for attention. I should have prevented it, especially since he's my guest. If he made you uncomfortable being here, I really apologize."

Alessandra allows such a long time to pass before replying I'm convinced she's about to tear into me. Instead, she says, "You're not responsible for the actions of someone else, but I accept your apology, anyway. He's already apologized multiple times. I'd prefer to move past it, okay?"

"Okay," I say, mentally pledging to still keep Asher on a tight leash.

My gaze drops to the kitchen island. A giant bowl of fruit has been placed on the table. Another platter has scrambled eggs and rice. There's coffee and fresh fruit juice, too.

Never in a million years could she eat this much.

I fold my arms over my chest. "What's all this?"

"What does it look like? Breakfast."

"Lot to eat for one lady."

She gives me a withering look. "Don't play dumb."

I sigh, uncrossing my arms and coming closer to lean against the counter. I glance down at the food. No, I shouldn't play dumb, not with what is clearly a nice gesture.

"Quite a feat for someone who likely has a personal chef back home."

"I can watch a YouTube video just as well as the next person," she says primly.

I laugh. Ain't that the truth. If I had a nickel for every time I had to watch a damn video to fix this place, I wouldn't have to watch videos for shit to get repaired around here.

Her eyes grow wide.

"What?" I snap.

"Nothing, nothing," she says, glancing down to take a towel and wiping furiously along the counter.

Hmm.

I motion toward the counter. "None of this is in your job description. I absolutely don't expect you to cook for people, just help my chef with dinner if she needs it."

She continues wiping, studiously avoiding my gaze. She shrugs. "It's an apology."

"Apology? What for?"

"For overhearing. Yesterday. That was obviously a

private conversation. I didn't mean to overhear, but I was already sitting there, and then he, um, jumped in the pool, and it kind of happened before I could announce myself."

I turn away from her, ripping open the fridge door with more force than necessary. I stare blindly inside.

"No apology necessary," I finally grumble.

"I disagree."

"This food wasn't necessary."

"I think it was," she says softly.

I slam the door closed, feeling restless. What the fuck is taking the guys so long? We should have left ten minutes ago, damn it.

"Well, it's appreciated," I say, "but don't do it tomorrow. All you have to worry about is cleaning their rooms."

"Do I have to clean your room?"

My head whips toward her. She stares at me, expression innocent. My eyes narrow. No question like that is ever innocent.

"Not necessary either," I drawl, trailing a gaze down her body. Her toes are painted flamingo pink. Damn it all, I want to suck them. My gaze jerks away, lifting to her face in what should theoretically be safer waters but so fucking isn't.

"What's your tattoo about?" she blurts out.

I just look at her, mind still back on her toes.

She throws up her hands. "You're right. I get it. Sorry. I just apologized for overhearing something personal, and here I am asking more personal questions. Forget I—"

"I don't talk about my tattoo."

Shiiit. I did not just say that, did I? Fucking hell, I just got done telling myself I don't want her to know anything else about me!

She takes a step toward me, then another. If I was smart, I'd snarl something at her, verbally shun this attempt at empathy, but something prevents me.

Alessandra sidles up a little closer, eyes locked on the exact place on my shoulder where the tattoo is hidden under my shirt.

"I understand," she says quietly.

I can make out every last streak in her hair, slightly lighter strands than the warmth of her brown hair. It falls to the middle of her back. Something uncivilized in me demands to bury my hand in that hair, to drag her head back and drop my mouth to the wildly beating pulse at her neck.

Her gaze lifts from my shoulder, those beautiful brown eyes searching mine with a guileless curiosity.

Something in me falls hard.

I look away, shift away, force away the strange intimacy that's snapped between us too many times to mean nothing. She doesn't actually want to know why I inked this permanent reminder on my skin. She thinks she does, but she doesn't. And even if I told her, she couldn't possibly understand. Not really.

"Ford ..."

I jerk my head, not wanting, *refusing* to share it with her. Because even if I believed she could understand if I told her—which I don't—the last thing I want is for her to know what this tattoo is.

A brand that I'm a broken man.

She remains silent. So do I, staring at the fucking fridge again. I can feel her gaze on me, quietly asking but not demanding.

I last only a few seconds before my gaze draws inexorably back to hers, before, unwillingly, it drops to her mouth. She sucks in a breath. I'm leaning toward her before I can think to—

"Yo, breakfast! Nice service—oh, shit, man. Sorry to interrupt."

Alessandra and I jump apart. I glare at Asher over my shoulder as Alessandra busies herself with the damn towel again as if the counter's not already spotless.

Asher glances from Alessandra to me, then mouths "sorry."

Before I can stop him, he says, "Hey, lady, I really want to apologize again for yesterday. I feel real sorry about it."

She nods. "You've apologized enough. And in the future, if you could ... I don't like being startled."

Asher laughs nervously. "You sound like Car, here. He hates it when someone sneaks up on him."

She blinks at him, the towel finally forgotten. She looks from him to me, her brows knit in confusion. I glare at her, daring her to get it.

"Car ...? What does ... oh. *Oh.*"

Alessandra throws a hand over her mouth but fails to smother the laugh.

"If you don't cut that laughing shit, I'll start calling you Ferrari," I grumble.

She laughs harder. Asher joins her, turning to me to

wag his eyebrows significantly. I mouth "I am going to kill you" at him.

His laugh turns sly as he gives the two of us another considering look.

"So happy you two could bond over the name I didn't choose for myself," I snap, then grab Asher around the neck and shove him toward the door. "Go get the gear around while I pack this up."

He snaps me a mocking salute, all the more irritating for its absolute smartness. "Sir, yes, sir."

"Get the fuck out."

Sighing, I turn, almost hesitantly, to find Alessandra studying me.

"What?"

She shakes her head slowly. "Nothing. You're just different around them, is all."

"No, I'm not."

Her mouth turns up in a sad little smile I instantly loathe.

"I'm going to get started on those rooms," she says, and disappears.

CHAPTER FOURTEEN

FORD

I wait for it all morning.

While we load up the gear into my vehicle, silence.

Eating the food she made during the ride out to the dive site, zip.

Coming up from the morning's dive, nada.

But as we sit down to eat the remains of breakfast for lunch on the deck of my outrigger ...

"So, bro, were you ever goin' to tell us you were into her, or were you plannin' on lettin' us think she was off-limits to *you* too forever?"

Aaaand there it is.

"I don't know what the fuck you're talking about," I mutter, taking another bite of the leftovers from last night I snagged along with what Alessandra made.

I can practically feel Asher roll his eyes. "Dude, I've got eyes. I know what I saw."

Tucker straightens up from his customary slouch in his

chair. "Oh, wait, now, what's this? What did you see? Is something sexual afoot?"

I send him a withering look. Tucker gives zero shits about whoever we fuck, but he does like stirring up trouble.

"I saw y'all almost kissing," Asher says gleefully. "He about looked like he wanted to suck her face right off."

"I knew there was a story, there," Jesse says, taking another swig of his water and then leaning back against the rail, his arms crossed behind his head.

"I'm not discussing this with any of you," I snap.

"Oh, so there *is* something," says Tucker.

"No," I say, "what I meant was Asher's far too stupid for his little brain to comprehend what his eyes supposedly saw."

Asher flips me off. "Rude, bro."

"How'd y'all meet, anyway?" Jesse asks.

"We ran into each other at the Golden Lotus," I say, not mentioning the plane ride. It feels too … private. Important. Not only because I don't want to embarrass her by telling the guys she's afraid of flying—a particularly difficult fear for any SEAL to comprehend—but also because of what happened after she calmed down. That moment of connection that still makes me uneasy whenever I remember it.

"Wait, wait?" Jesse says, arms dropping from behind his head. "What were you doing at the Lotus? I thought you were over that vigilante shit. Damn it, Ford, what the hell're you thinking?"

Aw hell.

This is what I get for letting Alessandra fucking Vitale distract my every waking thought.

Tucker stares at me in confusion. "Bro, I thought they banned you from the Lotus?"

Sipping my water, I say, working to keep my tone from becoming defiant, "No one has the balls to ever toss me out. And I think Chakrii likes knowing where I am, even if he allegedly banned me."

Jesse says, exasperated, "So leave him alone!"

"I don't want to hear shit about it; someone has to keep that fucker in line. He terrorizes everyone. This place is a paradise; people would be so much happier if the cloud of fucking Pravat Chakrii didn't hover over us all with his blackmail and assassinations and extortion. The locals don't deserve it and no one in the government dares touch the asshole. Who else is there but me?"

Tucker's expression flattens. "How many times are we going to have to tell you to quit this shit? This is not your fight."

Asher frowns. "Dude, but that means—"

"You know very well why I hate that monster—and why I'll never stop. And it *is* my fight, because I have a business here, too. I'm involved whether you like it or not," I snarl with such viciousness that they fall silent.

It only lasts about two seconds.

Jesse leans forward, waiting until I make eye contact with him to say, "Ford, you know we're right when we tell you this isn't a situation you can handle by yourself."

"I've been handling it alone just fine for years now."

Tucker makes a slashing gesture. "Sure, bro, but that's not the fucking point. *We* don't like you alone out here, dealing with this criminal."

"Yo, Car ..." Asher says, trailing off. I ignore him and keep my focus on the other two, who never live and let live.

"Hell, man," Jesse says, "we know you're competent as hell, but one of these days—"

"I'll be fine," I interrupt. "Chakrii's not about to make a direct move against me, not after I killed his right hand man two years ago. And none of it has ever been tied back to me explicitly. You *know* this."

Tucker paces back and forth, looking severely unhappy. "And we also know you could *still* get shanked for that if they can ever pin it on you! You're not a criminal, Walker. You can't go running around killing people."

"What did you do this time?" Jesse says. "Specifically. I want to know."

Asher frowns and says, "I think before that we need to discuss that—"

"He murdered the competitor of one of his suppliers," I say, still furious about it all. "Engineered a car crash. A bad one, y'all. Fucked up his brakes. The supplier's wife and three kids were in the vehicle along with him. They all died.

"Even worse, another car, someone completely unrelated who was just going to work, was hit by the supplier's car when the brakes failed. The guy is in the hospital. Multiple severe injuries. It looks like he'll be okay, but he's going to be in the hospital for weeks. All because the supplier thought he could move in on Chakrii's territory on Bangla Road! Sure, the supplier was a drug-dealing piece of shit, but his wife and children didn't deserve to be slaughtered along with him.

"And if he'd decided to drive just a few hours later in

the day, think of all the tourists who might have been injured or worse when the brakes failed. So yeah, I went to Bangkok and intercepted one of Chakrii's shipments of coke, then lit it the fuck up. After that, I went to the Golden Lotus for dinner as a reminder that *some* people aren't going to stand for letting Chakrii go around killing people. It had to be done."

Jesse shoots to his feet. "Christ, Walker! Could you have put a larger target on your back? You're all alone out here. *Shit*, you're getting worse, Ford. This has to stop. My God …"

Tucker plows a hand through his hair. "Yo, man, I can't act like both the supplier and Chakrii didn't get what they deserved, but this is over the top, bro, even for you."

I glare at them. "Do you think I want to do any of—"

"Shut the fuck up, all of you!" Asher yells, leaping to his feet.

"What?" I ask, exasperated. Asher and his penchant for dramatics.

"So you made her a target?" he growls, outraged.

My mouth drops open. Shit. Shit fuck. Christ, why the fuck didn't I think of that? All of Chakrii's little spies surely went right back to him with news of our dinner literally right after I blew up his supply. Like he would see that as a coincidence. He must think she's involved somehow. What the fuck else would he conclude? Fuck. Fucking *hell*.

"Damn," I whisper.

Asher jabs a finger at me. "Is that why she's here? You protecting her from Chakrii? You better tell us the truth, man."

"No, she showed up on her own," I say absently, but now I have to wonder. Why *is* she here? It never made sense why the hell she appeared here, out of the blue, willing to work a shit job I know she's overqualified for just to stay here.

How'd she even know how to find me? That's another thing I've been wondering since I opened the door to find her standing on my doorstep. Probably the woman driving her knew about me. The whole town does, although they're kind enough to pretend like I don't exist most of the time so Chakrii doesn't come after me. She must be an employee at the Lotus. Who else could Alessandra have met in the short time she's been here? So she knows all about Chakrii. Did she warn off Alessandra? Tell her about my feud with Chakrii? If so, just how much did she tell her? Why hasn't Alessandra brought any of it up?

What exactly happened at that resort in the days after our dinner? Surely nothing bad, not seriously, anyway. I would have heard if Chakrii had decided to torment a beautiful Italian woman, for I have my own spies.

Unless he's keeping it so hushed up not even his employees know ...

But why else would Alessandra come here? There is literally no other reasonable explanation she'd be here otherwise. Chakrii must have heard we dined together and thought he could get to me through her. Fucking hell. If that's the case, I'm responsible for all of it.

And I've been giving her a hell of a hard time.

"What are you going to do about this?" Asher says, his face furious. I barely look at him, still thinking about this turn of events, although somewhere in the back of my mind I register he's appointed himself Alessandra's protector.

"I don't know what I'll do yet," I say slowly, "but I do know one thing. Alessandra and I are going to have a little chat."

CHAPTER FIFTEEN

ALESSANDRA

I'm still struggling with the bathrooms for the second day in a row when the men return from their dive trip. I managed to avoid them all for over twenty-four hours after I left Ford in the kitchen, still reeling from our almost-kiss. I hid in my hot apartment, pretending not to hear him when they came back from their first day of diving and he marched over to my apartment, banged on the door, and said we needed to talk.

Yeah, right. Like I'm talking to him about that almost-kiss. I don't know what got into me, but I wanted that kiss way too much for my own good. No, I wanted *Ford* too much for my own good. And we mix like oil and water. Kissing him would be bad, bad news. So like any self-respecting woman, I plan to avoid every mention of it. And him, for that matter, so I'm not tempted to kiss him again.

That being said ... what was he thinking right before we were interrupted? I can never get a read on him. His discomfort talking about his tattoo was the first time I'd ever gotten an identifiable emotion from the man. Whatever that tattoo is about, it's bad. Sure, it's a mystery I want to solve, but with my consulate appointment today, what's the point? I'll be flying out soon.

It's better to just avoid him. Whatever that was in the kitchen, he must have forgotten how much he dislikes me. The last thing I want is for him to kiss me and then immediately regret it. Knowing him, he'd snap something surly at me, and a girl's got her pride.

Spoiler alert: I did not make them breakfast this morning.

Pushing thoughts of Ford aside, I stare at my last remaining bathroom. Why, on earth did I agree to cleaning these rooms? I haven't gotten any faster cleaning them; if anything, I think it might be taking *longer* to clean them. Instead of it getting easier, it gets harder to stick my arms in the bathtubs. How do people do this every day, day after day, for years? They must be superhuman.

Everything else is done. I even cleaned the bedroom in this one—Asher is weirdly clean for how loud he is—so all that remains is the damn bathroom. My stomach already roils, and I haven't even entered it.

I may have teased Ford about cleaning his room yesterday—for the life of me, I still cannot figure out why I did, although maybe it had something to do with how he looked so sad staring at the fridge—but if he'd agreed to it, I have no idea what I would have done. Cleaning an additional bathroom when I've already puked twice today would really suck.

Steeling myself, I plunge into the bathroom, determined to get it done. Within minutes, I'm hurling myself out of the room and puking in the shrub outside.

"*There* you are. We need to—are you okay?"

Oh great.

He waits while I wipe the back of my hand across my mouth, my stomach still quivering. Maybe if I take long enough to respond, he'll just go away. This man has already seen me freak out on a plane, and now he just witnessed me vomiting. Wonderful.

"Hey," he says, coming closer. A hand presses to the small of my back and I stiffen, shocked by the display of comfort. Ford isn't exactly touchy-feely.

The hand jerks away, leaving me feeling bereft.

"Alessandra," he says softly, his raspy voice sending shivers down my spine. Oh brother. I really am in trouble, aren't I?

"I'm fine," I say, straightening. Plastering a bland smile on my face, I turn to him. "The various cleaners just mix together into this awful smell that makes me nauseous, is all."

He studies me, his gaze trailing from my head to my toes. A lick of fire ignites within me; I fold my arms over my chest in a vain attempt to fight it off, to ignore the urge inside me that screams at me to throw myself at him.

His gaze drops to my chest. His eyes grow heavy-lidded.

My arms fall to my sides. Jesus, I know that look. Ew. For the love of God, I literally just finished puking and he's giving me the I-intend-to-stick-my-tongue-down-your-throat look. Men.

I extend a shaky hand to the cleaning cart I left outside,

shuffling the stack of towels I keep there so I don't have to keep trekking over to the linen closet.

"Did you want something?" I ask, hoping he won't notice my voice is as shaky as my hands.

"We need to talk about—Did you clean the pool today?"

"Of course," I say, busying myself with rearranging the cleaning bottles on the cart so he can't see my face, because I'm a lying liar. "I did it first thing."

I feel more than see his attention switch from studying the pool to studying me. "You sure about that?"

"Of course, why?" I say quickly. "Do you want me to do it again?"

He hesitates a long moment. "No, that's fine. You can just clean it again tomorrow."

"Okay, then," I say, my face still averted. There's no way I'll clean the pool tomorrow, just like I didn't today or yesterday, or the day before that. How much longer before he realizes I'm lying? My stomach twists with nausea, but this time it has nothing to do with shoving my arms into water.

When I first arrived, he annoyed me so much I almost *wanted* to mess with him. But now ... after the hint of vulnerability he showed me in the kitchen, the possibility that there may be some hidden tragedy he refuses to deal with, well. It's difficult to continue viewing him as the arrogant ass he's been from the start. Excusing his poor behavior because of past trauma—and those damn *eyes*—really is a stupid thing to do, and yet here I am, doing it anyway.

I really need to get out of here.

"You wanted to talk about something?"

He turns back to me. "Why did you leave the Golden Lotus?"

I blink. "I told you, I wanted to get away from it all. Have some anonymity."

He frowns. "So you came here. And not one of the many other nicer places in Phuket."

I shift on my feet, my mind blank as to what to tell him.

"Did you run into trouble at the resort?" he asks.

"Why would you think that?"

"Because there's no other reasonable explanation for you being here."

"Hey, my friend brought me here," I say, wondering if I should just tell him. We're not at each other's throats like we were before; I could say I pissed off Chakrii and am now hiding out here.

However, if Ford really is the Green-Eyed Tiger, wouldn't he feel compelled to involve himself? If he helps all the locals like Pranee told me, then he definitely would. He thinks himself some sort of white knight. And that has to have put a huge target on his back. I admire that, I admire that he would help others for no other reason than that it's the right thing to do—but I don't want to make it worse for him. Telling him Chakrii wants to kidnap me would definitely do that.

In all likelihood, I'm leaving tonight. All I need is that passport, and then I'm gone. There's even a red eye flight to Singapore this evening. I haven't booked it yet, because I want to be sure I have a passport before I potentially let Chakrii know I'll be at a certain location at a certain time. I won't be headed back to Europe, but I'll be out of the country, and I've always wanted to see Singapore. Soon I will put this whole thing behind me.

What if I told Ford now and then left but he still thought he should do something to Chakrii in retaliation? Would he try to clean up the mess I left behind? That's not fair to him. And that's not why I came to his resort, either. He's not responsible for me. I've still seen no indication either way that Ford has anything to do with Chakrii; I won't risk that criminal going after Ford just because I told him. I would be too worried about what might happen to Ford to leave.

Ford stares me down as I debate with myself. When I don't add anything further, he sighs and shakes his head. He leans down, just a little, until we're nearly eye-to-eye. "Alessandra. I'm not stupid. I know there's more going on here. Just tell me."

My lips press together. He lives here; I don't. I refuse to make his life more difficult by telling him.

"Fine then. Don't tell me," he says in disgust, straightening. "Are you done here?"

I glance at the room. Technically, no. The tub's not quite finished. I start to shake my head, but something awful must linger on my face, because Ford waves his hand.

"Just leave it. Asher's anal about his shit, anyway. The room was probably spotless, right?"

"Well…"

"Thought so."

I glance from Ford to the room and back again. "But it's my job…"

"And it's my job to assign you tasks. I'm un-assigning this one for today. Take the rest of the day off."

I squint at him. "You're not much of a boss, are you?"

"On the contrary, I'm a real hardass. My last employee quit, remember?"

"Then why are you letting me slack off?"

Ford just stares down at me, then shrugs and looks away. "The reason's not important."

Oh, but he's wrong. It's important to me.

A FEW HOURS LATER, I'm just finished dressing for my appointment with the consulate when a car starts. Shoving aside the curtain, I look across the pool yard to see Ford climbing out of the Range Rover, which is now idling. He cups his hands over his mouth and yells for his friends to hurry the hell up.

Without thinking, I snatch my purse and hurry outside. The men are already nearly to the vehicle by the time I've navigated a wide berth around the pool.

"Hey," I call, drawing their attention, "can I catch a ride into town with you?"

Ford turns to me and freezes. Something hot flashes in his eyes, his jaw clenching. I grind to a halt.

And then I remember what I'm wearing.

In my panicked packing that last night at the Golden Lotus, this was the only dress I told Pranee to grab. I have no intention of analyzing the significance of that, but I probably still will tonight, especially with the way Ford is looking at me right now.

"The green dress," he says quietly, giving me a once-over.

"What's the green dress?" Asher asks.

"Shut up," Ford says, not even looking at him.

"Uh ... yeah," I say. "This was the only one ..." I trail off before I can finish saying that it's the sole dress I took with me. He'll pounce on that in an instant.

Ford's eyes narrow. "Only one what?"

"Nothing," I say, smiling brightly. "Can I have a ride or not?"

"Um, yeah, I'm betting you can have a ride if you want one," Tucker snickers. Ford shoots him a death glare, which only makes Tucker grin wider. I bite my tongue to hide a smile myself, because, yeah, if Ford keeps looking at me like that, Tucker's probably not wrong.

Not that I'll take him up on any offer, of course.

"Why do you need a ride into town?" Ford asks, frowning. "Are you meeting someone?"

The other three men turn to look at me pointedly. I'd have to be daft not to pick up on the sense that they think I'm meeting someone when Ford and I have been developing ... whatever this is between us. The truth is, though, that I just wanted to dress professionally for an official government meeting.

The easiest thing to do would be to just let them all believe that. After all, wasn't I searching for an excuse for why I needed a ride into town? This one practically fell in my lap.

I'm already lying about the pool, though. And about why I left the Lotus. Allowing them to think I'm heading out for a hookup depresses me.

"No," I say calmly, smoothing my skirt down. I check my watch. "I have an appointment at the Italian consulate in about an hour."

It's like I've flipped a switch.

Ford steps toward me, his face serious. The rest of the men crowd in behind him. "Why the hell are you going to the consulate?"

"I lost my passport while shopping," I say smoothly, unnerved by their expressions. "They're issuing me an emergency one."

Ford steps even closer. We're so close now I have to crane my head back to see his face even in my considerable heels.

"How did you really lose your passport?" he growls.

"I already told you," I say, proud that my voice is steady.

He scoffs. "So you're still not going to tell me."

"I really did lose my passport."

He just shakes his head. "Get in. I know where the consulate is."

The men allow me to take the passenger seat. It's deathly quiet in the SUV as we head into town. Ford slams his door so hard the car rocks back and forth.

"I swear I'm fine," I say quietly, which is true. There's been no sign of Chakrii since I came here. I've been in this little bubble, away from everything else. Nearly a week has passed, and nothing. Chakrii may have already lost interest in me.

"We'll discuss it after your appointment."

"You don't have to do that. I don't want to ruin whatever it is you're doing, anyway. I'll catch a ride back on my own."

He says nothing. The men crammed in the back seat say nothing either. Finally, after a painfully long silence, Asher says, "We're not going to let some stranger take you home."

Well then.

When we finally arrive at the consulate, I practically want to throw myself from the vehicle, it's so awkward. Ford jerks the wheel toward the entrance, like he's about to drive right in there.

"Stop," I say. "You can't drive in there. You're not Italian citizens."

"We're your security team," he says tersely.

I laugh. When no one joins me, my laugh trails off. I look from Ford to the back seat. They're all glaring at me. I glance out the window. Literally no other cars are on the street. There is no one. This is ridiculous. Okay … I've had about enough of this.

"Pull over."

Ford keeps driving.

"Okay, fine, I'll get out here," I say, and make to open the door.

He slams on the brakes. "What is the matter with you?"

"You!" I snap. "All of you, for that matter. Do you see anyone on this street? Where's the danger? This is essentially foreign soil. What do you think is going to happen, I get gunned down right outside the consulate?"

When no one responds, I conclude that, yes, they do believe that. Jesus Christ. Pranee was right, after all. The Green-Eyed Tiger has just made his first appearance.

"I will see you back at your resort," I say coolly, opening my door and sliding out.

Before I can slam it shut, Ford reaches over and grabs my wrist. I stare at him, eyes narrowed, until he releases me.

"We'll be right here, waiting, until you're done."

"That's hardly necessary."

I shut the door, knowing they'll just stay parked there until I'm back no matter what I say. Ford isn't one to be made to do something he hasn't already decided to do.

I cross in front of the car, my heels tapping loudly on the silent street. I frown and glance around. It really is deserted. That's actually ... odd. Every road I've driven in this country has been crammed full of people, bikes, motos, and of course, vehicles.

My gaze sweeps back and forth. Maybe this is what has them all so spooked. Hell, now I'm getting spooked myself.

I've just crossed the street when the gates to the consulate begin opening. At first, I assume it's opening to allow me to enter, and I step inside, hurrying up the path to the entrance. A moment later an armored vehicle pulls out in my direction, and I realize they must be leaving. I ignore it, expecting the vehicle to turn out of the consulate and drive off, but that's not what occurs.

The car roars with sudden acceleration. It barrels right for me. I scream, staggering back a step on my heels. My balance slips out below me, and I begin to fall, my gaze locked on the grille of the car that in two seconds will splatter my head against the concrete.

The car suddenly swerves, narrowly avoiding me. It screeches to a stop behind me just as I hit the ground. Pain tears through me as I land on my ankle. I scrabble back from the car, terror squeezing my chest so harshly I can't even draw breath to scream again.

Men jump out from the back seat, guns pointed at my head.

CHAPTER SIXTEEN

FORD

I'm out of the car in an instant. "Glove box!" I shout as I sprint across the street. I've got seconds to get to her before she's dragged inside that vehicle and gone forever.

The driver sees my approach. An arm holding a pistol extends from the window, but I'm already sliding across the hood before he can get off a shot. He fires anyway, the sound ringing out in the sudden silence.

Fucking damn it. I *knew* this street was too quiet, too still. And I let her leave the vehicle anyway.

Two men are dragging Alessandra toward the vehicle. She's screaming; a fleeting look at her expression shows she's terrified, but I shove that down, focusing on the man closest to me.

My feet have barely touched the ground after sliding across the hood when I jerk the dive knife from its sheath around my calf and fall on the man closest to me. Wrapping my forearm around his neck, I stab once, twice up into his kidneys, then drop him. He screams, a raw, horrible sound as he bleeds out. I rip the gun out of his hand and kick him in the head, snapping his neck.

Seeing the treatment his compatriot has gotten, the second man releases Alessandra, not out of the goodness of his heart but rather to save his sorry ass. He eyes me warily as we point our guns at each other. My eyes remain locked on the second man; the slightest sign from him and he's as dead as the first guy.

He feints to the left. I watch him, stepping closer, leaning onto the balls of my feet, waiting for my opportunity.

It comes a moment later. A barrage of gunfire slams into the armored car, distracting both the driver and the man before me as the boys open fire with the firearms I keep in my glovebox. The instant the man's eyes flick from me, I fire into his heart and then his head. He drops, dead before he hits the ground.

I pivot to face the car; the driver is still exchanging gunfire with my boys. While he's distracted, I back toward Alessandra, making sure to keep myself between her and the vehicle. She's collapsed on the ground behind me, sobbing. I don't spare her a glance as I keep the pistol locked on the driver. He could still attempt to run us over.

Guards rush out of the consulate. "About fucking time," I growl, although I don't trust a damn one of them right now for one simple reason.

Someone in that consulate let the car inside.

The driver whips his gaze from the guards running toward him and my men. Sensing he's lost this round, he floors it, screeching out of the consulate onto the deserted road where my men have taken up a position behind my vehicle. The back end of the vehicle fishtails back and forth as he flies down the road, abandoning his two dead men inside the consulate.

I very slowly, very cautiously lower the pistol to the ground, then back away from the men, keeping my hands raised. Jesse, Tucker, and Asher follow suit, stowing my weapons back inside the glovebox and then stepping out with their hands raised.

A second later we're surrounded.

THEY INTERVIEW US SEPARATELY, one increasingly annoyed Italian after the other. My statement does not take long. I don't know why those men were after her, after all, and my actions outside the consulate were not only witnessed by many, but also recorded by a whole host of security cameras.

They take statements from my men as well, but those are surely even less helpful than mine since they've only been in the country for a few days.

I don't, however, tell them about my suspicions. I don't tell them I believe Chakrii is involved, and I certainly don't say a word about my feud with the man. That's a way to ensure I never get out of here.

Eventually, someone must discover my service background because a stern-faced guard comes in and then I'm brought to another room. This time I'm not alone; Asher, Jesse, and Tucker are there, either sitting at one of the chairs at the table or staring at what is clearly a two-way mirror.

"How much do y'all wanna bet they're on the phone with the Pentagon right now?" asks Asher.

Tucker snorts. "I don't take sucker bets."

Jesse unfolds his arms and turns away from the mirror. "They're already off the call. That's why they've got us in here together."

"How long do y'all think we're gonna be stuck in here?" Asher grumbles. "You'd think we're criminals or something. We weren't the ones tryin' to kidnap a woman, for fuck's sake."

"Perhaps it would be best if we remained silent," I say, leaning against the wall.

Jesse grunts. Asher shrugs. Tucker takes his turn glaring at the mirror.

Some time later, the door finally opens, and a woman dressed in an expensive black suit strolls in, a folder tucked under her arm. She's tiny; I doubt she'd reach my chest if she weren't wearing those killer heels. Her brown hair is pulled in a severe bun at the nape of her neck. Little makeup adorns her symmetrical face, making her seem even more serious.

"And who might you be?" Asher says, straightening in his chair and giving her his best I'm-a-good-boy grin.

"Interpol." She motions toward the table. "I'm Agent Marcella Bianchi. Take a seat, gentlemen," she says as she sits, her Italian accent clipped.

We take seats around the table. Jesse, a clotheshorse despite our constantly making fun of him for it, is studying the woman's clothes with avid interest. When she looks up from her folder, he hides the interest behind an expressionless mask.

Agent Bianchi studies me, then looks down at her file and says, "Your alias is the Green-Eyed Tiger, yes?"

"No."

Her head whips up. She stares at me, brow cocked. "Care to explain?"

"I don't go under that name. Locals have created the moniker for me, but I do not want it and I certainly don't act under it."

She closes her folder. "I see. So it's just a coincidence, then?"

"Correct."

"Hmm." She returns her attention to the file, opening it again and running a finger down the page. She flips to another, scans that, flips again. I resist the urge to roll my eyes at such an obvious stalling maneuver. My men and I are far too well-trained to let a little silence get us to talk. We wait as she flips to the last page. "My, my, you SEALs really do make other special forces look bad, don't you?"

"All special forces are important, regardless of which country they're from," says Jesse smoothly.

She regards him, then nods as if acknowledging a hit. "Too true."

"What's the status of Alessandra Vitale?" I ask to cut through the bullshit. If I don't move this along, we'll be here for the rest of time.

Bianchi returns her attention to me, summarily dismissing Jesse, who *really* doesn't like that. "She's fine.

Sprained ankle and some scrapes, but fine thanks to you. Thanks to all of you."

"So we can go? Great," Asher says, getting to his feet. "Today's kind of an important day, so if you wouldn't mind, we'd like to mosey."

"Ah, yes. The anniversary of the death of Chase Burnham is today, correct?"

She might as well have set off a grenade in our faces. She takes one look at our cold expressions and sighs.

"That is why you're here, yes? Why you're visiting Mr. Walker? The Pentagon told us this is a yearly trip, although it usually isn't quite so incendiary. But it's my understanding your group grows smaller each year; I can only imagine what might have happened had even more of you been here."

"The other guys have lives," Tucker snaps.

"An interesting way to put it," Bianchi says mildly.

"Why don't you just cut to the point," I snarl. "You going to hold us, charge us, what? If you've been chatting with the Pentagon, there must be something else."

She smiles faintly. "Yes, well, I'm afraid we find ourselves in a rather sticky situation, gentlemen."

Jesse leans his forearms on the table, staring at her. His jaw clenches when she ignores him. "How so?"

"The Thai government doesn't want to be involved in this situation due to the nature of who allegedly is behind it. They've abdicated jurisdiction for investigating this matter to the Italian government and Interpol since it technically happened steps inside the consulate.

"Now, I, of course, have already spoken to your government, and know that you're no longer in active service. That makes the fact that you've been involved in this little international incident all the more uncomfortable for everyone, including your government. They've asked us to keep your names out of it, which we are prepared to do, however ..."

"However, what?" Jesse snaps when she refrains from finishing her statement.

Agent Bianchi throws out her hands, then shrugs. "There's an opportunity here."

I sigh in disgust. "You told our government you'd keep our names out of the press if we help you catch whoever tried to kidnap Alexandra Vitale, and they agreed to it."

Bianchi shrugs again. "Need I remind you that you just *executed* two men right outside this building? They were hopelessly outmatched and you know it. It can't just be swept under the rug, although if you co-operate, we can certainly do our best. And as I said, there is a mutually-beneficial opportunity here to do some good. Chakrii is one criminal we've been trying to lock up for many years."

"Who's Chakrii?" Tucker asks.

Bianchi rolls her eyes. "Yes, yes, none of you will admit to knowing him." She looks at me. "We're already well aware of the bad blood between the two of you. Until now, Interpol has been content to leave you be, since no ... indiscretions have been tied back to you and it doesn't appear as though you are involved in any criminality yourself. But now ..."

"You've got one hell of a video from the cameras outside," I mutter, jaw tight.

"Correct."

"And if we don't want to involve ourselves?" Jesse asks.

Bianchi looks at him, then shrugs again. "Well, we can't force you to help us stop him. I suppose you could try your luck at keeping a low profile. But Ms. Vitale *is* a rather well-known figure back in Italy, and this incident *has* already started to circulate online. We'll do our best to keep the pertinent details from becoming public, but from where I stand, with such a famous person involved, I just don't see how—"

"We get it," I snap. "We know the score. But what I'd like to know is, how do you plan to do it? How are you intending to catch this guy?"

Bianchi leans back in her chair. She turns to the mirror, then nods. A moment later, the door opens, and a man comes in, leading Alessandra.

She looks at me. "They want to use me as bait."

CHAPTER SEVENTEEN

ALESSANDRA

"Absolutely not," Ford snarls, shooting to his feet. He jabs a finger at me, his gaze still on Bianchi. "She's already suffered enough from this asshole. Putting a civilian at risk is beyond the pale. Completely unprofessional."

"We'd keep her safe, of course," Bianchi says, her eyes sparking like she enjoys Ford's anger. "She'd never be in actual danger."

Ford laughs caustically. "How many times have I heard that one?"

Bianchi leans toward him. "This is the first time in ages that Chakrii has moved into the open. The first real chance we have to catch him. And for whatever reason, he wants her. That's valuable."

"I don't care. You're not using her," Ford says, crossing his arms. "You use her, I walk. Let my name be printed in all the papers in the damn world. I don't give a shit."

Bianchi frowns. "You realize my hands are tied, right? I've got my orders from above."

Ford leans forward and bangs a fist on the table. "She's at risk because of *me*," he growls, still not looking at me. "All of this happened because of a damn dinner between two strangers. One big fucked-up coincidence."

I suck in a breath. Holy God, he admitted it. He admitted he knows Chakrii. He really *is* the Green-Eyed Tiger. Is he right? Could the attack at the consulate have been avoided if I'd confided in him sooner? Would I still be, even now, residing at the Golden Lotus, if I hadn't felt compelled to invite him to dinner as thanks for helping me on the flight? Had I arrived even a minute later, would we have never crossed paths, never had dinner, and would any of this ever have happened?

Likely.

Ford finally looks at me. His gaze veers instantly away, like he can't bear to meet my eyes. I was right. The man feels responsible. And he's offering himself up on a platter instead of me.

This is exactly why I refused to tell him what Chakrii wanted with me. And now, what, he intends to let the international media vilify him for killing those men who tried to kidnap me? I know the media; they'll eat him alive. No one deserves that treatment.

"Sometimes coincidences break cases," Bianchi says.

Even Asher sneers at that one.

Bianchi makes a placating gesture. "All I'm saying is that this is the first real break we've had in ages. Chakrii could be permanently off the street in days. That's worth taking some risks."

"It's never that simple," Ford snaps. "And why the hell

should we believe you're competent? Chakrii's got a mole in this damn consulate. Or did you think we wouldn't put that together? The car that attacked her was *inside* the consulate. Which means it was let in. Which means someone knew ahead of time when Alessandra was arriving. Hell, who the fuck has an appointment this late in the day, anyway? Your fucking mole probably set it up so she'd come in when everything was closed so it would be easier to take her."

Whoa. Ford has a point. The last few hours have been so insane that little tidbit completely slipped past me. I *knew* it didn't feel right that they wanted to see me so late in the day!

"They had a legitimate appointment at the consulate. Once it ended, it was assumed they'd already left," Agent Bianchi says quickly.

Ford scoffs. "Okay, and how did they know *when* to make said legitimate appointment?"

The agent has no explanation for that.

Ford nods. "Exactly. Apologies for being blunt, but no one around here is running a tight ship. How can we trust you to keep her safe? To keep any of us safe, for that matter?"

"The staffer that made the appointment with Ms. Vitale will be dealt with."

"As soon as you can find him."

"Her," I say quietly.

Ford spares me another passing glance. I flinch. The fury rolling off him is undeniable. He looks about two seconds away from transforming into the animal that killed two men in seconds. Maybe he's never fully come back down from that adrenaline rush. I don't know. What I *do* know is that I've never seen anyone so lethal in my life as when he protected me from my abductors. The locals gave him an apt nickname, that's for sure. That he's angry on my behalf makes me feel ... something. Something I refuse to acknowledge.

"What I'd like to know," Jesse says into the silence, "is why you're here, Agent."

She gives him an irritated glance.

He raises one brow, an almost taunting expression flashing across his face. I glance between him and the agent. I don't know Jesse very well at all, but if I had to guess, I'd say the man finds this agent fascinating in a distinctly unprofessional way.

"What do you mean, why am I here? I'm the agent who's been put in charge."

Jesse shrugs. "Yes, but you're Italian. And we're in Thailand. And you seem to know a hell of a lot about a Thai gangster. Seems unlikely, no?"

She glares at him. So much for the professionalism. "I've been read in."

Jesse studies her, then says slowly, "Seems convenient, is all I'm saying. Maybe you know Chakrii a little too well because *you're* the one working for him."

"How *dare* you—"

"Agent Bianchi was on a temporary job in Singapore this morning when Ms. Vitale was attacked," says the agent I first gave my story to before Bianchi arrived. Until now, he's remained silent while all this testosterone clashes against the iron will of Agent Bianchi. "Since this thing happened at the Italian consulate, they figured she should consult on the case. That it would be more comfortable for Ms. Vitale to have an Italian working with her."

Jesse gives Bianchi a long look. "And what were you investigating in Singapore?"

"Something well above your pay grade, sailor. But I'll tell you it involves the *Italian* mafia, which is why, I'm sure you can understand, I was called in to handle this particular situation," Bianchi says, smiling much like I'd imagine a shark would smile before it takes a huge chomp out of some poor, unsuspecting sea creature. "That's what I do. I put away mobsters more terrifying than you could ever imagine. So this skepticism is getting old, and unnecessary. Is that good enough of an explanation for you? Have I established I'm not corrupt enough for you, Mr. Cohen?"

Jesse gives the slightest nod, but his eyes flash with something predatory. Almost like he's enjoying himself. I glance at Bianchi, who looks completely reserved and yet somehow still seems like she'd enjoy nothing more than to deck him. Oh boy.

"And who the hell are you?" Ford asks, turning his attention to the man standing next to me.

"This is Agent Made Subiyanto, out of Jakarta, but who has been in Bangkok for the last six months," says Bianchi, pronouncing his first name as a combination of "maw" and "day." "He's the Agent in charge of this case."

"Then why haven't we been talking to him?" asks Asher.

"Because I wanted to get a read on you before I introduced myself. And please call me Made," says Made.

"And what did you conclude?" Ford says.

Made shrugs. "If we all agree to work together, I believe we can put this man behind bars for a long time."

I smile. The agent, who insisted I call him by his first name, has this calm way about him. After I told the people in the consulate who was after me, they left me alone in a room. I'd been sitting in there for over an hour, nursing my injuries when he finally showed up and immediately took control of the situation.

Made has been on the team investigating Chakrii; my involvement with the criminal is just the break he's needed. When the Italian consulate filed the incident report with Interpol, my mentioning Chakrii must have tripped some wire, because Made flew over from Bangkok right away to take my statement.

Of course, then I had to repeat the whole thing to Bianchi when she arrived a few hours later.

"And you actually agreed to let yourself be used as bait?"

I jerk my attention to Ford, who's glaring at me from behind the table. We stare each other down, another one of our impromptu games of who-can-outlast-the-other. But this time, judging by the set of his jaw, he won't be the one to break. Ford has officially stopped letting me evade his questions.

I sigh. "I'm considering it."

He does a double take. "Are you for real right now?"

"Yes," I snap.

He throws up his hands. "What on earth could convince you to do something so unbelievably stupid?"

My eyes narrow. "I don't know, maybe getting attacked and nearly kidnapped makes a girl want to kick some ass."

"Damn it, that's all the more reason for you to remove yourself from being involved!"

"You mean like the way you're not involving yourself right now?"

"That's different."

I roll my eyes. "Oh really? How so?"

Ford comes around the table and gets right in my face. "Because I've made an entire career of dealing with dangerous people."

"And here I thought you were just a resort owner with a bossy attitude," I say sweetly.

He takes another step closer. Our chests touch: I feel it in my entire body as he sucks in a breath, about to tear into me. "If you think—"

"Why don't we all just take a breather," Made says. "Yelling won't solve anything."

"Neither is risking innocent lives," says Ford, staring down at me.

"I can do anything I want with my life," I snap back, just to be contrary. In all honesty, before I came in here, I was leery of helping them with their investigation. A large part of me just wants to go home. But something about this man just completely writing off that I could be in any way helpful really makes me want to hang around just to stick it to him.

Then again, doing that to prove a point when said point

includes a dangerous criminal who wants to kidnap me may really just be shooting myself in the foot.

"Out of curiosity," Tucker says, "how are you gonna use Alessandra to get this guy?"

I wouldn't mind knowing that myself. Bianchi shifts in her chair, dropping her gaze to the file in front of her. When it becomes clear she won't respond, Made clears his throat and says, "Well, we're still working out the details, but the plan is to put Alessandra in a public place and wait for Chakrii's men to make a move."

"She'll be a sitting duck," Ford snaps.

Yeah. I'm not so crazy about that idea, either.

"She'll have men on her the entire time," Bianchi says. "And as soon as Chakrii makes a move, we'll move in and capture—"

"Chakrii isn't stupid enough that he'd pick her up himself," Jesse interjects, rolling his eyes.

"I am aware of that," says Bianchi through gritted teeth. "Which is why we plan to catch some of his men and convince them to roll over on Chakrii."

"You're endangering her life for a maybe," Ford says, his jaw tight with fury.

"Like I said, we're still working on the details," says Made. "Right now we're just—"

The door bangs open, and an aide enters, holding a phone. We all turn to him, but Made calmly says, "Yes?"

"Sorry, sir. I've got a call."

"Tell them I'll return it shortly," Made says.

The aide's expression turns distinctly uncomfortable. "Sorry, sir, but ... uh, the call isn't for you."

Made's brows rise. "Then who is it for?"

"For her, sir," the aide says, nodding to me.

"How on earth did someone get a call through to a civilian?" Bianchi mutters.

The aide looks helplessly from Bianchi to Made. Made sighs and nods. "Yes, fine."

Shuffling over to me, he extends the phone. Feeling the eyes of everyone on me, I lift the receiver to my ear and say, "H-hello?"

"THANK GOD! WHAT THE FUCK IS GOING ON RIGHT NOW?"

I wince at the stream of furious Italian, pulling the phone away from my ear. I switch to the language myself, saying, "Jesus, Marco, calm down."

"Calm down? Calm down? Don't tell me to calm down. My baby sister almost just got kidnapped for fuck's sake in fucking Thailand. Do you have any idea what they do to women over there? I told you going alone was a terrible idea!"

I turn my back on the room, embarrassed by his outburst. Thank God only one other person here speaks Italian. Everyone I've met here has been wonderful. A few criminals are not emblematic of the rest of the country. "Marco, you need to lower your voice."

He says nothing for an unbearably long moment, then mutters, his voice a low growl, "Sorry, sorry. You're not alone, right?"

"Yes, that's correct."

Marco sighs. "And this call is surely being recorded."

"It is a government line."

"Fucking hell ... you're okay?"

"Yes."

"You're really okay? Don't downplay it just to calm me. Mother is having a damn conniption. She called from Lucerne an hour ago when I was trapped in the middle of a lunch meeting. About tore my head off. She had to read about it on a fucking website. *Our* website. Are you hurt? Do I need to send a doctor?"

"Only a sprained ankle and some scrapes," I murmur, my back stiffening as I feel the eyes of everyone on me. "Really. It ... it could have been much worse."

My brother curses again. "This is unbelievable. Something about a gangster? A Thai one? What the hell does a Thai gangster want with you? Now Sicily, on the other hand—"

"You know very well no one in Sicily is interested in us," I rush to say, not wanting whoever may be listening to think we're connected to the mob.

"Sure, sure," Marco mutters absently.

"Um, Marco," I say quietly, drawing one arm across my chest, "I'm glad you called, but ..."

"But what?"

"I'm kind of in the middle of something."

"What could you possibly be in the middle of? Aren't they holding you in the consulate?"

"Well, yes, but ..."

"But what?"

There is no way to say this that won't result in an eruption of epic proportions. "They kind of ... want my help."

"Help? What help?"

"Help catching the guy who wants me," I say, wincing.

The eruption of barely coherent Italian makes me even more thankful that only Bianchi can understand us.

"Help? Help? No. Absolutely not. Has everyone lost their minds? You are a civilian. Not even that, you're my sister! A Vitale! Do you have any idea the shitstorm that is currently being unleashed in Rome? I'm not even there, and already I'm getting hounded by calls."

"Yes, well, there's a reason you fucked off to New York, isn't there?" I say dryly. "To get away from those shitstorms, right?"

"As if I would just stand by while my sister nearly gets kidnapped in Thailand," he growls. "Is *every* woman in my life going to scare the life out of me?"

I sigh. Right. That's why he's so frantic. Marco's wife is six months pregnant with their first child, and there have been some mild complications. For Marco, who's used to being the captain of his own universe over there in New York, not being able to micro-manage away the issues with Izzy's pregnancy has pushed him over the edge.

"Marco, you need to calm down."

"I will be calm once you're home. Which is why I'll be heading there myself."

"You're flying here?"

"Like you want to risk a commercial flight now, when you couldn't even go to a consulate without being attacked?"

I sigh again. The man has a point.

"Fine. The jet can come, but you don't have to. You should be at home right now."

"Of course I have to come. You're my little sister! But the problem is I can't fly out until tomorrow evening, my time. Izzy has a doctor's appointment in the afternoon that I can't miss. But I'll fly out straight after and bring you home, okay?"

"I don't want to go back to Rome. That's why I left. I need some time away. Surely you, of all people, can understand that," I say, feeling a sense of futility; no matter what I say, my brother will worry until he's carted himself across the world to save me. Maybe once he's here, I can convince him why it's important I stay to help them with Chakrii, something I'm still on the fence about myself. In either case, I still have a little over a day to tie up loose ends before I go.

"So come to New York," Marco says, cutting into my thoughts. "Or go somewhere else. I don't care. I'll fly you anywhere in the world. But until then, I assume it's safe for you to stay at the consulate, yes? Or do you have somewhere else?"

"Yes, I'll be fine," I mutter, then tell him another three times I really am okay before he finally ends the call.

I turn back to the room. Ford rises out of his chair and stalks toward me, folding his arms over his chest.

"Who the hell is Marco?"

CHAPTER EIGHTEEN

FORD

"Her brother," Jesse says.

I flick a glance at him, then look back to Alessandra. The truth flickers in her eyes. Well, shit. Her damn brother. How fun to make a complete fucking ass of myself. But as much as that sucks, at least Marco isn't her husband. Or lover.

Of course, she could still have any of those.

"You speak Italian?" Bianchi barks.

"*Sì, signora.*"

"Americans never speak Italian."

"This one does."

"Is he coming here?" I growl, ignoring the little drama between my friend and Bianchi.

Alessandra quirks a brow. "Who?"

"Your brother," I say, jaw clenched.

"Yes. He's flying out tomorrow. The day after tomorrow, our time."

"Good," I growl. "You'll be out of here soon, then."

She frowns. "Just because he's coming, doesn't mean I'm leaving. Made told me I could really help—"

"You are *not* putting yourself at risk," I say, something like panic clawing up my throat. I shove the feeling away. It isn't happening again. Don't be fuckin' ridiculous. "It's not your job to deal with Chakrii. You've already suffered enough. These agents will just have to catch him some other way. I'll do it myself if I have to in order to keep you out of it."

"But it's my decision—"

"It is. But it would be a damn stupid thing to do," I snap. And I know I shouldn't, but the words fly out of my mouth before my mind can catch up. "Anyone else comin' to save you?"

She gives me an arch look. "Who else might that be?"

"Like a husband," I say, stepping toward her. "Or a boyfriend." I take the final step so our chests touch. "A lover, maybe?"

Her eyes widen as she flushes. She sucks in a breath, sending her tits sliding against my chest. My jaw clenches, feeling the wave of desire slam into me with enough force that I may shortly embarrass myself if I can't get it the fuck together.

"No," she says softly, eyes never leaving mine. "None of those will be joining me."

Is that because they don't exist? I don't ask; I've already embarrassed myself enough, damn it. Instead, I ask the question that should have been my first concern when Made led her in here.

"Are you okay?" I murmur.

She blinks. "Yes, of course."

I reach out and pass my thumb over a tiny scrape near her temple. She must have gotten it when she fell. Christ, she got lucky. They could have fucking taken her. They nearly managed to, damn it all. All because of me. All because I had dinner with her one night, and that psycho decided to take it out on her.

Fury snaps through me. I let my hand drop. Alessandra blinks and shakes her head a little like she's coming out of a trance.

"We need to talk," I say quietly, then nod toward everyone else, "away from these people."

"Why?"

"Because I want to know what the fuck Chakrii did to you to make you come to my resort. I assume these Interpol dicks have the full story?"

She nods. "I told them after they treated my injuries. Well, I've told it multiple times now."

"That tends to happen during a debrief," I say ruefully. I turn to the rest of the room. "Are we done here?"

Agent Bianchi jerks her head away from sniping something at Jesse—this time in Italian—and turns to me. "I'm the agent here. I will decide whether we're done."

"I thought that was Made's job?" Asher says gleefully.

I give him a withering look. I'm trying to get us the hell out of here; pissing her off won't speed things up.

Made throws out a hand. "Let's all just relax. That was your brother, Ms. Vitale?"

"Yes. And it's Alessandra."

"I take it he's coming to pick you up?"

"He'll arrive the day after tomorrow, our time," Alessandra says.

Made sighs. "I suppose you're not sticking around then, yes?"

Alessandra shrugs a little and looks uncomfortable. "He wants me to leave. It would be the smart thing to do. I'm ... you know ... rather well-known back home, and he's just worried about me, you know? If something were to happen to me ..."

She trails off, but we all get it, Made most of all. "It would create problems with the succession of your family's media company."

Alessandra shrugs again. "Pretty much. He moved the headquarters to New York now that he runs the company, but I've stayed on in Rome to run strategy for the subsidiaries that remain. We're supposed to inherit it jointly once our father dies, but he, um, got kicked out of the company early for, uh, poor behavior so we've been running it even though we haven't, you know, inherited it yet. If something were to happen to me, it would leave the company without one of its most important executives."

None of this makes sense. "I thought you were a party girl?"

Her eyes narrow. "And why would you think that?"

I shift on my feet, then finally admit. "I searched you. The articles made it seem like ..."

"Like I was a no-good partier with nothing to contribute to society?" Alessandra asks dryly.

I wince. "I didn't translate any of the articles. I thought

the pictures told it all. I just wanted to know why you'd show up at my resort."

Alessandra laughs bitterly. "Yes, well. When I was younger, I attended a lot of functions. It's expected, for people of my background. But I grew up, and when I started working for the company, I quit all that. Our competitors still love to smear my reputation, though, because it gives them clicks. And yes, I still have to attend many events as a representative of my company. My few indiscretions therefore were a bit more visible than most people's, but it was never anything out of the norm. Are you telling me you never did stupid things in college?"

"College? More like BUD/S," Asher snickers.

Alessandra looks at him blankly.

"SEAL training," I say.

"Oh," she says. "Well, that's why my brother doesn't want me to have anything to do with Chakrii. Our competitors will try to sell it like I've reverted to my old ways. Someone could even try to insinuate that I'm no longer fit to hold my position."

"And in the middle of all that you just picked up for Thailand?" I ask. How the hell is she here alone if she's such a bigshot back in Italy?

Her face flushes. "I really needed ... a break. It was beginning to interfere with my ability to work."

Bianchi considers her. "Aren't you like thirty?"

"Twenty-nine."

"Seems like a lot of responsibility for someone so young."

"Yes, well, originally, we should have taken over the

company much later. My father still has many years left in him. Unfortunately. We've had to figure it out sooner than we thought. My point is, the board could attempt something with me like they did with my father. Which is why my being involved in this situation does come at personal risk to me. Is that enough, now? Have I explained my personal life enough to you people?"

"Well," Made says, "I suppose that's it, then."

"What? She can't just leave," Bianchi says, outraged. "This is an investigation."

"She certainly can, if she wants," I snap.

Made makes a placating gesture toward me. "Agent Bianchi, you and I both know we can't force her to do anything. It isn't as if she's committed a crime. While I'd certainly welcome her help, ultimately it's her and her family's choice. And she raises a good point with the press, both those of her country and those in Asia. How do you think any investigation would go if it became public knowledge that she's working with us? Chakrii would see it coming from far away and it would drive him back underground. Using her could end up being a liability."

"Precisely," I say, glad someone in this building has sense.

Made turns to Alessandra. "We would, of course, prefer that you stay here in the consulate until your flight out. For your protection."

Tucker scoffs. "Seriously? Y'all're the ones who let those assholes inside to wait for her. What makes you think she's any safer here than somewhere else?"

Bianchi shoots to her feet. "Do you actually believe the

Italian government would dare risk the life of one of its citizens?"

"You already have, haven't you?" Jesse drawls, smiling without humor when Bianchi pales and then flushes with fury.

She opens her mouth, but Alessandra interrupts her. "Listen, it pains me to say it, but they're right. I don't feel comfortable here. I regret any offense that may cause you, but ... well, it's how I feel."

Made says, "Do you have another place to stay that is adequately safe?"

Alessandra stares at him blankly. Is she for real? Does she really believe she has nowhere to go?

"She's staying with me, obviously," I snap.

Made looks at me and says mildly, "And I suppose you and your men here are making it your responsibility to protect her?"

"Obviously," I say. "She's already been staying at my resort. And, I'll have you know, she was perfectly safe. Chakrii knows better than to move against me there."

"And why is that?" Bianchi snaps.

I just smile at her. I'd have to be a real dumb shit to admit it's because Chakrii knows I'll kill whoever else he sends for me. The man may be a criminal, but he is not stupid.

Made nods. "Fine, then. I assume you'll want to escort her to the airport?"

"Correct."

He nods again, "I will be staying with you as well, of

course. Until Ms. Vitale is out of Asia, she remains my responsibility."

"I'm coming, too," Bianchi says quickly.

"We figured," Jesse says dryly.

"Then let's go," I say. "Who knows which employees here might be sending word back to Chakrii."

MY BOYS and I drive home in tense silence, my bullet-ridden vehicle limping along. It's going to need new windows and everything. I might as well buy a new fuckin' clunker. Alessandra follows behind in a vehicle with Bianchi and Made.

I'm lost in my thoughts until Asher says quietly, "Looks like we're not doing much remembering today, huh?"

I stiffen, my hands tightening on the wheel. Christ, how did I forget again today is the day Chase died? It feels like a week has passed since the attack. It's well past midnight. Technically, it's not even the day of anymore. We missed it.

"We can still do that shit when we're back at the resort," Tucker says. "It's not like Chakrii's going to hit her twice in one day."

"He would have wanted us to take care of her instead of moping over him, anyway," says Jesse quietly. "In a way, this is the best way of honoring his memory."

I grunt in lieu of answering. Jesse's right, I suppose, but fuck, that doesn't make it any less painful.

"Five years," I murmur. "How the hell has it been five years?"

Asher reaches across the front seat and slaps me on the shoulder. "Too long, man. I'm officially older than him now. I realized that the other day."

"Still the baby, though," Tucker says.

"Hey, fuck you, man. I'm thirty-two years old."

"Still younger than the rest of us."

I run a hand over my face, feeling fucking ancient. "Cut the shit. I don't want any fighting tonight."

"True," says Tucker, "we can leave that for Jesse and Bianchi."

"Don't start," says Jesse.

Asher turns around in his seat to smirk at him. "Dude, bro, like, we have eyes, man. A pretty, Italian super-agent with a nice ass and fancy-pants suit? It's like your perfect woman just dropped down out of the sky."

"Cut the shit about her ass, you dipshit," Jesse says blandly. "I merely liked needling her."

Even I laugh at that one.

"Yeah, I bet you liked it. I'm pretty sure that's not the only needling you want to do to her," Tucker says. Asher reaches into the back seat to give him a high-five.

"Even I've never seen you lose your head over a woman so fast, Jesse," I say. "And we served together longer than anyone."

"I'm not here to fuck an Interpol agent," Jesse snaps. "I'm here because of Chase."

I snort. "Pretty sure Chase would have been egging you on with her."

"I'll discuss this with y'all just as soon as Ford admits he wants to bang Alessandra. I'm not the one who went all caveman in there," says Jesse, looking out the window.

"Thanks, asshole," I snarl as Asher and Tucker howl and then start in on me. I ignore them as much as Jesse, but that doesn't prevent Asher and Tucker from giving us hell the rest of the ride back.

"All right, shut the fuck up. That's an order," I say as the Interpol vehicle pulls in after us.

"Where are we staying?" Bianchi asks as soon as she exits the SUV.

"Why don't you stay in Jesse's room?" Asher snickers behind a fist. Tucker bursts out laughing, but Jesse simply turns and walks away.

"What?" Bianchi says, irritated.

"Nothing," I say, then motion toward the ground floor. "There're six available rooms on the bottom level. Pick whatever one you want."

Bianchi scans the rooms clustered around the pool. "Fine," she mutters. "Agent Subiyanto, do you want the first watch, or shall I?"

"Don't bother," I say. "We'll be up the rest of the night, anyway."

Her brows lift. "And why is that?"

We just glare at her. Bianchi must remember the significance of the date in her file, because she colors slightly and mumbles something about seeing us tomorrow. She stalks off toward the rooms, a small bag slung over her shoulder.

"Agent Bianchi is a bit ... prickly, but she's highly effective," Made says, breaking the awkward silence. When none of us reply, he adds, "Ms. Vitale, I'll be taking room six. I would ask that you relocate to room five, so that you are surrounded by people in the unlikely event that someone tries to go after you here."

"Um ... okay," Alessandra says, looking at me.

I nod. "You're not working for me anymore."

"I'm not?"

"Don't be ridiculous," I snap. "If I'd known the reason you showed up here was to avoid Chakrii, you never would have worked for me in the first place."

I give her a hard look. She looks away.

"I'll just get my stuff, then," she says, and heads for the pool house.

As she passes me, I reach out and gently take her arm. She looks up at me.

"We need to talk," I say quietly. "Not tonight. It's late, and you need rest after your ordeal. But I want to know exactly what Chakrii did to you once you're up tomorrow."

"I suppose there isn't any reason for me to keep those details to myself anymore," she says absently.

"Damn straight."

She glances from me to Asher and Tucker, then says more loudly, "Thank you all for saving me from those men, by the way. I haven't had the opportunity yet to thank you, but I want you to know how grateful I am that you were there."

"You bet, Alessandra," Tucker says, giving her a thumbs-up.

"We love saving people," Asher adds.

Alessandra laughs and shakes her head. "Okay, well. See you tomorrow, then."

We watch as she disappears into the pool house. Made leaves as well, taking his bag with him.

"Yo, we drinking' to Chase's memory or not?" Asher says, clapping a hand on my shoulder and giving me a shake.

"Fine," I say, "but no one's getting shit-faced tonight. We really don't know what Chakrii might do."

"I'll stand on watch," Jesse says, coming back out of his room. "Y'all can drink whatever you want."

I lead them over to the outside bar, then pour them all a shot of bourbon, Chase's favorite drink. Not even Jesse abstains, although we all know he won't drink another.

"To Chase," I say, holding up my drink.

"To Chase," they echo. We down our drinks. Jesse moves off to take one of the chairs at the end of the bar, so he can better see the pool yard and thus anyone who might try to enter. The rest of us continue to drink and quietly tell our favorite stories of the man who gave his life in service to his country. Most of the anecdotes have been told so many times we could all recite them, no matter who actually starred in each one, but it is in the recitation of them that we find solace.

We try to remain quiet for the agents and Alessandra to sleep, but we must fail in the attempt. When I look up from my current drink a few hours later, Alessandra is sitting in the chair outside her new room, staring at me.

CHAPTER NINETEEN

ALESSANDRA

"You're still awake?"

Ford frowns down at me, his drink held loosely at his side. I glance behind him to his friends, who are still drinking, although Jesse seems more sober than the rest, so maybe he's not consuming much alcohol.

Following my gaze, Ford glances over his shoulder and smiles wryly. "I guess I can see why. We tried to be quiet, but—"

"I couldn't sleep, anyway."

He turns back to me. I watch as he takes a drink, stares at it momentarily as if considering something.

"Couldn't sleep because of what happened at the consulate?"

I nod. "Whenever I close my eyes ..."

"You relive it."

I shrug. "Pretty much, yeah."

Ford curses softly. He jerks his head. "Let's go for a walk."

"A walk where?"

"Just come."

Without another word, he walks away. I'm on my feet and following before I can ask myself where he's taking me. Ford pauses at the edge of the pool, waiting. Just as I catch up, Asher spins on his barstool to face us.

"Yo, y'all want company or not?"

"Not," Ford says. Asher laughs and gives him the finger, then turns back to the bar, where Tucker is serving him another drink. How many have they had in the two hours since I moved into my new room?

Something about the way they're drinking, though ... it doesn't seem like a normal night of partying.

Ford motions for me to follow, then makes for the trees at the edge of the pool. I come up behind him, but once we enter the trees, I falter. It's so dark I can barely see in front of me, and while I've been here for a few days, I've never ventured past the pool. Certainly never anywhere near the ocean, which I can hear from my room, especially at night.

"Um ..."

Ford pauses, and then I hear him coming back to me. A moment later, a warm hand takes mine, the touch sending jolts of unexpected pleasure down my spine. I trip in surprise, nearly falling right over myself before the hand tightens around mine and keeps me upright.

A thumb brushes over the back of my hand.

"Are you okay?" he murmurs.

"Sure. My ankle is just a little weak."

He stops. "Are you okay to walk? Fuck. I forgot. Jesus. We can go back."

"N-no, it's fine. A very mild sprain. I should be okay in a day or two. I j-just can't see well," I stutter, hoping he believes I'm unnerved by the darkness and not by how the rough skin of his hand tempts me to do dangerous things.

I've felt this hand before. Just once, when he gripped mine tightly on that plane and kept me from going to pieces. There's that bond again, that feeling like we're linked for life.

Only this time, he doesn't sever the link. Instead, he pulls me closer, so close the heat from his body slides down my body like a physical caress. I follow along behind him in the dark until the trees open up to the beach.

It isn't large; a little cove in a perfect horseshoe shape. It's nearly a full moon, and the reflection flickers in the waves that gently roll to shore. Way out near the horizon a boat cuts smoothly through the water, so far away its warning lights are barely discernible. The air is still apart from a slight breeze, warm despite the lateness of the hour. But most noticeable of all is the silence, the stillness, the absolute unlikelihood of such a place ever being marred by violence.

It's beautiful, or could be, if being this close to the water didn't freak me out. It occurs to me that Ford has brought me out here to comfort me, that he's taken me to this beautiful place to keep my mind off the ugliness of earlier today. While my mind is definitely off the events of earlier today, he doesn't know, can never know, how terrified water makes me. A sharp, poignant sadness cascades through me.

Will I ever be normal?

Then Ford releases my hand, his face turned to the

ocean as if it is his own personal compass, the way he navigates through life. Always in the direction of water.

I tuck my hand against my side, feeling bereft. Unwilling to break the silence, I turn toward him, glad he has not yet seen fit to move closer to the water. If he stays just here, at the edge of the beach, I can keep it together. I can stay focused while we discuss whatever it is he clearly wants to say to me.

"I need to apologize to you," he says quietly, gaze still locked on the water.

Apologize? To me? The man saved my life today. He has to apologize for nothing. "Why?"

He laughs and shakes his head, index finger tapping on the rim of his glass. "Because you're in this situation because of me."

"That's not true."

"Of course it is. You had dinner with me, and Chakrii decided to target you because of it. Couldn't be more obvious. I should have thought of that before I agreed to dine with you. It was damn stupid I didn't." He laughs again. "If I'd been thinking clearly, I surely would have. But that night ... Chakrii was the last person on my mind, even though I came to the fucking resort to toy with him in the first place. But ... fuck ... but I took one look at you and forgot everything else."

My eyes widen, both at his admission and at the realization that he doesn't have the full story. But how could he? He wasn't there when I gave my statement. Good God, I can't let him think he's responsible for what happened today.

"Ford," I whisper.

He waves at me with his glass. "Don't say anything. I know you must resent me, especially now knowing that the only reason it happened was because of a fucking coincidence. I suppose that's the last time you invite a stranger to dinner, huh?"

He finally looks at me. In the pale moonlight, his eyes are only the faintest shade of green, unreadable.

"But I'm sorry this happened to you, Alessandra. Fucking damn sorry. You don't deserve any of this."

He stares at me, undoubtedly waiting for me to respond, but I'm too overwhelmed to think straight.

Ford steps closer. "Alessandra?"

"Can I have some of that?"

"Some of what?"

I point to his drink. Wordlessly, he hands it over, watching me as I raise the glass to my lips and drink. The liquor burns a trail down my throat, but it also lends the most pleasant warmth—and courage.

"Ford, you're under a misconception."

"I'm what?"

I take another sip. "You're not fully responsible."

"I most certainly am."

I shake my head. "No. I pissed him off, too."

"Explain."

I laugh, but it's devoid of humor. "You're right that he came after me because he noticed I dined with you. But what you don't know, and what apparently Bianchi and Made haven't told you, is that he invited me to dinner."

"He *what*?"

"Oh, yeah," I sigh, nodding. "I went, not knowing who he was. I just wanted a dinner companion. Almost immediately he started making terrible comments, and I got a bad feeling. So I told him I wouldn't be able to dine with him after all, and then …"

"You left him. In front of a bunch of witnesses. People who likely work for him."

I wince. "Yeah. Exactly. Pranee—the woman who brought me to you—said he couldn't allow that to stand."

"Christ," Ford mutters, plowing a hand through his hair and staring at the ground.

"So you see," I say, "it's not entirely your fault."

"That makes a lot of sense," Ford finally says. "But it's beside the point."

"No, it's not."

He looks up at me. "Alessandra. He wouldn't have even asked you to dinner if I hadn't first done it."

"Well, maybe—"

"Yes, entirely. For fuck's sake, a woman should be able to decline a dinner invitation without being kidnapped."

The warmth in my chest moves lower, pooling in my belly before sinking lower. I pass him back the glass. He takes a long sip, draining it.

"Ford, why does Chakrii hate you so much? Why do you hate him, for that matter?"

He glances at me, runs a hand through his hair. "I don't talk about it."

"Oh," I say, not wanting to overstep. "I'm sorry for intruding."

Ford doesn't make the standard noise about how I'm not

intruding. Instead, he turns back to the ocean, even takes a step forward as if he would cast himself beneath the waves. Then he halts, drawn back by some internal force. His fingers clench tighter on his glass.

"I've lived here for three years now. Two years after ... two years after, I decided to move here and sank all of my savings and every monthly pension check into this resort. After twelve months, I had built a new life for myself. Then something happened that ruined it all. *Chakrii* ruined it all. So I retaliated in kind.

"We've been at war for two years since, but he doesn't have the balls to come after me directly, not after I—not after what I did. And I'm always careful to never tie anything back to me. Chakrii recently suffered a loss, and I bet that has something to do with why he wants you so badly. Retaliation. It's always about retaliation. Before that, though, we were at an impasse. Until you."

"Me? What do I have to do with it?"

"Nothing. Not technically. But ... history has a way of repeating. Or perhaps rhyming. And your arrival here has stirred up unpleasant memories for many people."

He falls silent. I watch him, waiting for him to explain what any of that means, but he doesn't. I won't get anything else if I don't ask.

"Are you one of those many people?"

"Yes."

"If you're unhappy here, why don't you leave?"

He shrugs. "I'm a stubborn man. And I've invested so much already. Not many would be interested in buying me out. And I don't want to sell the resort, anyway. I like it here, mostly. The guys want me back in the States, but ... that was a different person. He's not me, now."

Which reminds me. "I know I shouldn't ask," I say hesitantly, "but it seems as though the four of you are drinking for a specific reason."

"We are," Ford says quietly.

"Is it about Chase?"

His head whips toward me. "How do you know about him?"

"You were discussing him that first day in the pool. And I was listening behind the two-way mirror when Bianchi mentioned him."

Ford sighs. "Yes, that's right. He was in our unit. Five years ago—today—we were inserted into Raqqa to acquire intel on enemy troop movements before coalition forces attempted to take the city. We were successful in getting the intel but didn't manage to exfil as unobtrusively as we were hoping. A smaller, previously undetected group came across us. We exchanged fire.

"Jesse got shot first, because he refused to leave Asher behind when Asher was late getting to the checkpoint. Asher was hit carrying him out. Chase, who'd already gotten out, went back for both of them. Nearly made, it too, when they got him. He didn't make it. The others did."

"What about you?" I ask, so horrified I can barely get the words out.

Ford is silent a long time. "I took one retrieving his body. My unit. My responsibility."

"Ford ... I'm so sorry," I say, knowing it's painfully inadequate.

Ford doesn't respond but jerks his head once in a sharp nod. In his stillness lingers a distinct sadness, a particular kind of pain I can never comprehend.

"That's the bone frog, by the way."

"What?"

Ford absently taps his shoulder. "The tattoo. We call it the bone frog. SEALs get one when a brother falls in the line of duty. It's to remember."

I step closer, wishing I could touch him, offer some kind of solace. But I know he wouldn't welcome it. I'm shocked he's even told me any of this.

"You came here to distance yourself from all those memories."

He slowly inhales a deep breath, but I don't miss its shakiness. "Yes."

"Thank you for telling me."

Ford laughs bitterly and shakes his head, refusing to look at me. "How could you possibly be thankful for that?"

"I want to understand you."

"You shouldn't."

But I do. So much about him makes sense now. Sadly so. No wonder he was so standoffish on the plane. Who'd want to talk to a stranger when it would likely mean touching upon such a horrible memory?

Even worse, for whatever reason, my being here brings up those painful memories for him. "I'm sorry," I whisper. "Sorry my being here hurts you. What happened today must have brought up awful flashbacks. I never wanted you to be involved in any of this. It was never my intention. On the plane I just wanted a distraction. And then at dinner I just ... I don't know. You said you couldn't look away; I suppose I couldn't either."

That catches his attention.

And maybe it's because of the secret truths we've shared with each other. Maybe it's the way everything seems just a tad unreal in the moonlight. Maybe it's the fact that our time together is coming to an end. Maybe he just looked so terribly sad telling me about his friend. In any case, he's barely turned to me before I step closer and drag his mouth down to mine.

Ford freezes, so still I only kiss him a moment or two before I pull away.

"Should I not have ..."

Ford tosses his glass to the sand and hauls me up, wrapping his arms below my ass as he lifts me clear off the ground. His mouth captures mine, teeth nibbling on my lower lip. I gasp and he groans in approval, tongue sweeping inside to stroke mine with blissful skill as he tastes me.

I kiss him back, tangling my hands in his hair and yanking his head closer to mine. My teeth sink into his bottom lip and he growls, a deep, satisfied noise rumbling in his chest.

Ford tilts his head, his kiss almost bruising in its intensity as it turns wild, ferocious. As if everything in this world has ended and his only hope of survival is this one single kiss. Electricity erupts within me, stars bursting behind my eyes as the wave of pleasure sinks lower, so acute it's almost painful. I writhe against him, frustrated he holds me so tightly I cannot move, cannot wrap my legs around his hips and alleviate this ache.

A hand trails up my back and fists in my hair. My head is jerked back; my eyes burst open in surprise as his mouth tears from mine and he trails a line of hot kisses along my jaw to my ear.

His grip tightens, holding me completely immobile as he whispers, his voice hoarse and furious, "Christ, you're the most gorgeous thing I've ever seen. How the fuck am I supposed to function when one look at you nearly sends me over the edge? Every time you glare at me, I ache to bend you over the nearest surface and fuck you until you scream. Do you know how many times I've nearly done just that? How many nights I've used my fist just to get you out of my mind? How many times I've wondered the exact taste of your wet pussy as you come on my tongue? Well? Do you?"

Oh God. Those words. Never in all my dirtiest fantasies have I imagined him with such a filthy mouth. I whimper, desperate, out of my mind to lessen the terrible throbbing between my thighs his words have set off. I grab for his shoulders, nails digging into him as I struggle to hold on, to anchor myself to his considerable strength even as I feel like at any second I might blast right off this earth. My chest heaves but I can't draw in enough air. The desire rolls through me, again and again, each crest higher, harder, but still not even close to what I want.

Ford sucks the skin behind my ear, a great shudder rolling through his body when it draws a long moan out of me, and then rasps, "What do you need? Tell me and I'll give it to you."

"I want my legs around you."

"Hold on, then."

My arms tighten around his neck as his hands slip down to the backs of my thighs. He jerks them apart and I mindlessly wrap them around his hips. An almost sob escapes me as I finally, finally grind against the full, hard length of him. The shorts I sleep in are so thin as to be barely there; I can feel every glorious inch of him. I'm too far gone to wait for him to even touch me. I need relief, and I need it now.

Ford drops his head back. His eyes drift shut; his brows furrow as I grind against him a second time. I bury my face in his neck, my breath ragged. His hips buck into me, sliding his cock along my clit. My body screams in approval at the desperately needed friction, so unbelievably good that I do it again. Then again. Ford's hands tighten on my ass, and he pants, helping me move against him.

"That's it, gorgeous. Take what you need."

I manage to lift my head from his neck. Ford's looking at me through eyes narrowed to slits, his face twisted in such desire I nearly explode just from the sight of it. His entire body is bowed backward from the force of driving me against him. I can actually see the tendons popping out on his neck. It's easily the hottest thing I've ever seen.

I've made him look like that. *I'm* the one who's making him delirious with need. My hips roll against him faster. I'm close, so *close*...

"Gorgeous girl. So fucking hot. Every inch of you is so damn perfect, you're burned into my mind. Let me see you come for me."

I shatter, crying out as I convulse against him. Ford's hands clench painfully hard on my ass as he works me through every last wave of pleasure. I collapse against him, exhausted, my fingers tangled in his hair. I bury my face in his shoulder, gasping for air, burrowing into him as close as I can, feeling drugged.

"Dear God," Ford mutters. I vaguely register the fact that he's shaking, still hard, somehow still holding me to him.

"Give me a minute," I manage against his neck. "Then I'll—"

"Ford? Are you okay? What the hell are you two doing out here?"

CHAPTER TWENTY

FORD

I lower Alessandra to the ground and turn, putting her behind me as I face whoever has the world's worst fucking timing.

Jesse grinds to a halt when he sees us. His hands lift in an apologetic gesture.

"Go away," I growl.

"Sorry, man. You had me on watch, and I thought I heard something."

Oh, he heard something, all right. He heard the sounds of a woman's orgasm that were so fucking erotic I nearly came in my damn pants. The precise sound she made when she exploded flashes through my mind. Then again. It takes a third fucking time for me to replay the instant and realize this means my friend heard her.

"Leave," I hiss, my hand steadying Alessandra behind me to ensure I'm blocking his view of her. "But before you do, apologize to her."

Jesse sighs. "My apologies, Alessandra. I thought something was wrong. And after everything else that happened today ..."

He doesn't say what we're all thinking. That after the shitstorm of today, another hit right now would damn suck.

"It's fine," Alessandra says at my back, her voice shaky, "I'm glad you were making sure we're okay."

"We'd be much more okay if you'd leave," I mutter, not caring if he hears me.

Jesse snorts and says, "Yeah, yeah. Try not to stay out here too long, okay?"

"Keep talking and I'll knock on Bianchi's door and tell her you want to spend the night."

Jesse gives me the finger, then turns and disappears back into the trees. When Alessandra steps out behind me, it really hits me what we've just done.

Fucking hell, I just got her off by grinding her against my clothed erection. And it was ... way hotter than it should have been. I stare down at her, proud I gave her such pleasure. I want to do it again. And again. And again. Until neither of us can move. Until we have to crawl back to the resort. I want her in my bed every hour, every last second that she remains here.

The thought might as well be a bucket of ice water, for all the effect it has on me. My erection dies a swift death. I battle the urge not to cuss a blue streak.

Jesus Christ, what was I thinking? I just nearly took her on this beach, ground her against me, growled any number of filthy things at her I can't even remember now, I was so far gone. She was damn into it in the moment, but after Jesse interrupting us, does she regret it now?

"I suppose I should apologize," I say slowly, stooping to pick up the glass I pitched to the sand when I could finally no longer resist touching her.

"Apologize?"

Alessandra stares at me, but since I stand between her and the moon, my height casts her face in shadow. A strange note has entered her voice, something I can't quite identify.

"I wasn't very ... tender just then," I say, but what I mean is *I just ground you against my body and praised you into orgasming.*

"I suppose you weren't."

What the hell is she thinking? Damn it, I don't *want* to apologize; I want to do it again. Twice. All night.

"Well, should I apologize or not?" I say, feeling grouchy.

Alessandra steps around me, heading toward the resort. But as she draws near, she lifts up on her toes and whispers, "Sex doesn't always need to be tender, Ford."

Before she can walk another step, my arm snags around her waist and jerks her to me. "Good," I grunt, "because I fuck like a wild animal."

A shiver rolls through her. "That is ... very enlightening."

"I'd be happy to provide another demonstration," I say, nibbling on her earlobe.

Alessandra shivers again, then shakes her head, sighing. She sags against me. I don't have to see her face to know she's yawning. "Mmm. I'm s-sorry, Ford, but suddenly I'm so ... tired."

I chuckle. "You're exhausted. Today has been horrible

for you. There's time tomorrow to pick up where we left off. I should have let you rest, but I brought you out here because I thought you might like to see the ocean at night. I always come here when I feel like shit."

She lets several moments pass, then squeezes my arm. "I thought that might be the case."

There's a peculiar note to her voice, but I don't push her on it. Instead, I bend down and sweep her into my arms.

"What are you doing?"

"Taking you back to your room."

"I can walk."

"I know you can, but isn't this more pleasurable? It certainly is for me."

She laughs, a quiet, lazy little laugh that does strange things to my insides. She wraps an arm around my neck, fingers playing with my hair as I head for the trees.

"Ford ... this feels a bit unfair to you."

"How so?"

"Well. I finished, and you, you know ... didn't."

"Oh, that," I say, shrugging. "Don't worry about it. I'll fuck myself after I deposit you in your room."

"*Ford.*"

"What?" I say, shrugging again. "It's true. Only this time, I know exactly what your face looks like when you come, so I'll no longer be forced to use my imagination."

Alessandra suddenly starts shaking as if she's holding back laughter. "Well, in that case, I won't worry about it."

"Please don't," I mutter, "I'm a military man, Alessandra. I'm used to using my fist."

TAKE ME IN BANGKOK

I WAKE WITH A POUNDING HEADACHE, the absolute last kind of pounding I wish I'd done last night. After leaving Alessandra at her room—and pressing her fully against the door for one helluva steamy goodnight kiss—I didn't go up to my room to finally take care of my painfully raging boner. As much as my body really needed a release.

Oh no. Not when Jesse told Asher and Tucker about what he'd seen on the beach.

I didn't hear the end of it for over an hour, the two of them absolutely refusing to turn in until we drank to my finally getting my head out of my ass. Then they insisted on another round for Chase. And after that we needed to toast Jesse for good luck in wooing Agent Bianchi, which Jesse despised so much we simply had to do it again just to piss him off.

And before I knew it, I was mildly drunk. By the time I stumbled up the stairs to my apartment, there was no question of my doing anything but passing out.

"Christ," I grumble, rubbing my eyes with the heels of my hands. "Those dipshits better be even more hungover."

Jesse laughs at me the moment I drag myself into the kitchen. "Well, hey there, sunshine. Aren't we looking spiffy this morning."

"Get fucked."

"But I thought that was supposed to be *you* last night. Don't tell me you didn't close the deal?"

Bastard's going to get a facer if he doesn't quit that chipper shit.

"You know very well I left her in her room."

Jesse makes a show of stroking his jaw. "Oh, that's right. I happened to interrupt your little interlude. So sorry."

I grab a fist of his shirt and drag him toward me. "You will never mention that again. You will certainly never allude to your having seen or heard her. Last night never existed for you, got it?"

Jesse laughs. "Boy, have you got it bad."

I shove him away. "Fuck right off."

"Hey, man, it's fine. Even preferable, if it means you're finally getting over—"

"Don't talk about her, either," I snap.

He grows serious. "Ford, you know I'm just giving you shit, right?"

I dig the heels of my hands into my eyes again. "Yes, yes. Now shut up until I get some coffee in me. It's like you *want* me to growl at you."

Jesse scoffs. "As if our entire relationship is not based on giving each other shit."

I grunt. Ain't that the truth. Christ, I never meant to drink so much bourbon. We weren't *supposed* to drink this much, damn it! So much for keeping a sharp eye out for any of Chakrii's men. Although realistically he wouldn't have tried something last night. Not after getting his ass handed to him at the consulate.

"Just let me get a cup of coffee in me," I say. "Then I can take all the shit you want to sling at me."

I'm just finishing my first cup when Asher drags himself into the kitchen.

"*Bro.* I feel like shit," Asher moans, dragging himself

into one of the stools at the kitchen counter. "Who made me drink that much last night?"

I glare at him. "That's my line, asshole."

Asher grunts. "Least I can clean a pool, man. You need to fire your cleaner."

My head jerks toward him. "The fuck you say?"

Asher blinks wearily at me. "Dude, I jumped in the pool this morning to shake it off. It's gettin' nasty, man. Don't you worry about bacteria and shit growing in there?"

"She said she ..."

Asher takes a good look at my expression and jerks upright. "Hey, man. It's not *that* bad. You had Alessandra cleaning it? Dude, what the hell? Even I can tell she's not up to that."

"Fuck," I say, plowing a hand through my hair. "My guy quit right before y'all came. She said she could do it. I didn't have time to find anyone else or do it myself what with getting everything ready for your arrival. And hell, we've been on the boat the whole time you've been here. She *lied* to me."

My cup slams down on the counter. Asher climbs to his feet. "Hey, now, boss. I'm sure—"

"I don't want to hear you make excuses for her," I snap, heading for the door.

Jesse and Asher follow along behind me as I make for the pool, emitting various possible explanations at my back that I ignore. Tucker runs into us in the hall, takes one look at my face and curses.

"Now what?"

Jesse says behind me, "Alessandra was supposed to clean the pool and didn't."

"Aw shit."

Tucker joins in with the guys in excusing her behavior. I say nothing, just stalk out to the pool and frown down at it.

Asher's right: this hasn't been cleaned in four, maybe … fuck. Probably not since my employee quit. A thin film of scum covers the surface, glinting in the sunlight, and a few leaves and other detritus have sunk to the bottom of the deep end. Bending down to the edge of the water and inhaling, I shake my head in disgust; the scent is way off. This water hasn't been cleaned in days.

Asher's been in this thing every day since he's been here. He's lucky he hasn't fallen sick, although knowing my luck, he might still fall ill if anything's been incubating. In a place as hot as Phuket, any pool of water can fill with all sorts of terrible bacteria and viruses within a few days. That's why I'm a real asshole about maintaining it; first, there are laws requiring it, and second, I'd hate it if anyone got sick from their stay at my resort. The resort itself might not be that fancy, but the entire reason people come here is to receive no-frills but excellent dive instruction. The basic requirement of that is having a fucking functional pool, damn it.

I cannot fucking believe this shit. I'm lucky she showed up when my friends arrived, and not when I had any guests. Someone could have gotten sick by going in here. How the fuck didn't I notice this?

The answer stares me in the face. I needed her to work for me, and wanted to screw us both blind, so I looked the other way when she assured me it had been taken care of. The other shit had been cleaned, and I wanted time with my friends, so I didn't bother to check.

And the entire time she was lying to me.

Fury whips through me, directed both at her, for her duplicitousness, but also at myself, for being a stupid shit thinking with his dick instead of his head. If she hadn't fucking lied, I could have squeezed in time somewhere to get it cleaned. Hell, my boys would have fucking helped, if their growing exhortations to calm down are any indication.

On the heels of anger rolls another emotion, something deeper, more catastrophic. Something that feels suspiciously like betrayal. I thought we'd turned a corner, moved past the animosity we felt that first night. After everything that happened yesterday, especially her ability to remain cool under fire, well, I'd started to like her. Hell, scratch that; I've liked her since I watched her slog her way through all ten rooms that first day. Last night I finally admitted it.

And that's not even getting into the erotic moment on the beach last night.

All of that feels dirty now. If she'd just been honest and told me she couldn't do it, it would have been fine. It's not like I would have bit her head off.

Well, not much, anyway.

I step away from the pool.

"Now, Ford," Jesse says. "This isn't the end of the world."

I turn on him, then jab my thumb over my shoulder. "You have any idea how many gallons of water are in that pool? It'll take twenty-four hours to shock it and I can't do that until tonight so the chemicals mix properly. So we're looking at almost forty-eight hours until I can even test the damn thing to see if it's suitable for swimming again. I've got guests coming in the day after y'all leave. Two of them want their open-water certs. They can't get them without a fucking pool for the fucking pool work!"

Tucker makes a placating sound. "Don't worry, man. We'll shock it this evening as soon as the sun goes down, and it should be ready by early evening tomorrow."

I step around them, my gaze locked on the door to Alessandra's new room.

"Don't yell at her," Asher shouts behind me. "You're just going to regret it later."

"Unlikely," I mutter to myself, reaching the door and pounding on it until she finally opens it wrapped in bedsheets.

CHAPTER TWENTY-ONE

ALESSANDRA

"What's wrong—"
"Why'd you do it?"

I blink and rub a hand over my face, trying to get my bleary eyes to focus. Twenty seconds ago, I was dead to the world, and now ... I get my first good look at Ford.

He's furious.

I blink again, this time in surprise. Oh shit. He is *pissed*. Has Ford ever been this mad in the short time I've known him? Doubtful. He crowds in the door, arms folded over his chest, his jaw so tight it looks like it could slice through wire.

"Well?" he snaps. Something flashes in his eyes. It disappears an instant later. Is it ... was that ... sadness? No, something deeper than that. *Disappointed* sadness, more like. As if I've personally betrayed him.

Only one thing could upset him that much after the intimacy we shared last night.

Oh no. Oh no, no, no.

"Ford," I rasp, mortified when my voice comes out still hoarse from sleep. I stand taller, clutching the bedsheet tighter around me that I brought because the nightie I sleep in barely covers the important parts.

Ford's gaze flicks down to where my fist clutches the sheet to my chest. His expression hardens. He jerks his attention back up to my face.

"The pool is a fucking pigsty."

I flinch. Yep. And there it is, what I've been hoping he wouldn't notice until I had already left. "I'm sorry," I say, the apology pathetic even to my ears.

His jaw rolls from side to side and he huffs in frustration. "What the fuck, Alessandra? Why didn't you just tell me? The entire pool needs to be treated. It will take a few days until I can safely let people back in there. Someone could have gotten sick. I could have lost business, thousands of dollars if people had cancelled and gone somewhere else to get certified."

Oh God. I didn't even think of that. I *should* have thought of that from the beginning. I run a company, for God's sake! That I didn't, that the thought didn't even enter my mind, is a thousand times worse. Shame tightens my chest, making my mouth run dry, cutting off my ability to answer.

I was too absorbed by my stupid fear to think about anyone but myself. That makes it even worse. I should have foreseen the financial consequences if this giant pool became unsuitable for swimming. It's clearly the one thing that matters to Ford. I should have just told him no, thrown a fit until he said I didn't have to do it. Anything. Even him thinking I'm a spoiled bitch would be better than the justified guilt I feel now.

"I'll pay for it—"

"Of course you will," he says, voice bitter. "It isn't about the money, gorgeous. This might come as a shock to you, but I'm not so damn poor I can't handle an unforeseen expense. I really should make you pay every damn penny for it, though, since it's your fucking fault it's out of commission in the first place.

"But no. What this is about is the fact that you *lied* to me. I asked you multiple times over multiple days whether you cleaned the pool and you lied straight to my face. Every time. I just ... in my previous life, people *died* if someone couldn't handle their shit and lied about it. No excuses. After last night—I thought we were being straight with each other. So again, one final time, I want to know why you lied. That's really the issue at hand, here."

My eyes drop to the floor, too ashamed to meet his gaze. I don't want to tell him I'm afraid of water. It's my deepest shame, the thing that embarrasses me more than anything else. Every particle of my being shies away from admitting it to this giant of a man, who jumped in front of a gun for me like it was *nothing*.

I'd rather have him despise me than believe I'm weak. That I'm so pathetic I can't even stand to touch water. As if I could admit such an embarrassment to a *Navy SEAL*.

Or any of them, for that matter. They're surely all right outside listening to him chew me out. Ford's not the only one who saved me; they did, too. Like it was their job. And ha-ha! It literally used to be.

No way could they possibly understand this phobia of mine. In fact, it's so ridiculous, I actually think if I told the sorry truth right now, if I actually admitted to Ford the real reason the pool went uncleaned, he wouldn't believe me. Because what idiot would come to Thailand if she's afraid of water? He'd think I'm using some pathetic excuse to keep him from being angry. Even worse, he might think this is some pathetic woe-is-me routine. He would despise that.

Maybe last night after ... after he made me feel more alive than any man has in my entire life, if I'd told him then, he would have believed me. We would have still had that fragile, newfound trust between us. Not now, though. That trust has clearly been broken.

It's just ... I can't do it. I want all of them, and especially Ford, to think I'm that fearless woman from yesterday. The one Interpol believes can help set a trap for one of the worst criminals around here. I'm so not. I have my own talents, but bravery in the face of real danger isn't really one of them.

Bravery in the face of *water* isn't one of them.

But the one thing I can't bear to do is lie again. So I tell the smallest truth I can. Maybe he'll understand. "I just ... couldn't do it."

He shakes his head like he can't believe the words that have just come out of my mouth. "You couldn't do it, or you just didn't want to?"

I wince. Well, that's the truth, too. "I did not want to, no. Pools make me uncomfortable."

Ford stares at me as if I've started spouting gibberish. "Pools. *Pools* make you uncomfortable? What? It's a fucking pool. What the fuck is it going to do to you? In my wildest dreams, I couldn't have come up with such an unbelievable excuse."

So much for him understanding. Now I'm really not going to tell him I'm afraid of water. He's essentially just said that's pathetic.

Ford shakes his head back and forth in bewilderment. He's still furious, but when he speaks now, there's also an undercurrent of hurt in his tone. "Why can't you just tell me the truth? Why are you lying? I know you are. There's something else. So I ask you again and you fabricate some bullshit reason? I thought ... fuck, I know we don't mean much to each other, but I thought after last night we meant *something*. I don't even know what to say right now."

Oh, God, he's right. He's entirely correct that I'm brushing him off. But I'm scared. I'm terrified to share this phobia with anyone, and I am even more afraid of what he might think of me if I told him. Because he's right. He does mean something to me. What, yet, I don't know, but it's not nothing.

I search for a response and can only scrounge one up that—knowing him better now—will offend his sense of personal honor, even if it was the original reason I told him I would when he asked me to clean the pool.

"I thought you would kick me out."

His head snaps back. He half turns away from me, shaking his head as he stares darkly at the pool. When he finally speaks, his tone is exhausted.

"And you were worried about what Chakrii would do to you if you weren't here."

He looks so disgusted with himself, I don't have the heart to reply in the affirmative. And now *I* feel disgusted, too, because it's like I'm gaslighting his justified anger about this entire situation, an unintended consequence of my desire to no longer lie to him. What a mess.

I can only add, "Now I know you'd never do that, Ford."

He laughs, a sound devoid of humor. He shakes his head again, still not looking at me.

"Ford ..."

He makes a slashing gesture. "Don't. Just ... don't. There's nothing more to discuss."

He stalks off, but my guilty conscience compels me to say, "That's it?"

He freezes, his back stiff. "Yeah. I think we've said all there is to say, don't you? What's the point, really? Tomorrow you're gone, anyway. We can leave things here."

The words are cooly uttered, the tone final. Ford has decided he's done with me. Or maybe it's the situation he's sick of. I don't blame him if that's the case.

But as he walks away, it feels worse than that. It feels like he's once again broken the bond between us. And this time, nothing will ever repair it.

CHAPTER TWENTY-TWO

ALESSANDRA

The yard clears out, falling quiet with the kind of silence that feels accusatory. I stare at his back, feeling the eyes of his friends on me, although I'm too guilt-stricken to do anything but head back into my room.

Tossing my sheet on the bed, I shower and dress, wishing I had told Ford I wouldn't clean the pool from the beginning. But what's done is done; all that's left is for me to find some way to make up for it.

When I leave my room, the pool yard is deserted. Frowning, I glance around a second time, as if this might somehow cause someone to appear before me, but no, there's no one.

A flicker of unease skitters through me. Has something happened? Some update about Chakrii? Surely they wouldn't have left me, though, right?

Maybe everyone is still eating. It's early enough, and after the excitement of yesterday, I'm suddenly starving since I was too tired to eat last night.

Weaving around the blasted pool, I head into the main building, then pad down the hall to the kitchen. Only Made and Bianchi look up from their coffees when I enter.

I grind to a halt. "Where is everyone?"

Bianchi snorts, not bothering to look up from the report she's reading. "You mean where are the soldiers? They disappeared about thirty minutes ago."

I sag onto one of the stools. Made quietly gets up and pours me a coffee. I mumble a thanks and wrap my hands around it, the mild heat soothing.

"Where'd they go?"

Bianchi shrugs, attention still locked on the report in front of her. "Out. Who knows where. They said they'd be back. Had to reiterate multiple times to watch you, I might add, which was really quite offensive. Like you wouldn't be safe with the two Interpol agents. Made was just coming to wake you if you weren't up yet. That Jesse really is an asshole. I don't care if he speaks Italian."

I stare down into my cup, sure that I'm the reason they've left. Needing a distraction, I say, "Have you heard anything about Chakrii?"

Bianchi makes a disgusted sound. "No."

"And we're not expecting to," says Made. "He's no doubt planning his next move, but with your brother coming in tomorrow, you'll be long gone before he'll be able to organize anything."

Another thing I feel terrible about. "I'm sorry I'm not helping you with him. Using me as bait, I mean."

Made shrugs. "It's okay."

Bianchi mumbles something that sounds suspiciously

like "no, it's not." Made sighs and flicks an irritated glance at her, the first time I've witnessed him depart from his customary politeness.

"It's always risky involving civilians," says Made. "And it would be even more so with you, due to your fame back in your own country. Perhaps it was wishful thinking."

"What about the mole? The person who helped the car enter the consulate before I showed up?"

Bianchi says, "We're working on that. They let us know who took your appointment; we're searching for her now."

"You mean the woman who answered the phone when I called the consulate?"

Bianchi nods. "Yes, her. We sent a few agents to her residence this morning. Guess who wasn't home even though it wasn't yet dawn?"

My eyes widen. "So it has to be her, then. Right?"

Made shakes his head. "It's likely, but not necessarily. She could have been threatened, bribed. She might not even know why someone needed you to show up at that time. She could know nothing about Chakrii."

I think back to how she insisted she needed to go back to her boss. "I thought there was something strange about her. She didn't seem professional. But it was the consulate phone number, so I figured she had to be legitimate."

"She was," says Bianchi. "An official employee of the Italian government, that is. But that doesn't prevent people from becoming corrupt."

"But if she's not home, then she's on the run," I say slowly, thinking it out. "That implies she's guilty of at least something."

The agents exchange a glance.

"What?" I ask.

Made says reluctantly. "Or she could have served her purpose and has been ..."

My eyes widen. "You think someone killed her?"

"Again, we don't know anything yet," Made rushes to say, "which is why it's imperative we find her."

"Wow," I say, my appetite gone. "Someone might be dead because of me."

Bianchi snaps, "You had nothing to do with it. A criminal is tying up loose ends. Or she stayed over at a friend's last night. Whatever. None of that is your fault."

"I guess," I say, but I still feel responsible.

"There's food in the fridge if you want it," Bianchi says, then dismisses me.

My stomach clenches just at the thought eating food right now. I was famished when I came in here, but I'll need some time to forget about what we've discussed before I believe I can keep food down. I place my cup down on the counter. Ditto for coffee.

Restlessness stirs within me. I study the kitchen, looking for something to do. I need a distraction. With a sense of dread, I know working in the kitchen isn't what would be truly helpful. There's something else, though. Something I can actually do about the pool. And also a way to make amends.

I can clean it.

Well, I can try, anyway. I can maybe clean it a little. Make it less filthy. Make the effort, anyway. Ford will surely understand the gesture. And then, when I leave tomorrow, it won't be on such awful terms. He saved my life, and I should do *something* as thanks. If I can clean it even a little, then he'll know I don't want to leave things badly between us. That I do care. That I'm grateful for everything he's done, even if at first we couldn't stand each other.

And, most importantly, that what happened last night on the beach meant something, at least to me.

Filled with purpose even if at the same time dread makes my throat dry, I push away from the table.

"I'll be out by the pool."

"That's fine," says Made. "We have some work to catch up on in here. But stay in view of this window so we can keep an eye on you."

"Don't go in it either," Bianchi says absently, reading a document. "Ford told us it isn't clean."

I wince, glad they don't notice my guilty expression since they're busy with their reports.

Once outside, I make my way over to the chemical room. Only one of the instruments holds any meaning to me. I'm pretty sure I've seen one of our own staff using something like that to vacuum our pool. And it comes with such a long hose, I won't have to get too close to the water to do it. It will reach the bottom without much from me.

I do another video search on my phone for the model of the vacuum to figure out how the hell to use it. I can suck up all the leaves and other crap that have fallen into it while I've been here. It won't do much help, but someone will have to do it eventually and it's the thought that counts. At the very least, for whoever ends up cleaning it for real it won't take as long.

It's all I can manage.

Still, as I drag the machine to the water and plug it into an outlet by the chairs, I'm not sure how I will manage. I creep toward the water, the hose clutched in my suddenly sweaty palms, dreading to do it yet still resolved. I've stuck my feet in the Golden Lotus pool for nearly twenty minutes the last day; I won't even have to *touch* the water now. I can do this.

Cautiously lowering the vacuum into the water, I turn it on and then watch as stuff begins sucking up the hose. I move slowly up and down, getting all the crap in front of me, then carefully sidle a few feet to my right, sending me ever so slightly farther from the shallow end of the pool. It's not fun, but it isn't awful. My heart pounds every time I extend as far as I can, but I manage. I'll have to go around to the other side to clean from that end, too, since the pool is so wide. It's wide enough there will be a middle portion I can't reach, but there's nothing to be done about that.

I don't think about how much water there is the closer I get to the deep end. I keep my eyes locked directly in front of me, carefully unraveling the hose each time I need more line and slowly dragging the heavy vacuum along behind me. After a while, I've gone halfway around the pool. There's just a small portion remaining in the very deepest part of the pool. I can get the leaves if I reach, but I shudder at the thought of extending that far out over the water. Nevertheless, I do it.

It happens so fast I'm still reaching out with the vacuum, trying to suck up that last couple of leaves. I yank to unravel the last few feet of the hose so I can reach the final spot. But the line has already fully unraveled, so instead of jerking on the slack line of the hose, I accidentally yank on a taut line, much harder than I should. The force of it sends the vacuum crashing into me. And since I'm already leaning way too far over, I don't stand a chance.

I crash into the pool.

Most people would kick to the surface, swim up, drag themselves out, whatever. Even people who don't know how to swim would thrash around, wildly kicking their legs and arms in a desperate attempt to save themselves.

I do none of that. My brain shuts down. In the instant between processing the fact that I'm going in and actually hitting the water, my brain decides that this is it. This is how I die. I can't save myself. Not this. Not a second time.

My heart clenches with such terror the sheer stab of pain actually makes me gasp. Water rushes in, along with panic. Only then do I begin to move, to thrash, to flounder, but in that moment of terror, my greatest fear coming to life, I forget how to swim.

And so I sink. Down, down, down, to the bottom.

CHAPTER TWENTY-THREE

FORD

"Shit, I forgot my wallet," I say, yanking the wheel to send the Range Rover back toward the resort. That really is a miracle in itself; when I sat behind the wheel this morning, I half expected the car not to start.

"Man, you really are distracted today, aren't you?" Tucker drawls.

I say nothing, my fists tightening on the wheel.

"Slick, bro," Asher snaps. "Dude's already pissed. You antagonizing him won't help shit."

"I'll cover it," Jesse says, "so we don't have to turn around."

"Y'all're *my* guests, remember?" I grumble. "What's the point of an apology breakfast if I don't fucking pay?"

"Maybe this will convince you we don't need an apology breakfast. It's almost like this is karma," Jesse says mildly.

"Well, shut up," I say. "We're doing it. I was a dick to all of you this morning, so as a courtesy, I'm not also subjecting you to my shitty cooking as well."

Out of the corner of my eye, I feel Jesse stare at me significantly. "So we deserve an apology for you yelling at us ... but not Alessandra."

I grind my teeth together.

"Yeah, Car," says Asher, reaching through the seats to clap me on the shoulder. "We all heard you yell at her, man. That was overkill. Way harsh. We told you not to do it. Said you'd regret it. And oh, look! Ya already do."

"I can apologize to her later," I say through gritted teeth. "Once I've calmed down."

Tucker laughs. "Yeah, man. Like being around her will make you *more* calm."

I give him the finger over my shoulder, eyes still locked on the road.

Jesse sighs and rolls his head back and forth along the headrest. "Why do I get the feeling you just want an excuse to get away from her?"

Because that's true.

"That girl's got him tied up in knots," Tucker says. "Don't think I've ever seen you get so worked up about a woman. Not even with—"

"Don't finish that thought."

Silence falls in the car. Then Jesse says, "Are you never going to talk about her, either?"

"Not if I can help it."

Jesse sighs. "It's like you can't even see how one situation might be affecting the other. That's impressive denial, really."

"As if you have room to talk," I say, "repeatedly getting into it with Bianchi like you're not a fully-grown man."

"Also true," says Tucker.

"That is entirely different," says Jesse.

Asher snickers. "Naw, dude. It's literally the same."

"How about we all just drop it," I say, pulling back into the resort. Leaving the car running, I shove open my door and add, "Wait here. I'll be right back."

I'm just heading into the main building when I hear it, the sound so ordinary, so inconsequential, at first I don't take note of it. Then I pause. A splash? Everyone knows the pool is closed. No one should be swimming.

I swear to God, if Asher is fucking around again ...

I change direction and head out back to the deserted pool yard. Where the hell is everyone? And why the fuck is the vacuum out? And why is it dangling—

Christ, no.

In three strides I'm diving into the pool, kicking for the body lying motionless at the bottom. In seconds I reach her, looping an arm around her waist and kicking off from the bottom. She isn't moving. Her head lolls on my shoulder, her body a dead weight as I swim up, horrified terror making me pray harder than I ever have before.

"Call an ambulance!" I scream the instant I breach the surface, but who knows if they can hear me over the radio and their own talking shit. Why the *fuck* was she out here alone, damn it!

Made comes barreling out of the building, his phone already clapped to his ear.

I lift her out of the water, then haul myself out. Made comes up to us, still speaking with emergency services, but I ignore the bastard, too busy clearing her airway and beginning chest compressions.

"Come on, come on," I groan, my hands pushing into her chest. "Breathe, damn it! Breathe so I can kill you myself."

"Yo, Ford, what the hell is—holy shit!"

Asher falls to his feet beside me, babbling about what he can do, but there's nothing. I've either gotten to her in time, or she's gone.

"Come on, gorgeous," I plead. "Come on!"

She heaves violently, water spewing out of her mouth. I quickly turn her on her side, rubbing her back as she coughs out disgusting pool water. Thank God, *thank God*.

Tucker and Jesse run up to us as Alessandra catches her breath.

"Christ, man, what happened?" Tucker asks.

I'm wondering that myself.

"It was close," I say tersely, still kneeling over her, my hands trailing all over her body to assure myself she's okay. There's no blood. She doesn't wince when I touch her head, so she didn't hit her head. Apart from the water in her lungs, I don't think she has any other injuries.

Alessandra shudders. Her mouth drops open. She tries to say something, fails, wets her lips, then tries again. We all bend closer to hear the faint rasp that comes out of her.

"Get ... away."

My head snaps back in astonishment. I just saved her

fucking life, and she wants me gone? My hands form fists against the concrete. I'm about to climb to my feet when another horrible cough rattles through her. I fall back down on all fours, my anxious gaze tracking over her, hating the sick sound she's making.

"Get ... me ... away."

What? Get her away from what? If not me ...

Her eyes collide with mine and the fear in them sends understanding crashing into place. Multiple events finally click into place. Why she wouldn't change seats with me on the plane. Why she didn't follow me when I stepped toward the ocean last night.

Why she never cleaned the fucking pool. Why she lied about doing it.

"Dear God," I rasp. "You're not afraid of flying at all, are you? You're afraid of water!"

She turns her head away, croaks, "Yes."

Something cracks in my chest, in the vicinity of my already bruised and broken heart. "Shhh," I hush. "It's okay. You're okay now."

Gathering her in my arms, I climb to my feet and walk to the chair the farthest away from the pool. I collapse into it, still holding her. She stiffens; my arms tighten around her, and she relaxes. I need the closeness as much as she does right now. I tuck her head into the space between my neck and shoulder and lean the rest of her against me, her feet dangling off to the side. I slide a hand up and down her back, waiting for it to hit her. After a few moments, her hand comes up to rest on my chest.

And then the sobs begin.

My heart breaks for her as she cries, great wracking sobs that shudder through her entire frame. A stream of soothing words escapes my lips, although it's unclear whether she even hears any of them. I barely register what I'm saying myself.

"You're okay now, gorgeous. I'm here with you. I've got you. Just let it out. Let it out, now. You're going to be fine. I won't let anything happen to you."

"What the hell is going on out here?" Bianchi says, coming out of the main building.

She stumbles back a step at the look on my face.

"I don't know," I say quietly, my voice tight with fury. "What *is* going on here? Care to explain why the fuck she almost drowned on your watch?"

Bianchi pales. Alessandra stiffens when I mention drowning. I press a kiss to her forehead and rock her gently, still glaring at the Interpol agent.

"I watched her fall in, Walker," Made says. "I was already on my way. You just got to her first. I didn't think—"

"Clearly you weren't thinking," I snap. "This situation has been fucked from the moment y'all fuckers got involved. I'm starting to think you're *trying* to get her killed."

Bianchi flushes in anger, but wisely chooses not to respond.

Made says quietly, "You're right to be angry. I apologize, Ms. Vitale. I should have been closer. It's my fault for not getting there sooner."

"No, it's mine," Alessandra says weakly.

"This isn't your fault," I say, "it's a failure on the part of the people responsible for protecting you."

Which would include me.

Christ in hell. I'm furious with Made and Bianchi, but I am just as angry with myself. Angrier. Our argument from earlier pissed me off and I left to get away from it, thinking she would still be safe.

I should only rely on myself when it comes to protecting the people I care about. And I didn't. I farmed it out to someone else. How many times am I going to have to fucking learn that?

Alessandra slowly leans away from me. Reluctantly, I release her, and she drags herself into the chair next to me. "I don't want to listen to all of you blame yourselves for my own stupidity," she says hoarsely, pausing multiple times before she finally gets the words out.

"What were you doing cleaning the pool, anyway?" Bianchi asks, turning to look at the vacuum that's still running. "I thought it had to be shocked or something."

My gaze has never left Alessandra, so I don't miss the instant embarrassment flashes across her face. And with sickening certainty, I know exactly why she did it.

"Because of our argument this morning," I say quietly, so quietly only she can hear.

She winces, but nods. "I'm leaving tomorrow and didn't ... didn't want to leave it that way ... between us."

"Christ," I mutter.

"I thought ... you would appreciate ... the gesture."

Fuck me. "Alessandra, my God. If I'd known you couldn't swim, I never would have asked you to clean it in the first place. Hell, I would have been teaching you how to swim this entire time instead."

"I know how to swim," Alessandra says.

Her words are like a gunshot, they cause such silence. Alessandra glances around at all of us, notes the confusion on our faces, then sighs a sound of abject misery.

"When I was eight," she begins, the sadness in her eyes already hinting I'm about to hate whatever story she tells us, "I almost drowned. My family's yacht was anchored in the Mediterranean, off the coast of Mykonos. Our family was hosting a few other families, close friends. A trip away, you know. One of the families had a boy who was my brother's friend, and he had brought along his cousin.

"Unfortunately, his cousin was a terrible human being. Even then when he was only a couple years older than me. One evening, when all the adults had left to go out for the night in Mykonos, leaving us kids with the security detail, this boy thought it would be funny to throw me off the deck. Sink or swim, he laughed. Well, I swam.

"But what none of us knew was that there was a current that day. A strong one, moving out and away from the island. When I landed in the water, I kicked to the surface, but I was no match for it. It started dragging me away. I was just out of swimming class, but no kid, no *person* can swim when a current is that strong."

Alessandra falls silent, staring unseeing in front of her. Then she says, "My body gave out right as the security team was coming toward me on the dingy. I went under, sank right down. Someone had to dive in and swim to me. They hauled me out, managed to save me just like you did, Ford.

"I remember the coldness, and how the light faded the farther I descended. How fast I sank, knowing no matter how hard I kicked—even if I had had any strength left to do so, which I no longer did—I would never reach the surface. The sensation of me breathing in the water, choking on it, feeling it move into my lungs, realizing I'd never breathe air again. It burned. All that water, and I felt like I was burning alive. You don't forget something like that. And ever since, I can't go near water. Can't touch it."

Jesus Christ. Getting towed by the current ... that can go bad quickly. Really bad. It's why we were taught in BUD/S never to remove our fins before we're on the ladder. You can come up out of a dive just feet from the boat and then be carried out to sea by a ripping current, which is always stronger on the surface than it is below. Without fins, it's almost a hopeless endeavor to swim out of a strong current.

It even happened to me a few times during an op; once I was carried nearly a mile away before the boat finally found me, forced to kick and kick and kick to stay alive. The ocean is an inhospitable place for humans when you're out in deep open water.

To think of that happening to a tiny child, a kid barely having learned to swim ...

"Well, shit," Tucker says, breaking the silence. "That's awful. Sorry that happened to you."

Asher and Jesse make similar sounds of agreement. Made tells a story of how he nearly drowned as a boy, which upsets Alessandra, but nevertheless she still sends him a look of gratitude. Even Bianchi has sobered, and actually apologizes for not being there when she went in. Jesse's brows nearly disappear into his hairline when that happens.

But I don't do any of those things. I don't say how sorry I am that happened to her or tell her about how many near misses I've had in the ocean, or vow again to protect her when I've clearly already failed to do so.

Instead, I just reach over and take her hand.

CHAPTER TWENTY-FOUR

ALESSANDRA

The paramedics pull up a few minutes later. The others clear out while they treat me, apart from Ford, who doesn't move an inch from the chair next to me. His hand never releases mine, even when they put a stethoscope to my chest and listen to my lungs. They decree my lungs clear and one of the medics gives me a prescription for antibiotics to prevent an infection caused by any water I inhaled.

The exhaustion hits when they finally drive off. It's not even noon, and all I want to do is crawl back into bed. My chest hurts, my throat is raw, any words I manage to get out are hoarse, the cuts from yesterday sting from the chlorinated water, and my sprained ankle throbs from falling into the pool.

"You should rest," Ford says.

My head lolls back against the chair. I can feel his eyes on me, studying me, cataloging my every last movement.

His expression is unreadable, but knowing Ford, he's probably wracked with guilt.

"Lessa," he says, "I can't apologize enough for this happening."

My head jerks toward him, startled by my brother's nickname for me.

"Sorry," he repeats, noticing my expression. "Should I not call you that? It just seemed ... right."

I smile. "No, it's fine. You can call me that."

I'm also quite partial to gorgeous.

He smiles back, a faint smile, one that doesn't quite reach his eyes. The desire to smooth away the line of worry between his brows rises up with such force my hand is moving toward him before I snatch it back. Ford's gaze drops to my hand, heat flashing in his eyes.

He clears his throat, but when he speaks, his voice still croaks. "Lessa," he says, "I'm sure it's private but I have to know ... why are you here? Why did you come to Thailand when there's water everywhere?"

I sigh. "I hate my phobia, and thought if I came here, I could get over it. Obviously, with the Chakrii thing, I haven't had much time to work on it. When I fell in ... my mind just shut down. It didn't even matter that I knew how to swim."

"Why didn't you say something before?" he asks quietly, practically begging. "Why did you let me think ... just why?"

My shoulders slump. "I was embarrassed to tell you. It's pathetic, and you're all SEALs."

"You're not pathetic," he says fiercely. "You're brave. Most people will never face their fears, never in their whole lifetime. In fact, they'll design their entire lives around never having to confront them. It's understandable, human even, which is why it's so remarkable when someone actively decides to get over something that scares the living shit out of them. That's why it's one of the first things they force us to do in the military. That makes you like us, Alessandra. You're not pathetic at all, and I never want to hear you say that again."

Whoa. He really thinks I'm as brave as him? No way. I don't jump in front of bullets like he does. Neither do I wrestle people to the ground, steal their gun like it's nothing, and then shoot them dead.

But Ford just keeps staring at me, his gaze intense, as if he won't look away until I believe he really means it. The thought is ... nice. Comforting.

Has anyone ever put it to me quite like that before? Has anyone ever cared enough to convince me that my greatest weakness is actually a strength? Certainly not the Italian media. They've laughed at me for years. Even my family, apart from my brother who was there when I nearly drowned, doesn't understand. Not really. Not truly. But Ford does.

And in a little over twenty-four hours, I will leave and never see this man again. We haven't discussed keeping in touch after I leave, not even a little. And what would be the point, even if we did? We live on opposite sides of the earth. He's not going to Italy, and now I'm certainly never returning to Thailand. This can't go anywhere.

Pain stabs through my chest again, but this time it has

nothing to do with inhaling water. How is it the man I originally despised understands me better than anyone else?

I should take advantage of whatever time is left.

I get to my feet. Ford leaps out of his chair. "Are you okay to stand?"

I smile. "Yes. I need to shower. I'm soaked from the pool and need it off me."

Ford runs a hand through his hair. "Christ, of course. Can you make it to your room okay?"

My smile widens. "Ford."

"What?"

"You're wet, too."

His hand slowly drops from his head. "That is true."

I step toward him. His gaze zeros in on mine, my eyes tracking back and forth over his face as he tries to guess my train of thought.

"I hate showering," I whisper. "Obviously. Right now the idea of more water exhausts me, but I feel disgusting. Maybe ... with you ... it would be better."

Understanding dawns on him. A look that's almost tender flickers across his face. "I would love to help you with that."

Before I can say a word, he bends and lifts me. I throw my arms around his neck and smile.

"Your room or my apartment?" he asks.

"You know, I don't know where you live, actually."

His lips twitch with the hint of a smile. "Half of the third floor is mine."

I tilt my head back to look at him. "So what you're saying is ... we'd be alone up there."

He grins. "That is correct."

"I think that settles it."

He makes for the main building, shifting me in his arms to free a hand so he can jerk open the door. My eyes nearly roll back in my head at this casual display of strength. I tuck my head into his neck, inhaling the masculine scent of him as he aims for the stairs.

"Hey, Car ... oh."

I lift my head to see Asher standing in the hallway, a shocked but smug look on his face.

"Go away," says Ford, turning for the stairs.

"You're supposed to be entertaining us, dick!"

"Not today."

"But—"

"See you at dinner."

"But I wanted to apologize again to Alessandra for pretending to throw her in the pool—"

"You hear him?" he asks me, not breaking his stride. "He's sorry. And to make up for it, he's *going away*."

I press my face into his neck to smother a laugh. Asher mumbles something behind us that sounds like "don't forget to wrap it up."

"Sorry about him," Ford grunts as he carries me up the stairs.

"I don't mind. My brother's friends talk shit whenever he's back in Rome."

"You have any other siblings?"

"No. Do you?"

"Only child."

"What do your parents think of you living all the way over here?"

Ford chuckles. "They hate it. They've pretty much given up any hope of having grandkids."

"Ah," I say. "I get that, too. Only for me, they're not grandkids, they're heirs."

"Jesus."

"Yeah. Story of my life."

Ford kicks open a door. "Well, I propose we forget that with lots of hot sex." He pauses, then adds, "That is what you meant, right? Because if I misinterpreted the shower request…"

I raise my mouth to his ear, nibbling lightly on his earlobe before whispering, "You didn't misinterpret a thing."

Ford groans. "Thank Christ."

"The thing is, though," I say, "I'm not exactly at a hundred percent after…"

Ford curses. "After nearly fuckin' dying? Shit, yeah. Perhaps we shouldn't—"

"I am leaving tomorrow, Ford. And I'd hate it if I left never having touched you."

Ford's arms tighten around me. He sucks in a shaky breath as he slowly lowers me to the ground in the bathroom. My eyes lock with his; Ford's apartment could be bright pink, for what I've noticed of it.

Ford tucks a wet strand of hair behind my ear. "Christ, you're beautiful. So gorgeous, even standing there dripping pool water all over my bathroom. Sometimes it hurts just looking at you. Do you know what that does to a man?"

I smile, stepping forward and sliding my hands under his shirt. "What do you think it's like for me when you're shirtless? I don't even like to swim, and I fantasize about you in your swim trunks."

Ford barks with startled laughter, his face flushing. It's beyond cute, to see this powerful man floored by my compliments. I remember the dirty words he growled at me on the beach, and vow to tell him in filthy detail every last thing he makes me feel.

I slide my hands up, working the shirt over his body. Ford lets it fall to the floor, his gaze never leaving my face. I take a nice long look, from his broad shoulders, down over his delectably developed chest, to the ridge of hard abs disappearing into his waistband.

"Mmm," I moan in appreciation. "You're even better up close."

He laughs again. "I'm not the only one."

I lift my arms over my head. His smile widens as he removes my shirt. My nipples instantly harden under his scrutiny, clearly visible through the wet bra. He groans, sucking his lower lip into his mouth. His nostrils flare from how hard he drags air into his lungs.

"I've made you come," he pants, eyes locked on my chest, "but I've never touched you. Do you know how many times I've imagined sucking your tits? Christ, every time you cross your arms over your chest, I want to fall to my knees and lose myself in you."

My hand flies out to his chest for balance, my head woozy from the white-hot flash of heat pooling in my core.

"Go ahead," I say.

Animalistic lust flies across his face. Ford drops to his knees before me. My bra is unhooked and dragged down my arms before I can give him another instruction. Ford wraps his arms around me, clutching me tight against him as he sucks one nipple into his mouth.

"*Oh*," I gasp, my fingers plowing into his hair, holding him against me as he sucks hard once, twice, a third time, his mouth moving in a lazy rhythm that sends languid heat pulsing through me. It's good. It's *very* good. I writhe against him, then sigh as he transfers his mouth to my other breast.

"I love your mouth on me," I say.

He releases my nipple and then stares up at me in the valley between my breasts. "That's convenient, because I intend to spend much time here."

He climbs to his feet. I almost protest before his fingers move to his waistband. Ford bends over and shucks his shorts and briefs in one motion. My knees go weak at the sight of his dick, I want him so badly.

I'm stroking his full length before he's even fully straightened. "This is an exceptional cock."

Ford's head drops back, and his eyes squeeze shut, his hands balling into fists at his sides as his jaw clenches. I stroke him again, gripping him more fully, giving the tiniest tug as I slide back up to the head. Ford grunts, a deep, wild sound. He thrusts into my hand, driving my fist back down his length.

"Mmm, yes," I hiss, "fuck yourself with my hand."

Ford's eyes pop open. He stares down at me, mouth working to form speech. His pupils have dilated so wide only a tiny ring of green remains. I stroke him again, and even that green disappears.

Eventually, he stutters, "You're ... you're ..."

"Not the prim heiress in bed? No. Not with you. No."

Ford's hand flies out and slams into the wall above my head. He crowds me back into it as his other hand slides up to cup my breast. He groans again, his hips thrusting into my hand.

"You like that?" I ask. "You like fondling me while my hand strokes you?"

"Fuck," Ford grunts, his head dropping down in the space between his arm and my head. He buries his face in my neck, inhaling deeply. "I'm not going to last. It's been ... a while."

"So don't," I say. "I want to feel you explode in my hand. I need it."

"Shit." Ford's legs spread wider, his hand cupping me harder, his thumb tracking back and forth across my nipple. He begins pumping into my hand, a strangled groan escaping him. I still, keeping a firm grip as I let him thrust up and down.

A shudder rolls through him. His entire body shakes. Sweat pours off him as his breath becomes ragged. His hips jerk harder, and the sight of his thick cock gliding in and out of my hand is the hottest thing I've ever seen. I'm transfixed, about two seconds from collapsing to the floor, I'm throbbing so hard. I need him inside me, but I want to do this for him, need to give him this orgasm without taking one of my own, just as he did for me last night.

"That's it, beautiful man," I pant, echoing his words from the beach. "Take it from me."

"Fuck!" he shouts, hips bucking wildly.

I moan.

He pinches my nipple.

I rub my thumb over the crown of his cock.

He bites my neck.

I cup his balls with my free hand and lightly squeeze.

Ford shouts and explodes, thick jets of cum spurting all over my fingers. I give him one last stroke as he finally stills.

He slowly lifts his face to look at me, his chest heaving. There's the most wonderful glazed look in his eyes; they're drunk with pleasure. Pride slams into me.

Ford stares down at my messy hands, still lightly holding him. "That shouldn't please me as much as it does."

I laugh. "Typical guy. There are plenty more places on my body if you'd like to repeat the performance."

He groans and grabs a hand towel off the sink to wipe us off. "Give a man a minute to rally, gorgeous."

Ford grabs for my shorts. "Need to get rid of these," he mumbles, his motions jerky, just erratic enough for me to know he's still reeling.

I rest my hands on his shoulders for balance as he pulls my shorts down my legs. My panties follow a moment later. Ford takes one look at my naked body and swears an impressive string of epithets. And I thought Italians could curse.

"A quick shower. Yeah, a real fuckin' quick one," he growls. "Can I turn on the water?"

I nod, wanting it over as well. Ford pulls back the

curtain and turns on the water. I can't help flinching at the sound. Ford waits for the water to heat, staring at me in sympathy.

"Is it always a struggle to shower?"

"I get in and out quickly. I can tolerate it because I must."

Ford straightens. "Wrap your arms around my neck."

I step closer, putting my arms around him. We both groan as our bodies glide together. For an instant, with waves of heat rolling off him, I completely forget the water. And when his arms come around my ass and lift me hard against him, I know that this will easily be the best shower of my life.

"Put your face against my chest, gorgeous. There you go. I'm going to step into the shower with the water at my back. You can tell me how far into it you want to go."

"Okay."

Ford cautiously steps inside the shower. A few droplets splatter across my hands and I stiffen.

"Are you okay?"

"Yes," I say through gritted teeth.

Ford slowly lowers my feet to the tub. "Shall I wash you?"

"Yes."

"You'll need to be wet for that. How do you want to do it?"

"I usually jump into the spray and then jump out and clean myself. And then I jump in again quickly to rinse it off."

"Okay. I'll step back further, then?"

"Yes."

He slowly steps back, moving into the water, giving me ample time to stop him. I keep my face buried in his chest, shuddering as the water rolls over me, remembering how the water enveloped me in the pool just a short while ago.

Ford's arms tighten around me.

"Shh, gorgeous girl. I've got you. Close your eyes and listen to my voice. Feel my body instead of the water. Listen to my heartbeat. Breathe. There you go. I'm going to step forward now, okay? You did it."

He moves me back out of the water. I relax against him.

"I have shower gel here," he says. "Does that work?"

"Sure," I mumble, struggling to resist the wave of exhaustion rolling through me.

I keep my eyes closed, then a moment later I feel his hands slide over my body, massaging softly as he soaps me. He doesn't linger, instead efficiently covering every inch of my body.

"Do you want me to shampoo your hair?"

I nod, stepping back so he can clean my front as well. A moment later, he lathers shampoo between his hands and then works it into my hair, massaging. Shockingly, it feels wonderful, a strange lethargy wrapping around me. My eyes flutter closed and I hum in approval.

Best shower ever indeed. It's not even close. And maybe after another hundred times, I might actually begin to enjoy it.

Ford's hands still. When I open my eyes, he's staring at me with the strangest look on his face. Before I can speak, though, he moves his hands away and says, "Rinse?"

I nod, looping my arms back around his neck. Ford steps into the water. His hands move, sliding all over me in every effort to rinse away the soap that much faster.

"Okay, you're done," he says.

I sag in relief, glad it's over. Ford picks me up and steps out, depositing me on the sink. I grab a towel and begin drying off.

Ford hops back in the shower and quickly washes himself, glancing at me from time to time to ensure I'm okay. The thoughtfulness of him not letting me stay inside the shower a second longer than necessary makes me smile.

My smile widens when I see his already half-hard dick.

A moment later, he shuts off the water and steps out. He grabs a towel and dries off, his eyes never leaving mine. He pitches the towel to the floor.

"Come here."

I step toward him even as he bends down to lift me into his arms. His mouth crashes down on mine, his lips moving in a deep, searing kiss, one that lacks the overwhelming eroticism of last night but is so damn sweet my heart aches.

Ford carries me into his bedroom, his tongue sweeping inside my mouth when I open for him.

He lowers me to the bed, then crawls on top of me. He kisses me slowly, thoroughly, his hand sliding down to cup a breast, before moving lower. My legs drop open for him, and he slides a finger around my clit, rubbing softly, so perfectly softly, in time with the lazy thrusts of his tongue.

I move against his hand, my own hands sliding into his hair, then down to his shoulders, across the hard planes of his chest, around to his back, before settling on his ass. I squeeze and a noise of approval rumbles out of his chest.

He tears his mouth away. "I'm going to taste you now. Lie back, gorgeous, and enjoy it."

His mouth moves down my body, kissing and licking, sucking every inch, skillfully seeking out and finding all of my most sensitive places. He moves slowly, in no rush at all. Each lazy kiss and slide of his tongue sends warmth through me, comfort. Peace. I am safe now. Safe in this man's bed, inside his arms, underneath him. The longer it continues, the drowsier I become. My eyes fall shut; my limbs feel as if they weigh a million pounds.

If I could ...

Just ...

Stay ...

I fall asleep. When I awake, it's dark, I'm alone, and a masked man is dragging me out of bed.

CHAPTER TWENTY-FIVE

FORD

After Alessandra falls asleep from my mouth on her body, I pull the sheets over her and then dress before heading downstairs.

Not wanting to talk to anyone, I head out to my boat that's docked in the little cove outside my resort. As I track across the sand, I remember what happened there last night. Hell, was that really less than twenty-four hours ago? How is that even possible?

It's like my life has been torn into a Before and After. Before what happened in that bathroom, and after. Somehow I'll have to let her go tomorrow. It will be beyond difficult.

Maybe even impossible.

But I need to do it. She doesn't belong here, and my life is not in Italy. I couldn't ask her to give up her life there, not when I'm not willing to do so myself. Once she's aboard that plane, that must be the end of it. It's the best thing to do.

That's a loss I don't take lightly. I have never wanted a woman as badly as I did five minutes ago. I'm fucking damn proud she felt comfortable enough to fall asleep in my bed. How right it felt seeing her there.

It's been three years since I felt that way.

Pain stabs through me, an echo of a previous agony I've long since buried. But it's also a warning, a dreadful foreshadowing of what might happen if I don't get her on that plane tomorrow.

Pushing such thoughts aside, I climb onto my boat. There's nothing to worry about; Alessandra is safe here—if she stays out of the damn pool—so I need not worry about Chakrii's men coming to my resort. He would never dare. He'd know the next day I'd fucking waste him. He might organize something once we step foot off the resort, but that's a different story.

Still, that echo of foreboding lingers, no matter how hard I rationally tell myself I'm worrying over nothing.

I spend the afternoon doing minor repairs on the boat, things I've been putting off because my friends are here. Even when they're not, there's a million other more pressing chores that need to get done, so boat repairs can take a backseat. It's hard but satisfying work, and I desperately need something physical to distract myself from the woman in my bed.

I half expect someone to come out and let me know she's awake, hope for it, even, but everyone leaves me alone. By the time the sun is slipping toward the horizon and I finish work for the day, I'm about ready to crawl in next to her and sleep myself, I'm so tired.

When I drag myself back to the resort, my guys are clustered around the bar, drinking, apart from Jesse, who's drinking what's likely carbonated water.

I raise my brows at them. "Really? Y'all're drinking when we haven't gotten her home yet?"

Asher gives me the finger. "We're only having two, asshole."

"Well, I'm not having shit," I grumble, snagging a seltzer from the outdoor fridge like Jesse.

"Someone sounds extremely sexually frustrated," Tucker says. "Where *has* Alessandra been all day, anyway? I haven't seen her."

I flick him a look that has sent lesser men running. He just grins.

"She's upstairs resting," I say. "Hard to believe she's slept this whole time, but clearly she needed it. No doubt you dicks would have woken her up if she'd been on the ground floor."

Tucker and Asher laugh. Jesse just stares moodily into his drink.

"We were wondering why you've been hammering away on that boat all day. Hey, Car, don't sweat it," Asher drawls, elbowing Tucker. "I get it. It's understandable. It's also fuckin' hilarious. The first time a woman falls asleep when I'm screwing her is the day I hang it all up."

"How about I wipe the floor with your ass and you hang it up now?" I snap.

"Not necessary, dude."

"Then I suggest you stop talking about her. She nearly fucking died. She *should* sleep it off."

Jesse lazily looks up at me from his drink. "You are very far gone, my man."

"Your opinions are neither solicited nor warranted."

Jesse's gaze flicks behind me. He frowns. I turn to find Bianchi coming out of the main building.

"She's going to be gone tomorrow, Ford," Jesse says, still looking over my shoulder. "Your time with her is dwindling."

"Are you sure it's me and Alessandra you're referring to?" I ask dryly.

Jesse's gaze snaps to mine. "I don't know what you're talking about."

"Oh, come on," Tucker crows. "We have brains, bro. You've haven't taken your eyes off her since we got hauled into the consulate. *And* you're half Italian. If you don't hit that, I'll—"

"You'll do what?" Jesse says softly, his head whipping to Tucker. The rest of us fall silent; Jesse doesn't use that tone often. When he does, violence is imminent.

"Not a damn thing," says Tucker meekly, backing down. "Just trying to get a rise out of you, man."

Jesse says nothing, just gets up and walks around the edge of the pool to his room. He and Bianchi ignore each other as they grow closer, but at the last moment, just as she passes him, Bianchi mutters something. Jesse grinds to a halt, his hand forming a fist at his side. His back is stiff with tension; I very nearly call him back, but then he continues with such casual ease I know it's a front.

"What did she say to him?" Tucker mutters.

"Something in Italian," Asher says.

"Whatever's going on between them," I say, "it isn't going to end well."

Asher looks thoughtful and then says, "Well, he was right. Perhaps he should take his own advice. She'll be gone tomorrow along with Alessandra."

"Possibly," I say. "Even with Alessandra gone, I doubt they'll be done with us. Not now that they've gotten the Pentagon involved."

Asher grunts in agreement. Tucker plays with the condensation on his glass.

"Hello, boys," Bianchi says. "I was about to order takeout. You want in?"

"What are you getting?" Tucker asks as he rubs his stomach. I roll my eyes; the man is a bottomless pit.

She shrugs. "Whatever looks good on Bangla Road."

Asher grins. "Looking to party, are we?"

She frowns. "I'm on duty. Just want to get something to eat." She looks at Tucker. "How about you come with me? I'm pretty sure whatever you'll want to consume will weigh more than I can carry, so you might as well be the one to lug it back."

Tucker grins at her, but then his grin fades as he glances at the rooms on the ground floor. "Why don't you take Jesse? He'd probably go with you."

"No."

She offers no additional reasoning. Tucker glances at Asher and me; we both shrug. Jesse's clearly staked a claim there, but it isn't like we can force him on Bianchi if she's not interested.

"Okay, then," Tucker says with one last look at Jesse's room.

"What do all of you want?" Bianchi asks.

Asher asks for three orders of *pad thai*—we give him shit for his lack of originality—and I ask for green curry and *tom yum* soup since I've discovered that hot liquids can actually cool me down on days when the weather feels like it's melting my face off.

And I'm fucking flaming right now.

Bianchi looks up from typing the orders down on her phone. "What about Alessandra? What would she want?"

I haven't the faintest clue. She hasn't eaten out since she's been here. I don't know if she likes spicy food, which is common in many of the dishes here. I've seen her eat fruit, but that's not substantial enough for dinner.

I don't know much about her at all, really.

Frowning at that realization, I say, "She's sleeping. I'm not sure what she'd want. Get her a spicy curry and something milder like a *pad thai*. Whatever she doesn't want, I'll eat."

Bianchi glances at the door to Alessandra's room. "She's sleeping? Still? How long has she been out? Made and I have been sending reports in the kitchen all day. We were able to find the woman who set up the consulate appointment with Alessandra. Turns out she spent the night with a boyfriend, and eventually showed up back at her apartment. We're grilling her now."

"Good," I say. "Let's hope she leads us to Chakrii."

Bianchi shrugs. "So far she's keeping her mouth shut.

Are you sure I shouldn't go knock on Alessandra's door? I'd hate to get her something she doesn't like."

"She's not in her room," I say, my tone leaving no room for discussion. "And she's been sleeping for most of the day. I don't want her disturbed."

Bianchi turns back to me in confusion. A moment later, her eyes widen when it dawns on her where Alessandra must be sleeping if not in her room. I stare her down, daring her to comment on it.

She holds up her hands. "Not my business."

She and Tucker are just reaching the agent's SUV when Asher cups his hands around his mouth and yells, "Yo, and I want mango sticky rice for dessert! Like five of 'em!"

Bianchi looks at him like he's lost it, but when Asher doesn't recant his order, she shrugs and types it into her phone, then climbs behind the wheel. We watch as she pulls down the drive.

"If you eat that much rice, your stomach is going to swell up and explode," I say mildly.

"Naw, dude. I have an extraordinary capacity for digestion, and mango rice is the shit. I've barely had any of it since I came here. We haven't gone out at all, man. The Kangaroo Bar is calling my name."

I roll my eyes. "You can party your ass off once Alessandra is out of the country."

"I am holding you to that, dude. I have not fucked *one single woman* yet and that is a fuckin' travesty of a vacation."

"Sometimes you can be a real ass, Asher, you know

that?" I say, watching the last of the sunset fade from the sky.

"Naw, dude. The ladies love me."

"You keep telling yourself that."

I climb to my feet, tossing my seltzer can in the trash. If I shower now, I'll be finished by the time the food arrives.

And if Alessandra happens to be awake, I'll be missing dinner entirely ...

"I'll be back," I mutter.

"Say hi to her for me," Asher says.

I give him the finger over my shoulder, not bothering to look. Treading along the edge of the pool, I'm nearly to the door when Asher suddenly shouts my name.

For the love of—I turn in time to catch the arm of a man who's slashing at me with a knife. My fingers constrict around his wrist, crushing it; he screams and drops the knife even as my knee is coming up to smash him in the balls. He doubles over and I grab his holstered gun with my left hand while simultaneously kicking the knife out of the way.

I fire two shots into a second man barreling my way, clad in the same all-black fatigues as the first guy. One round enters his head and the other his chest. He drops. I fire two rounds into the first guy, barely pausing to register they've hit him as I turn to Asher, who's struggling with two men of his own. Asher disables one; I put a bullet in the skull of the other. Asher stoops to snag the pistols of both men as I gather one from my second attacker.

Jesse comes flying out of his room the instant another four men descend over the row of hedges. I shove a pistol at Jesse as I aim at the first man I see.

This group, however, must be higher up the food chain, because they have flak vests and helmets, making the prospect of shooting them more difficult. Their pistols are holstered. Two of them hold knives, but none of them make a move toward us.

"They've got orders to take us alive," Jesse says tersely.

"Yep."

"Where the hell is Made?" Asher yells, taking up a position next to us as the group before us hesitates.

"Right here," says Made, appearing out of nowhere, his chest heaving. "Where are Bianchi and Tucker?"

"They went for food," I say.

The other men step cautiously over their fallen comrades, inching closer to the line we've made to defend the door to the resort.

"Why the fuck aren't they moving?" Asher mutters. "This is fuckin' weird."

"Leave or you're dead, too!" I shout. "And take these assholes with you."

"Walker," Made whispers to me. "We need one of them alive. This is precisely the kind of people we were hoping to flip on Chakrii. And I can't sanction a bloodbath with ex-Navy SEALs. Interpol would have a field day."

"Then go grab one," I hiss. "I'm not leaving the door unprotected."

One of the men steps forward. "Give us what we want, and we'll leave without killing you."

Asher laughs. "Bro, we're not the ones who just got merked. Fuck right off."

"What do you want, assholes?" I snap.

The man motions toward the resort. "You know what we want. The woman. Chakrii must have her."

"He sure as shit won't get her," says Asher.

The man holds out his hands. "Let us have her. Be reasonable about it. If you don't, we'll come back here with thirty men and burn the place down with her inside it."

"Chakrii won't allow that," I say, my quiet voice carrying in the silence.

"And why is that?" another one of them jeers.

"Because he remembers what I told him I'd do to him if he ever killed someone I cared about again. Call him up. Ask him. He's not getting her."

They remain silent.

I pull my phone out of my pocket. "Shall I call him, then?"

Made's head whips toward me. "You have his number?"

I ignore him, my phone held out menacingly. The men glance at it, proving my suspicion correct; they're not supposed to harm anyone.

I slide my phone back in my pocket. "Understand this, gentleman. If you so much as cause one instant of discomfort to her, I will obliterate you. Leave now or I'll—"

A scream rips through the air behind us.

"They're a diversion!" Jesse yells.

The men rush us.

"Go," says Made.

I'm already gone, sprinting for the door. I'm up the stairs and down the hall in moments, ripping my door open. Three men are dragging a naked Alessandra out of bed, *my* bed, and toward the window. She screams again and one of them backhands her across the face.

I snap.

A thin red film descends over my vision. Wave after wave of rage rolls through me. I don't resist. Instead, I welcome it, let it wash over me, allow the full force of righteous fury to take me. These fuckers think they can take her? They dare to hurt her? They are *nothing*. I will annihilate them.

A single thought courses through my mind: *They will not take her. They will not take her. They will not take her.*

Theywillnot—"Ford? Ford? Ford! Oh, thank God. There you are. It's over. I'm safe. They didn't take me. You can stop now, Ford."

Through the dissipating red haze, my gaze slowly fixates on Alessandra. She's staring at me, my face pressed between her hands. She's making little comforting noises like a mother might make to a distraught child as she rocks us back and forth. My hands cover hers. I wince, then glance down to discover my knuckles are destroyed.

Slowly, I turn my head, taking in the devastation. I can't be bothered to feel a second of remorse. The broken bodies of three men are dead on the floor, their limbs twisted at odd angles. Weapons and bedding are strewn everywhere. My mattress hangs halfway off its frame. A table is knocked over. My desk chair is smashed. Broken glass crunches under my shoe from an obliterated lamp.

But Alessandra is safe in my arms.

CHAPTER TWENTY-SIX

ALESSANDRA

He killed three people with his bare hands.

Feet come pounding up the stairs. Ford whirls on the door, pushing me behind his back. God, is it not over? Are there *more* of those monsters?

I scan the room, trying to search for a weapon to help Ford attack whoever comes through the door. Not that I bet I'll be much help.

To my relief, however, Jesse bursts inside. He takes one look at the destroyed room and his mouth drops open. "Holy Mother of God."

Ford yanks the sheet up from the ground and wraps it around me. Confused, I look down, wondering why he'd do such a thing. I'm naked! But of course I am; I hadn't dressed before I passed out in Ford's bed. How did I not even *notice* until now?

Ford lifts me into his arms. He tracks out into the hall, Jesse following him.

"Is she okay?"

"Clean up that trash," Ford snarls, not even looking at him.

"But—"

"Do it!"

Ford moves into the hall, leaving an astounded Jesse behind him.

"I'm okay. It's over," I tell him as Ford carries me down the hall. He tenses under me, his body still vibrating with that awesome fury that erupted from him the instant he flew into his room.

He snapped their necks. One by one. Three against one, and he just destroyed them. I've never seen anything like it. No wonder the locals call him a berserker. It was like he wasn't even there, his mind blank. Just cold hard wrath, fury the likes of which I've never seen before. An avenging angel.

He killed three men to protect me. I should be terrified of him, but all I am is grateful. A fate much worse than I could imagine was waiting for me if he had failed to stop them.

Ford reaches a door halfway down the hall and kicks it open. After we're inside, he kicks it closed and makes for the bed in what is another guest room. He gently lowers me to my feet, then rips the sheet away.

I yelp. "What are—"

He starts running his hands over every inch of my body. My shoulders, down the length of my arms, between and underneath my breasts. Lower, so very much lower. There's nothing sexual in the touch.

My eyes widen as he turns me around and repeats the

caresses on my other side. Oh God. Ford still hasn't come down from his adrenaline spike. I thought I had gotten through to him, but I must have only just barely returned him to rationality. Or maybe the sound of Jesse coming upstairs sent him back under. In either case, he's still in protector mode, his entire focus on carrying out the mission.

To protect me.

My knees go weak. I need to do something, say something, to snap him out of it, but this primal display of masculinity is arousing. Tempting. Part of me yearns to push him that last bit over the edge, to feel that power unleashed in a different direction, one of pure eroticism, but another part fears neither of us would survive it.

He turns me around again. My attention lands on a gun tucked into his waistband. "Why didn't you just shoot them?"

Ford removes the gun and places it on the table next to the bed, his focus locked on inspecting the space between my collarbone and throat. He says absently, "As if I'd ever point a gun in your direction. As if I'd let any of them draw a gun on you themselves."

"Ford."

He ignores me, or perhaps he doesn't hear. He drops to his knees before me, trailing his hands down my legs.

"You're okay," he mutters, more to himself than to me. "They didn't get you. You're safe now. Don't be afraid, gorgeous."

The sight of him kneeling before me unravels my last bit of resolve.

"*Ford.*"

His head snaps up. We stare at each other for an instant before he's on me, arms lifting me at the waist to toss me on the bed. He falls on top of me, shoving my thighs apart with his knee as his mouth captures mine.

I moan, a deep, tortured sound torn from the depths of my soul. I grab the hem of his shirt and drag it up his body. He breaks the kiss just long enough for me to rip his shirt over his head, and then his mouth is on mine again as my hands clasp his shoulders, clutching him to me.

"I'm going to take you so deep you never forget the feel of me," he says, driving his hips into mine.

"*Yes*," I moan, wrapping my legs around his waist and meeting him as he thrusts against me. Ford shivers, a delicious shudder rolling through him. He grips my chin, tongue sweeping into my mouth when it falls open on a gasp. Ford sucks my bottom lip into his mouth and then bites down, sending a wave of fire radiating from my mouth to my core.

He breaks away, beginning a trail of kisses down my throbbing body as I shove the rest of his clothes down over his hips. He kicks them to the floor then returns his mouth to my stomach, the stubble on his cheeks brushing a line of heat along my skin.

"Ford," I moan, writhing under him. "I need ..."

"What do you need?" he asks, nipping my stomach. "Do you need me to fill you? Taste you? Eat you? Stroke you? Tell me what you want. Tell me now."

"I want your mouth on me until I explode."

"Very good," he grunts. An instant later, his tongue dips inside me as his thumb swipes around my clit. I come off the bed, grabbing his hair and yanking. "Very good, gorgeous," he groans. "Tell me how good you feel."

I chant his name as his tongue dips in and out, his thumb rubbing infuriatingly soft circles over my clit.

"More," I moan. "Harder. I want your fingers."

"You can have them," he says, licking up the entire length of my pussy to suck on my clit, sending shockwaves rolling through me.

"Yes," I sigh, fingers twitching in his hair. "Like that."

Ford slides a finger inside me, curving it to hit the most perfect spot. He adds another finger slowly, slower than I need, softer than I want. He strokes in and then out, slowly, so slowly. My head whips back and forth, my hips riding his hand, desperate for release.

"Pinch your nipples," he commands. My hands move to comply. I squeeze, pull my taut nipples, but the sensation still isn't enough. A frustrated cry escapes me, and a moment later, Ford's free hand lands on top of one of mine. The rough pads of his fingers interlace with mine, rubbing and teasing and pinching as his other fingers finally, *finally* begin to thrust faster inside me.

"So good, so perfect," he mutters against my skin. "The prettiest little pussy I've ever had. I want to eat you in tiny little licks, but I know you what you need, gorgeous, and I'm prepared to give it to you."

He spreads his fingers, stretching me in the most delicious way as he sucks my clit into his mouth, his lips moving back and forth against me. His fingers move faster, harder, finally giving me what I need. I scream, then moan, my hips bucking against him as my release finally takes me. Stars burst behind my eyes, his hand spasms on top of mine as I buck up off the bed. His fingers fuck me over and over until I finally fall still before him.

Ford looks up at me between my thighs. "You look absolutely exquisite when you come."

I whimper, filled with such an unimaginable lethargy and yet still desperate for more.

"Ford," I pant, staring down at him, my voice pleading. "I feel so empty."

His eyes flash and a growl escapes him. He crawls up my body, spreads my legs wider with his own and then grinds his cock against me.

"Is this what you want?"

I nod, past the point of speech.

Ford grinds against me again. "This cock is what you need?"

I nod, grabbing his ass and jerking him against me.

He stills, grabbing my chin and whispering against my mouth. "I expect you to tell me with actual fucking words."

"Yes," I gasp, sucking his upper lip into my mouth and reveling in the way he thrusts even harder against me in response as I bite down. "I want that exceptional cock of yours deep inside me."

Ford immediately rolls onto his back, taking me with him until I'm straddling his hips. "Then take it."

I rise up, rolling my core against the full length of him, coating him with my wetness. Ford curses and his eyes roll back in his head.

"Yes, take it, take it."

My hands land on his hard stomach, nails digging into

him. He tenses, his hips bucking under me. I lift up farther, all the way up until his head glides against my entrance.

Ford looks at me through eyes narrowed to slits. "I'll fuck you if you put my aching cock inside you, gorgeous."

I smile, circling my hips around him. Ford answers my smile with a feral one of his own, his teeth bared. His hands grab my thighs and spread me wider. His body tenses under me, ready to give me precisely what I want.

But I rock against him, denying both of us, drawing him inside the tiniest bit but moving no farther.

His face turns animalistic. "Alessandra ..."

My grin turns wicked. "I expect you to tell me to fuck you with actual fucking words."

Triumph flashes in his eyes. "Take every inch of me inside and fuck my cock with your sweet, tight cunt."

I give us what we want, finally letting him slide inside me. He's barely entered an inch when Ford thrusts up and positively impales me with his dick. I shriek with pleasure, hips circling madly to sink down on every last inch. Ford's hands tighten in approval on my thighs, gripping me so hard I know he'll leave marks.

"Ride me," he groans, gaze locked on where we're joined.

I lift up and then sink back down. Ford meets me with a thrust of his own, full and thick inside me. I moan and nod, my eyes drifting closed as I ride him another time and he thrusts up into me again, harder.

"Fuck me faster," he rasps.

I rock faster, circling my hips as I move up and down.

He's the perfect stretch; thick enough to feel it and yet long enough I can take him and take him and—

"Fuck me harder."

I crash down on him with more force, my nails gouging his stomach.

Ford's hands move to my ass, squeezing hard as he helps lift me up and down on his cock.

"I want you wild. Fuck me like it's the last time we'll ever have."

I let go, my eyes closed, gasps and moans and cries escaping me as I ride him with everything I have. The sounds of our bodies slapping together echo in the silent room, an erotic noise that winds me tighter. The wave of pleasure rises within me. I chase it, rocking faster and faster, my heart pounding so quickly it's nearly impossible to breathe. My eyes open and I stare down at him.

"Y-yes, there you are," he pants, his eyes wild, his feet planted against the bed so he can drive up into me with every roll of my hips. "Take every last inch. Again. Oh, God. *Again*. That's it. Fuck, that's it, gorgeous. Gorgeous, beautiful Alessandra, fucking me so perfectly. You're so ... fuck ... take me. Again. More. Lean back so I can watch you take me. *Fuck*. Perfect. So pretty. *Look at that*. I'm going to ... I'm going to ..."

His thumb slides against my clit, rubbing in firm circles. I cry out, sobbing, needing to come again so badly I'll do anything. Any strength I had remaining suddenly seeps out of me. I lift my hands from the tops of his thighs and slump forward onto his chest.

In an instant, I'm flipped on my back. Ford spreads my

thighs and kneels between them. Taking my left leg, he lifts it, resting the back of my calf on his shoulder as his right hand cups the top of my thigh. His left hand wraps my right leg up and over his hip, before anchoring my foot behind his ass. He reaches under me with his left hand and lifts, bringing me into perfect alignment.

And then he begins grinding, rocking in tiny circles. He's deep, so very deep inside me I cannot move, can only moan and grip the bedsheets in tight fists as he slides out slowly, before gliding right back in and grinding again. He alternates, grinding and thrusting, thrusting and grinding, gradually building up the tempo until I'm screaming, incomprehensible words babbling out of my mouth as I plead for him to finish me, so overwhelmed with pleasure my eyes slam shut.

"Look at me."

Somehow I manage to open my eyes. His brilliant green ones glitter down at me, flickering from naked lust to smug pride to wild need. Sweat pours off him, his mouth dropping open to drag in a ragged breath.

"Please," I beg.

"Lean up on your elbows."

I do, but it takes every last bit of energy. My entire body throbs, my blood pounding so hard I can actually hear my heartbeat *whooshing* in my ears.

"Watch as I make you come," he growls.

I stare, transfixed, as his thick cock continues moving in and out of me. The pressure builds, beginning to break into the first crest of the wave. Ford suddenly releases my thigh and slides his hand down. The heel of his palm glides over my clit, rubbing in a tiny circle in time with his thrusts. His fingers press into my belly, immobilizing me, trapping me between the hand squeezing my ass and the one pressing into my stomach.

"Come now, gorgeous. I demand it."

I explode, shattering into a million pieces. I thrash against him, writhing as wave after wave of pleasure rolls through me. My back arches off the bed and I cry out, sobbing from the glorious release.

Ford throws his head back, a hoarse shout escaping him as his thrusts grow wild, unsteady. He shoves my leg off his shoulder and falls on top of me, his mouth capturing mine as he pumps again and again. And when he finally comes his body goes rigid. He groans into my mouth, his tongue stroking against mine. Then he falls still, the considerable weight of his body crushing mine in the most delightful way.

I've barely caught my breath when he rolls off me, off the bed entirely. He stares down at himself in astonishment.

"C-Christ, I'm still hard," he cries, his voice tortured. His head drops back and his face twists in what looks like agony. He strokes himself once, twice, moaning. "Fuck, I can't ... I can't come like that again. That took everything in me. Fuck. My balls are *aching*. Look at what you do to me, gorgeous. Look how much I need you. Shit. *Shit*."

I crawl unsteadily to the edge of the bed and roll onto my back, letting my head extend off the side. I look up to find Ford's gaze locked on my body, his eyes glazed.

I let my mouth drop open. "Take my mouth, Ford. Finish yourself off."

He staggers a step forward. Then another. And another, until he's straddling my head. He fists his cock, sliding it against my mouth. A bead of moisture escapes him, and my tongue flicks out to lap it up.

"Holy fucking God," he groans, his voice utterly unlike any time I've ever heard him speak. It's utterly wrecked, devastated, beyond the point of rational thought.

Ford clasps his hand around my neck, his thumb and index finger cradling my jaw.

"Open wider."

My mouth drops open all the way. My eyes fall closed, every last depth of my soul focused on the way his breath catches as he begins feeding his cock into my mouth.

"No, you can't ... Oh Christ, you *can*. All the way. Fuck me, I can see my cock moving up and down your throat. *Shit*, Alessandra, how can you ..."

I slide my hands up the back of his thighs, squeezing his ass for balance. Ford emits a low, almost pained sound. I moan around him, and he whimpers.

"It's too much. No, it's too much. I can't take it. Christ, yes, I can. Good God, that's good. You take me so fucking good, gorgeous. Shit. I can't ... I can't stop. I'm going to fuck your mouth harder, you understand?"

His hips move faster, rougher, but his hand cradles my neck so gently, so tenderly, like he hardly dares to believe he's receiving such a gift.

I moan again, loving the disbelieving sounds he's making, the way he tries to hold back and yet fails to do so whenever I suck him hard just as he's about to pull out completely. He chants my name, pleads with me, a constant stream of words about how good I'm doing, how wonderful he feels, how no other woman's mouth will ever satisfy him again.

I slide my hand down my body and between my legs to touch myself. Ford's hips buck faster.

"Fuck yes, gorgeous. Touch yourself. Slide your fingers inside that wet pussy. Get yourself off while my cock is down your throat."

It won't take me long at all, but I don't want to. If I come, I'll be too far gone to continue. I want to feel him explode inside me and then collapse to the ground, unable to move another inch from how thoroughly I've sucked him. I reach between his legs, sliding up to grip his balls as they slap against my face. I squeeze him.

Ford instantly comes, my name roared from his lungs as he erupts down my throat. He twitches once and then a final time before he finally stills.

Ford gently removes himself from my mouth and then kneels before me, his hand still cradling my throat.

"You have ruined me," he says, and then kisses me with a trembling mouth.

CHAPTER TWENTY-SEVEN

FORD

I crawl off the floor, up onto the bed, my heart still hammering so hard I clutch my chest because it hurts. I collapse next to her and pull her onto me, my hands moving up and down her back.

My heart twinges for another reason. She's leaving in less than twenty-four hours. Just one little day, and she'll be gone from my life. I don't want to make her any promises; I tried that once, and it ended disastrously. I simply can't lose another woman like that. I don't want to risk feeling that pain again. It's the reason I swore off women after Achara's death. And Alessandra deserves more than me pretending otherwise; it's better for us both if we end this now.

But it's more than the fact that I don't want a relationship. Chakrii has no intention of stopping his vendetta against me, and frankly, I have no desire to leave him alone, either. The man needs to be stopped. Alessandra is just one in a long line of people he's hurt. So unless Interpol miraculously puts him behind bars, any woman I'm with is a target for Chakrii's evil. And if how Interpol has handled all of this so far is any indication, I'm skeptical they're capable of stopping Chakrii. So it falls to me.

I'll be damned if I risk Alessandra's life doing that. After what we just shared ... shit. What if Chakrii decided to track her down in Italy because he believed he could go through her to get to me? Fuck no. I won't let that happen.

As painful as it will be, she has to get on that plane. She has to leave. And that has to be the end of us.

Which after being inside her will be one hell of a sacrifice. Christ, she felt *incredible*.

"That was the best sex of my life," I blurt out. Alessandra laughs in my ear. My fingers thread into her hair and pull her head back until our eyes meet. "Seriously. Shit, gorgeous. I'm floored right now."

She smiles, and buries her head in my neck. Tenderness rolls through me.

Along with a realization.

"Fucking hell," I croak, my body stiffening. "I fucked you without a condom."

She kisses my cheek. "I'm on the pill and test regularly."

Relief crashes through me. I rub my face. "Fuck. Sorry. I should have ... Jesus ... God, Lessa. I think I've been out of my mind the last half hour. I never would have not used a condom otherwise. You must—"

"Ford," Alessandra says, lifting up on my chest to look at me. "You might have been out of it, but I wasn't. I *wanted* you wild like that. That was hot as hell."

I chuckle softly, rubbing my face so she can't see the blush on my cheeks. Fuck. That was hardcore, even for me.

"Still," I mumble. "It feels like I should say something."

"Say nothing. That was perfect, Ford. All of it. Don't ruin it with embarrassment or regret."

I clutch her tighter against me.

A thump comes from down the hall. I jerk, remembering the rest of it. How I slaughtered those men in front of her.

"Lessa, you know I had to kill those men, right? It was you or them."

She lifts her head to look at me. "Of course."

"Yeah, but ... you aren't upset? We can talk about it, if you want. I don't want you to think that I'm violent."

Or a killer.

She's silent for so long I begin to worry. Just before I'm about to tell her it will never happen again—a promise I'd fail to keep, because Chakrii could do anything next—she says, "I know what those men were going to do to me. I may never have been found again. They could have hurt me, or worse. I'm sure later it will hit me, and I may be troubled by it, but right now all I am is thankful to you."

How is she so reasonable about this? "Just ... like that?"

"You forget I'm Italian," she says dryly. "We have our own criminals. And if you're a well-known businessperson, you're going to come across the mafia eventually. It's inevitable."

I consider that, frowning. "Do you mean to say that you're in danger at home?"

Fuck that if that's true.

She shakes her head. "No, nothing overt like this situation with Chakrii. It's more like ... always in the background, you know? Certain people my family needs to please. Certain vendors that occasionally must be used. Things like that. They mostly leave us alone."

"I don't like the sound of that."

She shrugs. "No one does. That's the point."

I roll to my feet, running a hand through my hair. "I need to go downstairs. Help them with everything. But I don't want you alone up here. Can you get dressed and come out by the pool? I want you to remain in my sight at all times."

"Yes, I'll do that. My clothes are ... well, they were in your room. Everything else is downstairs."

Like I want her to see the bodies again. "Use the sheet on the floor and I'll distract everyone so you have privacy to go downstairs to your room."

"Okay."

I lean over and press a quick, hard kiss to her mouth. "Good. They'll probably need to interview you, but hopefully I can push that to tomorrow." Trailing a line of softer kisses to her ear, I add, "And I hope you're well-rested from napping all day, because I don't intend for us to get any sleep tonight."

She smiles.

I stoop to pull on my clothes, trying to ward off the faint tremor in my hands. Christ, I'm never going to be the same again. Even now, as I reach the door and turn back one last time to look at her, I'm unsure if I'll ever get over the intensity of the last ... holy fuck, it's been an *hour*?

Where the hell is everyone?

Shutting the door quietly behind me, I set off down the

hall, feeling both exhausted and wired at the same time. An image of my cock moving in and out of Lessa as she rode me flashes through my mind, and my dick twitches. Jesus. Get it the fuck together, man. Another few rounds like that, and I'm going to become insatiable.

Which would suck, because she's leaving. Soon.

Fuck. I resolutely push that thought aside—and the one that quickly follows about what the hell I'll do when it happens—and enter my apartment.

Jesse stands in the middle of it, arms folded over his chest, glaring at me.

"What?"

His eyes narrow. "You about shook the damn house down."

"So?"

He rolls his eyes. "So you left me with the bodies while you went and got fucked. We all had to listen to you two, man."

"I thought we had a discussion about you never mentioning overhearing her."

"Well you should have thought about that before you let her suck your cock."

"You were listening?" I growl.

"No, man. Believe me, I was not trying. I did my best not to hear a damn thing. Made no difference. That is what I'm trying to tell you. The Interpol agents are having a field day; this situation is so fucked."

"I don't give a flying fuck what they think. Now shut up and help me with the bodies."

"You're welcome for me cleaning up the broken furniture, you ass," Jesse grumbles, but nevertheless grabs the feet of the man I'm dragging from the room.

I cast a quick glance around the room. Sure enough, he's removed everything I smashed in the process of protecting her. I shrug. "Thanks. Although why you cleaned that first and not the bodies, I don't know."

"That would be because no one wanted to come up here while you two were going at it. I only made a show of thumping the chair against the floor when y'all finally finished so you'd remember we're in the middle of a damn problem."

I don't bother with a response. He and I both know incredible sex always trumps getting rid of dead bodies.

Jesse and I carry the bastard down the stairs and out the door, depositing him with the pile of other bodies littered around the pool.

Asher and Tucker, who apparently returned with Bianchi during my absence, take one look at me and hightail it over.

"Dude, you blew out my ears, man," says Tucker with mock seriousness.

"That was the hottest shit I've heard in a while," says Asher. "And I was downstairs the whole time. Y'all're makin' me jealous."

"Tell me how much I don't care," I snap, then add furiously, "and if *any* of you so much as even *hint* to her you heard us, you're going to end up like one of these assholes."

"Threatening the lives of your own friends. Nice, douche," says Tucker, rolling his eyes.

"I am letting you know now," says Asher, "you are never

living this down. As soon as we're Stateside, all the rest of the buddies from the platoon are going to—"

"You will not so much as breathe a word of it to anyone."

Asher frowns. "They're just going to be happy you found someone, Ford."

"But I haven't!" I practically shout. They stare at me. I drag a deep breath into my lungs in an attempt to drum up a measure of calm. It doesn't work. "She's leaving tomorrow. *Tomorrow*."

Tucker and Asher look away, but Jesse stares at me with sympathy. I ignore them all and stalk over to Made, who's conversing with two men wearing vests with "Interpol" blazoned across the chest.

Jesus Christ, I really was upstairs a long time, wasn't I?

Made looks at me for a significant moment. "I take it Ms. Vitale is unharmed from the abduction attempt?"

I give him a flat look.

"I'm glad to hear it," he says mildly, then motions to two men who have been handcuffed. "We need to debrief. And we need to discuss when you were going to tell me you have Chakrii's number."

"I don't have it," I say, sneering at the handcuffed assholes. "I was bluffing. But he does know I can easily contact him if I wish to—and he damn well knows I'll make good on my threat."

The men glare at me.

Made sighs. "Fine. Let's go through it all."

"Give me a minute," I say. I make sure everyone is busy with other tasks so that Alessandra, who has been waiting just inside the door, has the opportunity to slip inside her room. She gives me a grateful look and then quickly moves down the walkway.

Once I'm certain she's safely inside, I turn back to the handcuffed men. They're seated on the floor and have been divested of their flak vests and helmets. They still glare up at me, seething. I resist the urge to give both of them the finger. They're lucky I don't reach down and beat the shit out of both of them for being part of the team who tried to take her.

"So these assholes caused the diversion."

Made nods. "Part of the group, anyway. We were able to take them alive in the fight, while you went off to save Ms. Vitale. And while you needed to go to her this time, in the future it's best if you waited for back-up before charging into a situation alone."

"And leave her to defend herself? Not gonna happen," I say, not even bothering to look at him. I'm too interested in the men who glare up at me. "I take it you're going to get these men to turn on Chakrii?"

"We'll *never* betray the Golden Dragon for the likes of you," one of them snarls. I roll my eyes at the theatrics.

"You gentleman would be surprised by the incentives I can utilize," Made says, his tone again excruciatingly mild. I consider the agent and wonder just what kind of lethal danger may be hidden behind that calm facade.

"So essentially," I say, "we've done what you've wanted of us, given Interpol someone from Chakrii's organization so you can get a man inside his outfit."

Made nods.

"So you're done with us, once we deliver Lessa to her plane tomorrow? Our involvement is over?"

Made looks at me, then nods again, this time more slowly. "We'll need to debrief all of you, but yes, I expect my superiors will be satisfied. I suppose it all worked out in the end."

I grunt, then spy Bianchi coming out of a van that's parked next to my battered Range Rover.

She notices me and shakes her head. "I see someone's decided to join us."

"Oh, you mean you? The person who missed the entire confrontation?"

She glares at me. "Don't start with me. I've already been getting it from Tucker. How was I supposed to know they'd launch a full-scale assault when we left to get takeout?"

"You should have had it fucking delivered."

"You may recall you all were fine with me leaving!" she snaps.

That's infuriatingly true. "Why don't you focus on removing this trash from my property so we have a hope of getting some rest tonight, huh? We need to be alert to deliver Lessa to her flight."

"Oh, so she's Lessa now," Bianchi says, then shakes her head again. "Good God, I didn't sign up for this shit. It was supposed to be a quick seventy-two hour trip to Singapore to iron out a few new leads, and now this nightmare. Don't worry, Walker; we're processing these men you *killed* and rest assured, you won't be hauled up for actual homicide. Something you think you'd be thankful for, but no, no gratitude to Agent Bianchi, apparently."

I nod my head in acknowledgment. She's not wrong. "Obviously, I and my brothers, and likely the US government would be grateful to you for keeping this quiet."

She rolls her eyes. "You're lucky I wrote you in as consultants before any of this happened. If it had been some other hardass agent, you might have been stuck with someone unwilling to bend the rules like I am this *one* time. You cannot go around killing people."

"Understood," I say. "And after tonight, I don't see that happening again, do you?"

She just looks at me, then steps away. I frown; I have a dreadful feeling I may be wrong.

CHAPTER TWENTY-EIGHT

ALESSANDRA

My phone rings just after Ford and I finally drift off. After he fucked me so many times during the night I can no longer move.

"Huh?" I groan into the phone.

"Christ, sis, are you okay?"

"It's not yet five in the morning here," I whisper, trying not to wake Ford. I roll out of bed, thinking to take the call in the bathroom, but an arm snakes around my waist and pulls me back. Ford rolls me onto my back and throws an arm and leg across me, his face nestled between my breasts. I smile, my fingers threading through his very tousled hair. Ford makes a contented noise and relaxes on top of me.

"Lessa? Lessa? Are you listening to me?"

"What? Huh?"

"Christ. I was apologizing for waking you and saying I'm getting on the jet now. We should touch down in Phuket in fourteen hours."

Ford tenses on top of me.

"Oh, okay," I say. "Have a safe flight."

"We're landing on a private runway just outside the city. I'm texting the details to you now. I don't want you going anywhere near commercial areas. Do you have a safe way to get there?"

"Yes," I say quietly.

"Perfect. *Ciao*, Lessa. I'll see you soon."

I've barely placed the phone on the bedside table when Ford rolls on top of me.

"I can't possibly go again," I groan, although heat still rolls through me when he caresses my breast.

"We have to," Ford says with a hint of desperation as he takes my nipple into his mouth and sucks it. I moan again, my body so completely attuned to him by now, it knows exactly what pleasure I'm about to receive. "We don't have much time left."

He's not wrong, so I pull his mouth up to mine.

FORD IS a different man when we awake late in the morning. Cool. Silent. Vibrating with a barely-leashed intensity. Watching as he dresses in a black outfit of what can only be fatigues, it dawns on me that this is the military man; the soldier. The trained killer. The man who touched me last night with passion and coaxed such unimaginable pleasure out of me is gone.

I dress also, trying to ignore the pang of sadness at the distance he's put between us. Perhaps it's for the best; perhaps now I'll have the wherewithal to leave him.

My body certainly can't handle more. After my attempted abduction and the all-night sex marathon, I'm sore pretty much everywhere, but it's the kind of soreness I'll treat as the fondest of memories.

I finish dressing to discover Ford is staring at me, his expression unreadable.

"What?" I ask.

He shakes his head. "Nothing."

It's not nothing; it can't be. But I don't push him on it, knowing that neither of us wants to discuss what's about to happen.

Ford leads me down into the kitchen, where the rest of the group is already assembled. I scan the group and notice a few more Interpol agents.

Made comes over to me. "Ms. Vitale. How are you feeling after the excitement of yesterday?"

I refrain from laughing. How tactful of him to put it that way. I should be embarrassed that the rest of the house probably heard us all night long, but I'm not. Or perhaps only a little bit. What I shared with Ford was far more important, and I'm glad I never, not for one second, held myself back from him.

"I'm managing," I say.

He nods. "Then if you're rested, I'd like to get your official statement about what happened last night, when those men entered your room. It should be the last thing we need from you before you leave."

"Okay," I say, glancing at the other agents. Bianchi nods at me from over her cup of coffee. "Where should we do it?"

"You can debrief her in my office," Ford says, leading us

down the hall to it. He turns to me. "I'll be planning your extraction with my men in the kitchen while he interviews you."

I blink at him. "Surely that's an exaggeration. You're not *extracting* me from anything, Ford. I'm leaving."

He just looks at me. I flinch, realizing how badly I put that, like there aren't extenuating circumstances.

Like I'm just leaving him, nothing more.

Made clears his throat. "If we could begin?"

Ford disappears after shutting the door behind us. I answer Made's questions thoroughly and carefully about my entire stay in Thailand, not just last night. I know it needs to be done, but I still grow increasingly frustrated the longer it continues. Every minute wasted here is one fewer moment I can spend with Ford.

After three hours, I can't take it anymore. "Do you think you have everything?"

Made glances up from the notes he's been taking. "I believe we're about finished, yes. I apologize for how long it's taken, but I want to be thorough. Your statement, combined with any intelligence we receive from the men we captured yesterday, will go a long way toward convicting Chakrii, should we ever manage to arrest the man."

My brows raise in surprise. "You mean you caught people yesterday? I thought everyone was ... dead."

"Well, yes, of course. We managed to capture two men from Chakrii's organization. Didn't Mr. Walker tell you that?"

I blush. "We, uh, didn't do much talking."

"Ah. Well. I understand."

Hopefully he doesn't understand *exactly*. "Is there anything else I should tell you? I'd like to have time to express my thanks to everyone before we leave."

Made stands. "Of course. And I'm sure there will be many details of our departure to go over. We want to ensure you make your flight safely, Ms. Vitale."

"You don't really think he's going to try *again*, do you?" I ask, already knowing it's exactly what Ford believes.

Made considers. "It's possible. Chakrii really does appear obsessed with taking you. And ..." he trails off, studying me, "there is the question of the leak at the Italian consulate."

"What do you mean?" I ask carefully.

"We interviewed the woman who made your consulate appointment. She was paid to schedule you after the consulate had closed. We're still working on her to see if she knows more than she's saying. It will take some time to figure out the full extent of her involvement. In the meantime, we'll need to be extra careful with your safety."

I sigh. "I suppose that's true."

Made escorts me back to the kitchen. Everyone stands around a tablet in the middle of the kitchen island that has a map of the city pulled up. Bianchi is running her finger along a route in red, highlighting which checkpoints could potentially be the most dangerous.

"There's a two-kilometer length of road coming into the private airport. There are no intersecting streets on that stretch. No escape. If they block us in any way, we'll have to fight our way out."

"No intersecting roads means nowhere for them to hide, though. That makes it safer," says Jesse, frowning.

Bianchi shoots him a scathing glance. Jesse ignores her, but something about the way his jaw tightens tells me he doesn't miss the look. Do they really hate each other *that* much?

"We will be alert regardless," Ford says, interrupting Bianchi before she can say something terrible to Jesse. "In any case, we've gone over the route multiple times already. Three cars, Vitale in the middle, simple for any of us to peel off to engage if necessary. Does anyone have any questions? The flight should be arriving in three hours and it's going to take just over two to get there. We need to get moving."

A chorus of mumbled agreements echoes out around the room. I glance at everyone; their deadly serious demeanors are beginning to freak me out. It's going to be fine. Right? It has to be ...

Made motions to the other Interpol agents. "We'll head out to begin readying our vehicles. I trust you and your men can prepare Ms. Vitale yourselves, Walker?"

"Yes," Ford says, staring at me. He spares a fleeting glance to his friends. "I'll meet you in the basement, boys."

He takes my hand and leads me out of the room on the heels of a few agents. His hand holds mine tightly, trembling. I'm wondering where the stairway to the basement is when Ford suddenly shoves open a door and drags me inside a bathroom. He kicks the door shut and an instant later his mouth is on mine.

It's a harsh kiss, harder than others I've received from him. A soldier's kiss, not a lover's. I kiss him back with enthusiasm, hands clawing at his shirt. Ford rips his mouth away and sucks along the line of my jaw.

"One last time, gorgeous," he whispers in my ear, already unbuttoning my shorts. "Let me love you one last time before you leave me."

Pain slams into my chest. "We can't ..." I pause, needing to say it, even though I already know the answer. "There can't be anything between us after I leave?"

Regret flashes across his face. "I'm not in a position ... to want a relationship. And even if I did, I'd never risk Chakrii coming after you again. He needs to believe you're gone for good. But if things were different, if *I* were different ... you are who I'd choose."

"I understand," I choke out, wishing my heart did not feel as if he had just punched a hole in it. I shove away the pain, refusing to acknowledge that he's right, that this will be the last time I feel him so perfectly inside me.

I claw at his waistband, shoving his clothes to the floor as Ford does the same. Neither of us bother with our shirts as he spins me around and bends me over the sink. He slides a finger inside me, stroking deep. I thrust back into him, riding his finger as he makes me ready for him.

"So wet, gorgeous," he whispers, adding a second finger. "You're ready for me, aren't you?"

"Yes," I gasp. "Please, Ford."

"Quickly now," he grunts, kicking my feet apart until I'm spread wide before him. He grabs my hips and thrusts all the way home.

A moan escapes us. I bite down on my lip to keep from

making another sound, knowing everyone is outside the door and that we must be both quick and quiet.

Ford hammers into me, his grip punishing, so forceful I'm shoved forward into the sink again and again. It's deep. Overwhelming. Perfect. I raise my head high enough to watch him in the mirror. He thrusts with a frenzied abandonment, his eyes locked on the place where his body enters mine. He thrusts particularly deep inside me and it's so pleasurable I clamp down on his cock, bucking back against him, straining to keep quiet. A look instantly flashes across his face, one of such sadness, such bittersweet regret, such *longing* that I gasp.

His eyes collide with mine in the mirror. Something in my face must echo how he's feeling, because he suddenly withdraws and spins me around. He lifts me, slamming me down on top of the sink. A moment later he's inside me again, moving forcefully, passionately. He reaches up with both hands to cradle my face and leans closer until he's inches from me.

His eyes track back and forth across my face as he whispers, his hips pumping into me, "I am never going to forget you. *Never*. Never going to forget this. You have made me feel more alive these last few weeks than I have in months. In *years*, gorgeous. You've made me a man again, whole, not the empty husk of a person just going through the motions before you appeared in my life."

"Ford," I sob, heartbreak shattering me even as his skillful thrusting sends me closer toward my orgasm. "I—"

He kisses me, a perfect, soul-wrenching kiss of passion and yearning and tenderness. He kisses me so that I don't have to say—so that he doesn't, either—that this is a goodbye. Final. And he kisses me so we need never acknowledge what our parting will do to us.

I wrap my arms around his neck and cling to him, giving him my body and my mouth and my soul, and when I shatter a moment later, he follows me, too, filling me with his very essence for the last time. Tears spring to my eyes, but I force them away, determined these last moments with him won't be ones of sadness.

CHAPTER TWENTY-NINE

ALESSANDRA

Ford rests his forehead against mine as we catch our breaths. My eyes drift closed, wishing to prolong the moment as long as possible. Far too soon, he withdraws, grabs a hand towel on the sink to clean us up, and then slowly draws his clothes back up his body, his gaze never leaving mine.

I slide off the sink and do the same, feeling empty. Alone. Brittle. Ford stares at me one last time, and then his expression goes hard, a permanent severing of the bond we forged between us last night.

My heart squeezes painfully, but I manage to prevent the tears from falling. Crying right now will only distract Ford.

He takes my hand and leads me out of the bathroom, along the hallway to a door that opens to reveal a staircase. I follow Ford down, hearing the voices of his men below me. When I reach the bottom, my mouth drops open.

It's an armory.

Racks of guns line the walls, along with many cases of what might even be grenades and other kinds of artillery. Tucker, Asher, and Jesse are suiting up in vests and helmets with an efficiency born of many repetitions.

"I thought you said you *used* to be in the military ..."

Ford releases my hand and walks over to a case of vests. He digs through them. "We were."

"But ... this can't be legal."

Ford barely spares me a glance. "It's not."

"But ..."

"Alessandra, it's easy to get weapons when you need them," Asher says helpfully, sending me a grin.

"There are agents just upstairs!" I hiss, glancing at the ceiling.

Ford walks over to me holding a vest. "And Made has extended me the courtesy of not asking any questions. I'm well-known to both the authorities here and the Pentagon. If I ever went off the reservation, they'd know. No one thinks I'm that stupid."

"But ... but ..."

Jesse sighs. "Governments look the other way all the time, Alessandra. It's normal. More importantly, Ford is a mitigating force on crime in this city. In a way, he helps them. So they don't ask questions."

"And I thought Italy was corrupt," I murmur.

Ford begins strapping the vest around my chest. "All governments are corrupt," he says thinly, yanking the vest so tight my chest jerks toward him. He gives it a rap. "Comfortable? Can you breathe?"

"It's tight."

"It needs to be."

I shiver. Not "it's supposed to be," but rather it *needs* to be.

I am so unqualified to handle this.

Giving me one final check and then a satisfied nod, Ford starts equipping himself. I watch in astonishment as the four of them outfit themselves with pistols at both their hips and in holsters at the chest of their flak vests, before loading rifles with magazines that look like they have about a zillion rounds in them.

"I think we'll be well-prepared for an airport trip," I say weakly.

Ford pulls back on the bolt of his rifle and releases it with a loud *clang*. "We're not taking any chances."

"That is apparent, yes."

Ford hustles me out to his Range Rover, along with my lone suitcase and backpack I hastily packed when I woke up. God, the rest of my belongings are still at the Golden Lotus. That's probably the last I'll ever see of them. Even worse, I never got to see Pranee again, or thank her for everything she did for me.

"If I leave a note with you, will you give it to the woman who dropped me here? She works at Chakrii's resort."

"Yes," says Ford. I'm wedged between Ford on my right and Jesse on my left in the backseat, while Tucker drives and Asher rides shotgun. Ford no longer looks at me but instead scans our surroundings as Tucker pulls in between the two Interpol SUVs. The other men remain silent as well, their rifles pointed toward the ceiling.

Hastily, I take a piece of paper from my purse and

scribble a note for Pranee, thanking her for helping me out of the resort, and also telling her she can do whatever she likes with the rest of my clothes. Perhaps if she sells them, she'll have enough money to spend time looking for a different employer.

Once I finish, I'm about to give the note to Ford when I realize there likely won't be time for me to say all that I want to him when we arrive. So I take out another piece of paper and write a second letter, to him this time. I tell him how glad I am to have met him, and how wrong my first impressions of him were. I thank him again for helping me on the plane. For understanding about the pool.

For giving me the most incredible sex of my life.

That last part is too depressing to continue. I don't have the heart to keep writing, and I especially lack the courage to tell him I wish we'd had more time together. That's what those final moments in the bathroom were meant to say.

When I finish, I fold both letters, placing Ford's under the one I've written for Pranee. I tuck both into the flap of the seat in front of me.

"The letter is there for later," I say.

Ford barely spares it a glance, but nods, his eyes tracking back and forth out the window. The car remains silent, each man scanning his respective quadrant; even Tucker glances repeatedly in the rear view mirror.

I shift uncomfortably in my vest, wedging a finger under the edge so I can give my ribs a moment's relief. I can't imagine actually fighting someone in this thing. It's heavy, too; no doubt I'd struggle to move at all if I suddenly had to flee.

I pray it doesn't come to that.

With nothing better to do, I stare out the window as well, watching as my final moments in Thailand stream past. Will I ever return? Or is this country permanently off-limits to me?

Will I ever see Ford again?

I try to imagine a world in which Ford meets me somewhere else, or I can return. The idea feels quaint, it's so unlikely. He's made it clear he doesn't intend to see me after today, even if he does value the time we had together.

This really is the end.

Ford tenses beside me after we've driven through Phuket and continue on through the other side. I haven't memorized the route like the others have, but I know we'll soon reach the portion of the road that Bianchi was worried about. The roads become increasingly less-traveled, reminding me of how deserted the road was outside the consulate before I was attacked.

I'm not the only one wary of the deserted area.

"This reeks of Raqqa," mutters Asher, shifting toward the window.

"Don't even put that out there, dude," Tucker grumbles.

Ford and Jesse don't join in nervously like the other two, but Ford's grip tightens around his rifle.

Asher shakes his head, his gaze locked out the window. "There's nobody here, man. I don't like it. Fuck this shit."

Jesse swears under his breath. I scan around but see nothing. No one who could be after us. The only thing I can see is a half-falling down structure that looks like it might once have been a garage.

Ford's head whips toward it. "Tucker, watch that—"

A truck plows into the driver's side of the SUV in front of us, launching so fast out of the building it could only have been waiting for us.

"Back up!" Ford roars, but Tucker already has the car in reverse. "Get down!" He shoves me toward the floor, his arm thrown over me as he stares out the back.

I lift my head high enough to stare out the front window. The two vehicles are smashed together, the frames completely crumpled. I watch in horror as men drag themselves out of both vehicles, but the driver's side of the Interpol vehicle is too destroyed for anyone to climb out.

Was Made on that side? Dear God, please, no.

"There's another one!" Tucker yells. I try to lift higher to see, but Ford shoves me down harder, my vest digging into my side as I bend in half.

A crash sounds behind us, followed by a squeal and what must be the sound of metal tearing.

"That's Bianchi's car," Jesse says dully. I roll my head to the side in time to catch anguish flash across his face.

"We can't help them now," Ford snarls above me. "Tucker, get around the crash in front of us while they're still recovering."

"They've completely blocked the road, Ford."

"Then clip them on the side if you have to! I don't care; get the fuck through!"

A barrage of bullets slams into our vehicle, which already was worse for wear after the consulate attack. I glance to the side and can see daylight through Ford's door.

"Fuck!" Asher yells, flinging his door wide and sticking his rifle through the window so he can return fire.

Jesse throws out his door, too, but instead of facing forward, he directs his rifle behind us.

"Two more cars approaching from behind. Bianchi is out of her vehicle with the other men, but they aren't going to hold them off long."

"Tucker and Asher, clear the way forward for us. Jesse, help Bianchi and the rest hold them off," Ford says, his voice tight.

A second rain of gunfire slams into us from behind. I scream as the back window blows out, smattering me with shattered glass.

"You're okay," Ford breathes, shoving me to the floor and throwing himself on top of me. "We'll get you out of here."

I turn my head to the side to watch as Tucker and Asher fire into the crash ahead of us. Another turn of my head shows Jesse aiming behind us, the gunfire so loud at this close range that my teeth rattle. I can't watch; I hyperventilate, eyes locked on the carpet of the floor three inches from my face.

"Almost clear, almost clear," I hear Tucker say, although how I manage to hear it with Asher firing I have no idea.

A tremendous *boom* echoes behind us, the force of it rocking our vehicle.

"They're through!" Jesse yells. A second later he screams, followed by a thud.

"Jesse's down!" Tucker cries.

"Fuck!" Ford yells. He climbs over me and out through Jesse's door, shouting, "stay down!"

I lift my head. "But—"

"*Stay down!*" he roars. Our eyes collide for one final instant before he slams the door shut. "Get her out, damn it!"

I'm dragging myself up when I'm shoved to the floor again as Asher lands on top of me.

"No!" I sob, thrashing under him, trying to break free, to drag Ford back inside the vehicle, but it's as good as useless. I can't move.

"Go!" Asher yells, and I feel the Range Rover charge forward. "Brace yourself, Aless—"

"No!"

We slam into something; my temple smacks against the driver's seat. Asher curses and shouts my name, but stars burst in my eyes and I'm falling, falling, falling.

III

THE DRAGON

CHAPTER THIRTY

ALESSANDRA

I wake to the sound of my name and a slap across my face.

"Ford?" I mumble, batting away the hand.

A short silence, then, "No, honey, it's not Ford."

I bolt upright. "Ford!"

"Shh, shh," says Asher. "Take it easy. You've hit your head."

"Where is—" I roll over on my side and vomit. Not much comes up, but what little does spews out of the open car door. Wait, what? Last I remembered, I was on the floor of the vehicle, not stretched out on the back seat. Just how long have I been out?

I attempt it a second time, more cautiously sitting upright, wincing as my head pounds.

"Shit, I think she's got a concussion," Asher says to Tucker.

"I'm fine," I mumble. Already the nausea is subsiding. "Where are we?"

"You're at the airport."

I stare dully outside. Sure enough, our bullet-riddled vehicle is parked at the base of a runway. No Vitale private jet waits, though, so my brother hasn't yet landed. He must be any minute, though.

"We have to go back."

They remain silent.

I focus on them. Tucker and Asher are wearing twin expressions of agony, but also mulish determination.

"We *have* to."

Asher reaches toward me. "Alessandra—"

"We can't just leave them there. Are you insane? We've abandoned them!"

Asher flinches, but Tucker says, "It was what he wanted. He wanted you to get out."

"What about what I want? What about what you want? Jesse got shot! He could be …" I trail off when twin expressions of horror flash across their faces. They know better than I do what Jesse could be like right now. "No man should be left behind."

"And we're going back as soon as we see you safely onboard," Tucker says, folding his arms over his chest.

"That could be minutes from now!" I cry. "An hour! And I'm not going."

Asher's head snaps back. "Not going?"

"Of course I'm not."

"Men got shot to get you here!" Asher roars. "You're getting on the plane!"

"And I'm telling you I'm not leaving until I know they're okay! No one gets left behind on account of me!" I yell right back, ignoring how much I hate that he's right about people getting shot to protect me. I *never* wanted that.

"Let's just cool it," Tucker says, then curses. "Christ, since when am I the rational one?"

"So leave me here," I say instead, desperate for them to go back. "Give me one of your guns and I'll hide out with the people in the control tower.

Asher gives me a disgusted expression. "We're not leaving you alone."

I practically scream with frustration. "If I were one of your men, you'd have already left me to go back for them! Just do it! My God! And I thought my biggest problem coming here would be getting over water! What was I thinking?"

They glance away. A pang of sympathy for them courses through me; I know what this must be doing to them. How much they must yearn to save their brothers-in-arms. And while I hate myself for using that against them, I *have* to know that they're all okay.

That Ford didn't sacrifice himself for me.

Because that I couldn't take. My head pounds harder; I grip the sides of my head and will it away, which helps not one bit.

Then inspiration strikes. "So one of you go, and the other can stay with me. Problem solved."

This tempts them. Asher and Tucker look at each other, brows raised. I hold my breath; they're really considering it. Before I can push them over the edge, something occurs to me.

"How long have we been here?"

"What?"

"How long was I unconscious? How long since we arrived at this airport?"

Tucker frowns. "About twenty minutes. You hit your head when we rammed the SUV to get around them and have been out since."

"Twenty *minutes*? But that's a year! Where is everyone? Isn't someone running this airport? What about the control tower? We can't possibly be alone."

They shift on their feet, exchanging a glance. Finally, Asher says, "Alessandra. We drove in with a bullet-ridden car. They're not going to roll out the welcome committee. They probably took one look at us and decided it was best if we went about our business."

"Yeah, but what about the people pursuing us? There were more cars coming up on Bianchi's car, weren't there? Presumably, if you got around the first crash, then they could, too. If they're after me, why haven't they come?"

"Ford probably stopped them," says Tucker.

"Really? All by himself? Multiple cars?"

"It wouldn't be the first time he did something like that," mutters Asher.

"If that's the case, then why isn't he here?" I ask. "Why didn't he come after us? None of this makes sense!"

"There probably isn't a functional vehicle for him to drive."

"So go pick him up!" I yell.

They shake their heads.

I erupt. "This is *ridiculous*! I'm fine! There's no one around! Just do it! What is the matter with you!"

"We have our orders."

"You're not in the military anymore! Fuck your orders!"

They glare at me.

I've had enough. I crawl out of the backseat.

"What are you—"

"I'll do it myself, then," I snap, springing into the front seat. My hands haven't even touched the wheel before I'm hauled back out. "Damn you!"

"We know it's hard," Asher says, his arms wrapped tight around me, "but this is how it has to be."

I'm saved from having to answer such stupidity by the sound of an approaching airplane. Tucker mutters a prayer of thanks as we watch the plane drop lower.

"That yours?" Asher asks.

"Too far away to tell, but it must be."

We watch in silence—Asher's arms still locked around me—as the plane lines up for its final approach and drops down out of the sky. The wheels squeal as it rolls to a stop, then taxis toward us.

The hatch has barely opened when three men jump out with rifles.

"Release her!"

"Get on the ground!"

"Do it now!"

"Holy fuck," Asher shouts, releasing me only to shove me behind him. He and Tucker lift the rifles slung across their backs.

"Identify yourselves!" shouts Tucker.

"Put down your weapons and release the woman, or we'll blow you away!"

I cower behind Asher, hands over my head as everyone shouting sends pain stabbing through it. Why is this *happening* to me? Ford could be hurt—he could be *dying*—and we're wasting our time with whatever the hell this is!

Summoning my courage—if these men wanted to harm me, they would have blown us away already—I peer around Asher's back, barely poking my head out from his side to study the plane.

The Vitale logo is blazoned across the side.

I nearly collapse to the ground in relief. "It's okay, guys," I say. "That's my family's plane."

They don't lower their rifles an inch. "Frankly, Alessandra," Asher grunts, "until we see your brother and know he hasn't been kidnapped himself, we're not taking any chances."

"That's highly unlikely," I say. "He flew nonstop from JFK. Chakrii couldn't have done anything to him."

The words are barely out of my mouth when my brother himself appears on the top step of the hatch.

"For fuck's sake, stop pointing guns at my sister!"

No one moves. One of the men says something unintelligible to my brother, whose gaze snaps to the very worse-for-wear condition of our vehicle. He pales.

"Release my sister, fuckers!" he says, trying to shove his way around his men, who block him and shout their heads off.

"Oh, for the love of *God*," I snap. This has gone on far enough.

Before Asher has the chance to stop me, I dart out from behind him and into the gap between our car and the plane. Asher and Tucker shout and grab for me, but I just dance out of their way.

"See?" I shout. "I'm fine! These men saved my life, Marco! Stop this nonsense!"

Marco says something to his men, who lower their weapons, but only slightly. I turn to Asher and Tucker.

"Lower them."

"Come on, Alessandra," Asher pleads. "This is the height of stupidity. We're taking their word for it."

"It's my *brother*. Captive? Really, Asher? Does my brother look like a captive to you? Now lower them, or so help me I'll shoot you myself."

Asher snorts, glances at Tucker, then says, "Well, let's see if they shoot us. They haven't shot her, so at least there's that."

Tucker rolls his eyes. "Might as well. This thing's been fucked from the start."

He lowers his rifle a smidge. Asher follows suit. Tucker says, "And you don't even have a gun yourself, Alessandra. No way you're shooting us."

"I'd snag it from your holster," I say, but I'm smiling now.

Tucker scoffs. "I'd like to see you try. Truly."

I roll my eyes and turn back to my brother, who's barreling down the stairs. We meet in the middle of the tarmac. Marco pulls me into a huge hug, his arms so tight I feel my ribs protest even through my bulletproof vest.

He steps back enough to look at me. "Christ, Lessa, what the hell hap—"

"Marco, who are those men?" I say, my gaze locked on them.

"What? Them? You thought I'd come here by myself when some lunatic's trying to kidnap you? They're a security team I hired in New York. Ex-military. I don't know which branch. Real tough assholes and thank God for that." Marco starts pulling me toward the plane. "Come on; let's go. I want you out of here."

I literally dig my heels into a crack in the pavement. "No! I'm not going!"

Marco does a double take. "What? The hell you're not!"

I try to yank my arm away, but my brother holds fast. "You have to send them with them! They need help!"

"What are you talking about?"

I look over my shoulder at Asher and Tucker. "This security team can help you save them! You need more men!"

Asher's eyes widen with understanding and Tucker punches the air. Marco yanks my arm again and wheels me around. "What are you talking about?"

"There were two other men who saved me, multiple times. We were nearly taken, and they stayed back to let me out. Your men can help save them if they go quickly. Please, Marco, I owe them my life! They have to go! Now!"

"Is there a problem?" one of Marco's men asks, coming up behind us.

Marco half turns toward him, his gaze still locked with

mine. I plead with him silently, ready to hold them all at gunpoint myself if that's what it takes.

My brother sighs.

He motions toward Asher and Tucker. "These men saved my sister's life and lost two of theirs. They need help going back for them. Can you provide it?"

The man sizes up the former SEALs. His eyes narrow. "Did I hear y'all right with that American accent?"

Asher grins. "You bet, baby."

His gaze narrows further. "That's a Navy asshole if I ever heard one. Absolutely no discipline."

Tucker scoffs. "You've gotta be a Marine."

His lips twitch. "I'm not, but Ace is."

Asher sizes him up. "And you?"

The lips twitch again. "Ranger Battalion."

"The shittiest branch!" Tucker crows.

"That would be the Air Force, dipshit, and don't you forget it, or I'll make your shitty-ass swab the deck with it, sailor."

But he grins and extends a hand. "You can call me Diamond."

Asher takes it. "Army man, continuing with the shittiness. What kind of a name is that, asshole?"

"The kind you'll use if you want someone to save your sorry Navy asses, fuckface. Yo Ace! Jack! Get over here."

The two men clamber down from the plane and jog over. In seconds they're all cramming into what's left of the Range Rover and wheeling out of the airport.

"What the fuck just happened?" Marco says in astonishment as the car fades away.

I hug him again. "Welcome to my life for the last few days."

Marco stares at where they disappeared. "Alessandra. I could swear they were *excited* to go off to get shot at."

"I'm not saying it made any sense."

Marco sighs, "Let's wait in the plane."

I follow him inside and collapse into one of the seats, thankful for the little piece of home. I've been dreading returning to Italy, but this seat right here, where I always sit, makes me feel safer than anything has since I arrived in Phuket.

"How's Izzy?" I ask. "Did her appointment go okay?"

Marco runs a hand through his hair. "Yes, she's okay. We're at twenty-eight weeks. Her blood pressure is stable for now, but the worry is eating me alive. She never had blood pressure problems before she got pregnant."

I reach over and squeeze his arms. "Sometimes it's like that."

"I know," Marco says, like he's been told that a million times.

"I'm really grateful you came over here despite all that."

Marco laughs and shakes his head. "She practically kicked me out of the house, Lessa. I bet she's dancing on the deck of our penthouse now that she has some time to herself."

Based on what I know about his wife, yeah, she's probably thrilled to have my overprotective brother out of her hair for a while.

Marco throws out his hands as if pushing away the topic. "I can't talk about it. I'll start obsessing, and there's nothing I can do all the way over here. You need to tell me what the hell is going on. Wait ... what the fuck happened to your head?"

"Oh," I say absently, lifting my hand to gingerly poke my temple. I wince. "I hit it against the seat when we rammed through the other car."

"*What?* You were in a car accident? Jesus Christ! Barnes! Get out here!"

I jump. "Who's Barnes?"

My question is answered when a man steps out from the other room carrying a medical bag.

"Examine her," Marco says. "She's been in a car accident."

"I'm fine—"

"You'll be fine when Barnes proclaims you are."

I sigh, leaning back in my chair as the doctor comes over. There's no use trying to argue with my brother. He'll just worry until I submit.

"Hey, can you treat a gunshot wound?" I ask Barnes in English as he peers at my temple.

Marco leaps out of his chair. *"You've been shot?!"*

"No, but one of the men they went to retrieve is. And there ... might be more injuries," I add faintly, praying Ford isn't one of the casualties.

"You had better start explaining," Marco growls.

I fill him in on everything that happened since I arrived in Thailand, my brother's eyes growing wider the longer I talk.

"You almost drowned? Yesterday? How are you ... I don't know whether to be proud or appalled."

"Let's go with the first one."

He shakes his head, opens his mouth to respond, but the sound of vehicles roar into the airport. I shove the doctor away and run to the hatch. Two cars pull up in front of the plane. I'm running down the steps before they even come to a halt.

Tucker and Asher are first out of the Ranger, their expressions blank. They carry out Jesse, who's cussing a blue streak about how he doesn't need to be carried but thankfully is alive.

Bianchi limps out of the second car, her left arm cradled against her chest. Two of Marco's men carry out an unconscious Made, whose leg is clearly broken. A couple of the other Interpol agents I met this morning exit, but that's it.

No one else gets out.

"Where is he?" I ask.

His friends flinch, avoiding my gaze.

"Where's Ford!"

Jesse finally looks at me, his expression filled with pain. "They took him, Alessandra. Those bastards grabbed Ford and then just left us."

CHAPTER THIRTY-ONE

ALESSANDRA

"They *took* him?" I cry, my gaze ping-ponging from Jesse to Asher to Tucker. The men can't meet my eyes. "If you'd gone back, you could have stopped them from taking him! I told you to go back!"

"They couldn't have," Jesse grunts, his eyes glazed with pain. "Y'all had barely broken through the crash when they came up on us. We were completely outnumbered. They wrestled us to the ground, dragged Ford off. He put up a hell of a fight ... I tried to stop them, but this fucking gunshot. Why the fuck didn't they kill the rest of us? Makes no fucking sense. It happened so fast I could still see the Rover in the distance by the time they'd taken Ford. And then they just left. It's like they didn't even want you."

No. Jesse must be mistaken. That can't be true. It surely couldn't be. Because if that's the case, then—

I fly at Asher and pound my fists against his chest. He winces, still avoiding my gaze.

"You *knew*!" I turn my fists on Tucker, not that it does

anything to either of them. "You both knew he'd been taken this entire time! You saw it happen in the rearview mirror."

"You were unconscious, and he was already gone, Alessandra," Asher says quietly, finally meeting my gaze, his eyes pleading. "There was nothing we could do."

"Why did you lie?" I ask, but I already know the answer. "Never mind. Because I never would have gotten on the plane otherwise."

They nod.

"Bastards," I say without heat, utterly exhausted by the betrayal. I turn and head for the aircraft.

"We had to do it," Asher says to my back as they carry Jesse after me. "Ford has never lost his mind over a woman like he has with you, not even when he was with—all I'm saying is it would have been his last—"

"Don't you *dare*," I snarl, whirling on them. "Don't you dare act like he's already gone."

"We're not," Tucker says. "We just don't want him chewing us out for endangering you when he's back."

"That's not something you need to worry about."

Asher does a double take. "Are you serious? He'd yell at us for that first thing."

"We'll focus on it later," I say. "Jesse, are you okay? When I heard you get shot …"

He grimaces. "Pretty sure it went clean through."

"We need to get him to a doctor," says Tucker. "We came back to let you know we're okay, and also to deliver those dicks your brother hired, but then we need to take him—"

"Oh, we've got a doctor," I say.

"Wait, what?"

"Are you serious?"

"I would appreciate some pain meds right about now."

"Come on," I say, "my control-freak brother brought one in case I needed it. Lucky for you, he seems competent."

"And he still hasn't given you a clean bill of health," Marco says, frowning as he comes down the stairs. His brows raise as he takes in Jesse. "Has he been shot?"

"So much for the vest, huh?" says Asher.

"I'm telling you, it went right through. Hit high in the shoulder, nowhere near anything important," Jesse says through gritted teeth. "I'm fine."

"We'll have the doctor verify that," I say, shaking my head. What the hell has happened to my life that I'm calmly discussing a man's gunshot wound? Was it really too much to ask for a quiet vacation in Thailand?

"I wouldn't mind getting my arm popped in," Bianchi grumbles as they carry Jesse past.

His head whips to look at her, his gaze locked on her shoulder. "Fix her first."

Asher and Tucker laugh. Asher says, "Gunshot trumps dislocated shoulder, jackass. Isn't that right, Bianchi?" he adds over his shoulder.

"I'm managing," says Bianchi. Sweat has broken out over her brow, though.

"Dislocated shoulders are far more painful than what I'm dealing with right now," Jesse growls. "I insist the doctor works on her first."

"Naw, dude, you go first. We saw all the blood you lost

from your supposedly no-big-deal gunshot. That's why we're carrying you."

Jesse jerks his uninjured arm. "Another thing I don't need. You two jackasses are liable to drop me. Let me down, damn it."

"No can do," Tucker says cheerfully as they haul him up the stairs. "We're enjoying this too much."

Jesse swears the whole way into the plane. When they plunk him down into one of the chairs in the living area, the doctor takes one look at him and pales.

He turns to Marco. "I wasn't informed about the potential for gunshots."

Marco waves him away. "I'll pay you whatever you like. Just do it. My sister is safe because of these men."

"Gunshots must be reported to the respective authorities."

"Of which I am one," Bianchi snaps as she enters the plane. "Interpol, got it? All of this shit will be in so many reports it's ridiculous. Believe me, you don't need to worry about it."

The doctor remains uncomfortable, but nods. "Very well. Young man, you're going to need to remove that vest so I can see to your wound."

Jesse stares at him like he's grown two extra heads. "Young man? I'm thirty-seven years old."

"And I'm fifty-eight. Which makes you a young man. Some day you'll understand that. Now if you gentlemen could assist in removing his vest—"

"Fuck my vest. Bianchi first," Jesse growls, batting away Asher's attempt to remove his flak vest.

The doctor straightens, giving Marco a helpless look. "Who's Bianchi?"

"I am," she says flatly, stepping around Marco's men who have just finished hoisting Made up the stairs.

The doctor stares at her, frowning unhappily. "A dislocated shoulder and God only knows what you did to that leg of yours."

Jesse's gaze drops to her leg. "What did you do to it?"

"Nothing," she says. "Their car hit on that side, is all."

Jesse's face grows furious. He jabs a finger at Bianchi. "Doctor her, now."

Bianchi steps up to Jesse and peers down at him, her expression haughty. "You need to have that looked at. I can handle a little pain."

Jesse's eyes narrow. "And I don't give a flying fuck. Doctor, do your fucking job."

The doctor throws up his hands, looking from one to the other. "I can't attend a patient who won't consent."

Jesse smiles grimly. "And I don't. Not until she's been looked at."

He stares at Bianchi. She glares back at him. The rest of us watch, spellbound, as this little drama plays out. Blood continues to trickle from his shoulder. Bianchi's gaze follows the line of it, and she finally makes a noise of disgust.

"You're a real piece of work, you know that?" she says, and turns to the doctor.

Triumph flashes in Jesse's eyes. He watches, transfixed, as the doctor examines Bianchi's shoulder. A few moments later, he asks if she's ready. When she nods, he quickly relocates the shoulder. Bianchi gives a loud grunt of pain. Jesse pales.

Bianchi rotates her arm, and nods in thanks to the doctor.

"Someone get her ice," Jesse snaps.

"I'll do it," I say, although I'm loath to miss even a second of this interaction. I'm dying to just straight-up ask them if they're hooking up, but they both seem to despise each other. No way would I get a straight answer out of either of them.

I come rushing back with a bag of ice from the bar fridge in time to hear Jesse is insisting that the doctor look at Bianchi's leg. Now even Tucker and Asher protest along with Bianchi that Jesse is being unreasonable. My brother catches my eye and mouths the word "goner." I shrug. Probably.

Suddenly Bianchi turns to Jesse, unbuttons her pants, and rips them down her body. Dead silence falls. No one even moves.

"There. You see?" Bianchi snaps. "Just a bunch of bruising. No bones out. No mangled limb. I'm fine."

She turns her back to Jesse, and from my vantage point behind him, I can see what's rendered the other men mute. Bianchi's wearing a thong, and she *really* wears it well.

Jesse's breath whooshes out.

"See?" Bianchi says again, turning back around and yanking her pants back up her legs. She fixes him with a deadly glare. "Now let him sew you up, you stupid man."

Jesse says nothing, just nods to the doctor, who looks like he's about to faint. Jesse's face has flushed bright red.

"Dude," Tucker says to Asher in a stage whisper. "Did I really see that? Those bastards didn't get me after all and I'm now relaxing in heaven?"

The other men laugh, even my brother. I roll my eyes. Bianchi's looking at something on her phone, like she doesn't even care she flashed the entire plane.

"Shut it," Jesse snaps and the men shockingly fall quiet. Asher nudges Tucker and then Tucker nudges Asher, like two little boys gleeful that Mommy and Daddy are no longer fighting.

They pull Jesse's vest off him, then cut away his shirt. Everyone is busy helping him, but I don't miss the hard look Bianchi gives his hard chest before she quickly returns her attention to her phone. *Very* interesting. It's only a matter of time with those two if it hasn't happened already.

"Well, it did go right through," says the doctor. "You were right about that. I can sew it up and prescribe a course of antibiotics, but it should obviously be checked out at a hospital."

"Just sew it up," Jesse grumbles. "I'll be fine."

Barnes shakes his head like he expected such a response. He pulls on gloves, then goes about cleaning and anesthetizing the wound before sewing it closed. Jesse stares resolutely ahead, his jaw tight.

The doctor is just finishing when Made stirs. He groans, his eyes slowly drifting open. He blinks around at us. "What ... they got away?"

"Yep," says Asher.

"Where's Walker?"

"They took him," I tell him, struggling to keep my tone level.

Made frowns, taking in this development. His leg shifts and he groans. "I don't suppose you could set a broken leg?"

Barnes turns on him and pales. "Absolutely not. I can tell just looking at you it's broken in at least two places. You likely need surgery if it's shattered. Good God, people. I'm a private physician, not a miracle worker!"

Made shifts uncomfortably in his chair. "Then we'll have to table the rest of the debrief until I've been treated."

"I've already got a medevac helicopter on the way," says Bianchi, still tapping away on her phone. "And a transport to take the rest of us to the hospital. My other agents, here, need attention as well."

"Finally, someone with sense," says Barnes.

Bianchi flicks a look at him. "No, just efficiency so we can return to the task at hand as quickly as possible."

"How are we going to find Ford?" I ask, no longer able to bite my tongue now that the most urgent of medical care has been administered.

Made winces as another wave of pain takes him. "We'll get the men we captured last night to give up Chakrii's location. It will have to wait until I'm in better shape—"

"I'm already on it," says Bianchi. "I'm having them moved into interrogation rooms as we speak."

"We want to be present during those conversations," says Jesse.

"So do I," I say quickly.

Marco turns to me. "Absolutely not. Alessandra, this is no place for you."

I barely look at him. "I'm not leaving until he's back. This is not open to discussion. What happens once we find out Chakrii's location?"

Bianchi says, "What always happens. We go in and get him out."

"You'll need a diversion for that, won't you? To give you time to find him?" I ask.

"Yes."

I nod. "You'll use me."

CHAPTER THIRTY-TWO

FORD

The men are efficient; I'll give them that.

I've barely been taken when I'm hustled onto a helicopter a few miles from the scene of the crash. At first, I figure we're headed to the Golden Lotus.

But they head off in the wrong direction. We're going elsewhere. With dread, I analyze the men who've taken me for any sign of momentary weakness, a lapse in judgment for even a second. Any instant I can utilize to disable them and make my escape.

There are none.

These men appear more experienced than the individuals we dealt with outside the consulate or at my resort. They may even be ex-Naval Special Warfare Command, which would really be disappointing, because they're the Thai equivalent of the SEALs. Chakrii has finally pulled out the big guns.

In any case, it's going to be a damn bitch escaping them.

My eyes squeeze shut as I try to erase the mental

picture of Jesse bleeding out on the ground while they dragged me away. Bianchi was trying to fight her way to him, but no one was getting through.

Christ, what if he's dead? It looked like a clean round through the shoulder, but everything happened so fast I can't be sure. All I cared about was defending the line until Tucker and Asher cleared the way forward for Lessa.

She should be on the plane by now.

Thank God for that. Getting captured was worth it if we got her out. Nothing else matters but that. If only I could have said goodbye ... Fuck, I miss her already. Even had we managed to get her there with no trouble, I would have never seen her again.

With being captured, that's all but a certainty. If I can't find a way to escape, I won't be alive much longer.

Someone cuffs me over the head. I swear and glare at the asshole who stares at me expressionlessly from behind dark sunglasses.

"You. Time to leave." He drags me out of the helicopter. We've landed at another airport, this one hidden by overgrown vegetation.

This must be a drug runway, used for the transport of any number of illicit goods. No way this place is listed with any official aviation authority.

It's also my last opportunity for escape. Once they get me on a plane, I could be sent anywhere.

Testing the bonds around my wrists reveals little hope for snapping them; the man who tied me knew what he was doing. This won't be easy.

Seven men are situated around me in a loose circle,

firmly gripping their rifles. Each surveils the area with extreme alertness. Getting away will take a miracle, but I'm attempting it anyway.

Lacing my hands together, I swing up toward the man standing next to me, using my hands as a club. I catch him in the Adam's apple. He bends over, hacking, as I slam my fists down on top of his back while simultaneously swinging my knee up into his stomach.

He groans, but being the consummate professional these men clearly are, he doesn't loosen his grip on the rifle. I attempt to steal it anyway, not that I'll be able to use it much with my hands tied.

My fingers don't even reach the gun before I'm tackled to the ground. The butt of a rifle slams into my head and stars burst in my eyes. A second later, darkness descends over me.

I STARTLE AWAKE IN A CELL. Groaning, I wipe the ice water out of my eyes, the better to glare at the man who just tossed the bucket of frigid water all over me. Dick.

Christ in hell, where am I? This dank cell is a grimy piece of shit. And is that ... yes, that is a rat. Awesome. This shithole easily rivals some of the places we were inserted into during the Raqqa campaign.

Unease skitters through me. That's not something I want to compare my present situation to.

Another bucket of ice water lands on me. Sputtering, I shoot to my feet.

"Hey, asshole, I'm already awake!" I shout, flicking the water off me and hoping the source of it wasn't too unsanitary.

My jailor sneers at me. "That is because you stink."

"Fuck off," I snarl, although in the heat of this cell, I'm not exactly fresh. I reach up with my bound hands to rub my face, my fingers gently probing the lump I received when they knocked me out. Shit, that hurts. I'm lucky I don't have a concussion.

"Where am I? And how long was I unconscious?"

Quicker than my battered head can process, the man leaps forward and kicks me in the stomach. I topple to the floor, heaving and swearing. I roll onto my back, unwilling to let this asshole out of my sight as I struggle to draw air back into my lungs.

He hauls me to my feet which is no mean feat considering my size.

"You are not in a position to ask questions."

He drags me out of the cell. When I try to resist, he smacks me in the head where I'm injured. I bend in half, dazed, wondering if the precision of his punch means he's originally the person who knocked me out. He's dressed like a prison guard, so I doubt it.

"Where are you taking me?" I demand, still trying to shake sense into my head after being hit yet again.

The man grins at me, the expression feral. Fucking fantastic. This will be fun.

"The Golden Dragon has requested your presence," he says with great ceremony, as if expecting me to be excited about this dubious honor. "However, before we bring you to him, we must make you presentable."

Presentable? What? Yeah, right. Pretty sure his definition of that and mine are two separate things.

Sure enough, I'm taken into a room where three very tall, very brawny men await. They chain my bound hands to the table in the center of the room and then work me over. Each fist lands with precision. I receive one very thorough beating.

When I attempt to kick out in a vain attempt to defend myself, they snag shackles around my ankles and then beat me there, too. None of the blows create any lasting damage. I'll be bruised for days, but any internal bleeding won't be life-threatening. Instead, it's a steady procession of fists, landing one after the other, until my entire body feels as though it's been tenderized.

This is about humiliation. Chakrii and I have been at odds for two years now, and here I am, finally his captive. He won't let me forget that, and as I futilely try to free myself from my restraints, I definitely don't.

After they've finished beating me to their hearts' content, I'm stripped and blasted with a hose, the water just as freezing as the buckets. They laugh at my shriveled state; I stare down at the mottled bruises already forming on my naked skin, and with weary resignation accept the fact that this is only the beginning.

One of the men tosses a crumpled white linen suit at me, cut of expensive cloth that's all the more mocking due to the fact that I must wear it while aching with pain. They unbind my hands long enough so I can dress; I'm too weak to even consider resisting. Pulling the clothes onto my wet body is a struggle, one final insult to my beating.

I'm rebound, then marched down a hall and up a flight of stairs. They must be keeping me in the basement. Trying to get a sense of my surroundings, I catalogue the area outside every window, but all I see is a city, which is answer enough.

We're in Bangkok.

The men deposit me in what might otherwise be called a throne room, were this not the home of a criminal. I'm shoved into a chair at a long and ornate dining table, then tied to the arms; even my ankles are shackled to the legs.

"Chakrii afraid I may do something to him?" I ask dryly.

For this I'm rewarded with another punch to the face. Lovely. My right eye is already swelling up; we might as well work on the left, too.

They step away, fading back along the walls. I slump angrily back against my chair, furious to be in this situation. The beating will make it much more difficult to escape.

Thank Christ I was taken in her place.

I shudder, thinking of all the horrible things they might have done to her had she been captured. A beating might have been the least of her worries. No matter what happens to me next, I must ensure they never find her.

Because he won't stop looking for her. He'll want to torment me with her suffering before he finally kills me. Not that I'll let him do it.

I've lapsed into a painful torpor when Chakrii finally enters, his walking stick rapping smartly with every other step. The asshole smiles, entirely unaffected by the glare I send his way.

"Mr. Walker. We meet again at last."

"Not too soon for me," I grunt.

Chakrii emits a distasteful noise. "Let's be civil, shall we?"

"No."

Chakrii holds out a cigar that one of his staff rushes to light, his gaze still locked on me. "But finally together again after all these years. Surely that must count for something?"

I sneer at him, knowing it's a stupid thing to do and yet not caring one tiny bit whether I piss him off. This ends for me only one way if my friends fail to rescue me.

"You killed someone I loved," I snap. "So no, I have no desire for civility."

Chakrii takes a thoughtful puff on his cigar. "You can't find it in yourself to let it go, then."

I laugh bitterly. "You know I cannot."

"But surely you knew your actions would require a retaliation of my own?" he says mildly, blowing smoke up toward the ceiling. His hand tightens around that fucking walking stick.

How I ache to beat him to death with it.

Chakrii notices the direction of my gaze and smiles as if he knows my train of thought. "It is a shame," he says thoughtfully. "You are a considerable man, Mr. Walker. As I am. We could have accomplished great things together."

I scoff. "Even if you hadn't killed her, I never would have worked with you. I spent nearly my entire adult life protecting innocents from monsters like you. That's why

I've made it my mission to fuck up your operation. Nothing could convince me to do otherwise. Especially not now, after what you've done."

Chakrii sighs, stamping out his half-finished cigar in disappointment. "Yes, you always seemed a man whose morals could not be bought for the right price."

"Did you come to that conclusion before or after I killed your nephew? Perhaps if you'd gotten a clue sooner, we could have avoided the bullshit."

Chakrii's expression grows furiously cold. "You have insulted me one too many times!" he hisses. "Bringing that up, as if it is *nothing*. You have taken the one thing I cannot replace, no matter how much money I acquire."

"Well, back at ya, asshole," I drawl, knowing I've pushed him well past the point of no return and just not giving a fuck.

Chakrii suddenly grows sly, his fury hidden behind a mask of smugness. "Oh, well, but that is the interesting part of all this, isn't it? You've stupidly allowed yourself to fall into the same situation a second time. How happy I am knowing I shall be able to enact your punishment not once, but twice."

"Speak plainly," I snap.

Chakrii smiles. "By all reports, you love her, don't you? That bitch, the Italian heiress. Such a whore, parading herself around my own resort and then declining my invitation. Insulting me to my face. And in front of half my associates, too. I had to coordinate three assassinations just to keep them in line. All because of some woman. A woman I've failed to take three times now. Infuriating."

"Your inability to inspire loyalty is not Alessandra's fault."

"Perhaps not, but it is yours. You see, I find myself with a delightful opportunity. You must know you are here because I intend to kill you. Slowly. Painfully. But purposefully. What everyone in my organization shall learn from *your* death is that no matter how long it seems that a person has gotten away with it, no one will harm me and live to tell about it."

Chakrii leans forward, his eyes glinting with triumph. I remain expressionless, refusing to give him the satisfaction.

"And what they will learn from her death is that I am not a man to be trifled with. I am not a man to be insulted. My reputation is not to be tarnished.

"The irony is, I never would have been interested in her had she not first dined with you the night of her arrival. She would have remained a random guest. But you just *had* to join her, so soon after you intercepted my shipment. Did you think I wouldn't put it together? Of course I knew it was you. Terribly obvious."

"I *wanted* you to know it was me."

"Yes, well, I'm having the last laugh, aren't I? In any case, I needed to teach you a lesson, and she was so conveniently right there."

"We were complete strangers when that happened. She meant nothing to me."

Chakrii laughs. "Yes, indeed. She *meant* nothing to you. Past tense. But she does now, doesn't she? I had hoped you two would develop feelings for each other. I never believed her line that having dinner with you was happenstance. It was clear she liked you, and she's not hard to look at. Odds were good that, even if you didn't already want to fuck her, eventually you would.

"When she smuggled herself off my resort—I *will* find the person who helped her, I assure you—I figured she would end up at yours. Where else could she go? I own the rest of this city, if not in actuality, then by proxy. While I wanted her right away, it could only work to my advantage to let the two of you spend time together. Sometimes others can clearly see what we refuse to believe ourselves, yes? It all worked out so nicely."

"Fuck you."

His face darkens. "Be careful how you speak to me, or I shall prolong her agony before I execute her."

I fall silent.

He laughs again. "See? So simple. Of course, she also insulted me herself. She must be punished for that as well. A second strike against her. She must not be particularly lucky, eh? If she had just shut her mouth and dined with me, I may have seen fit to be merciful, to not visit your sins upon her."

"You never would have left her alone. As you said, she was a way to get to me."

Chakrii shrugs. "Alas, we'll never know. But her death will serve another benefit, namely that my organization will learn that if they ever do try to betray me, I will not only kill them, but all their loved ones as well. You would think they'd understand such things already, but people can be surprisingly stupid. And who knows, perhaps after I kill her, I'll kill those friends of yours. They're still in the country, after all. We wouldn't want them to get in their heads to avenge your deaths, would we?"

A sick feeling slides through me. "They're not here. They left with Alessandra when she flew out. So you won't find any of them. You failed, Chakrii. Go fuck yourself."

His smile grows wider. "Oh, but she didn't leave."

My breath catches. Chakrii smiles in triumph.

"Yes, that's right. When she learned that you had been taken, she refused to leave. So you see, your great sacrifice in coming here was all for naught. And she will surely walk right into my trap, thinking she can save you. Poetic really. If predictable."

"Harm her in any way, and I will beat you to death with that cane," I snarl, but fear has sweat breaking out on my brow.

Chakrii leans back in his chair, satisfied. "And finally, there will be something *you* learn, Mr. Walker. I will make you watch as I execute her, and you will learn that you are not untouchable. That you can be more miserable than you can possibly imagine. When I kill you, you will welcome death."

CHAPTER THIRTY-THREE

ALESSANDRA

"We finally got one to turn!" Made says triumphantly, wheeling himself in from one of the interrogation rooms.

Asher and Tucker leap to their feet. Jesse stays seated, still stiff from his wound. While we tried to convince them, neither Made nor Bianchi would let us sit in on the interrogation, so we've been forced to wait outside in another part of the Italian consulate, which has allowed Interpol to use its facilities since there isn't an adequate office in Phuket.

"It only took two days," Asher drawls, but he's still grinning. "What did he say? Where's Ford?"

Made rolls his wheelchair over to the table and plops his folder down, wincing. The car accident broke his leg in three places, requiring surgery and a full leg cast, but it could have been way worse. In fact, it *was* for the two Interpol agents who died sitting on the driver's side when the other car broadsided them.

Add that to the list of crimes Chakrii has to answer for.

"So? Where is he?" Tucker asks.

"Well, we captured the man before the attack heading to the airport, so he can't know for certain, but he believes they've relocated to Bangkok. That's where they were supposed to take you after they took you from the resort, Alessandra. And it's Chakrii's base of operations, although he spends a lot of time in Phuket now too."

I shoot to my feet, arms folded across my chest as I begin pacing. My brother's gaze drills into my back as I move; he's still furious with me for staying here. He doesn't know for certain why I remained, although he must suspect. The last thing I'm telling him is that I'm involved with Ford. He'd lecture me that our family back in Rome expects me to marry an Italian—no matter that he set off a firestorm when he married his American executive assistant a couple years ago.

Like brother like sister, I guess. Marco and I are the only Vitales who picked someone with our heart and not our head.

"Do we have the address?" I ask.

"Yes," says Bianchi. "I had to threaten him with a prison term so long he'd never live to see the light of day as a free man again, but we got an address out of him. It's surprisingly close to the royal palace; Chakrii's poor attempt to elevate his station above that of a common street thug, I'm sure."

"So what's the plan?" Jesse asks her.

She considers him for a long moment, her gaze trailing down to his shoulder and then back up to his face. Jesse's gaze, however, never strays from her face.

"That's what we need to decide," Bianchi says. "And another thing. We finally got the woman at the consulate to admit who paid her to set up your appointment."

"And who was it?" I ask.

"An Interpol agent," Made says quietly. "One of the men on my team that's investigating Chakrii."

Tucker whistles. "Damn."

"We're sending agents to pick him up now," says Bianchi, "but surprise, surprise, he's in the wind. Either that or Chakrii assassinated him because we were getting too close."

"It just doesn't make any sense," Made says. "Agent Onsi was always so dedicated."

Bianchi rolls her eyes. "That's the job of a mole."

I return to the table. "Well, we can't do anything about that now. We need to decide what we'll do once we're in there with Ford. I've already told you I'll act as bait."

"You absolutely will not," my brother snaps. I look at him, daring him to say something further. He does, "I'm not letting my baby sister sacrifice herself to some mobster. I won't let anything happen to you, and there's the family company to think about."

I wave him off. "You already unofficially took it over when the board kicked out Father. If something happened to me, they'd just make it official."

He pales. "No, I'm going to run it from New York, like I've always done. But you still need to handle things in Italy. There's a whole bunch of people—"

"Now isn't the time to discuss this," I cut in, "it's hardly a relevant topic to everyone. They don't need to watch us bicker over our line of succession."

Marco's face darkens with fury. "The hell we're not discussing it. You're talking about walking straight into the lair of a criminal, a man who actively wishes you harm! No man could possibly be worth that kind of risk."

Asher sucks in a sharp breath. Tucker drops his gaze to the table. Jesse's jaw looks like it could cut granite, but his attention remains locked on Bianchi, who's tapping away on her phone.

Is my brother serious right now? What a thing to say in front of all his friends, the men who have also sacrificed so much to defend their country, losing many men in the process.

Idiot.

"Ford is worth it to me," I say quietly.

Asher releases his breath on a slow exhale. Tucker grins. Jesse gives me a look of admiration. My brother glances around at everyone and seems to realize what he's said. He curses under his breath, extending a placating hand toward me.

"Look, I meant no offense. What I'm trying to say is that you're hopelessly unqualified to attempt something like this, Lessa. These people need to handle it. You're liable to do more damage than good."

I chew on my lip, because out of everything, this is the one point I've already considered. What if I make things worse? What if my trying to help only gets Ford hurt—or worse?

But I can't just stand by and let everyone else risk their

lives. Not when the reason we're in this mess in the first place is because of me. If I hadn't met Chakrii that day, none of this would have ever happened. Walking out now just because I'm scared or can conveniently use the excuse of being a potential liability seems ignominious at best and downright cowardly at worst.

Ford would move heaven and earth to get me out, and I'm not about to forsake him. Even if I don't know what I'm doing, there's bound to be a way I can help.

"I'm not proposing I go in as part of the assault team," I say calmly. "But you'll need a diversion, won't you?"

Made and Bianchi seem reluctant to answer with my brother present, but eventually Bianchi shrugs and says, "It always helps. Better than a straight assault, which they'll surely be expecting. And frankly, since Chakrii already wants you, you would be a more useful diversion than most. He'll *want* to be diverted."

"But he'll also be expecting it," Marco says impatiently. "All of you are insane for actually contemplating this. You, most of all, sis."

"Marco," I say. "I'm twenty-nine years old. I can make my own decisions."

"And Ford is thirty-eight, right? That's *definitely* old enough to make the one he already made."

Asher stalks around the table and gets right in Marco's face. "The decision where he chose your sister's well-being over his own? That one? Didn't anyone ever teach you a little gratitude?"

Marco's mouth thins. "Yes. But I've also been taught to understand when I'm ill-equipped to deal with a problem."

"Which is why you hired a bunch of men to handle it for you," says Jesse mildly.

"That's right," Marco snaps. "And if my sister actually goes through with this, you better believe they'll be going right along with her."

They all turn to me. I shrug. I don't actually have a problem with that. The more people we have available for this, the better our chance of success.

The guy who introduced himself as Diamond cuts in, "You would do better to use us as part of the insertion team; this Chakrii guy doesn't know about us. If we're the group tasked with getting out your friend, and all of you show up with her as part of the diversion, then he won't assume you have anyone else with you."

"Absolutely not," says Tucker. "No way. We're not leaving someone else to save our guy. No offense."

"It's the logical thing to do, though," says Bianchi. "Besides, the two of you aren't enough for this situation, anyway. You might as well stay with Alessandra and let the other men team up with our agents."

"Two of you?" Jesse echoes softly, his gaze locked on her.

She turns to him. "Of course. You're shot. It's not like you'll be participating."

Something dangerous glitters in Jesse's eyes. "You expect me to sit back while my brother is in danger? After he got caught protecting me when I took a hit?"

Bianchi stares him down. "You've been *shot*."

"A flesh wound."

"A liability."

Jesse grows still. "You think I'm a *liability*?"

Bianchi says nothing, which is answer enough. Jesse's face goes gray. In anger? Dismay? Embarrassment? It's impossible to tell, but I'm putting my money on his being pissed.

Bianchi dismisses him, which only serves to piss him off more. She surveys the rest of the room. "Now. Under what pretext are we going to have Alessandra meet with Chakrii? If she just shows up, offering herself to him, he'll be suspicious. That's far too easy."

"My sister isn't—"

"Actually, I've thought of that already," I say.

"Really?" Made asks curiously. He and Bianchi trade a glance. "What were you thinking?"

I send my brother an apologetic glance. He won't like this. "We use our company's connections to contact the mob, and arrange a meeting between their organization and Chakrii's, with me as the intermediary. We could play it like the Italians want to expand to this part of the world and are looking for a new partner. Even if he doesn't fall for it, Chakrii can't afford to piss off a rival crime syndicate. He'll have to take the meeting if the Italians approach, if only to prevent a turf war."

A pin could be heard dropping, it's so silent. Made and Bianchi look at me thoughtfully. Marco's security team looks on with open admiration. And Ford's brothers have huge shit-eating grins on their faces.

But my brother? My brother's pissed.

"*Christ*, Alessandra. Are you that dead-set on putting your life in danger? As if you don't have enough problems, now you want to involve the Family, too? Are you out of your mind?"

"Your family is related to the mafia?" Bianchi asks with just a little too much interest.

I remember that this woman's job is to put away Family associates back home. Hastily, I say, "No. It's not like that. We know a guy who knows a guy. You know what I mean. The mafia is never difficult to get in touch with when you really need them, you know?"

"But what incentive do they have to help you?" Made asks. "This would in essence be a fake meeting, right? They won't be very pleased to discover your contacting them was merely a ruse."

"I haven't thought that far," I admit. "But maybe they can just fight it out. Or we can be honest, and they'll do it as a personal favor to my family. They would ... it would be advantageous for them to be owed a favor from one of the largest media companies in the country. A way to provide cover to the public when inevitably some scandal of theirs breaks. Something like that. It doesn't have to be a win-lose situation."

Marco runs his hands through his hair. "I can't believe this. This is absolutely mental."

"You can always go home," I say sweetly. "Leave the jet and I'll meet you in New York in a few days."

Marco glares at me. "Absolutely not."

"Well, then get on board," I snap, "because this is what I do, remember? Strategy. I've done it for our company for years, and this isn't anything different. I may not know how to shoot a person or save someone who's been kidnapped, but you know very well I'm excellent at finding advantageous solutions for all parties involved during negotiations. That's why *I'm* the head of strategic partnerships, and you run the US subsidiary. It's about time I did something useful here."

I turn back to Made and Bianchi, waiting for the verdict. The rest of the room waits in silence as the two of them consider. Finally, Made turns to me and says, "Set it up."

CHAPTER THIRTY-FOUR

FORD

Chakrii never allows me a moment's comfort. Every morning I'm brought into the room with the table and beaten. Some days are worse than others, leading me to wonder whether the severity of each beating stems from Chakrii's mood that day. After they're finished with me, I'm hauled back into my cell in the same linen suit they gave me when I arrived. It's decidedly worse for the wear by now and perfectly mirrors how I feel.

Gingerly I roll to my feet, the shitty cot that's barely an excuse for a bed creaking ominously. I half expect it to collapse every time I sit down, but this grimy floor is so disgusting I don't dare chance sitting on it.

My body protests every movement. Fortunately, in the seven days I've been here, they haven't hit my face again—Chakrii must have told them he doesn't want to stare at my mangled mug—so I can see out of my eyes again, although I assume there must still be nasty bruising around them.

But that's the least of my concerns; today is the day that I escape.

With nothing better to do and much motivation, I learned every last detail of the guards' schedules. One of them should be coming along any minute now to take me for my morning beating. For the next twenty minutes or so, they'll gleefully punch me anywhere that can be concealed under clothing. Then I'll be stripped down and hosed with the oh-so-delightful frigid water, reclothed in the same disgusting outfit I've been wearing, and then returned to my shitty cell, where I'll be fed a shitty meal of rice and not much else.

Beating me must have become boring because only one man serves as my daily brutalizer now. After I disable him, I'll have nearly half an hour before anyone thinks to verify whether I'm back in my cell. By then I'll be long gone.

I inch my way down the length of my cot, wary of getting to my feet when all it will accomplish is make me dizzy. I must conserve my energy for this next critical hour. If I can escape this compound, then I can lose myself in the busy streets of Bangkok.

Reaching between my legs, I grope around the underside of the cot until I find the jagged piece of metal jutting out of the bottom that I discovered during a search of my cell. I pull my wrists apart as far as I can manage with the zip-ties, then rub the plastic against the metal shard.

It's slow going. A few times I miss and accidentally scratch myself. Blood pools around my binding, making it slippery and prolonging the process.

"Come on, you stupid fuck," I growl. "Break already."

Footsteps ring out down the hall. Shit. The guard is ahead of schedule. Fucking figures they'd change their schedule on the day I decide to escape.

"For fuck's sake," I mutter, working furiously. My plan falls to shit if I don't break this binding in the next few seconds. With a great heave, I scrape it against the shard one final time. The bond releases with such force I fall forward; I only prevent myself from falling face-first onto the floor by throwing out my blissfully free hands at the last moment.

There's no time to rejoice over my freedom. As quickly as I can manage in my battered state, I grab the zip-tie off the floor and rearrange myself on my cot. Wrapping the tie across the back of my left wrist, I place my left hand over my right and grab the ends with my right fingers, my hands dangling between my knees. On close inspection it will be obvious I freed myself, but that's more time than I need. I slump over, my head down, pretending to be utterly dejected, which couldn't be further from the truth.

"Hey, you." The guard rattles the door. "Time to reintroduce my fist to your face."

I ignore him, still slouched over. *Come on, come on.*

The guard unlocks my door, the keys rattling as he shoves them back into his pocket. "Given up already? That didn't last long," he snarls.

My teeth grind together but I remain still. Come on, asshole. Come get me. Just a little farther ...

The guard growls in frustration. "Get over here."

I don't move.

He stomps over to my dejected form. Just as he reaches

down to grab my arm, my hand flies out and punches him in the balls. He howls, doubling over. I slap my other palm over his mouth, trying to muffle his caterwauling, then punch him in his Adam's apple. The guard emits a gurgling, choked sound. I surge upward, hand still clapped over this mouth, my thumb and forefinger pinching his nose as my other fist slams three vicious jabs into his stomach.

The guard drops, but he's not completely out yet. I straddle him, wrapping a hand around his throat and squeezing. He struggles, weakly attempting to buck me off, but I grind down harder; this is my only chance to escape.

His thrashes grow weaker and weaker until he finally passes out. I rap his head twice against the ground to ensure he won't be waking any time soon.

For a second, I take a breather; my breath comes out a rasping wheeze. Anyone will hear me from a mile away. My ribs protest with every battered inhale; my knuckles are split and swollen. Shit, that hurt. I drag myself off his body and search his pockets, smiling grimly when I find another zip-tie.

The cot isn't going to work; it isn't bolted to the floor. Grumbling under my breath, I drag the dead weight over to the cell bars. I grab his wrist and shove it up against one of the bars, then tie him to it with the zip-tie. All the times he delighted in hurting me flash through my mind and I squeeze the zip-tie as tight as it will go. He'll have lost feeling in the hand long before he ever regains consciousness. Get fucked, asshole.

The man thus incapacitated, I search him again for a firearm, but the asshole surprisingly isn't wearing one.

Damn it. Chakrii probably ordered them not to carry in the likelihood this very thing happened.

Well, fuck it. I can get out of here unarmed. I dig into his pockets again, pulling out his set of keys. There isn't time to figure out which key goes to the lock on my cell door. Instead, I creep out into the hall and close the door as quietly as possible. My gaze stays resolutely steered clear of the security cameras lodged in a corner of the ceiling; looking up is the surest way to draw attention to my face.

Shoving the keys in my pocket, I stagger down the hall, trying to walk as normally as possible and yet still failing. I just need to make it to the end of the hall. Then I can climb the stairs and make my way out of here. Just a little bit farther. A little farther and I'll—

"Hey!" someone cries behind me.

Fuck. I take off running, my bare feet pounding down the hall. Just a little farther. Footsteps slam behind me; whoever it is can run faster than I can in my injured state. I throw a glance over my shoulder to discover two guards are sprinting toward me. The door to the stairs is just a few yards away. I can make it. I just need to—

The door flies open. A third guard leaps out in front of me, holding a baton. Shit fuck. I jerk backward, trying to slow my momentum, but I'm sprinting too fast. I literally run right into him. We topple to the floor. I thrash out, trying to slam his head into the ground. If I can disable him, then I can steal his baton and use it against the guards who are running up behind me.

It's no use; I've barely wrestled the baton away from the guard when the other two land on top of me. I kick and punch as best as I can, but I'm too injured and malnourished to put up the kind of fight I'm capable of. They rip the baton from my hands and shove me onto the ground. A moment later my arms are yanked behind my back and the restraints once more are tightened around my wrists. A frustrated roar escapes me. To get so close!

And yet, for that third guard to jump out from the stairwell so quickly, he must have been posted there. As soon as I came through, he would have been on me. I wouldn't have made it out.

The guards swear and shout as they haul me to my feet. I receive an elbow to the stomach and back. With a groan, my body goes limp, too battered to put up more of a fight.

"Fuck you," I pant as they literally drag me down the hall. "And your asshole buddy I dropped in my cell."

Someone elbows me in the ribs. "Shut up."

They drag me through the door into the stairwell.

"Where are you taking me?" I croak, stumbling up the stairs as quickly as I can. It isn't fast enough; a moment later I'm lifted and carried up the stairs.

Chakrii stares at me with a bemused expression when they haul me back into his special little throne room. I'm tossed down into one of the chairs, my back screaming in protest.

"Surely such theatrics is unnecessary," Chakrii says. "Untie him."

"But sir—"

"I said, untie him," Chakrii snaps. "We're about to receive guests, and I wouldn't want it said I don't treat my prisoners with respect."

I bite back a snort. If the man is stupid enough to allow me free, I won't give him an excuse to change his mind.

"We caught him trying to escape, sir," the guard says, glaring at me as he nevertheless reaches around behind me and unsnaps my restraints. "If you hadn't requested us to retrieve him when you did, he may have gotten away."

"Is that so?" says Chakrii, turning his attention to me. I sneer at him as I rub my wrists. He better understand I'm taking advantage of the slightest opportunity. "Oh, but I wouldn't worry about it. He won't want to miss this."

It's a blatant attempt to bait me, but I still find myself asking, "Miss what?"

Chakrii smiles. "A meeting with your lover, of course. I must say, it took them long enough. An entire week just to figure out my location and engineer a reason to meet with me. Rather a disappointment, don't you agree?"

"You're lying," I snarl. No way she's coming here. My brothers wouldn't let her do such a thing. This is Chakrii fucking with me. Throwing me off so I'm not tempted to find a way to escape. Something. Alessandra wouldn't *actually*—

"I can see you don't believe me," says Chakrii, smiling wider.

"I don't believe a single word out of your lying mouth, no."

"That's too bad," Chakrii chuckles, "because I was just about to tell you that she should be here any minute, with those awful soldier friends of yours, all in the hope of breaking you out of here."

Dread slides through me. No, I can't believe it. They

wouldn't betray me like that. They *know* the reason I'm here is because I wanted her to get away. But ...

Chakrii nods. "Yes, I can see you begin to believe it. And why shouldn't you? I've known about your movements from the start, haven't I? I knew when that woman was heading to the consulate. I knew precisely when to strike your resort. I knew what route you'd take to the airport. So why would you doubt me now when I tell you she's coming here?"

I remain silent, refusing to acknowledge that he has a point. We *have* known from the start that there is a mole within either Interpol or the Italian government. We just haven't found him.

"So she's coming," I shrug, hoping I can downplay it. "So what? Fine. It'll be that much easier to escape while you're distracted."

Chakrii shakes his head, sighing dramatically. He slaps his hand twice against the table and withdraws a cigar. One of his many servants scurries out of nowhere and elaborately lights it for him. Chakrii's attention remains locked on me the entire time. Fuck this asshole using cigars to intimidate me. It doesn't work.

But Chakrii hasn't finished. "Your little woman, Alessandra, has taken it into her head to contact the Italian mafia, of all things. Imagine her thinking she could facilitate a meeting between their organization and mine. Like I'd ever work with such people. I don't need a partner; I already dictate my terms to everyone. They obey *me*.

"But even more implausibly, they intend to send in a second group to free you while we have our special little meeting. It's all a lie. Imagine what their surprise will be when *I* surprise *them* with a second team of my own, carefully hidden exactly where they believe you're being held. It's almost too easy, really. Boring. From the start, I gave you more than enough opportunity to flush out my spy, but apparently, no one managed it."

Chakrii leans toward me, his smile so irritating I want to leap across this table and throttle him. I'd do it, if I thought it would make any difference. But his guards would shoot me before I made it to the door.

"Tell me, Mr. Walker. Are you looking forward to my men slaughtering everyone who's come to save you? Because I certainly am. How do you think it will ruin their carefully laid plans when instead of you being somewhere else, I have you here with me now? It's never been so easy in my life. I am going to kill every last one of you and enjoy each second of it."

I launch myself at him; one of the guards slams me back into my seat. Chakrii just smiles that sickening smile and glances at his watch.

A knock comes at the door.

His smile turns feral. "Ah yes. Right on schedule."

He motions to the door. One of the guards jumps to open it. I watch, my breath sawing in and out of my chest, as not only Alessandra, but Tucker and Asher enter. Even Jesse walks stiffly behind them.

Alessandra scans the room. Her eyes land on me in horror.

CHAPTER THIRTY-FIVE

ALESSANDRA

He looks *terrible*.

I ache to run to him, to smooth my shaking fingers over his bruised face, to inspect every inch of him to assure myself he's okay. But any fool can tell he isn't fine. He's badly beaten and has lost weight in the week he's been captured.

I am going to kill Chakrii.

A quick glance at Ford's friends shows they're thinking along the same lines. I'm tempted to let them, to just unleash them on this room until nothing is left.

What do we do now? Ford wasn't supposed to be present at this meeting. What do Marco's men and the Interpol agents do now? We can't very well have a diversion when the object the diversion is for is in the same room!

Asher mutters something under his breath as he scans the room. I throw my shoulders back and glare at Chakrii; our plan may have already fallen off the rails, but we are going to get Ford out of here. The second team can fight their way to us if they need to. Even if it means shooting someone myself, I'm not leaving here without him.

Chakrii gets to his feet. "Right on time, I see." He makes a sweeping motion toward the banquet table. "Please take a seat."

I turn to the man beside me. Luciano, a member of the Family out of Sicily. It took us days to convince him to come here. Part of me thinks he's doing it for fun, in addition to accepting the future favor Marco and I promised we'd do for him.

As if being a mobster isn't enough drama.

Luciano extends an arm solicitously toward me. I stiffen but wrap my hand around his bicep. He leads me to a seat across the table from Ford. I keep my eyes averted; if I stare at those bruises, I'll lose it. I can't afford the distraction, as much as I yearn to go to him. Chakrii will take advantage of any second of weakness.

Luciano folds himself into the seat next to me and carelessly unbuttons the coat of his three-piece suit. He rakes a hand through his hair, then smiles at Chakrii.

"So," he says. "We want to use you to move some product. Arms, right? And a little women and blow thrown in as well?"

Chakrii blinks at him. For fuck's sake, Luciano! Chakrii would resent any implication that he's not the ringleader at this little circus. Luciano just insulted him thirty seconds into the meeting. At this rate, we won't have enough time for me or one of Ford's friends—hell, or even Ford—to think of a way to get him out of here. Luciano will goad Chakrii into attacking us long before we have the opportunity.

"You seem to be laboring under the impression I'm interested in having a partner," Chakrii says coldly.

Luciano smiles at him, revealing a row of predatory white teeth. "So you aren't hoping to sell our arms in this country, then?"

Something flashes in Chakrii's eyes, but it disappears an instant later. I glance at Asher and Tucker, who have taken up a position behind Ford. They shake their heads, silently telling me this Italian mobster may be more of a liability than an asset.

My gaze drops lower, colliding with Ford's. His gaze drills into me, trying to telegraph something. His eyes track over my face, as if assuring himself I'm alright. Something intense brews behind those green eyes. But I can't focus on that right now; though it pains me, I dismiss him.

"Let's cut to the chase," I say coolly. "We're not here to insult each other."

Chakrii considers me, smiling faintly. "And why *are* you here, then?"

I brush imaginary lint off my skirt. "To arrange for his release, of course."

Chakrii laughs. "Is that so?"

"Obviously," I say coldly. "There's no other reason I would be caught dead in a room with you."

Chakrii bangs his golden walking stick on the floor. The door opens and a group of men stream in, holding rifles. We're easily outnumbered two-to-one, and that's not including the fact that we're also outgunned. The concealed pistols strapped to Ford's men are nothing in comparison.

Chakrii turns back to me, then motions to his men.

"And what makes you think you have any negotiating power?"

"Because you wouldn't be so stupid as to assassinate one of the most powerful people in the Sicilian Family," Luciano says, looking bored. "It's not exactly good business practice, is it?"

Chakrii shrugs, the gesture indolent. "Perhaps not the best practice, but accidents can happen to anyone."

Luciano rolls his eyes. His head turns just far enough to glance at me. "You didn't say he would be so boring."

I blink. The energy in the room shifts, grows taut with acrimony. Chakrii stiffens and his men jerk upright, their rifles swinging toward us. Asher swears under his breath. Tucker folds his arms over his chest, a deep frown on his face. I can't see Jesse, who's come to stand behind me, but he can't be happy, either. Luciano's bodyguards, however, remain stone-faced, a silent wall before us. This can't be the first time they've witnessed their employer's antics.

"You would insult me in my own home?" Chakrii hisses. I swallow hard, reminded of that dinner long ago, how Chakrii seemingly changed in an instant from someone unremarkable to insanely dangerous.

"Luciano ..." I murmur.

Chakrii studies the two of us. A sly smile steals across his face, and he turns to Ford. "It seems we've both misread the situation, Mr. Walker. You have more competition than you've been led to believe."

Luciano slings an arm along the back of my chair and grins wickedly. "Well. She is gorgeous, isn't she? One of the finest women in my country. A woman without equal. All the men ache to touch her." He trails a finger along my shoulder, then down along my arm. "Few have managed to."

It takes everything in me not to react. That bastard. Ford's eyes are on me, questioning. I don't look at him. He's not the only one. I can feel the attention of his friends, too. They're all wondering if Luciano and I ever had something between us. If we *still* do. We never did—although I've met him at various functions and had to rebuff him every time, much to his displeasure.

But my family warned me off from him long ago. Even if they hadn't, I would have known better than to involve myself with the man, who is rumored to have made more than one of his so-called paramours disappear. When Luciano wants something, people scramble to give it to him. Being in the Family can do that. My disinterest in Luciano has only made him want me to submit to him more.

And now that I've asked him here and willingly stepped into his world? Well. He'll be even pushier.

But that doesn't matter. What matters is getting Ford out of here alive. Even if the hurt and betrayed look he's sending me now is the price I must pay to ensure he goes unharmed.

Chakrii suddenly laughs. Turning to Ford, he says snidely, "Oh, but this is perfect. She's not available to you after all, is she? That must be quite painful, Mr. Ford. How ironic. Tell me, how does it feel, knowing the person you've sacrificed so much for feels nowhere near what you do? That must hurt."

Ford glares at him.

"I would advise you to think twice before you insult her again. I wouldn't want to have to hurt you," Luciano says idly, softly stroking his finger down my arm a second time. I dig my nails into the soft underside of my wrist. Damn him! It's like he *wants* to antagonize Chakrii.

I still. But of course. That is exactly what he wants. The bastard probably hopes that this confrontation will end in a firefight—one that gets Ford killed. In Luciano's twisted mind, that would clear the way for him to swoop in, comforting me in my grief, paving the way for something to finally happen between us.

The sick fuck. It won't work.

I turn back to Chakrii. "My personal life can't possibly interest you. You're a businessman, and a successful one at that. So let us return to the task at hand. You are interested in expanding your shipping lane between Singapore and Kuala Lumpur, yes?"

Chakrii straightens. "How do you know that?"

I smile thinly. "Did you think I'd walk into this meeting without knowing about your organization? I'm not a fool, no matter what you think. So. It's my understanding that you've struggled to get a foothold in the waters outside this country. We are prepared to give you that."

Chakrii considers me, his mouth curving in a faint smile. "You've surprised me, Ms. Vitale. I somehow ... was not aware you were prepared to make such an offer. How do you propose to accomplish this?"

Luciano leans forward. "She won't do anything. I will. My outfit, that is. We are willing to bring you into our network. Your organization will be granted access to our people who transport goods around the world. That will allow you to establish a foothold in your neighboring countries with little risk. Once you've expanded your operation, you can then create your own smuggling network. In short, we are giving you a free ride for expansion. Risk free. Once it is profitable, you can then work on making it entirely your own."

I have to hand it to Luciano; it sounds good. Really good.

But it's all bullshit.

The Family has no footprint in Southeast Asia. They rely on the very network that Luciano is teasing Chakrii with; other people, other *criminals*, who are familiar with the area and can move illegal goods around with little effort. It wouldn't take much to verify the Family isn't a big player over here. Luciano is sticking his neck way out, and he's doing it entirely because I asked him.

Chakrii studies Luciano as several moments pass. Will he go for it? How much longer do we have to stall before the Interpol agents launch their offensive? What will they do since Ford is here with us? The basement cells Chakrii's man mentioned are no longer our target because the person we hoped to smuggle out is with us now.

"No."

Luciano tilts his head, surprised. I resist rolling my eyes. Luciano's likely never been told no in his life. Apart from me, that is.

"You are not interested in my proposal?" Luciano asks, finally lifting his hand from me as he straightens.

"I am not," Chakrii says. "It is not a real offer, after all."

"And why do you believe that?"

Chakrii dismisses Luciano and turns to me. He motions toward Ford, his eyes never leaving mine. "All this effort for one man. Tell me, is it worth it?"

Everyone turns to me. I shift in my chair. This is a trap, somehow. My eyes land on Ford, who stares back at me, silently trying to communicate something. *What? What are you saying?* But no answer comes to me.

"I wouldn't be here for no reason," I say cautiously.

Chakrii smiles, as if I've given him exactly what he wants. "Yes, that is so. And it really is remarkable, considering all of your problems have stemmed from this one man. After all, if I had never been told you dined with him that first night you arrived at my resort, I wouldn't have bothered with you. You were merely a means to an end. A way to torture Mr. Walker, here. And if you hadn't accepted my dinner invitation, you therefore would never have insulted me by later turning me down. All of this could have been avoided, had you only avoided *him*. My, my, does history repeat itself."

"How so?" I ask slowly.

Ford turns to me. "Ignore him. He's just trying to get in your head, Alessandra. You should leave. This has nothing to do with you. I don't want you involved. I can deal with him myself."

Seriously? He wants me to go? Just like that? After everything we shared together? Yeah, right. The man can barely breathe without wincing in pain, and he thinks he's going to fight his way out by himself. Ford and his hero complex. Well, he can't fight his way out this time. It's too late for that. He—all of us—are only getting out of here if we work together.

Chakrii laughs. "You two really are entertaining. So willing to sacrifice everything for the other. And you've only known each other for a few weeks. So tragic. Such little time to get to know one another. Tell me, Ms. Vitale, has it come up yet that your Ford was engaged to marry the very woman my own nephew had selected as his future bride?"

CHAPTER THIRTY-SIX

FORD

Alessandra turns to me, her expression unreadable. Furious with Chakrii for telling her, I say quietly, "She was terrified of his nephew. Achara had already broken it off with him by the time she met me."

"Mine is not a family you can simply *break off* from!" Chakrii shouts into the silence. Spittle flies from his lips as he heaves air into his mouth, his eyes bulging with rage as they lock on Alessandra. The change is instantaneous; one moment he is in control, and the next he's absolutely lost it. Have I ever seen him so enraged?

Only once before.

I launch out of the chair as Chakrii lunges for his walking stick. My hands collide with his throat as I barrel into him. His chair knocks over backwards; we're catapulted to the floor. Chakrii snarls, his hand tightening on the stick. My arm lifts just before he swings it down toward my back.

The heavy stick slams into my forearm. I roar in pain and smash my fist against Chakrii's wrist with such force the bone cracks. He screams and drops the stick, his other hand flying out to claw at my face. I jerk my head back out of the way, bearing down on him with my weight as I snatch that hated fucking stick and raise it above him.

"What did I say I would do to you if you ever again threatened someone I love?" I ask softly.

Fear flashes across Chakrii's face, real, honest, raw fear. He remembers. That's right, asshole. You're getting a taste of this stick. I raise it behind me—

"Look out!" Asher cries as he shoots a guard in the chest.

I swing reflexively, the stick slamming into Chakrii's guard as he tackles me. He grunts but still wraps his arms around me and squeezes. We roll off Chakrii, who is shouting his head off to kill us all. Out of the corner of my eye, my men open fire on the guards before they have time to draw weapons.

I'm still grappling with the guard, my weakened state making it more difficult to disarm him than it should be. My arms trapped, I wiggle the stick up between our bodies and shove it into the guard's throat, crushing his windpipe. He releases me to claw at his throat. I roll from him in time to ward off another guard as he breaks through my men's line. I swing at him with the stick, and he backpedals.

The guard rushes me again. I stab out with the stick, hitting him in the stomach. He goes down, gasping, but his hand slides to the pistol holstered at his waist. I slam the stick down on his wrist with all my might, breaking it before he has the chance to shoot me.

We have to get out of here. I turn to discover my men

have finished off the last of the guards. Bodies are strewn everywhere, the scene grisly. Blood is slicked across the marble tiles. The entire room looks like a slaughterhouse.

Gunfire erupts outside the door. An answering volley erupts a moment later. Fuck. More guards are coming. My hands tighten on the stick; there isn't much time left. But where is Alessandra? I scan the table, but only find Chakrii crawling across the floor to another door, one that must open to his personal quarters.

Where is she? *Where is she?* If she's been hurt, I swear— Luciano is dragging a protesting Alessandra toward a window that's been shot out.

Red descends over my vision. That asshole is *touching her*. Hands clutching the stick, I sprint toward her, barely slowing to jump over Chakrii.

"I'm coming for you later," I snarl. He barely has time to turn his head toward me before I crack the stick into the back of his head. He collapses, unconscious. But I'm still moving, not bothering to check his condition as I sprint toward her.

"Ford!" Alessandra screams, her hands clawing at Luciano's arm, who barely pays her any mind as he steadfastly drags her toward the window.

"Stop!" I shout. He sneers at me and continues dragging her.

"She's played with you long enough," Luciano says, patting Alessandra's head like one pats a child. "And look at what almost happened? This insane fucker nearly killed her. We can't have that. She's better off with me."

"*Lasciami andare, stronzo!*" Alessandra cries and kicks him between the legs.

"*Puttana,*" Luciano groans. He backhands her. Alessandra's face snaps back with a sharp *crack*.

I drag him off her and haul him up against the wall. "And you say *I'm* the problem," I growl, shoving the stick up under his chin. Luciano snarls at me and socks me in the stomach.

"I'll kill you!" he shouts.

"Not if I kill you first."

And I will. I should, if this asshole thinks he can take her. It would be so easy; his associates would never know it wasn't Chakrii who killed him. He's likely hurt other people, other women, too. Someone should put him down like the dog he is. My hand tightens on the stick—

"Ford, no!" Alessandra screams behind me. I turn my head just enough to see her tear-streaked face. She's shaking her head back and forth, her eyes pleading. "He's not worth it."

Luciano struggles under me. Fucker thinks he can free himself. I knee him in the groin, and he sags against the wall.

"Ford," Alessandra says. "We don't have time for this."

"Fine," I mutter. Grabbing the lapels of his suit, I glance out the broken window. It's a short drop; less than ten feet. This hall apparently is on the ground floor.

I return my attention to Luciano. I get right in his face. "Touch her again, you die."

Luciano bares his teeth at me, but I don't give him the

chance to respond. Without another word, I haul him off the ground and hurl him out the window. He lands with a loud thump, a scream tearing from his throat as he lands on his leg.

"You broke my leg, *stronzo*!"

"Be glad that's the only thing I broke!" I yell out the window.

My side erupts with pain. I double over. Oh, fuck, that hurts. One, maybe two of my ribs are cracked. Shit. The fucking guards probably started the job and tossing Luciano out must have finished it.

A wave of dizziness rolls through me. My vision tunnels to a narrow speck. Nausea roils in my gut. Fuck, I don't know ... no. I have to get her out.

"Jesse!" Alessandra calls. "We need to get out of here!"

"Through the window," I pant, still doubled over.

"We can't go through—"

"We have to," I say. "I'm not wasting time figuring out how to get out of this hellhole. They're going to regroup and then we'll be outnumbered."

"I'm here," Jesse says. He looks out the window and winces. "That must have hurt."

"It's far less than the asshole deserved," I snap.

"Yo, Car, man, it's really good to see you," Asher says, coming up to us, Tucker on his heels.

I take a quick scan of the room. Chakrii is still out cold. The dead guards are still dead. But people are pounding on the main door, which my men shored up by dragging the banquet table over to wedge it against the door. It's only a matter of time before whoever's on the other side knocks through the barricade.

No doubt about it. We're going out the window.

"Asher, climb through and then we'll lower her out after you," I pant, doubling over again. Christ, it hurts.

"No, you first, Ford," Alessandra says.

I level a death glare at her. We're having a discussion *real fucking soon*.

Tucker takes one look at me and rolls his eyes. Without ceremony, he slides his legs out and then drops lightly to the ground. Turning, he holds his hands up. I nod to Asher, who lifts Alessandra out and down, waiting until Tucker wraps his arms around her waist before releasing her.

Asher turns back to me, still leaning halfway out the window. "You good, boss? Jesse can't—"

"I'm fine," I say. Asher shrugs and drops to the ground. I jerk my head at Jesse. "Go."

"You're more injured—"

"I said *go*." I'll be damned if I let anyone else get captured because of their dumbass fucking plan. And to drag Alessandra into it! My men deliberately disobeyed my orders. Deliberately!

They knew I wanted her safe. They knew I wanted her out of the damn country. And instead, they fucking brought her here! If I hadn't moved faster, if I'd been just *one* second slower, Chakrii would have hit her with that fucking stick. My own men put her in harm's way. She was safe, damn it!

Jesse takes one look at my face and pales. *That's right, asshole. There's going to be hell to pay once we're out of here.*

He climbs out the window. He's barely hit the ground when I'm following, my entire body screaming in protest. I land with a bone-rattling thump, barely preventing myself from landing much like Luciano.

Asher is staring at the Italian, who has lifted up to a sitting position, babbling a string of Italian that is probably every curse known to man.

"Let's go," I say curtly.

Asher's head snaps up. "We're just gonna leave him?"

My teeth grind together. "That's exactly what we're gonna do. It's better than the fucker deserves."

I turn away, but Alessandra says, "We absolutely cannot leave him here!"

I glare at her. She doesn't want to leave him? After the bastard *hit* her? Just what the fuck are they to each other?

Alessandra notices my expression and her eyes narrow. "Think rationally, if you possibly can right now," she hisses. "He's one of the most important heirs to the Family in all of Italy. What do you think will happen to you if you just leave him here to die? He obviously won't make it. They'll hunt you to the ends of the earth. As it is, you've already broken his leg; they're going to be pissed, Ford. Use your brain."

"She's right," Luciano says, his smile a taunt. "They'll never rest until you're in the ground."

"Shut the fuck up. None of this would have happened if it weren't for you. Not that you should have ever been involved," I mutter, glaring at the Italian.

"You're not implying it's *my* fault?" Alessandra asks.

"You're the one who involved him. It couldn't have been my men. They don't know him," I say thinly. I jab my thumb at Asher. "Carry him, then. Tucker, I want you in front. Someone give me a fucking firearm. Apparently I have to protect her myself."

Tucker draws a pistol from his waistband and extends it to me. "I'm going to ignore that one because you're injured and upset, man. But you're starting to skate on thin ice."

"Later," I growl. "Let's go before whoever's shooting decides to start looking for us."

"They're with us," Alessandra says. "And they're the diversion that allowed us to escape in the first place."

"Oh, really? The plan was to go out a fucking window, then? Just how many windows have you jumped out of?"

"Let's just go," says Jesse. He steps around me, gun drawn, and begins making his way along the wall of the building. Tucker catches up to him.

"Stay behind me," I tell her, stepping in front of Alessandra. She mutters something unintelligible but follows. Asher comes up on the rear, a furious Luciano slung over his shoulder in a fireman's carry.

We creep along the building, expecting an armed guard to jump out at us at any moment. But no one appears; they must all be tied up with the so-called diversion.

"The van is waiting," Jesse says when we reach the edge of the property. A man-sized hole has been blown in the stone wall, just barely large enough for us to slip through. The gunfire must have masked the sound of the demolition.

Jesse goes through, then I shove Alessandra into the gap, relief cascading through me when she's finally safely off Chakrii's land. I follow and find Bianchi standing by a large black van, its door open.

Alessandra and Jesse climb inside as the rest of us

follow. Jesse pauses beside Bianchi, taking a long look down her body.

"I'm fine," she says, tossing her head with impatience.

Jesse leans down until his mouth hovers an inch from her ear. "You better be."

Something flashes in her eyes.

"Flirt later," I say, shoving them both into the van. I climb in, sitting as close to Alessandra as humanly possible. Asher deposits a complaining Luciano on the seat across from us, then climbs inside. Tucker follows then slams the door shut. The driver, who must be an Interpol agent, screams away from the compound.

Alessandra stares out the window at the retreating building. "The other team?"

"Already retreating," says Bianchi. "They'll meet us back at the safe house." Her gaze drops to Luciano, and she begins tapping away on her phone. "Medical attention will be ready when we arrive."

The leash on my barely-controlled fury snaps. "Well, that's fucking fantastic. Then why don't y'all tell me what the *fuck* y'all were thinking?"

CHAPTER THIRTY-SEVEN

ALESSANDRA

"What the hell does that mean?" Asher says, glaring at Ford.

"You fucking know damn well what I'm talking about, asshole."

Tucker sighs. "Ford—"

"I don't want to hear the excuses."

Bianchi sighs. "What is he going on about now?"

"He's furious we brought her to Chakrii," says Jesse.

I bolt upright in my seat. "Oh, is *that* what we're doing?"

Ford whips his head to me. "Yes, that's exactly what we're fucking doing. What the hell were you thinking, going in there? Do you have any idea what he wants to do to you? He wants you *dead*, Lessa. And you just delivered yourself up to him on a fucking platter!"

"What was I supposed to do, just leave you with him?" I cry. Why is he so upset about this? I mean, yeah, if our positions were reversed, I would have never wanted him to endanger himself for me. But that's just it; he'd never leave me with Chakrii. He'd claw his way through a brick wall if he had to in order to save me from that monster.

And so would I.

"That's exactly what you were supposed to do. Leave me," Ford says, his face inches from mine. My mouth drops open and his gaze drops to it. Frustration flashes in his eyes. He adds, "You could have been hurt. You could have been killed."

My teeth grind together. "You don't get to just dictate what everyone around you does when they're worried about you. That's what friends do. They're there for you when you're in trouble. That's, like, the most basic requirement of being a friend."

Ford scoffs. "Being there for someone doesn't mean sacrificing your fucking life. You're not a soldier."

"But we are," Asher says. "And we made the call."

Ford glares at him. "Yes, you *did*. You used her when you knew I specifically never would have allowed it in the first place. You did it *knowing* it would upset me."

"It was her call, too," says Jesse, crossing his foot over his ankle. He looks dead at Ford. "And you know what? It was a damn good plan. Shit always goes sideways during an op. We made it out fine. You need to calm down before you say something you truly regret."

Ford stabs a finger at Luciano, who's sneering at him. "Yeah? Involving this guy was a good idea? He was in the middle of *kidnapping her* while y'all were fighting off Chakrii's men. Was that part of your plan? Good job!"

Asher pales and glances at me, his eyes trailing to my

cheek. I rub it, grimacing when a flicker of pain stabs through me. There must be a mark from when Luciano hit me, the *stronzo*.

"Yeah," says Ford mockingly. "Real good plan."

Tucker gives me an apologetic look. "We didn't know he'd—"

"That's my entire fucking point!"

"Oh, fuck off, Ford," Bianchi suddenly says, interrupting us all. "You have people that love you and couldn't stand to see you suffer. Life is dangerous. It requires taking risks. Your friends were willing to take it. So buck up and accept they care that much about you. I'm sick of hearing your whining. This shit is why men are useless in relationships."

"Is that so?" Jesse says softly.

Bianchi glances at him, rolls her eyes, then returns to her phone. "Let's all just shut up until we're at the safe house, all right? Then you can take her off, Ford, and yell at her until you're no longer afraid something will happen to her."

Tucker snickers, then quickly wipes his mouth when Ford levels him with a furious look that promises retribution if he doesn't shut up.

I stare out the window. And here I thought he'd be *grateful* we saved him. But this is Ford, and he can't stand that someone might have endangered herself to get him out. It's more than fine if he does it, but the other way around? Apparently not.

Luciano says into the uncomfortable silence, "You should be with a real man, Alessandra. One who can control his women. Protect her. *I'd* never endanger you like that."

Asher smacks him across the face; a loud, quick, slap meant to mortify—just like Luciano did to me. "Well, you're a fucking psycho, so your opinion doesn't matter."

Luciano's face twists in fury. He lunges for Asher but before he can do anything, Bianchi pulls a gun out of her holster and levels it at him.

"I'm sick of your bullshit, too."

Luciano slowly turns his head to look at her. His gaze moves from the gun to Bianchi's face. Slowly, he smiles. "I like this one, too."

In one swift motion, Jesse reaches out and squeezes Luciano's leg where it's broken. "No, you do not."

Luciano howls, his face flushing. *"Vaffanculo!"*

Jesse turns to Bianchi, smirking. "Should I tell him I speak Italian?"

Her mouth twitches. She re-holsters her pistol.

Luciano lets loose with a stream of profanities, impressing even me with his creativity. Jesse chuckles, and shoves him back against the seat.

The vehicle falls silent again. I shift my attention back to the window, watching the city stream by. Ford stills beside me, his breathing faintly labored. I frown and turn to him.

"Are you okay?"

He nods sharply, which as good as tells me he's in horrendous pain.

I sigh. "Where are you hurt?"

He shrugs. "Everywhere."

I frown. "Do you need a doctor?"

He shakes his head.

"Well, Marco's doctor can look at you."

"Marco? Your brother's still here?"

Asher laughs. "Oh, yeah. Refused to leave. He's real pissed Alessandra set this up today."

"So he has sense, then," says Ford.

Tucker groans. "Not this again."

Ford shakes his head. He reaches over and takes my hand. There are bruises all up the back of his hand. I suck in a sharp breath. If his arm is this battered, what about the rest of him? All this damage after only a week with Chakrii. What if it had taken us longer to get to him? What if we'd failed? What if—

"I'm okay, gorgeous," Ford says quietly.

I nod shakily, unable to voice a response. It came so close. I came so close to losing him forever. I shudder.

Ford squeezes my hand. "So where is this safe house? Is it Interpol's?"

"Yes, it is," says Bianchi. "Made is waiting there for us. And I just got word that the other team made it out. They're en route also. We should be back five, maybe ten minutes ahead of them."

"Who's this other team?" Ford asks.

"My brother hired some ex-military men in New York," I say. "They helped get Jesse out after you were taken."

Ford nods thoughtfully. "How's your shoulder?"

Jesse shrugs. "How're your ribs?"

Ford shrugs.

"Men," Bianchi mutters. I have to agree.

The van turns into the safe house a few minutes later. Iron gates pull back as we drive inside. A man in a security booth checks the ID of the driver, then waves us through. We wind back up the path to the villa we only left a few hours ago, and I finally sigh in relief. A glance down shows my hand is shaking.

My brother flies out of the house when I step outside the van. He pulls me into a hug, gripping me tightly. "Never again," he says. "Don't you dare pull another stunt like this again."

"I won't," I say, knowing full well I'll do it again if something ever happens to Ford.

Marco steps back from me, staring over my shoulder at Ford, who's watching him. Ford steps forward and extends a hand. Marco gives him a considering look before he finally takes Ford's hand.

"You've saved my sister's life multiple times," Marco says. "Thank you."

Ford nods.

"But if you expect me to stand by next time and let my sister head into danger just to save you, you better think again."

Ford smiles. "I wouldn't want it any other way."

Marco's eyes narrow, like he's not sure whether Ford really is agreeing with him. Finally, he shrugs and heaves a sigh.

"Christ, Lessa, I'm glad this shit is over," Marco says, raking a hand through his hair."

"Not quite over yet," says Bianchi, holding the door open so Asher can carry Luciano inside.

Marco's face sours. "What the hell happened to him?"

"Ford tossed him out a window after he hit me," I say.

"He *hit* you?"

"He did. So I decided we should see if he could fly," says Ford neutrally. "Spoiler alert: he can't."

Marco considers him. "I think I like you after all." He claps him on the shoulder.

Ford winces.

"For heaven's sake," I say. "He's injured. He needs to be checked out."

Marco nods toward the house. "Barnes is still here, very much against his will. Luciano will need a hospital, though."

"I've already arranged an armored transport," Bianchi calls from inside the house.

"Come on," I say to Ford. "I need to look at your injuries."

"I *knew* it," says Marco. "I knew there was something more between you."

Now Ford claps a hand on his shoulder. "Remember you said you liked me."

"And you can be sure I'm reconsidering that right about now."

Ignoring my brother, I take Ford's hand again and lead him into the house. Barnes is already fretting over Luciano, who's yelling that if he doesn't fix his leg immediately, he's going to send the Family after him.

"I really don't need a doctor," Ford says to me. "Just some binding for the ribs."

"Your ribs are broken?" I say, my voice rising to a near shriek.

"Just cracked, I think. Broken is a sharper pain. You can wrap them, and I'll be fine."

I shake my head. "Barnes can do it better."

Ford just looks at me. "I don't want Barnes to do it. I want you to."

I swallow hard. "Okay, then. I'll just get some bandages from him."

Ford rubs his chest, wincing. "Great. Is there a bathroom around here? I haven't showered in a damn week."

"You can shower in the room I've been using," I say. "It's upstairs. Second door on the left."

Ford heads upstairs. I stare after him, still unable to believe he's really here with me. Marco catches my eye and gives me a worried look. I shake my head; I don't want to discuss my relationship with Ford. Instead, I walk up to Barnes and tentatively touch him on the arm.

"Yes?" Barnes turns to me. "Don't tell me you're injured, too."

"No ... but I need some bandages to wrap Ford's ribs. He, uh, cracked two of them."

"Of course he did," the doctor mutters. "No one in this group ever needs a doctor, do they? Oh no. As long as there are some bandages lying around, we can just slap those on our bodies. Medical staff? Pfft. Who needs them?"

"Um ..."

"Here are painkillers instead," Barnes grumbles, digging around in his bag for a bottle. "No more than two every four hours. And that's a 'no' to the bandages. We don't wrap ribs anymore because the patient may catch pneumonia. Tell *that* to your he-man who thinks he knows everything."

"R-right," I say, staring at the bottle.

"Go on, then," Barnes says irritably, his attention already turned back to Luciano.

I hightail it up the stairs to my room. I close the door behind me, taking a deep breath for what I'm about to see.

"Ford?" I call softly.

"In here," he answers.

He's still in the shower when I enter the bathroom.

"Are you okay?" I ask. "Do you need me to help you with the shower?"

"I'm already done, just toweling off."

I blink in confusion. "Then why are you still in the shower? Wouldn't it be easier for you to do so out here?"

Ford doesn't answer immediately. It takes me a good fifteen seconds to figure it out.

"Ford ..."

"I'm fine, gorgeous."

"*Ford.*"

"I don't want to upset you."

"Let me see you now!"

"It looks worse than it is."

"I highly doubt that."

"In fact, maybe I should just take care of it my—"

I whip the shower curtain aside. I gasp. No. *No.* "What did they do to you?" I whisper.

Ford's entire body is covered in bruises. Head to toe. Black, green, blue. Purple everywhere. How is he even standing? He looks like a fucked-up Jackson Pollock painting—if only someone splashed fists across his body instead of paint. He's lost weight, too, noticeably so. For him to lose that much in a mere week means they *starved* him.

"That's ... that's ... Ford ..." I choke on my own words. I'm literally robbed of speech.

He steps out of the tub, wrapping the towel around his waist. I reach out for his chest, but my fingers halt just inches from his skin. What if I touch him and it hurts?

His hand wraps around mine, then places it above his heart.

My eyes leap to his. Ford stares at me with an emotion I'm afraid to identify in his eyes. "Never be afraid to touch me, gorgeous."

CHAPTER THIRTY-EIGHT

FORD

She stares up at me, eyes still filled with horror at the sight of my injuries. Guilt whips through me. This woman put herself in danger to save me, and in return I yelled at her for being stupid.

I'm the dumbass.

"I need to apologize," I say.

She blinks, her gaze locked on a particularly nasty bruise on my chest. "For what?"

"For the things I said in the car. You found a way to get me out of there, and I'm grateful. I should have never lashed out at you, but I was just so damn terrified about what could have happened. When I saw him raising his stick to hit you—"

"Wait, what?" Alessandra drags her gaze up from my chest. "How do you know he was going to—"

"He beat her to death with it, Lessa," I say quietly. She gasps, her hand flying over her mouth. "When Chakrii found out that Achara had left his nephew, he was furious.

But by that point, she had already met me, and I wouldn't let him intimidate her. He tried, many times, to get her to dump me and return to his nephew, but when I pushed back at him every time, he dropped it. Or so I thought. Months went by, nothing happened. I figured it was over. I never believed—I didn't think he'd actually hurt her. Not when she had already left his nephew.

"Then I proposed to her. We'd been together for a year. Looking back, I think I wanted a life as different from the one in the SEALs as possible. I never even considered getting married in the teams. Never would have put a woman through that, wondering if I'd ever come home. In Thailand, though, it was like ... Chase dying, being in the teams, all of it, had happened to a different person. It had been three years since his death. I thought I was healing. I thought I *had* healed.

"We were so happy together. Achara was going to run the resort and I would run the boat. It was perfect. Like everything I'd ever wanted just fell into my lap. And then ... and then ..."

Alessandra steps closer, lifting her other hand to place it on top of mine that still holds hers against my heart. "He killed her," she whispers.

I nod, forcing the words past the lump in my throat. "One day I was out on a dive. Just myself and one other guy. A local. Turns out, he was a diversion. One of Chakrii's men. When we came back ... he was in the kitchen with her, guards standing all around him. He was sitting at one of the chairs, just waiting. Smoking a fucking cigar. That fucking stick had blood and ... brain matter on it. She was ...

she was already gone. Long gone. There was nothing I could have done.

"And he had this *look* on his face. Such rage. Just maniacal fury. He said he now owned me; if I didn't do what he said, he'd use his contacts in the Phuket police to pin Achara's murder on me. Apparently, he wanted an ex-military white guy to deal with all the tourists. He must have thought he'd get me to sell drugs to them or whatever. Something. He didn't even *consider* I might retaliate. The bastard probably believed I'd be so terrified of the murder rap that I'd just do whatever he said."

"My God," Alessandra says. "What did you do?"

I run a hand through my hair, pulling at the roots. My ribs creak in protest, but I welcome the pain, welcome the temporary distraction from my mental anguish in dredging up all these awful memories.

"I knew it wouldn't stop unless I put an end to it. So I ... I killed his nephew. The man was a monster. I'd heard three separate stories of how he brutalized women. I could only imagine what he must have done to Achara. He could never be allowed to inherit Chakrii's organization like Chakrii intended. So I killed him. A bullet to the brain while he was sleeping. In and out before anyone had any clue I'd been there.

"And I left a note for Chakrii. I told him if he ever hurt someone I loved again, I'd beat him to death with his walking stick. Just like he did to my fiancée. And he knew I could make good on the threat, because his nephew lived in the same house as he did. I'd already demonstrated I could get to him.

"He left me alone, never tried to pin Achara's murder on me like he threatened. In the two years since, I've disrupted his business whenever he gets too violent with the locals. It all came to a head when you arrived. Chakrii was waiting for an excuse. Someone I cared about. Like before. He is a patient man."

"Ford ... that's so awful. I'm so, so sorry that happened to her. And to you."

I crush her hand against my chest, drop my cheek on top of her head. "Thank you. That's why ... fuck. Tonight he had that same look on his face as he did that day in the kitchen. The same rage. He was going to hit you with it, just like Achara. I couldn't ... it brought it all back. I haven't been thinking straight since. Not until I got into the shower. I don't want you to believe that you're not capable of anything you set your mind to. You are. You're so damn brave, gorgeous. Sometimes that's what scares me most."

"I'm the one who was scared," she says. "Scared I'd never see you again. Scared you might die for me."

My hand slides up to cradle her face. "I would always die for you."

Her eyes widen. Mine do, too. But I don't take it back. Why would I, when it's the truth? Only a few hours ago, I was prepared to do just that.

I kiss her, pulling her against me as my tongue slides into her mouth. Alessandra moans, stretching up on her toes to better fit against me. Her arms come around my neck as she kisses me back, the bottle of pills she's holding falling to the floor.

She freezes, then draws away. "We can't."

My arm wraps around her. "We most certainly can. Why not?"

"You're injured! Everywhere! You have cracked ribs, for heaven's sake. I don't want to injure you further."

I bury my face in her neck, rubbing my mouth up the column of her throat to her ear. "You can't break me. And I don't care how much it hurts. I thought I'd never see you again. Never touch you. Never taste that sweet mouth of yours. Never stroke my aching cock inside you and listen as you scream how good I make you feel. I can't wait another moment. I *need* you. Need to feel alive."

Alessandra melts against me, a hand threading through my hair as she holds my face to her neck. "Okay, Ford, but we do it my way."

"Whatever you want," I say lazily against her neck, my tongue darting out to taste her. Fuck, I've missed that taste, the unique flavor of her skin against my tongue. Blood rushes to my head. I grow dizzy, warm, restless. I wish I could take us to the floor and drive into her again and again. But even I know I'm not up for it.

Alessandra walks backward, a slow smile spreading on her face. I follow, entranced, as she peels articles of clothing off her body. My chest grows tight when she tosses her panties away and stands before me naked.

"You're so beautiful, gorgeous," I say, my gaze trailing down her body. "It hurts to look at you."

She pauses. "Does it?"

Yes, but fuck it. I cup her breast, my fingers kneading, my thumb swiping back and forth across her nipple in tantalizing circles. Alessandra gasps and drops her head back, and I grunt in triumph. All the pain I received this week was worth it, if it led me to this moment.

I step closer, working her other breast as my free hand trails down her body to cup between her thighs. I grind the heel of my hand against her clit, circle her entrance with my middle finger.

"So wet already," I groan, my heart hammering in my chest. "Look at me."

Alessandra lifts her head, her eyes slowly opening. I circle her entrance again and then slide the tip of my finger inside her. Her eyes flash as she sucks her lower lip into her mouth, her face growing flushed.

I curl my finger and slide against the sensitive spot, still barely entering her, slowly stroking in and out, in and out. My other hand pinches her nipple, then tugs. Alessandra whimpers, her hands clawing at my forearms.

"Work my finger inside you, gorgeous."

She rolls her hips, taking my finger deeper.

"Yes, that's it," I groan. "Carefully now. That's it. Spread your legs wider for me."

She does. "Very good," I rasp. I plunge my finger inside her all the way, swirl it in a circle before withdrawing. She's so slick, so swollen for me, my cock throbs with the need to take her. "Would you like another finger?"

"Yes," she pants, "let me ride your hand."

A shudder rolls through me. "Take them, Lessa. There you go. Mmm you're so ready for me, gorgeous. I want to feel your hips grinding against my hand. Use me for your pleasure."

"Ford, *please*," she gasps, throwing her arms around my

neck. I bury my face in her neck, kissing and nibbling on her throat as she rides my hand, her hips rolling faster and faster.

"Come for me," I moan against her neck. "I want to feel you pulsing around my fingers. Squeeze me. You're so close, gorgeous, I can feel it. Throw your head back and let me watch you come."

"Oh!" Alessandra cries. I lift my head to watch as her head drops back, her mouth falling open as she shatters against me. I groan with pleasure, and need, and even a little pain as she tightens around my fingers, her hips bucking against me. She quiets a moment later, looking up at me with eyes that have grown drowsy.

I withdraw my hand and bring it up to my face. My eyes never leave hers as I suck each finger into my mouth, licking her taste from my hand.

"If I weren't injured," I say hoarsely, "I'd lay you out on that bed and feast on you until you couldn't come even one more time."

She shivers, her chest heaving. Her gaze drops to my towel, which is tented absurdly from the hard length of my erection. She smiles, slides her fingers inside the towel, and then with a quick yank, it falls to the floor. She wraps her hand around me, pumping slowly up and down as she looks up at me and says, "I think you need to be inside me."

"Right fucking now," I growl, thrusting into her hand.

"Sit on the end of the bed."

I drop onto it with a hard sigh, surprised by the relief I feel to no longer be standing. Alessandra smiles knowingly.

"Spread your legs," she teases. Something twinges in

my chest as she places her hands on my shoulders and straddles me.

She rocks against me, drawing a groan from both of us. She does it again, saying, "Do you want to be inside me?"

"More than anything in this fucking world."

She leans closer until our faces are just inches apart. "Take my hips and work me onto you."

"Fuck," I grunt, my hands sliding up her thighs to those beautiful hips. My hands dig into her skin as I squeeze her. I stare down between our bodies as my cock slowly disappears inside her. "Shit. Fuck, that's perfect, gorgeous. You fit me so good, so fucking well."

Alessandra rolls her hips in a tiny circle, working herself down the final inch. I moan, my eyes squeezed shut.

"Are you okay?" she whispers. "Does this hurt you?"

I manage to open my eyes. "The only pain I'll be in is if you stop. Put me out of my misery, Lessa."

She grins, then starts to ride me, working up and down, drawing farther up each time until she's nearly lifted off me. Then she slams down, taking me fully inside her in one swift movement. I shout, my hands grinding her down harder onto my cock.

"Faster, gorgeous. Truly fuck me."

She moves faster, sliding up and down, rocking in tiny circles, grinding for all she's worth. I moan. Gasp. Plead. Coax her on with filthy phrases I barely register saying.

"Fuck yes, baby. Shit, that's it. Such a perfect cunt you have, taking me over and over. You're going to make me come so hard. So hard, gorgeous girl, so fucking hard. I'm going to explode ... *damn it all, yes!* A little more, Lessa, that's it. Make me come inside you. God, I need ..."

Alessandra suddenly takes my face in her hands, her eyes tracking back and forth.

"Ford," she whispers as her hips slow down, grinding against me slowly, passionately, forcefully. She's keeping me deep inside her as she watches every last expression of pleasure flash across my face. "How are you so perfect?"

The breath slams out of my lungs. I can't breathe, can't move, can't think. My chest aches, throbs with a different kind of need, one that demands an echoing one from her.

Oh, God. This *feeling*. I know what this means. It's only gripped me once before. I never thought I'd feel it again. But it's too soon. It must be. It's too fragile, this bond between us. I can't bear to ruin it by speaking it aloud.

And so I tell her with my eyes, the clutch of my hands gripped tight around her waist. The way I drive perfectly home with every thrust. The moans I make as I start to come. I call her every beautiful name I can imagine, and then all the filthy ones, too. And at the very last, as I start to spill inside her and she explodes around me, I capture her mouth with mine and tell her with a kiss.

CHAPTER THIRTY-NINE

FORD

Alessandra lifts herself off me, her body slick with sweat. I grin up at her, out of breath myself.

"I'm going to need another shower now," I say, running a hand through my hair. Hell. Thirty seconds in a room with this woman and all I care about is being inside her. That'll really be an issue once we're together for real.

My heart clenches. Shit. I glance up at Alessandra, who's glancing at the bathroom. We need to have a very serious conversation pretty soon because I can't live without her. If my last week of hell wasn't enough for me to figure that out, the last fifteen minutes certainly was.

"Hey," I say softly, getting to my feet. "Do you want to shower?"

She gnaws on her lower lip. I groan. If she keeps that up I'll want another round, and with the way my chest burns from all that physical exertion, I really couldn't manage it.

"Well ..." she glances down at herself.

"You want me to shower with you again?"

She looks up at me through her lashes, almost shyly. "Could you? It was ... way better with you."

My chest squeezes again. Taking her hand, I lead her into the bathroom. "It would be my pleasure."

"You don't have—"

"Believe me, I want to. You can shower with me for the rest of your life if you want," I say, winking at her.

She grinds to a halt, her eyes wide. "You can't mean that."

Oh, but I really fucking do.

Instead of going there right now, I just wink at her again and rip the shower curtain back. Her eyes drill into my back as I turn on the water and make sure it's a comfortable temperature. I can practically *feel* her wanting to say something.

"You've never winked at me before," she suddenly blurts.

I laugh out loud. "No, I guess I haven't."

"You're not the kind of man who winks."

"I used to be, gorgeous."

Perhaps one day I will be again.

Alessandra says nothing. I lift her into the shower, and we proceed as we did the night before I was taken. After we finish, I'm toweling her off when my stomach growls.

"God, Ford," Alessandra says, "I should have gotten you food right away. You need food. You've lost so much weight."

"Nah," I say, tossing the towel at the sink. "I think I got it in the right order."

"The right order?"

I grin. "Shower, sex, food."

She rolls her eyes. "You forgot your second shower."

"Bonus."

"Can you make it down to the kitchen?" she asks skeptically. "Do you want me to grab something and bring it up?"

"No, I'll head down, too," I say. "If I don't keep moving, I'll stiffen up."

She snickers.

I swoop down and kiss her neck, then growl, "Careful."

We dress quickly and are heading down the hall when a shout rings out behind the door next to us. Alessandra and I exchange a glance.

"Hide in your room," I say quickly.

"But it sounds like—"

"Do it!"

Alessandra retreats. I wait until she's back inside before creeping to the door and throwing it open. I swear to God if Chakrii has somehow gotten inside here—oh.

Fuck.

Jesse has Bianchi shoved facedown on a bed, his hand between her shoulder blades as he rails her from behind. Neither of them are wearing a scrap of clothing. Bianchi's face is turned toward me as another scream escapes her. Her eyes drift open as Jesse thrusts into her again with such force her head bounces against the bed.

Her eyes collide with mine. "Planning to watch?" she pants.

Jesse's head whips to me, his face feral. *Get out.*

I throw up my hands and back out the door. "Sorry, man. My mistake."

I shut the door behind me, then actually have to slap a palm over my mouth to muffle the laughter bubbling out of me. A moan comes from the other side of the door.

Shoulders shaking, I turn away. Alessandra is peeking halfway out her door. When she sees my expression, she rolls her eyes. I jerk her to me and practically run for the stairs in my haste to get away before I can hear another sound.

"You knew they were screwing, didn't you?"

She laughs. "I mean, I didn't *know*. But ... I was pretty sure I heard them late last night. They weren't, um, very quiet."

I scrub my free hand over my face, like that will do a damn thing to erase the image of them that's now burned into my brain. "How long has it been going on?"

"Don't know. Something's up with them. I'm pretty sure it's just hate sex."

"Christ," I mutter. "I don't think so. Not on his end. I've known Jesse a long time. I've never seen him lose his head over a woman like he has with Bianchi."

"Is he half-Italian?" Alessandra asks. "He speaks Italian like it's his mother tongue."

I nod. "His mother was Venetian."

"Was?"

"Yeah. She died when he was a kid. Really young. He used to spend the summers in Venice with his grandmother to stay in touch with his Italian family. His dad never really got over her death."

"Poor Jesse."

I send her a wry look. "Don't ever let him hear you say that."

"Noted."

Alessandra helps me prepare a meal from their lunch leftovers. I eat everything in sight, only remembering how hungry I am when the food is in front of me.

"I'm so sorry Ford," Alessandra says as she watches me eat, her voice small. "If Chakrii hadn't wanted me, you never would have been captured."

I swallow slowly, then toss my fork down. "It would have happened eventually. Don't blame yourself. And he'd decided to make a move against me, too. He told me he wanted to make me watch you die. As an example to his organization, but also to make me suffer."

"My God."

I shrug. "Fuck him. He'll be out of action for a bit, anyway, since I injured him. But I do need to debrief with the team. They were nice letting me get cleaned up, but you and I both know Bianchi won't want to wait much longer."

"And then what?"

I consider, wondering if I should broach the topic now. "Tomorrow I'm going to personally escort you home. We're leaving this to Interpol."

She blinks. "You're coming with me to Italy?"

I give her a hard look. "Until the mole is found and I can guarantee your safety, I'm not leaving your side."

I'll never leave your side, if you allow it.

Her mouth drops open. "B-but ... but ... what about your business? Don't you have guests?"

I sigh. "Yeah. There were supposed to be a few in the

week I was held by that bastard. I assume one of my guys canceled them?"

Alessandra shakes her head. "No, actually, Asher and Tucker took them out on the dives for you. They were worried about you losing income on top of everything. And ... um ... the pool is clean again."

"Don't worry about it," I say, running a hand through my hair. I stare at my empty plate for a moment and then curse. "Shit. They did all that and the first thing I did was bitch them out."

"I'm sure they understand, Ford," says Alessandra. "They've been just as angry this entire week. Furious you were taken. They know you didn't mean it."

"Still," I sigh. "I need to go talk to them. Clear the air. Figure out if I can hire a local overnight to handle my guests. Otherwise, I'll have to cancel on them indefinitely until we get this situation worked out. I'm sure my friends will accompany me, and if they don't, they'll probably want to return home."

"Do you need help with that?"

I smile, reach out and squeeze her hand. "No, I can handle it. Go relax. You've earned it." She looks like she's about to protest, so I add, "Get some rest because I fully intend to try out that bed again later."

She rolls her eyes. "Might I remind you, you're injured."

"That means absolutely nothing." I pull her to me, cradle her face in my hands. Staring into her eyes, I say, my voice suddenly hoarse, "I would suffer another thousand injuries if it meant holding you in my arms, gorgeous. The pain means nothing. The pain means I'm *alive*, and here with you."

"Ford ..." she sighs, then reaches up to press her mouth to mine. I instantly respond, losing myself in the kiss. In the wave of hope that cascades through me.

"Get a room," Bianchi says, tromping into the kitchen. We startle; I glare at her over Alessandra's head. Bianchi just rolls her eyes. "What? This is a common area. Or have we all dropped the pretense of keeping this a professional operation? Pretty much everything else has gone out the window."

"I don't know," I say, giving her a hard look. "You tell me, is what I just saw in that room what you would call professional?"

Alessandra slaps a hand over her mouth. Bianchi shrugs. "You think I'm going to put my personal business in my report to Interpol?"

"Oh, so this thing with Jesse is personal, then?"

She pokes at a container of curry, then grabs a fork and starts eating. "I guess. Actually, no. Not really. It's temporary. A distraction."

Alessandra and I exchange a glance. Fucking hell. Jesse didn't look like he thought it was temporary.

Alessandra says, "Maybe you both should—"

"Oh, by the way," Bianchi interrupts, gesturing to us with her fork, "you need to debrief. Now. You've clearly showered and now you've eaten. We need to know what went on in that compound. And you'll be happy to know that our agents caught up to Agent Onsi an hour ago. He's in custody."

"Who's Agent Onsi?" I ask.

"The mole," says Alessandra. "They got the woman I spoke to at the consulate to turn on him. What a relief they have him."

My brows raise. "So your operation is no longer compromised."

Bianchi shrugs. "Yeah, looks like. Not much good it does us now that we just got out of Chakrii's compound. He's probably in the process of relocating as we speak. But yeah, at least now our plans won't be leaked back to him."

"And our involvement is over," I clarify.

"Correct."

"I'm glad to hear it," I say. "We're shipping out to Italy tomorrow until everything is wrapped up. I want Alessandra out of the country until everything dies down."

Bianchi glances between us. "You're leaving tomorrow morning?"

Alessandra nods. "On my brother's plane."

Bianchi returns to her food. "That's for the best. You'll all be safe there."

I extend my hand, "Thank you for your help. You kept Alessandra safe while I was gone, and I'm grateful for that."

Bianchi glances up from her food, stares at my hand for a long moment, then shakes it perfunctorily. She grabs her container and heads for the door. "Jesse is looking for you, by the way," she calls over her shoulder.

I sigh, then turn back to Alessandra. "She's so much fun."

Alessandra snorts. "Being a female Interpol agent in a male-dominated field must have toughened her up."

"Yeah, something like that. I need to talk to the boys and debrief, but I'll be up later, okay?"

"Sure," she says, then gives me a quick kiss. "I'll be waiting."

I head out in search of my friends. I find them in a makeshift command center that's been set up in the living room on the ground floor.

Made looks up from a report he's reading. "You feeling recovered?"

"As much as I can at the moment," I huff, then extend a hand to him. "Glad to see you up and about. I never knew what happened to the people in your SUV."

A flicker of sadness crosses Made's face. "We lost the driver and the man behind him. I'm lucky to be laid up with just this broken leg, although the whole-leg cast is uncomfortable."

I wince. "I can imagine. I broke my leg, too, a few years back."

"Doing stupid hero shit," says Asher, grinning.

I shake my head. "Like you weren't right there with me. Listen, guys, I need to apologize for—"

"Don't sweat it," Tucker says, waving me off. "We know you were just worried about your woman."

I sigh. "But that didn't make it right for me to act like an ungrateful shit. I know you were doing your best, and just wanted me back."

"Damn straight," says Asher. He sobers. "We really hated using her, Car."

I groan, collapsing into a chair. "This whole thing is fucked. I'm glad I'm getting her out tomorrow."

"You're going with her?" Jesse asks, brows raised.

I nod. "Yeah. I won't be satisfied until I walk her into Rome. And even then, I'm not leaving until I know Interpol guarantees that Chakrii isn't going to follow her to Europe."

"We're coming too," says Asher, crossing his legs one over the other on the coffee table before him. "We're seeing it through."

"Thank you," I say, wondering what I've done to deserve these men.

Tucker pantomimes washing his hands. "Well, now that that sappy bullshit is over, can we discuss the fact that Jesse's been railing Bianchi every chance he gets?"

"Don't speak of her that way, asshole," Jesse snaps, barely sparing him a glance as he continues staring out the window, a frown on his face.

Asher laughs. "Yep, total goner."

"What's up with you two?" I ask. Tucker and Asher turn their heads to look at Jesse. "I thought you hated each other."

"Like that's ever stopped anyone," says Tucker.

Jesse finally turns his attention away from the window. "It's none of your business."

Asher opens his mouth, but Made interjects, "And let's keep it that way, please. Agents getting involved with civilian contractors is frowned upon at Interpol, and I don't want to be forced to make a thing of it."

Jesse nods his thanks. Asher looks at me and mouths "later." I just shake my head.

"Speaking of which," says Made. "If you're going to be

leaving tomorrow, I'll need to get your statement now. Are you up to it? It will take a while."

"I figured. Go ahead," I say, getting comfortable in my chair. Good thing I had the sense to eat before I came in here.

My friends listen as Made asks me about my time with Chakrii. When I describe the beatings, their faces grow furious.

"That fucker," Asher growls. "I'm gonna kill him."

"Get in line," says Tucker.

"This will go faster with fewer interruptions," Made says mildly.

But it still takes forever. At least three hours pass while Made grills me on every little aspect of Chakrii's compound. How many rooms, the number of guards. My estimates on the size of the cell. Any conversations I overheard. By the time Made is happy with my statement, I'm exhausted.

"Where's that asshole, Luciano, by the way?" I ask, rubbing my temples. "Not that I want to ever face the fucker again, but ..."

"We transported him to a local hospital," says Made. "He needs surgery like me. You really didn't do yourself any favors with that one."

I shrug. If I have to deal with him, fine. The asshole deserved it.

"And the second team? Didn't Alessandra's brother hire people that were supposed to exfil me?"

"Hey," Asher asks, "yeah, where are they? The men

Marco hired in New York. I thought they were supposed to meet us here. That was hours ago."

Jesse says, "I asked Marco about it while you were upstairs with Alessandra. You're welcome for that distraction, by the way. Apparently, something came up in Guatemala that they were hired to handle. Hostage situation. Time sensitive. Since we're finished here, Marco figured it was fine to put them on a flight to South America."

"And that really is convenient for me, as it will make it so much easier to kill you all."

I leap to my feet, but it makes no difference. Chakrii stands in the doorway, gun pointed directly at me.

CHAPTER FORTY

ALESSANDRA

"Thank God you're alright," Marco says yet again, giving me another hug, as he has done for hours now. "Do you have any idea how terrified I was, letting you go in there?"

"You didn't *let* me go anywhere," I say, but hug him back. "It was scary, though, Marco. If anything had happened differently ... he could have ..."

"You're in love with him, aren't you?"

My head jerks up.

He smiles at me ruefully. "What is it about us and Americans? I fell in love in a New York elevator, and you ..." he makes an all-encompassing gesture, "with a guy who could be picked right out of central-casting for a commando movie."

"I haven't ... we haven't ..." I throw up my hands. "God, Marco, I haven't even told him. It didn't hit me until you straight-out asked me."

"Love hits you like that."

I run a hand through my hair, pacing back and forth. "I've only known him for a few weeks. This whole situation is insane. He can't possibly feel like I do. It's just too soon. Now he's taking me to Italy. God, Marco. The media will have a circus."

"He's taking you back to Rome?"

I shrug. "Yeah. He doesn't want to leave me unprotected until Chakrii is in custody."

"But that could take a long time."

I blink. "Yes, I suppose that's true."

"And he has a whole life, a business, here that he's just going to pick up and leave?"

"Um ... yes?"

Marco rolls his eyes. He cradles my face and places a big smacking kiss on my forehead. "I think you already have your answer, sis. The man is in love with you."

"No," I say, "he just has an overdeveloped sense of duty."

Marco just looks at me. A parade of moments crash through me.

You have ruined me.

I am never going to forget you. Never.

You can shower with me for the rest of your life if you want.

I would suffer another thousand injuries if it meant holding you in my arms, gorgeous.

I fall heavily into a chair. "Oh. *Oh.* Oh my God, Marco."

Marco laughs. "Hits you all at once, doesn't it?"

"Yes," I say, dazed, "it really does."

"This is all so very touching," says Bianchi, stalking into the room, "but save the declarations of love for later. They want both of you down in the command center. They're planning out how to get you to the airport. Again."

Marco nods. Glances at me. "One more day, sis. Then it's over."

Bianchi steps back to let him proceed out into the hall. As he passes, she strikes out and hits him behind the head with a gun concealed against her side.

I scream. Marco collapses to the floor, unconscious. Bianchi lifts the gun and levels it at me.

I gape at it, my mouth opening and closing. "Bianchi, what are you doing?"

"My job," she snaps. "And my employer will *really* be pissed that I've had to burn my cover this way, so thank you *very* much for that."

My mind sluggishly tries to process what she's saying, but when it finally does, my gaze jerks to hers. She glares at me with unconcealed hatred. "You're the mole."

She makes a sound of disgust. "Yes, you stupid girl. Or did you think I was just waving this gun at you for fun?"

"But ... but ... Agent Onsi—"

"That incompetent? Really? Obviously I pinned it all on him. Had to, when every single fuckup could have been led back to me. Had anyone bothered to look too closely. But I ensured they didn't. It was a real hard sell to Made, too, since Onsi was such a dedicated employee. A real kiss-ass. But those people always make the best moles simply because they're so unexpected. Bitchy agents like myself, on the other hand? Not so much. Too obvious."

"I just don't understand," I say, shaking my head. "You bribed that woman at the consulate to schedule my appointment? But weren't you in Singapore then?"

"I had nothing to do with that. That was one of Chakrii's men who bribed her. I had to clean up the shit after the fact, bribe her a second time to say it was Onsi who bribed her. Everyone really can be bought for a certain price, you know."

"How did you even get involved in the first place?"

"My employer read me in after those American assholes ruined Chakrii's kidnapping attempt at the consulate. Chakrii was pissed, wanted professionals from then on. I was one of the professionals. So my employer shipped me over from Singapore, got Interpol to put me on the case. And I thought 'Kidnap some spoiled bitch? Child's play.' But no. Those fucking men downstairs kept interfering."

I stare at the gun pointing at me, then glance back up to Bianchi's face. Her expression has gone completely blank, unreadable, no matter how hard I try. This woman has been betraying us the entire time?

"How didn't I see it?" I say, startling myself by speaking aloud.

Bianchi shrugs. "If you had seen it, I would have had to kill you. And think of how sad poor little Ford would have been. I mean, come on. Someone should have seen it. Every *single* time someone tried to take you, I'd just left, tapping away at my phone, fucking texting them they had the opportunity. And they fucking bungled it every time. What a joke. The first time at the consulate, I wasn't even involved, so that's not on me, but the rest? Infuriating."

"They attacked Ford's resort right after you left with Tucker to get dinner," I say slowly, the pieces falling into place.

"Very good. I even took one of their men away! Made the numbers even *more* in our favor. They still fucked it up. Couldn't have been more obvious, and yet still no one put it together."

"That's why you made sure to be in the last SUV," I say, "when we went to the airport. You knew exactly when they were going to attack."

"Obviously. I told Interpol the most vulnerable position on the route, then set up the attack for immediately before, when no one would be expecting it. Boring, so simple. But yeah, I put myself in the back. A dislocated shoulder is better than being pulverized in a car accident."

"Then how did we get out of Chakrii's compound today?" I ask. "If this is all true, I would have thought you would sabotage us so we never escaped."

She gives me a sour look. "How the fuck was I supposed to know you'd go out a fucking window? The entire place was surrounded, guards were everywhere in the hall. It should have been easy. But your brother's team ended up being useful, which really pissed me off. And now you're leaving tomorrow. I'm officially out of time. My employer will be *very* displeased if I fuck this up. So here we are."

"Your employer is not Interpol."

"Obviously. Interpol is my cover, and a convenient one it really is. I can get into all sorts of interesting places as an agent."

"Who's your employer?"

She laughs. "As if I would tell you."

Something sick occurs to me. "And the thing with Jesse? That was all a distraction, wasn't it? A way to keep him from figuring you out? You *used* him."

Something flashes in her eyes, there and gone in an instant. "Unlike the rest of you, that man suspected me from the start. Could sense there was more to me. Kept asking all these probing questions. Damn annoying. So yeah, I fucked him. Multiple times. I have to say, I really did enjoy it; the man knows how to use his body. So unexpected bonus. But surprise, surprise, he caught feelings the instant his dick entered me. So typical. So easy. And look, it worked. In the end, even he didn't see this coming."

I stare at her in horror. "See what coming?"

She smiles, but her eyes remain dead. "Oh, you're about to find out."

I glance over her shoulder. Oh God. I screamed, and no one ran up here. Where is everyone? Why is the house so quiet. They should be—

"Yes, you've got it," says Bianchi. "We've got a couple of visitors. You're not *quite* as stupid as I originally thought you were. And less spoiled. So there's that. Congrats. You're still gonna die, though."

My attention drops back down to the gun. It's rock steady in her hand. No tremors. No hint of vacillation. She'd shoot me in an instant if she wanted and not care about it for a second.

"Just ... just let us go," I say, my voice shaky no matter how hard I try to remain calm.

Bianchi's mouth twists again. "Not gonna happen. My

employer has decided it would be beneficial to please Chakrii. If we help him now, my employer believes Chakrii may become a client later. And like I said, you're all leaving tomorrow morning; my window of opportunity evaporated. I had to engineer this within an hour. So here I am, carrying out Chakrii's bullshit. And it only will require blowing my entire cover with Interpol. Such a fucking waste of the last three years of my life. Now walk."

"Where are you taking me?"

"You'll figure out soon. Now walk or I'll shoot your brother. Chakrii told me to take care of him, but that can be left up to interpretation, can't it? A whack to the head. A gunshot. Really, it could go either way. But maybe I should just shoot him to be sure..."

"Don't hurt him," I cry, staring down at my brother's body. He's so still. God, please let him be unconscious. Please let him be okay. If Izzy was left without a father for their baby, and during a risky pregnancy, too—No. No. I can't possibly go there. I'll never remain calm, and I need to if I'm going to get out of this alive.

Bianchi pushes me in front of her. The barrel of the gun digs into my back. I try to hold back a whimper but fail. Bianchi shoves it harder into my spine.

"Where is everyone?" I ask.

"I'm taking you to them. Now down the stairs, and don't even think about doing anything stupid."

When we reach the ground floor, I say loudly, hoping to draw the attention of someone, anyone, in the hope they'll save me. "Where are you taking me?"

"Nowhere. We're going outside. To the pool."

"The pool?"

"Yes. Walk like you mean it. Funny, isn't it, a safe house having a pool? Apparently, Interpol had to guard a Saudi sheik once, when he visited here for a state visit. He refused to stay anywhere that didn't have a pool. I guess Interpol never saw fit to dispose of the property."

No. That I won't do. I'm not going out there. I won't. There can be only one reason for Bianchi to take me near a pool. If I can just escape—Bianchi grabs my shirt and shoves me outside.

"No!" I cry. I stagger back against Bianchi, who shoves me another step forward.

"Watch it," she snaps. "Unless you *want* to be shot by accident."

I barely hear her. Asher, Tucker, and Jesse are tied to the metal fence on the opposite end of the pool, their faces ashen. They strain against their restraints, swearing and cursing, uselessly trying to free themselves. Their faces are already swelling up and there are rips in their shirts, like they put up one hell of a fight. When they see me step outside, they fall silent.

Then they notice who's behind me.

"*Bitch!*" yells Asher, his face contorted with fury.

"I am going to kill you all," Tucker snarls. "And I am going to enjoy every minute of it."

"Yeah, you really look like you're capable of doing some damage," Bianchi says snidely.

Tucker and Asher lose it again, hurling a bunch of obscenities at her. My eyes snag on Jesse, and I shiver. He says nothing, absolutely not a thing, but his eyes fixate on

Bianchi with single-minded intensity as he silently works at his hands restrained behind him. He acts like everything in his world has narrowed to the one simple task of utterly destroying the woman behind me. His face promises violent vengeance. I think about what Bianchi callously did to him, think of the little boy who lost his mother so young, and pray Jesse didn't actually fall for her.

"Alessandra."

My head whips to the other end of the pool. Ford is kneeling by the water's edge, his hands tied behind him. Beside him sits a giant boulder, the kind of rock you'd find jutting up out of the ocean.

There were never any rocks around this house. This has been brought in for one purpose, and that is to act as the anchor to the rope that's tied around Ford's ankle.

"No!" I cry, my eyes flicking up to Chakrii, who stands behind him with a gun pointed at the back of his head. My gaze skitters around the pool, landing on each of the ten armed guards that stand expressionless, their rifles promising exactly what they'll do if any of us try to fight back.

"Ah, I see you've finally joined us," Chakrii says in delight. "We've been waiting. I take it you've handled her brother?"

"He's no longer a problem," Bianchi says, lifting the gun to my temple as she grabs the collar of my shirt and shoves me forward. Ford's face twists with fury, before his eyes return to mine. He stares intently, silently trying to communicate something.

"Well, now that we're all here," says Chakrii, "it's time

to finally finish it. You can't imagine how *disappointed* I was when the two of you slipped through my fingers yet again. And at my own home, too. You even broke my wrist, boy. You're lucky I haven't shot you. Yes, very displeasing. Drastic measures had to be taken, so here we are."

"Are you going to kill us?" I ask woodenly. Ford stares at me pleadingly. What does he expect me to do, run away? Fight off all these people? I'm the least qualified out of everyone here to do that, and Chakrii knows it.

He smiles. "No, I'm not going to kill you, Alessandra. I've changed my mind. There's a much better way to make my point. You deserve it, girl, for insulting me that night at my resort."

"Don't do it," I say, striving to sound calm but my voice still hitches with terror. My eyes lift to Chakrii, afraid he'll shoot Ford right then. "Let them go. I'll do whatever you want. My family has money, connections. They'll give you anything. Just let them go.

Chakrii says, his eyes lit with excitement, "No, I think not. I have connections and wealth. What I want is to kill your American in front of you. No, scratch that; I want to watch while I grant you the chance to save him."

"What—"

"Isn't it obvious? The man is tied to the boulder. The boulder is going in the pool. It'll sink right down, taking your lover with it." Chakrii reaches into his pocket, frowning as he struggles with his broken wrist, then withdraws a long knife. With a flourish, he steps up next to Ford, gun still trained on him, and places the knife on the edge of the pool a few feet from him.

Ford's jaws clench. He never looks away from me, so he must know the instant I put it together.

"No," I moan. "You want me to go in ... there."

Chakrii smiles. "Yes, indeed. Fitting, isn't it? Ford will die knowing you feel the exact pain he felt when I killed his fiancée. There's not a damn thing he can do to stop it. He'll die knowing you could have saved him and didn't. That's even worse. A lovely tableau, I must say. I could never have thought of it had Bianchi not told me you're afraid of water."

"No," I plead. "Don't do this. I beg you; don't do this."

Chakrii just shrugs. "You should never tell people your greatest weakness, girl. It gives them a way to control you. What a show this will be. At least Ford knows if he'd gotten there in time, he could have saved her. You, however, won't lift a finger to save him because of your fear. Poetic, really."

"Bianchi, stop him!" Jesse shouts. "You know this is sick."

Bianchi shifts the gun from me to Ford's chest. "Fine."

"No!" I cry, shoving her arm. Her hand flies wide, but she's too disciplined to accidentally discharge the firearm.

Ford's friends yell oaths to enact revenge, to hunt Chakrii to the ends of the earth if he does this. It falls on deaf ears.

I stumble a few steps forward, my stomach heaving as I near the water's edge. "Don't do it," I beg. "Please don't."

Chakrii laughs. "Oh, but I'm having so much fun."

"Let him go!"

"You fucking bastard!"

"You won't get away with it!"

"Please," I beg again, the word barely escaping my mouth, my voice is so faint. Tears are streaming down my face so hard I can barely see.

"Alessandra, look at me!" Ford shouts. My eyes helplessly drop back to his. He gives me the saddest smile, his face wracked with pain. "I love you, gorgeous. It'll be okay. I understand."

"Touching, so touching," says Chakrii gleefully. "Very cinematic. It's time."

He motions to one of the guards, who shoves the boulder into the pool.

CHAPTER FORTY-ONE

ALESSANDRA

Ford's eyes stay locked with mine until the instant he hits the water. I scream and fall to my knees at the edge of the pool. My stomach roils with nausea, and I lean to the side and wretch.

"How disgusting," Chakrii says with delight. "So much for your *good breeding*. Look at him, already at the bottom. Must be nearly five meters down in a pool this deep. Twice his height. How long are SEALs trained to hold their breath? Three minutes? You think he's still got that ability? He is retired, after all."

"Please," I gasp. "Please, someone. Save him."

"Do it, Alessandra!" Asher bellows. "Jump in and save him!"

"You can do it!" Tucker cries. "Don't let him die."

I stare helplessly at the pool. Through the water, I can make out that he's utterly still. Calm. Can he really hold his breath that long? Does it even matter? He doesn't expect me to save him. He knows it's too much for me. That's why he told me he loved me, why he said it would be okay. He was forgiving me for it, saying he understood.

Oh God. Oh God no. He's going to die. He's going to die, and it will be my fault. I never even told him I loved him. He told me, but he'll die not knowing I love him in return.

All because I'm a coward. A useless, scared piece of shit. I gag, wretch again, thankful my stomach is too empty to expel anything.

"This is pathetic," Bianchi says above me. "And unnecessary. I'm leaving."

"I'm not done with you," Chakrii says.

"My services were to get you inside," she snaps. "You're stupid if you don't think it's only a matter of time before those three get free. And since you've just killed their friend, I don't want to be anywhere near them when they do."

"Alessandra!" Jesse suddenly yells. "Just throw it in. Just throw in the knife and it'll sink. You won't need to go in. Just grab it and throw it to him!"

"Now that isn't very sporting," says Chakrii. He lifts the gun to my head. "Do that and you'll be dead before it hits the bottom."

I scrabble along the edge of the pool, sobbing, desperately trying to see how Ford is doing. But there's little point, isn't there? I can't do it. I can't. I nearly drowned a week ago. If I try again, I'll panic, and Ford will die. But if I don't try, Ford will drown. He's dead either way.

"I hate you," I snarl at Chakrii. "I will kill you myself."

He just laughs again. "I don't think so, my dear. Not so

high and mighty now, are you? Funny how easily we can learn how unimportant we are. Imagine if you had just had one little dinner with me. Imagine if you had never met Ford Walker. Although, they say it's better to have loved and lost than to never love at all. Tell me, do you find that to be true in this moment?"

"You sick fuck," Asher snarls.

"Get the knife, Alessandra," Jesse says to me, his voice urgent. "Pick it up. You can do this. Don't let him die this way. I know you can do it. Close your eyes and jump straight down next to him. When you hit the bottom, hand it to him and he'll do the rest. He's trained for this. If you just give him the knife, that's all he needs. He doesn't need you to free him from the restraints. He can do that on his own. Just sink right down, hand him the knife, and then kick up with all your might from the bottom. You'll be back up in ten, twenty seconds at most. That's less time than when he saved you last week. You can save him. You *can*. But you have to go now. It's already been a minute. You must go now."

"Look at him," Chakrii crows. "Breaking it down into tiny tasks. Why, even I think you might manage it. Or not."

Bianchi makes a disgusted sound. She comes up behind me and puts her foot on my back. "How about I just kick you in? Then this stupidity would be over. Just kill yourself trying to save him already so we can be done with it."

"Shut the fuck up," Jesse snaps at her.

"That's my line, handsome," Bianchi says sweetly.

"You better hope I never get free of here," he says. I spare one quick glance at him and pale at the viciousness in his expression. How the hell can Bianchi see that look and *provoke* him?

Chakrii sighs. "This grows tiresome. It's taking longer than I—"

Sirens ring out down the street.

Chakrii looks over his shoulder. Bianchi's head snaps up, scanning back and forth.

Jesse laughs darkly. "Looks like your gunshot didn't kill Made right away. Thought he wouldn't be much of a threat since he's got a broken leg, huh, Chakrii? Thought you could leave him bleeding out on the floor, right? He must have somehow managed to call in reinforcements. And here you thought you'd get away with it."

"Shut up," Chakrii snaps. He snaps his fingers at two of the guards. "Go see if he's right."

They peel off, fading back toward the edge of the property. They're back within seconds.

"Police coming in from all directions," one of them says, his tone grim.

Chakrii curses, his gun waving around wildly. "I should just kill you all and be done with it."

"There's no time," says Bianchi. "I don't care what plans of yours are interrupted; I'm not going to prison for you." She makes for the property line.

Chakrii, as if unnerved by her sudden desertion, motions toward his guards. "Five of you go to the front and the other engage them from back here. I want a damn good diversion; if they capture me, your families die."

The men scatter.

Out of the corner of my eye, I see Chakrii turn back to

me, but I'm still focused on the pool. A pathetic whimper escapes me.

"Consider yourself lucky that only Mr. Walker dies today," Chakrii says. "If I ever hear you're in Thailand again, I will hunt you down."

He turns and jogs toward the open gate that Bianchi has already disappeared through.

"Throw him the knife!" Jesse yells.

I scrabble along the edge of the pool, too unsteady to trust myself to get to my feet, scraping my knees and palms from the rough pavement. My shaking fingers grab up the knife. How long has it been? A lonely bubble escapes up from the bottom of the pool. Thank God. He's still alive.

But still ... I shake my head.

"No, I can't," I say, shaking my head. I climb to my feet. "I'll free you; you go in and save him."

"They thought of that and used metal chains on us," Jesse snaps. "Don't bother. Only he has rope."

"No ..." I sob, falling back down to the edge. Another bubble escapes. The last of his air. Maybe ...

"You're running out of time!" Asher shouts.

"Ya gotta do it!" says Tucker, his voice hoarse.

I lean out over the water, so far out I shudder in revulsion.

"Carefully!" Jesse yells.

I shift the knife so I'm holding the blade, then aim it as close to Ford as possible. I release it, a wave of relief rolling through me as I watch it sink to the bottom. I did it, I've saved him, he can use it to free himself. He won't die. Everything will—

The knife falls to a stop a few feet from him. No hand reaches out to grab it.

"No!" I cry, the tears falling harder now. It didn't reach him. He's not going to make it. I *still* failed, and now we are going to have to watch him die. "Nonono."

My eyes flash to his friends. They stare back at me with resigned, heartbroken faces. They know I can't do it. They don't expect me to save him. None of them do. They know I can't do it.

Not even Ford believes I can. That's why he made sure to forgive me. His *dying words* were forgiveness for my failure. No one believes I can do it. I am going to have to live for the rest of my life knowing I killed the man I love because I couldn't get over my fear. I will have to look at myself in the mirror every morning knowing what a complete failure I am, that I had the chance for a lifetime of love, and I quite literally threw it away.

I cry, rocking back and forth, shrieking and moaning and pleading. I don't want to do it. I have to. I can't, but I must. It hurts. It hurts so bad. I will never survive it. I'm not strong enough.

"Alessandra. Please," Jesse says one final time, his voice exhausted. Resigned.

I reach out, my fingers dangling an inch above the water. Ford's words suddenly burst into my mind from only a few hours ago that now feels like a lifetime.

I would suffer another thousand injuries if it meant holding you in my arms, gorgeous. The pain means nothing. The pain means I'm alive, and here with you.

I dive into the pool.

CHAPTER FORTY-TWO

FORD

I'm dragged to the bottom in seconds. The boulder lands with a dull thud in the silent water. I land a moment later. My feet fall directly on top of the rock, a jarring impact that knocks me onto my side. With my hands tied behind my back, my prospects for working myself free aren't too great.

There is some time, though. Chakrii may be a bastard, but he must know I can last a few minutes down here. The SEALs trained me for just such a scenario. During BUD/S our arms were literally tied behind our backs, and we were shoved in the pool and forced to swim for five minutes, bobbing up and down, unable to use our arms. They called it drown-proofing. So being tied to a rock in the bottom of a pool doesn't terrify me as it would other people. It's real shitty, no doubt about that, but I've been trained not to panic.

I can't last here forever, though. And if I do get to the

surface, Chakrii will execute me. If I *don't* get to the surface, he'll execute Alessandra.

Her terrified, resigned eyes flash through my mind. She doesn't believe she can do it. Fuckin' hell, Chakrii's right; he's going to give her the same anguish I have with Achara from not being able to save her. I don't hold it against her; a person can't overcome her fear at the drop of a hat.

I roll up into a sitting position as shouting erupts above. The words are garbled, but I get the picture. My friends and Alessandra are pleading with Chakrii to have mercy. My chest twinges; there will be no mercy to be had, here. Chakrii is either certain Alessandra will never get in the water or intends to kill her if she tries.

I have to get out of this pool myself.

Placing my feet on the bottom of the pool, I bend my knees and kick up for the surface, hoping they've let the line long enough that I can reach the top. I only make it about four feet before I'm yanked back down. Damn.

Letting myself settle back on the bottom, I feel around the restraints on my wrists, hoping there's a knot I recognize. I've been taught to tie underwater many kinds of knots. Damn it all; I'm not familiar any of these. I give them a few quick tugs, just to test for weakness, but the rope holds.

Maybe I can move the rock instead. Groping around behind me, I feel for the rope that connects my ankle to the boulder. It could be light enough that I can drag it up the slope of the pool to the shallow end. Try as I might, however, I can't bend back far enough for my hands to grasp the rope behind me. If my hands were free, it would be simple, almost absurdly so, but with my hands restrained, simple becomes impossible. Fuck.

I kick back until the boulder is in front of me. Maybe it's small enough I can kick it up to the shallow end, moving like an inchworm. Placing my feet together, I give the blurry object a hard shove. The rock budges a few inches, but it's much heavier than I thought. How the hell did that guard push it in so easily? They must have already placed it on the edge of the pool, because this fucker ain't moving.

The first tendril of fear ripples through me.

I may not be able to get myself out of this.

Shit. Fuck. I give the rock another couple of kicks, but it's useless. No way am I fighting it up gravity into the shallow end. I've already wasted a good fifteen seconds trying. I need to conserve my energy and air in the hopes she gets the knife to me.

Come on, come on. Just toss it in. Toss it in and I'll free myself. I'm *trained* to do it, damn it! But all I hear is muffled screaming, both male and female voices.

At least I told her I love her.

I can go without that regret, at least. I should have told her sooner. I should have told her when I was deep inside her, so I could feel her clench around me the moment the words hit her. I should have whispered them against her mouth as I stole kiss after kiss.

It'll never happen now.

But I saw it in her eyes. That brief flash between my telling her and slamming into the water, I saw it. She loves me, too. We love each other. Fuck, to lose it *again*. I don't want to die. Christ, I want to live!

Please, God, give me enough time. Give me the strength to overcome this, to push back on the terror creeping into my mind. I grow still, as still as I can possibly be, conserving my energy before the panic response sets in. Before my body demands I inhale, no matter the water around me.

My chest burns. My head pounds so hard I half expect it to explode. My ribs send pain stabbing through me with every movement. I close my eyes to ward off the sting off the chlorinated water.

A muffled noise erupts above. My eyes fly open. I look up to the surface, not that I can see much. Hell, it's so close and yet impossibly far away. What was that sound? Is that a siren? The voices drop off for a moment or two, then redouble in intensity before fading away.

Is Chakrii *leaving*? The bastard. Oh God, what if he killed them? What if they're all gone? I can't hear anyone. Is anyone up there? Have I been left down here? Please, please, someone, anyone, save me.

I'm still looking up when a blurry object floats down. *Yes!* The knife. Good Christ, she got it to me. Which means Chakrii really has left, or something else has happened. I squint past the stinging water, staring where the knife falls, my chest screaming, the urge to inhale threatening to choke me. My vision wavers, growing fuzzy. I don't have much more time. I need to get to the surface now.

The knife lands a few feet away. I throw myself toward it, am nearly there when I'm yanked back by the boulder. Fucking hell! I strain against the boulder, trying to drag it with me, but it only budges an inch or two. My face is probably a hand's breadth from the knife. Inches more and I could grab it in my mouth, then release it down closer to where my hands could reach it.

It just sits there, taunting me. So close and yet so far. Despair overwhelms me at the enraging unfairness of it all.

I am going to die. Fuck, I'm actually going to die.

A splash sounds above me. I look up as Alessandra falls down toward me. My God, she came! My beautiful, gorgeous woman came for me. She actually came in to save me when she saw the knife didn't reach me. Such awed love slams into me I nearly waste it all by gasping in shock.

She doesn't move. She's absolutely still as she sinks down face-first. Her eyes are wide, terrified, her face twisted in horror. But her gaze never strays from the knife. She doesn't even look at me, and I know in that moment that all she can focus on is that knife. Her entire world has narrowed to a tiny flash of metal; if she becomes distracted, her control will snap.

She hits the bottom. Her hand snatches out and grabs the knife. She freezes, as if shocked she's made it this far. I thrash my head, trying to get her attention before she panics, because the panic is coming. If I can't free myself before that happens, we're both dead.

Alessandra finally looks at me. I stare at her, my head growing increasingly fuzzy. My vision narrows further. I force down a gag, my lips smashed together, refusing to let the water in. I have reached the limit. There are just seconds now. Precious seconds standing between us and death.

Alessandra grabs my shoulder, her nails digging

painfully. The pain is a hit to my system, momentarily jolting me out of the growing lethargy stealing over me.

She rolls me over, going for my hands, no doubt thinking to cut them free. No, no, we don't have time! I thrash, rolling onto my back, preventing her from reaching them. I buck my legs, trying to signal for her to slash the rope that binds me to the boulder.

In a moment she understands. She crawls down my body, her knee banging my head as she scrambles over me. Her movements are jerking; the panic has arrived. If she can't slash the rope in the next few seconds, she'll inhale, and we're finished.

I stay as still as I can manage. I feel a jerk, and a sawing motion as she slashes at the rope. Bubbles stream from her mouth; she twitches. Her movements become less fluid, more jerky, less confident. The rope is taking too long to cut.

I pray. Pray to God. Pray to everything I can think of. A little more time. Just give us a little more time. But there is no more time; I have run out. My vision grows darker. The lethargy rises up, beckons tantalizingly. I am tired, after all. This has been so exhausting. Perhaps it's time to rest. Perhaps there was nothing that could be done, after all.

The rope snaps free.

It takes me a precious moment to realize there's slack from my ankle. I blink, trying to orient myself. My body is so heavy. Fuck, I can't move. But I can. I must.

Alessandra isn't moving, either.

My fuzzy vision struggles to focus on her. Why isn't she moving? I'm free! Swim to the surface! Go! But as my eyes focus on her, I realize she's thrashing, her movements growing slower.

She freed me, but she doesn't have the air or the courage to get to the surface. The darkness is descending on her as well, and in her panicked state, she can't get out.

Her terror gives me the strength to try. I roll onto my stomach, then bring my knees up under me. I can kick up to the surface now.

But Alessandra is panicking in earnest now. Her frightened mind sees one thing and one thing only: me, an object for her to latch onto. She grabs at me, her hands nearly dragging me over backward as she claws her way upward. She'll drown us both if I don't get us up. I turn my head, trying to catch her attention, but she can't focus on me. She's too far gone. Her hands claw my arm instead.

It's what I'm waiting for. I launch myself at the surface, kicking up as hard as I can, hoping it's enough to propel us both to the surface. I furiously kick, even as my vision tunnels once more, thankful Chakrii didn't think to tie my ankles together. We surge toward the surface; Alessandra falls still as I swim up, her body becoming a dead weight against mine, slowing our progress. I kick harder, eyes locked on the surface. Just a little more. A little more.

When we break the surface, my men roar with triumph. I drag a precious breath into my lungs, never so thankful for a lungful of air in my life.

"Alessandra?" I croak. "Say something, gorgeous."

She's silent, so still. I roll onto my back and kick for the shallow end, praying she doesn't let go of me. I can't haul her out of the pool with my hands tied behind my back.

"Thank God!" Asher yells, his voice raw from the kind of true terror I've only heard from him on one or two occasions.

"I can't believe she did that," Tucker says in shock.

"She isn't breathing," I rasp, still kicking for the shallow end. "One of you assholes help us."

"You think we're fucking sitting here for fun?" Jesse growls.

I give one final kick and reach the shallow end. I stand up, swaying on my feet as a wave of dizziness rolls through me. Fucking hell, I can't faint now.

"Where the fuck is—ALESSANDRA!"

Marco sprints out of the house, his eyes lit with fury.

CHAPTER FORTY-THREE

FORD

Marco flies into the pool, hauling his sister off me. "What the fuck happened?"

I limp out after him as he puts her down on the ground. He does a hurried check and begins performing CPR. I fall to my knees beside them, shuddering with relief as I drag air into my lungs.

"Come on, gorgeous," I rasp. "Don't go. Don't leave me here alone."

"What the fuck happened?" Marco growls while giving compressions.

"Chakrii weighed me down, shoved me in, told Alessandra she could save me if she wanted."

Marco gapes at me. "She went in there? Voluntarily?"

"Bravest thing I've ever seen!" Asher yells.

"Warrior shit right there," Tucker adds.

Jesse says nothing, but I can feel him seething. Chakrii —and more importantly, Bianchi—is getting away.

"Come on, come on," I pray, staring at Alessandra.

And like she's heard me, she convulses, water spewing out of her mouth. She coughs and rolls over onto her stomach. Marco sags next to her.

"That's my girl," I say, my voice tight. "Breathe, gorgeous. Just breathe."

"F-Ford," she gasps, rolling over to look at me. Her eyes land on me, register that I'm fine. Tears stream down her face. "You're okay."

"I am, gorgeous. You saved me."

"Ford, damn it, now is not the time!" Jesse yells.

I cut him a glare, even though he's right.

"Go," Alessandra whispers, her voice hoarse. "Go get that asshole."

"Marco, get over here and release us!" Jesse yells.

"Go," Alessandra says to him. "Free them."

Marco stumbles over to the men.

"Me first!" Jesse roars. I exchange a glance with the other two; they give me worried looks. Heaven help us if he finds her; I've never seen Jesse so enraged in his entire life. So much for remaining cool under fire.

Marco goes to work on Jesse's chains. He curses, unable to disable the padlock, but cries in triumph when he instead manages to loosen the chains just enough for Jesse to slip one, then a second hand free. Jesse erupts, sprinting around the edge of the pool like a man deranged. Maybe he *is* deranged.

"You're unarmed, you stupid fuck!" Tucker shouts, but it falls on dead ears.

Marco releases Tucker and Asher. Asher sprints into the house as Tucker takes off after Jesse. Marco snags a knife from the pool bar, since I left Chakrii's at the bottom of the pool; by the time he releases me, Asher has come back out of the house, loaded to the gills with firearms.

"Made needs help," he pants. "He called out to the emergency services before he fell unconscious."

"Marco, help him," I growl, taking a pistol from Asher. Turning to Alessandra, I haul her to her feet and place a hard kiss to her mouth. "Stay here. Barricade yourselves inside. I love you."

Her mouth opens but I kiss her again. "Not yet," I say, then nod to Asher. "Let's go."

We sprint after Jesse, who's hurling himself over the wall at the opposite end of the property, Tucker on his heels.

"Christ, he's really gonna make me scale that thing," Asher mutters.

"Least you didn't almost drown," I pant. My ribs burn with every breath, but this ends now. Chakrii isn't walking another day free on this earth.

Asher climbs up onto the wall, then extends his hand down to help me up. I mumble a thanks, groaning when I drop down on the other side. Fuck, everything hurts.

Asher and I catch up to the other two as we creep up the alley between the safe house and the one next door. Jesse is deadly silent, his moves quick, calculated, controlled. The wildness in his gaze back at the pool has hardened into lethal resolve.

"Jesse, we were all taken in by her," says Tucker as Asher hands them pistols.

"You weren't fucking her," is all Jesse says.

And that's really all there is to say about that.

Gunfire rings out as we near the street. We throw ourselves against the side of the building. Jesse risks a glance around the corner and jerks his head back as another barrage of gunfire erupts.

"Well, that's why no one's made it to the safe house. Police are engaging with Chakrii's men. Bloodbath. Chakrii and Bianchi are hidden behind a car behind them all, letting them shoot each other. There's another alley down the street and opposite us. They go down that, they slip away."

He makes as if to dart out into the street. We grab him and haul him back.

"We can't run face-first into a hail of gunfire, you idiot!" I hiss.

"I'm not letting her get away," he says, his gaze locked on the street.

"Exercise some caution. Fuck, man, you're the cautious one!" Asher says.

"Not anymore."

He darts out, sprinting to the nearest car in between another burst of gunfire.

"This is fucked," Asher says.

Jesse runs to a second car. He's a quarter of the way out into the street now.

"Fuck it all," says Tucker, and sprints out after him.

"I am going to be *pissed* if I get shot," says Asher before following.

The mental image of Alessandra coughing up water flashes through my mind. She faced her fucking fear to save me. I am finishing this asshole, so she never needs to fear him again.

I move out into the street at the same time as Chakrii and Bianchi make a break for the alley. Jesse sprints after them and we follow. The police yell something over a loudspeaker, but whatever it is, Chakrii's men don't comply. With Chakrii's threat to their families, they aren't about to obey law enforcement.

We cross the street just in time to see Bianchi disappearing into the alley. Jesse's sprinting like I've never seen him run before, fueled on nothing but unhinged rage. We fly into the alley to discover Bianchi and Chakrii have run into a dead end.

"It's over," Jesse snarls. "You lost."

Bianchi pivots and levels her gun at him. Jesse ducks to the side just before she fires. We dodge, then return fire. Chakrii ducks behind a parked car. I fire off another round when his head pops up. He ducks back down.

"We don't have authority to go around killing people," I say quietly. "All we can do is hold them until the police arrive."

"Meanwhile, they'll kill us," Jesse snaps. He takes a few steps closer to Bianchi, who defiantly stands in the middle of the alley, gun raised. Asher and Tucker keep their pistols trained on her while mine remains locked on Chakrii.

"You're right," she says. "I wouldn't come closer if I were you."

"You're fucked in the head if you think I'll let you walk out of here. There's nowhere left for you to go."

She glares at him. "You know, for such a pretty package, you really are insufferable."

"If I'm so insufferable, you shouldn't have fucked me."

Bianchi laughs. "Oh, like you didn't enjoy it."

Jesse inches a few steps closer.

"What is he doing?" Asher mutters.

"Stalling them," I whisper. "Keep them talking until the police get here. They must have seen them come down this alley."

Jesse suddenly says something in Italian. Bianchi loses it, shooting at him. He throws himself to the ground, narrowly avoiding getting shot. Her pistol clicks; the magazine is empty. Before she can reload, Jesse launches himself at her. He tackles her; they hit the ground and roll, arms tangling, legs kicking. Bianchi punches him in the jaw. Jesse's head whips back before he rolls on top of her. His legs straddle her waist as he immobilizes her.

His hands grab for her wrists. He manages to secure one. Bianchi arches up, driving her hips into his in a useless effort to dislodge him. She head-butts him. Jesse groans, then curses. He shakes his head, trying to clear it. Bianchi punches him in the jaw a second time with her free hand.

Chakrii steps out from behind the vehicle. He raises his gun toward them. "I grow tired of this."

"Don't even think about it," I snarl, my gun trained on him.

Chakrii swings his weapon to me, hatred burning in his eyes. "You just won't die, will you?"

"You gave Alessandra the opportunity to save me. She took it," I sneer.

Surprise flickers across his face. He turns to Bianchi, who's still grappling with Jesse. "You said she was afraid of water."

Bianchi doesn't bother answering. Jesse wedges his forearm under her chin, squeezing her windpipe. Bianchi's free hand slams down on his back again and again.

"Stop resisting," he growls. "It's over."

"You don't have the slightest clue what you're talking about."

Jesse leans down, whispers something else in Italian in her ear. She shrieks with rage, thrashing against him, but Jesse has her completely immobilized now. He just laughs.

"I am really going to enjoy seeing you in prison."

"I will never go to prison."

Jesse laughs again. "Yeah? If not prison, then where? You going to let them shoot you dead?"

Bianchi remains silent.

Jesse falls still. He stares down at her, and when he speaks, something new has entered his tone, something I can't define. "I said, you going to let them shoot you?"

"Get on the ground now!"

"About damn time," Asher mutters.

A swarm of police stream into the alley, yelling in English and Thai to put down our weapons. I very slowly lower mine to the ground, then follow suit myself, placing my hands over my head. Asher and Tucker do as well.

But Chakrii isn't having it.

"You bitch!" Chakrii yells at Bianchi. "You were supposed to help me kill these people. So much for the recommendations of your employer. I should shoot you myself. In fact, I think I will."

Jesse's head whips up just as Chakrii swings his gun at them. He throws himself over Bianchi, shielding her with his body. Bianchi shouts something in Italian.

But before Chakrii can squeeze off a single round, the police open fire, multiple rounds hitting his body. He stumbles back as he stares down at himself in shock, like he can't believe they actually had the gall to shoot him. Blood blooms across his body. His gun drops. Shaking hands attempt to hold back the blood from escaping, but it's no use. He collapses to his knees, then topples over. Dead.

"Damn," says Tucker.

Jesse lifts his head from Bianchi, who's staring at him with a blank expression on her face. "What?" he mutters.

She blinks. "You're a very stupid man, aren't you?"

"No dumber than you," Jesse says as he looks behind him to the police officers who are now coming down the alley, rifles lowered, to check Chakrii's body.

Bianchi's face hardens. I shout. Jesse's head snaps back to her as she draws a knife from a sheath at her side and stabs Jesse in his thigh. Jesse roars with fury. Bianchi bucks upward, slamming the heel of her palm up under his chin as she slams her thigh into his injured one. He flies off her, bellowing with anger.

In an instant, she's on her feet. Before anyone can even lift their rifles, she throws herself through the window of the building next to her and disappears inside. Glass explodes, scattering everywhere, but she's already gone.

Jesse staggers to his feet as police rush in after her, his

face furious. He hops forward a step or two, like he's actually attempting to go after her. I launch to my feet, keeping my empty hands out where they remain visible to the police as I go to him.

"She fucking stabbed me," he says, shocked. He teeters, almost losing his balance. Then he rights himself and staggers another few steps forward. "I have to stop her."

"Bro, you are stopping no one," Tucker says, wrapping his arms around Jesse's chest.

Asher strips off his shirt and holds it against Jesse's thigh. "The only thing you're doing now is getting medical attention."

Jesse stares at the broken window his gaze obsessive. "I'm fine. She didn't hit the artery. She just wanted to injure me in the one place she knew would prevent me from following."

"She's not going anywhere," I say, trying to cheer him up. "Where could she possibly go?"

"I put nothing past that woman."

"Well at least she chose not to kill you," Asher says with false cheer.

Jesse's eyes swing to him. "What did you say?"

Asher stares at him in confusion. He glances at the rest of us. "Well, my dude. She seems like the kind of person who would know where to stab to hit the artery, right? If she wanted? And she didn't, so ..."

Jesse's gaze flickers back to the building. His jaws clench. "I am going to hunt her to the ends of the earth if I have to."

Fucking hell.

I turn to the police still standing in the alley. "I need to get back to Alessandra."

"Yeah, if they let us leave," says Tucker.

"I know the safe house number," I say, then head over to one of the policemen, asking around until I find someone who speaks English. I give him the number, hoping someone there has the authority to allow us to leave. Made is, at best, unconscious after taking one to the chest. The officer calls. He has a short conversation in Thai, then hangs up.

"You can head back to the house, sir," the officer says. "We will interview you about this there. Should we send him in an ambulance?"

"No," says Jesse. "I'm staying here."

Asher sighs. "Dude, you can't just wait here for them to bring her out."

"I'm not leaving until I know for certain she's been detained."

I exchange glances with Asher and Tucker. Without a word, we bend down and lift him off the ground. Jesse protests, but he's clearly outnumbered. We carry him out of the alley and back onto the main road where an ambulance is attending to people who were injured during the shoot-out.

"I'll go with him," says Tucker.

After we deposit Jesse with medical services, Asher and I head back to the safe house. Alessandra is waiting for me just inside the door when I finally drag myself inside.

She throws herself at me. I slide my arms around her, burying my face in her neck as I hold tight.

"You're okay," she says, her voice still raspy.

"Because of you."

She pulls back enough to look at me. "I ... I ... I almost didn't do it. I was so scared. You were so still. And I knew it would be my fault."

"It would never be your fault," I say quickly. "Only Chakrii's. He's the one at fault. Never you."

"Is he ..."

"The police shot him."

Her eyes grow wide. "It's over," she says, her voice dazed.

"It really is," I say, then, unable to resist any longer, I lift her off her feet and kiss her with all the pent-up emotion I've ignored to get me through the last few minutes. Alessandra kisses me back, her arms wrapped around my neck. My tongue strokes into her mouth, heat snapping through me when she answers in kind.

Reluctantly, I put her down. We'll be giving our statements for the next few hours; I don't want to start something I don't have the time to finish.

Instead, I kiss her forehead, then say, my mouth slowly stretching into a wide grin. "You can say it now, if you want."

Alessandra melts against me. Her hands slide up to cup my face. I wait for what seems like an eternity before she smiles and says, "I love you, too, Ford Walker."

I tuck her into my side. "That's a helluva good start."

EPILOGUE

ALESSANDRA

Rome
Five months later

Sun glints off Ford's mirrored sunglasses as he stares at me from across our table at the Piazza di Spagna. It's sunny now, but shortly the summer sun will set low enough that the buildings will block it out, casting shadows across our walk home. We always like to end our days in this piazza, where we can sit and talk and have a drink, or even just read quietly. Ford is just as big a reader as I am, something I should have remembered from that first flight we shared. But it's okay; we've had plenty of time to discover each other in the months since Chakrii's death.

The deep tan of his skin and his tousled hair, a little longer now than it was cut in Thailand, contrast remarkably with the crisp lines of his pale blue linen suit. He lounges negligently, one immaculate Italian loafer crossed over his opposite knee, his attention flicking from one crowd of tourists to the other. With his gorgeous outfit and slightly amused, even indulgent, expression, he fits right in with the locals lounging about for an early evening espresso in Rome's fashion district.

"Rome looks good on you," I say, still marveling over how at home he looks here.

He smiles, reaches across the table to take my hand. Leaning forward, he gives me a wolfish grin and then says, "No, *you* look good on me."

I throw my head back and laugh, drawing the attention of the tables around us. Ford's grin grows wider, delighted he's elicited such a reaction out of me when he knows I'm typically more reserved when out on the streets.

"I see you're rapidly picking up that Italian charm, as well."

"Perhaps I've always had it."

My brows raise, my head dipping toward his as I whisper, "Then I'd really like to see more of it."

Heat flashes in his eyes. "Your wish is my command, gorgeous. Shall I start right now?"

"I'd like that."

He gets to his feet, pulls a few euros out of his pocket and tosses them down on the table. He extends his hand toward me. "Let's go for a walk."

I slip my arm around him, ignoring the stares as we stroll across the piazza. We're stared at wherever we go now; to say that our relationship took Italy by storm is an understatement.

To be fair, what could be a more irresistible story than a handsome American military man saving the life of a famous heiress and the two of them falling in love in the process? We were hounded for days when we first arrived, by my own family's company most of all, who wanted to capitalize on a good story.

Ford was great through it all, sat through all the interviews, attended all the events with aplomb. Perhaps he's used to it, though, since SEALs are famous themselves in a way.

Ford looks behind us as we stroll out of the piazza, up the Via del Babuino in the direction of my family's compound.

"I take it he's still there?" I ask lightly, not bothering to turn around.

Ford looks back to me and nods, pulling me tighter against him. "Yes, Antonio's following, blending in as always. I could have really used that man on some of the ops I've been on; he has a gift for blending in."

I sigh. "I really think that now, after five months, a bodyguard—"

"You remember what Luciano said when we ran across him at that party. Not even here a week, and he strolls—well, hops up on crutches—at a charity gala and straight-out says the Family is *displeased* with how things went down in Thailand."

I sigh again. "He can't actually hurt me, Ford. We've discussed this. I'm too visible. And it's not the Family who is angry, it's Luciano. The Family got all that glowing press about how their *resources* helped me leave Thailand. It got the government off their backs temporarily. We can only imagine what sort of trouble they got up to during that time.

We probably made them millions. No, it's Luciano himself who is the problem, and that's because he lost. You bested him."

Ford's grip on me tightens. "And he wants you. I'm not putting anything past that man; if he sees an opportunity, he's going to take you, no question."

"I think you're probably reading into it too much."

Ford looks at me. "I'm a man, gorgeous. I know when one looks at a woman thinking he possesses her."

I sigh. We navigate around a child screaming her poor head off because her barely-eaten chocolate gelato has slipped off her cone and splattered on the concrete.

Ford winces, glances around for her parents. "I remember those days. Where are her parents?"

"She's probably just a kid running around for the day."

When no one comes to comfort her, Ford kneels down and retrieves his money clip. He pulls out a couple of bills and hands them to the kid, then points at the gelato stand across the way.

Her eyes widen in delight, and she shrieks with joy. Wrapping her arms around his neck, she places a chocolate-smeared kiss to his cheek and then sprints to the gelato stand, the euros still crushed in her gelato-sticky hand. Chuckling, Ford wipes his cheek with the back of his hand as he stands.

I slide my hand around his arm again and tuck my head into his shoulder as we continue walking. "Have I told you today how much I love you?"

"I think I could stand it if you told me again."

I lift up on my toes to kiss his cheek almost exactly

where the girl did. My mouth slides to his ear, and I whisper, "I love you *very* much."

"Will you show me how much later?"

"I think that could be arranged," I say, taking another step. "You'd make a great dad, you know."

Ford grinds to a halt and turns to stare down at me directly. A soft smile steals across his face. "Yeah?"

"Oh definitely. Did you see that little trio of *nonne* at the table next to the gelato stand? They were about three seconds from coming over there and kissing you themselves."

He leans closer. "And are *you* impressed with my fatherly skills?"

I grin. "Very."

His head dips, trailing a line of kisses up my neck right there in the middle of the street. Heat pulses through my core and I melt against him.

"Well, good," he says, "because you'd be a great mother."

The heat slides up to my heart, which skips a beat. I jerk my head back to stare up at him. He grins and winks at me but says nothing further about the subject. But I know what he's on about; these little comments have increased this last month, and they can only be heading in one direction.

Why doesn't he just ask me already? He can't possibly believe I won't answer yes, can he?

But I don't push him; men need to move at their own pace with these things, and really, where else is this relationship going? We have all the time in the world now.

"Speaking of children," Ford says as we continue our stroll. "How're Izzy and the baby?"

I smile. "She's as adorable as ever. I did a video call with them this morning and Izzy had her in the cutest little outfit. Thank God the delivery went well. Although, Marco's even more overprotective now that Sienna is born."

Ford laughs, shaking his head. "Do you know how many times he called me in the middle of the night freaking out? I swear, I should start charging him for therapy."

I snort. "As if you'd be any different, sailor."

A few moments pass before Ford says, his tone thoughtful, "No, I suppose I won't be."

I stare down at the street to mask my smile.

"How's Asher?" I say, "The resort still running? Did you get those photos yet?"

Ford groans. "The resort is fine. Asher's thrilled he gets to run it six months a year. Eventually I'll have to figure out a more permanent solution, if he ever wants to settle back in the States, but for now it's fine. We're booked up."

I give his arm a squeeze. "I'm glad to hear it."

"Hey, again, good call with Pranee. She's really been indispensable with the repairs. Maybe we can look into your suggestion of setting up a salon in the resort for Pranee to run. I can't imagine it myself, but ..."

"I keep telling you, Ford," I say excitedly. "Think of all the new guests you could attract if you had a nice salon to occupy their family members who don't dive. They wouldn't even have to leave the resort; they could be pampered all day. And you're always telling me how tired you are at the end of a dive. A massage would be perfect for that."

Ford chuckles. "Yes, yes. I know. You're going to wear me down eventually. But speaking of which, Asher sent me the photos this morning. The facelift is finally finished; the place looks incredible. We both know it's because of Pranee's direction. Asher couldn't pick colors to save his life. The only thing he's good for is leading dive trips."

"Ooh, let me see them," I squeal, holding out my hand. Ford laughs and hands over his phone. I scroll through the photos, smiling at the one of Pranee and Asher posing before the car I bought her. Her family got a boat, too, and I'm investing in their fishing business. If I can convince Ford to open the salon, then Pranee has already agreed to leave the Golden Lotus, which is now under a new owner.

"They did a great job," I say, still scrolling. Oh yes. It's gorgeous. I can't wait to return in a few months. Ford and I have decided to split the year between Italy and Thailand, with a few trips to the US sprinkled in to visit his parents.

I might even be able to enjoy the pool, now that I'm getting a better handle on my phobia. Saving Ford and showering with him every day—sometimes more than once—has gone far in making me more comfortable around water. I'm not completely over it yet, but I will be.

Speaking of being comfortable. I hand his phone back. "Hey, are you sure your parents are going to be happy staying at my family's compound? We're ... a lot to take in right away, and they may be more comfortable in a hotel. There's a whole bunch of beautiful places right down this street. They might want the privacy. It's just in Italy—"

"Lessa." Ford brings us to a halt. We've reached the Piazza del Popolo and are surrounded by tourists. Ford pays them no mind as he cups my face between his hands. "You absolutely do not have to be nervous meeting them. We've already zoomed them multiple times and they're in love with you as much as I am. Well. Maybe not quite as much. But just about."

I blush. With the kinds of delightfully filthy things Ford does to me, I would hope his parents don't love me *that* much.

"I just want it to be perfect," I whisper.

Ford kisses me on the lips, then on the forehead. "And that's why I love you. Always dedicated when it comes to strategic negotiations."

"Well, it is my job."

Ford leads me around the edge of the piazza. "I was thinking more of a merger this time around."

My head whips to his. Ford feels my gaze on him and smiles but doesn't turn his head to mine. He gives my hand a squeeze.

Needing to distract myself from what he's hinting at or I'll never be calm enough when I meet his parents for real, I search for a different topic of conversation.

"Have you heard from Jesse?"

Ford's grin fades, transforming into a hard frown. He jerks his head no.

"Nothing? At all? Hasn't it been like—"

"Two months and seven days. Eight days now, since he's probably in Asia and they're ahead of us. Tucker's gone after him but hasn't been able to find him."

"God, Ford, I'm so sorry."

Ford runs a hand through his hair. "Bianchi ruined him. He's obsessed with her. Obsessed with catching her. He's always been the best of us at reading people and in the end, she tricked him. He suspected something was off about Bianchi, but still couldn't keep his hands off her. Then she stabbed him. He's the most moral one of us, completely uncompromising about doing what's right. This shit was like his personal kryptonite."

I let a few moments pass, considering. Bianchi got away that day in the alley. She sprinted right up to the roof of the building and jumped across to the next one before the police had even thought to head upstairs. She was long gone by then. As soon as Jesse healed, he was after her. His own personal vendetta.

"Ford, I know we've discussed this like a million times, but I just think there's more to the story, there."

"Lessa—"

"No, really. She could have killed him when she stabbed him like that. And he shielded her from Chakrii. I don't think either of them have *no* feelings for each other."

"That's just lust, gorgeous. The desire to fuck a hot partner."

I shake my head. "No. It's more than that. She ... I don't know. I can't describe it. She could have killed my brother. Instead, she just knocked him out then told Chakrii he wasn't a problem anymore. Then he helped us out of the pool. What if he'd woken up sooner? He's a strong swimmer. He could have saved you. And me. And Bianchi was trying to move it along, get Chakrii to leave. What if she really wanted Marco to save us?"

Ford sighs. "She's the one who led Chakrii to us in the first place, Lessa. That's all just too convoluted."

"No, you weren't there," I say stubbornly. "It was like ... I don't know, it was like it was outside of her control. She kept going on about her employer. Who we *still* have no clue about. It was like she resented her employer or something. I don't know. Maybe she's just a bitch and hates everyone. It doesn't fit, though. Not entirely. Chakrii was about to shoot us, and she said there was no time. She left, and it spooked Chakrii, and he fled without killing us all. Does that make sense to you? Because it doesn't to me. The better thing to do would have been to kill us. If they had, Chakrii might still be alive. Her employer would have wanted that. *And* she threatened to push me in the pool. After you went in."

Ford rolls his eyes. "You're right. We have discussed this a million times. I can't believe you think her threatening to *drown you* was really some sort of obscure help."

"She knew I'd never make it in myself! Maybe she figured I'd manage it if I could just get in the water. Maybe she thought I needed a literal push to make it happen."

"Well, I'm glad she didn't. And she caused enough damage, nearly killed you multiple times by informing Chakrii about our movements. She better not come across me in a dark alley one day, because she won't come fucking crawling out of it. And a whole host of government agencies are on her ass for framing Onsi, who at least got released, along with everything else she did. Even Made is after her, and it took him two months to recover from getting shot. With all these people gunning for her, it won't be much longer before she's caught. Good riddance, I say. But until she's captured, it *is* yet another reason Antonio, back there, still has a job."

I sigh, letting the matter drop. We're just not going to agree about it.

Ford sighs as well, then turns to pull me into him. I wrap my arms around him, bury my face in his chest, breathing in so very deeply as I listen to the beat of his heart.

There's nowhere else I'd rather be.

Ford lifts my mouth to his. "Me neither, gorgeous," he whispers against my lips, and I realize I've spoken aloud. "Me neither."

He takes my mouth with his, both of us lost in the sweetest, most passionate kiss of our lives. And then we continue our stroll, the sun finally slipping down below the buildings behind us.

AUTHOR'S NOTE

The setting of this book is based on a trip I took to Thailand in 2018. As I am not Thai myself, I cannot comment on Thai culture and customs, but I do hope I came close to depicting what it is like for a foreigner in Thailand.

Bangkok is a massive, wonderfully dynamic city that I encourage you to see if you are able. One of my favorite things to visit was The Grand Palace where you can learn about the empire of Siam.

The lotus fabric really is the most expensive fabric on the planet, and Buddhist monks really do wear them. Essentially, the way it works is you break apart the stalks and then rub the fibers together to form a thread, which is then woven into fabric. You can see a demonstration here: https://youtu.be/S9F-u4T7leQ

Lotus fabric is mostly made in Myanmar, but areas in Cambodia, Vietnam, and to a lesser extent Thailand are beginning to make it as well, since it has the potential to be an extremely profitable industry. I took a small artistic

AUTHOR'S NOTE

license in creating a fictional lotus-making shop in Phuket as I wanted to bring awareness to this new industry. Most of the process is by hand and with traditional loom-weaving technology, so it is a more sustainable way of creating fabric.

The Thai *chao pho* are active in many provinces in Thailand. Like in Italy and other countries, they tend to work a specific territory. I made Chakrii active in both Phuket and Bangkok for the purposes of my story. There are also many crime dramas featuring the *chao pho* similar to our beloved *Godfather* movies. You can find a list of some here: https://mydramalist.com/list/W3rWXGm4

Finally, human trafficking sadly remains a large issue in Thailand. Most of the people taken in Thailand for sexual slavery and forced labor are Thai, as well as economic migrants from neighboring countries. According to the 2018 Global Slavery Index, Thailand has nearly 610,000 slaves in the country, which corresponds to about 1 in 113 people living in the country. While it is less likely a woman like Alessandra would be taken in Thailand, I wanted to bring awareness to this topic. The organization Walk Free publishes the Global Slavery Index; you can visit their website to learn more here: https://www.walkfree.org/projects/the-global-slavery-index/

That being said, I would like to make the point that human trafficking is one very small facet of Thailand, like it is in all our countries. I met many lovely, kind, and caring people in Thailand who are the real representatives of their country and culture.

ALSO BY K.D. ELIZABETH

Take Me Abroad
Take Me in Bali

Take Me in Bangkok

The King Brothers
Monster

Devil

Rascal

The King Cousins
Lush

Rogue

Hellion

Vixen

Construct My Heart Series
Miss InstaPrincess

Miss ManKiller

The Bright Series
The Christmas Cadeau

The Season Bright

Christmas of White

ACKNOWLEDGMENTS

Thank you, Cassie, for your great work editing.

And of course, thanks to Alison of Red Leaf Proofing, for making sure my final text is clean.

I could never release without my awesome street team and everyone else who promoted this book. You are such an important part of my book's release.

THANK YOU to all my wonderful readers. This book took me completely by surprise and I hope you have just as much fun with it!

Finally, to my family, I so appreciate the love and support you continue to give me.

With love,
    K.D. Elizabeth

Follow K.D. Elizabeth on TikTok at @kdewrites or visit her website at www.kdewrites.com.

Made in the USA
Middletown, DE
11 July 2023